8-2017

MVFOL

Shattered

ALSO BY ALLISON BRENNAN

Make Them Pay
The Lost Girls
Poisonous
No Good Deed
Best Laid Plans
Compulsion
Dead Heat
Notorious
Cold Snap
Stolen
Stalked
Silenced
If I Should Die
Kiss Me, Kill Me
Love Me to Death
Carnal Sin
Original Sin
Cutting Edge
Fatal Secrets
Sudden Death
Playing Dead
Tempting Evil
Killing Fear
Fear No Evil
See No Evil
Speak No Evil
The Kill
The Hunt
The Prey

ALLISON BRENNAN

Shattered

 MINOTAUR BOOKS 🅜 NEW YORK

SHATTERED. Copyright © 2017 by Allison Brennan. All rights reserved. Printed in the United States of America. For information, address St. Martin's Press, 175 Fifth Avenue, New York, N.Y. 10010.

www.minotaurbooks.com

Library of Congress Cataloging-in-Publication Data

Names: Brennan, Allison, author.
Title: Shattered / Allison Brennan.
Description: First edition. | New York : Minotaur Books, 2017. | Series: Max Revere novels ; 4
Identifiers: LCCN 2017011890| ISBN 9781250129277 (hardcover) | ISBN 9781250129284 (ebook)
Subjects: LCSH: Women journalists—Fiction. | Serial murder investigation—Fiction. | Cold cases (Criminal investigation)—Fiction. | BISAC: FICTION / Thrillers. | FICTION / Suspense. | FICTION / Mystery & Detective / Women Sleuths. | GSAFD: Suspense fiction. | Mystery fiction.
Classification: LCC PS3602.R4495 S53 2017 | DDC 813/.6—dc23
LC record available at https://lccn.loc.gov/2017011890

Our books may be purchased in bulk for promotional, educational, or business use. Please contact your local bookseller or the Macmillan Corporate and Premium Sales Department at 1-800-221-7945, extension 5442, or by e-mail at MacmillanSpecialMarkets@macmillan.com.

First Edition: August 2017

10   9   8   7   6   5   4   3   2   1

More than thirty books ago, Marti Robb (known to readers as Mariah Stewart) read and endorsed my first book. Thank you so much for being a mentor and a friend.

Acknowledgments

My fellow writers are generous souls, many of whom are experts in areas other than spinning tales. In particular, I want to shout out to Dr. D. P. Lyle, who has been a blessing. He never blinks an eye when I shoot him an e-mail beginning, "So I have this dead body . . ." Once again, Doug has been instrumental in helping me with the small details. Any mistakes are on me.

Legally, there's no one better than former prosecutor Allison Leotta, who always responds so quickly when I have a question about the justice system. This time, she really saved my butt. Thank you!

I needed some details about prisoners, bail, and the Maricopa County legal system. Thank you to Sergeant Patrick Regan with the Scottsdale Police Department for answering my questions. Apologies if I got anything wrong!

My editor, Kelley Ragland, always has a keen eye for problems in my books; with *Shattered* she saw the potential and with one eye-opening comment helped me see the solution. A good editor is worth her weight in gold; thank you, Kelley! And thanks once again to my agent, Dan Conaway, who always has my back.

As always, my family is my rock. They let me work when I have to and make me play when I need it. I love you all.

Shattered

Prologue

She sat on the edge of her son's bed, clutching his favorite stuffed toy. A dog. Matthew had wanted a puppy for years. She'd convinced her husband that they should get a puppy for Christmas.

But their son would never see another Christmas.

She didn't know how long she sat there, but it was dark when her husband came into the room.

"Please, honey, come to bed."

She stared at the man she had once loved. The man who had fathered her only child. The face she had admired, the smile that made her heart flutter, now made her physically ill. She hated him. She had never hated anyone more than the man she had sworn to love, honor, and cherish. The man she had promised to be faithful to, the man she had promised to stand by in everything life threw at them.

She could barely speak, but she said, "You should have been here."

"Don't—please don't."

Tears flowed, but they didn't soften her heart. Tears of rage were so very different from tears of grief.

"I can't look at you. I can't live with you. It's your fault our son is gone!"

"You don't mean that. Please, I'm sorry. I'll say it as many times—"

"It'll never be enough! *Sorry* doesn't bring Matthew back!"

"I know you're hurting, honey. I'm hurting, too." His eyes wandered to the wall of photos. Of Matthew growing up. Baby. Toddler. Kindergarten. And the last photo, second grade. His last school picture.

His voice cracked. "Stay with your mom for a few days. Until—"

"I'm not coming back."

He reached for her. "I know you're hurt, but we can survive this together."

She jumped up before he could touch her. She didn't know what she'd do if he put his hands on her . . . if he tried to console her.

She might kill him.

Death would be too good for him. He should suffer for the rest of his life. Suffer because *he wasn't here.* Suffer because he had lied, he had cheated, he was a selfish, disgusting excuse for a human being. How had she loved him? Why hadn't she seen the truth before it was too late?

She ran to the door of Matthew's room. The anger and hate bubbled up and overshadowed the deep, numbing pain.

She had never realized how much it would hurt to lose her only child, but if she dwelled on it, let the pain in, she would drown in her grief. Instead, she focused on the reasons Matthew had died. The anger that would keep her breathing.

"I hope you suffer for the rest of your miserable life. I hope you know that because of *you,* my son is dead."

Through the sobs that shook her husband's body, he said, "He's *our* son. Please—don't. Don't do this to me. To us."

"I hate you." Those three words changed everything. There was no going back.

She walked out without another word, without looking at her husband, leaving him sobbing in the middle of their dead son's room.

She hoped he suffered twice as much as she did.

I hate you.

She should have been speaking to a mirror.

Chapter One

Maxine Revere, investigative reporter, learned the hard way that insinuating herself into the middle of an active police investigation was a recipe for disaster, which is why she focused primarily on missing persons and cold cases. Law enforcement was usually willing to talk when the case was dead in the water. Unsolved cases grated on the nerves of most cops. If Max used her extensive financial resources and media access to gather actionable information, cops would often work with her.

Worse than shaking things up in the middle of an investigation was showing up right before a trial. The bad guy was behind bars, the powers that be were a 1,000 percent positive they had the right person, and Max's involvement caused the chief of police, district attorney, and prosecutor to lose sleep. She didn't much care—if they were confident with their evidence, there was nothing to lose sleep over.

But Max rarely did anything the easy way, so when her old college friend—okay, old college ex-boyfriend—called her weeks before his wife was to go on trial for the murder of their only child, desperately believing that she was innocent, Max agreed to fly to Scottsdale, Arizona, to listen to John's theory which—she had to admit—sounded intriguing over the phone.

Still, in Max's experience, while occasionally the wrong person was accused and imprisoned, the prosecution rarely went forward with a costly trial when they didn't have ample evidence for a conviction. Not only because of the cost, but politics. A high-profile case such as a wealthy mother killing her eight-year-old son? Everyone was under a micro-scope from the beginning. With such scrutiny, the DA wouldn't let it go this far without *something* solid to sway a jury. So even though it was John Caldwell—a man Max respected and even admired—asking for her help, she needed more than his faith in his wife's innocence.

It was the cold cases that had her flying from New York to Phoenix. Three cold cases in the southwest that were eerily similar to the murder of Peter Caldwell.

Max had interviewed many defendants and witnesses during her decade-long career as an investigative journalist. Most of the lawyers she dealt with either wanted nothing to do with her or attempted to manipulate her into printing only information favorable to their client.

She didn't know what to expect from Charles North, the respected criminal defense lawyer who represented Blair Caldwell. But a condition of her interview with Blair was that she would first meet with North, where he would "lay down the rules."

Max always enjoyed these conversations.

Boxer, North, and Associates had the top floor of a high-rise in downtown Phoenix, boasting views of Chase Field. As Max waited for North in the lobby—decorated in subdued desert hues—she wondered why Blair asked that the interview be conducted in her attorney's office. Blair had expressly said she hadn't wanted Max to come to her house. Originally, she'd planned to meet with the Caldwells yesterday, but in-stead John came alone to the Biltmore, where Max was staying, and gave her what she considered a lame excuse for Blair's absence. They'd talked for several hours, and the anguish in John's voice was clear.

His son's death had gutted him and John was desperate to protect his wife. She was innocent, the result of a legal system gone awry, accord-ing to John.

"Blair couldn't kill anyone, let alone our son. But the police couldn't find a suspect, they twisted everything around, and arrested Blair. They have no evidence. None."

Max had reminded John multiple times—because he didn't seem to absorb her meaning—that she would give him the truth, but that maybe a private investigator would be more appropriate than an investigative reporter.

"Blair's attorney has a private investigator on staff," John had said. "They don't care who killed Peter. They only want to prove it wasn't Blair."

John was correct, but Max had explained—twice—that she didn't work active homicide investigations. Cold cases were different because—usually—the crime was more than a year old and the police didn't have a suspect. The only time she stepped into a hot case was a missing person because a media spotlight could often be helpful.

John was convinced that if Max solved the three cold cases that were similar to Peter's murder, that she would de facto solve Peter's murder. Max thought he was stretching. Yet here she was, waiting to talk to Blair and her attorney. John was one of Max's few close friends. How could she say no? How could she turn her back on a friend when she didn't have many to spare?

Besides, the three cold cases were more than a little intriguing. Peter Caldwell aside, if her staff had presented her with the cases as a possible investigation for her monthly crime show, *Maximum Exposure*, she would have seriously considered them.

Her phone rang and she almost sent it to voice mail, but it was a call she'd been expecting. She stepped away from the receptionist and answered.

"Counselor," she said, her voice warm and smooth, "I've been expecting your call."

"You threatened me, and I've had enough."

She went from cordial to heated in a heartbeat. "I didn't threaten you, Mr. Stanton. I gave you a courtesy call."

"Courtesy? That's what you call exploiting my son's murder?"

She went from heated to angry in the next heartbeat.

"I said I didn't need your permission, but I want your help." Her voice was even but sharp. "You're the one who has been avoiding my calls."

"Let me explain something to you, Ms. Revere," Stanton said. "Without me, you have nothing. No one will speak to you. You step out of line, you will be arrested. My son is off-limits. Are we clear?"

"Your son's murder is unsolved, and I believe I can solve it." Why did she say that? She'd never solved a murder nearly twenty years cold. It was next to impossible.

But she was angry, so she didn't backtrack—not that she would have. Showing doubt, showing weakness, wouldn't get her what she needed.

"Do you think I haven't used every legal resource at my disposal to solve Justin's murder? He was my son, I'm the district attorney, and I have never forgotten."

Max dialed back her anger. Just a bit. "My track record speaks for it-self, Mr. Stanton. I have connected Justin's murder with two, possibly three similar crimes, but I need more information. Meet with me. Please," she added, "I'll explain my theory and share everything I have learned." Which was very little at this point. "If after we meet you are still adamant about not helping, I'll respect that."

"And back down?"

"Of course not," she said. Obviously the San Diego District Attorney didn't know her reputation. "I'll still investigate. I simply won't include you. I'll fly to Idaho and speak with your ex-wife."

"Leave Nelia out of this." She could hear the venom in his voice. Score one for her—she knew how to ensure his cooperation.

"Justin was her son, too."

"Blackmail now?"

"Really, that's what you're going with? Blackmail." Max was trying to give Andrew Stanton some leeway because he had lost his son, but the lawyer was making it difficult for her to play nice.

"Nelia has been through hell, I won't allow you—"

"Stop," Max said. She spotted who she presumed to be North's assis-tant standing by the reception desk looking at her. "You have my pro-ducer's phone number. Call him. He'll answer your questions and you can feel free to browbeat and threaten him over the phone. Ben lives for conflict. But I *will* be in San Diego tomorrow afternoon. Either you work with me or you don't, but you're not going to stop me."

She ended the call and took a long, deep breath. She needed to re-gain her composure if she was going to be on her A game with Blair Caldwell.

Max was digging a deep hole for herself. The four cases—Peter Caldwell's murder and the three others—had many similarities, but similarities didn't solve crimes. She'd been pulling together research for the last two weeks, and she still had very little to go on. The police had connected none of the four cases, and proving they were linked would be impossible if she couldn't access police records and forensics reports. The first two homicides were unsolved; in the third the father was in prison; and the last—Peter—was built on circumstantial evidence.

She and her staff were working several threads, but so far nothing she pulled led anywhere. Max could neither prove—nor disprove—a connection. She needed to be in the field, talking to people who had been there, reading the files, analyzing the data, reinterviewing witnesses and suspects. And even then, she had never tackled an assignment of this magnitude.

Yet, you tell Stanton that you can solve his son's murder.

She had put her reputation on the line with one angry comment. That deep hole she saw herself standing next to had just gotten a whole lot wider.

"Ms. Revere?" The young man who had been standing at the reception desk walked over to her. "I'm Ron Lee. Mr. North is ready for you."

"Thank you," she said formally and pulled herself together. She didn't know why this investigation had gotten under her skin. She prided herself on maintaining a level of detachment from the victims, the surviving family, and law enforcement. But lately, she'd found herself more wrapped up in the lives of the people involved in an investigation than she was comfortable with. She couldn't seem to find the personal detachment that had served her well for so long.

Max followed Ron down the wide hallway, which turned before reaching double doors with CHARLES NORTH engraved on a gold plaque. The assistant knocked, waited for permission to enter, then grandly opened both doors.

"Ms. Maxine Revere," Ron announced formally.

North rose from his desk and crossed the large corner office. Blair wasn't in the room.

He took her hand. "Ms. Revere, I'm Charles North. We spoke on the phone." He turned to his assistant. "Ron, please sit with Mrs. Caldwell until I need her."

"Yes, sir." Ron closed the doors on his way out.

North motioned for Max to sit at a conference table that could comfortably sit twelve. He sat at the head. Common tactic. Max smiled and took a seat two down from him. "Thank you for arranging this meeting."

"As I told you last week," North said, "I disapprove of Mr. Caldwell's investigation and his ill-conceived theory. He is a man grasping at straws who doesn't understand the legal system and the primary goal of my team. Our goal is for the jury to return a not guilty verdict. We believe that the State will not be able to prove their case against my client."

As with many lawyers who Max had met over the years, North spoke clearly and formally.

"You indicated during our earlier conversation that the prosecution lacked evidence, but you were not specific."

"I will not outline our legal strategy to the media prior to trial. As I also said over the phone, I would consent to an interview after the trial is concluded. It is my understanding that you will be covering the trial for NET?"

It was worded as a question, because Max hadn't actually said anything about media involvement in Blair's trial.

"NET will be covering the trial."

"But not you?"

"Either myself or Ace Burley, NET's crime reporter." She didn't want to cover the trial, but she was already out here. She might be stuck with it. NET gave her a lot of leeway to run her show and her investigations as she wanted—a condition of her agreeing to host *Maximum Exposure* in the first place. So when they asked for something—like coverage of a trial—she generally agreed. It was her least favorite aspect of her job.

"Then what is your interest in this case? Other than the fact that you're John Caldwell's ex-girlfriend."

Had John or Blair told the lawyer about her relationship with John? She hadn't expected the information to be kept secret, but she certainly hadn't intended to lead with the fact that she'd dated John for a year while they were both at Columbia University.

Max leaned back in the leather chair. "Mr. North, Blair already agreed to talk to me. Please bring her in."

"I advised Mrs. Caldwell not to speak with you. She overruled me, but be aware that she is only doing this for her husband. I ask that you consider that before using anything she says."

Max already suspected that Blair agreed to talk to her because John wanted it. She said, "Over the past decade, I have covered dozens of trials, investigated hundreds of cold cases, and interviewed thousands of witnesses, victims, suspects, and family members."

"Your point, Ms. Revere?"

"You have a job, I have a job. Let me do my job. Because whether or not Blair Caldwell speaks to me is irrelevant. I'm not packing up and going home."

Charles sighed. "I doubted you would, though I had hoped."

"Does the truth scare you?"

"The truth is subjective."

Max laughed, but she wasn't amused. "Truth is *objective*. It's neither good nor bad. It's what we do with the truth that is subjective, because *we* are flawed."

The defense lawyer sat there for a moment. "I think you and the Caldwells are making a huge mistake."

"I'm not making a mistake," Max said. "I can't speak for John or Blair." She leaned forward, kept her voice calm and friendly. She may not be able to sway the lawyer, but she didn't want him to actively oppose her efforts. "Charles, I have one question for you and I promise that I will not quote you, I will not even mention the situation except for what has already been reported in the press."

"I can't promise to answer, but you may ask."

"The local news reported a leak out of the DA's office that they'd offered Blair a plea deal and she declined. I'm not asking for the details," she added quickly, knowing what his primary objection would be, "but did you recommend to your client to accept or decline?"

He stared at her for a long moment. He would make an outstanding poker player—maybe that's why he was so good as a trial lawyer.

"Wait here."

He walked out of the interview room without answering her question. She liked him.

Charles North was a top criminal defense attorney, and his firm wasn't cheap. He'd made his name after defending a professional athlete charged with killing his mistress. The jury had been hung, and the prosecution retried the case, and then lost—a not guilty verdict. North had made a small fortune on the two trials, but the ballplayer had walked free. Max didn't know if he was guilty or innocent. She'd never looked into the case. But North had been praised by his colleagues, including the prosecution, for his professionalism.

She'd always wondered what motivated lawyers to specialize in criminal defense. Some, perhaps, because of the money. A big defense trial could be extremely lucrative. She'd known enough lawyers in her life to know that most didn't take cases out of some noble cause of righting wrongs, believing that their clients were always innocent and they were champions of a corrupt court system. Most treated their clients as a job. They did due diligence, ensured legal rules were followed, and worked out plea deals to the benefit of their clients. The most *noble*—for lack of a better word—defense lawyers believed in the system just as much as the prosecution. They went into practice because they believed in their hearts and souls that every person, rich or poor, black or white, deserved a fair trial. That the goal wasn't to win or lose per se, but to ensure that the police behaved, that the prosecution played aboveboard, that the accused was treated appropriately. And yes, that the evidence was fair and untainted.

North's goal was clearly to get a not guilty verdict, which didn't mean he thought his client was innocent. That only meant he thought the prosecution had no case.

There was no way in hell the DA or the cops would meet with Max. She'd gone through the motions—if necessary, she could say so-and-so declined to comment. But she wasn't expecting a quote or cooperation. The only way Max could learn about the case was through the defense and it was clear North wouldn't give her anything—except allowing her to talk to his client against his advice.

She was going to have to get everything she could out of Blair Caldwell.

Sometimes what someone said—or didn't say—wasn't as important as how they behaved.

Chapter Two

Blair Caldwell was thirty-five, a year older than her husband, and a successful corporate attorney in Scottsdale—at least until she was arrested for murder. Her specialty was tax law, which Max supposed made her compatible with John, a financial consultant.

Blair was an attractive woman. Her long blond hair was straight, clean, and brushed back into a neat ponytail. She wore minimal makeup, an expensive but subdued suit not unlike something she might wear in court. Her blue eyes were sharp, focused.

Max had a bad habit of judging people instantly at first meet. Nine times out of ten, she nailed their core personality. Sometimes she was wrong, so she tried to avoid snap judgments.

Okay, she didn't really try to avoid such judgments because being right 90 percent of the time helped her.

Max had Blair pegged from when they'd first met more than ten years ago, and time had only confirmed Max's assessment. Smart—to the point of being shrewd—ambitious, and image-conscious. Never a hair out of place, never a style out of date. Max knew the basics: Blair was born to an upper-middle-class family in Boston, graduated from Boston College, and attended law school at Fordham in New York. The one thing she and Max had in common was their love of art and art history, and Blair had exquisite taste in that field. That had been the one thing Max liked about Blair—they'd first met at an art gallery after John and Blair started dating, and Blair had a keen eye.

While smart to the point of thinking herself an intellectual, Blair had a deep disdain for stupidity. A lot like Max, she realized, so maybe it wasn't surprising that while Max respected Blair, she didn't like her.

Maybe, perhaps, because Blair wanted everyone to know that she was smarter than most people. Image and status were extremely important to her, and that separated her from Max—Max couldn't care less about what people thought of her.

Blair sat down at the conference table, directly across from Max, and crossed her hands in front of her. Blair seemed a bit harder around the edges today compared to when she'd been a law student, but being accused of killing your son might do that to a person.

With her chin tilted up, Blair said, "I'm only here because John asked me to meet with you."

Just as Max expected. Didn't mean she couldn't learn something.

Blair continued. "Maxine, you and John have been friends for a long time. I respect that. You don't know me as well, but I'm asking you for a favor. You *must* convince John to drop this—for now. After the trial, after I'm exonerated, we can hire a private investigator to find out who killed our son. And if you want to help us then, I would appreciate it. But right now, my freedom is at stake. I just need . . . I need John to understand that this isn't helping me."

"You think that I can convince John to forget that Peter's murder is similar to three other crimes spanning twenty years."

"The trial begins in less than three weeks. I need him to be with me, supporting me during the trial, showing a united front. That is extremely important to the jury. I can't have him chasing answers that he may never find. John respects you, Maxine. If you tell him there's nothing here, he'll believe it."

"I won't know if there's anything to his theory until I investigate."

Max found it interesting that Blair was doing all the talking. Max had yet to ask a question, but sometimes, she learned more by letting her subjects talk at will than by focusing the discussion.

"I'm not going to discuss my trial with you, Maxine."

"I didn't ask about the trial, Blair."

She looked perplexed. "Then why did you want to meet?"

"Because John is convinced that you're innocent and he felt it was important that I talk to you—as if by talking, I would agree with him and take on this investigation."

"And what? You don't agree?" Did she sound defensive? Or angry?

"I'm not here to investigate Peter's murder. I'm here because there are compelling similarities between his death and the deaths of three other young boys. As you well know, Blair, I only investigate cold cases."

"Then you obviously don't need to talk to me because I don't know anything about those crimes—other than what John has told me."

"Based on what John has uncovered, what do you think?"

Max glanced over at North, who was surprisingly quiet. But again, this was the first real question Max had asked.

"I think it's awful that three other mothers lost their only son, like I did. On the surface—yes, there seems to be a pattern of sorts. But I can't focus on that right now. This trial is tearing me apart. It's eating John up from the inside out. He wants answers, and the police aren't getting them because they think I did something so awful—" She stopped, took a breath. She reached for a decanter of water on the table. North took it from her, poured a tall glass, and handed it to her.

"Thank you, Charles."

"Ms. Revere?" North asked.

"Thank you."

Charles poured her a glass, then walked over and placed it in front of her. "I think you'll agree, Ms. Revere, that the stress of the trial coupled with the strain at the Caldwell house over this theory of Mr. Caldwell's is severely affecting my client's well-being." He sat back down, looked at Blair then Max, and said, "It would benefit everyone, including Mr. Caldwell, to . . . temporarily put aside any hunt for the real killer, and focus solely on clearing Mrs. Caldwell's name."

"It would seem to me that the only way to clear Blair's name is to find out who killed Peter," Max said.

"Yet she's the one standing trial. This is the legal system. Not always swift, but there is a process. Bringing up alternate theories of what may have happened is not the defense's role."

"I've covered enough trials, Counselor, that I'm surprised that you would even say that."

"There are on occasion strategic reasons to suggest to the jury possible alternatives to interpret evidence that the State has presented, but that is *my* job, not yours." He had a sparkle in his eye, knowing she would immediately recognize him using her earlier comment against her. Yes, she definitely liked Blair's attorney.

"And wouldn't it benefit your case if I uncovered evidence of similarities that may give the jury reasonable doubt?"

"Yet if you conclusively prove there is no connection," North countered, "and word gets out that you were investigating these cold cases with the goal of exonerating Mrs. Caldwell, then that information could sway the jury against us."

"My goal isn't to exonerate Blair," Max said.

"Then why are you here?" Blair snapped, her composure crumbling. "Do you think that you can just waltz back into John's life when I'm in prison?"

Max hadn't expected Blair to be . . . *jealous*. It didn't seem to be in character for Blair.

"I'm here because of three cold cases: Justin Stanton, Tommy Porter, and Chris Donovan." Max was calm, more amused than irritated at Blair's comment. "I found John's research compelling. I think there's a connection. I will find it."

She realized that there was a distinct philosophical difference between what John wanted and what Blair wanted. She knew exactly what she needed to do—starting with postponing her next interview.

She rose from her seat. "Thank you for your time."

"What are you going to write about?" Blair said, suddenly worried.

"I'm not writing anything at this point," Max said. "I don't print theories. I print the truth. And I don't know the truth." *Yet.* "I'll talk to you later."

"Call my attorney, I'm not talking to you without someone to protect my interests."

"I only want the truth," Max said. "And if the person who killed Peter is the same person who killed three other boys over the last twenty years, I will find out."

Wow, that must be a record. Max telling first Stanton then Blair that she would solve this case when she had no idea how she was going to do it. But there was a fundamental difference between this case and the other three: she wouldn't be able to access any information about Peter Caldwell's murder until after the trial. In the other cases, most of the information was public.

North called in his assistant to sit with Blair, then walked Max to the lobby. "My client is under stress, and her husband's insistence in pursuing this theory isn't helping."

"He wants the truth."

"He wants his wife cleared of all charges."

"On the contrary, Mr. North, John wants the truth. *Blair* wants to be cleared of all charges. I don't know if they can both get what they want."

She walked out. While in the elevator, she sent her producer Ben a message to postpone her interview with Peter's teacher—she needed to make a stop first.

She wanted to see where John and Blair lived—and where Peter had died—before Blair got home.

Chapter Three

Max convinced John to meet her at his house. He questioned her on the phone, but she said she'd explain in person.

He was already there when she arrived, dressed in a business suit and looking just as handsome as ever. But the events of the last nine months had taken their toll: he had lost weight and slouched as he walked, his hair was longer than he should keep it, and he couldn't hide the dark circles under his eyes.

She could relate. Insomnia was a way of life for her, and eye cream her best friend.

"What's wrong?" he asked immediately. His dark eyes were watery and red. If she didn't know better, she'd think he was on something. But grief had the same effect on people. John had been grieving since the night his son disappeared.

"I thought it was best if I walked through the house with you— without Blair."

"I don't understand. What happened?"

"Nothing happened."

"But you know Blair's innocent."

"I didn't ask, and even if I did, her attorney wasn't going to allow any questions about her case. I talked to her because you wanted me to, but she made it clear she doesn't want to pursue any theories about Peter's murder until after the trial."

"That's her attorney talking!"

"She's listening to him. You must understand their point of view. The trial starts in less than three weeks."

"All the more reason to find out what really happened!" He ran both hands through his hair as he turned to his front door. He stared at the panel as if he'd forgotten the code.

"I told you last night that they wouldn't be able to answer my questions. But you can."

"Anything. Anything to find out who did this." He typed in a code. It took him three tries before the door clicked open.

John told her he wanted the truth. "And if Blair killed Peter?"

"She didn't. How can you even say that? Is that what you're going to write about?"

Max stepped inside the cool house. It was spacious with large, open rooms and a view of the golf course from eighteen-foot windows in the great room. Everything was light and airy, with tile on the floor to help keep the place cool in the desert heat. January felt like a New York spring, but without the wind.

"I'm not writing about this case, John—I'm writing about the three cold cases you uncovered."

"That's what you said, but—"

"I said it because that's what I'm doing. My staff went through all the information you sent, and we found additional information that makes me believe that there is a connection. I won't know for certain until I talk to the individuals involved with those three cases. Whether they connect to Peter's murder, I won't know until I find answers to the first three." She'd told him all this last night, but she would repeat it as many times as it took for John to accept. "Blair's attorney, the police, the DA—none of them are going to give me any information that isn't already public. But you, John, know the details."

She felt uncomfortable asking him to do this, but the police always held back information in any homicide investigation. John might know those details, and if she could use them to connect this case to the three cold cases, then she could do exactly what he wanted—exonerate his wife.

The other three cases were so similar it was eerie—and Max's gut instinct told her there was a connection. Peter seemed to be an anomaly, but there were enough surface similarities that if the details started to match, maybe John was right—that Blair was innocent and Peter was the victim of a serial killer who had been killing young boys for nearly twenty years.

"I trust you, Max." His voice was so pained Max hated that she had to push him, but if she didn't, she was wasting both of their time.

"I need to know if you trust me to find the truth or you trust me to exonerate Blair."

He opened his mouth, then closed it. John might have been scattered these last few months, but he was a smart guy. He knew exactly what Max was saying.

His voice was a mere whisper. "I want the truth."

Max knew that John was struggling, but if she coddled him, he would break, and that would do neither of them any good. She didn't know when Blair would return home—if she had left the law offices right after Max, they might only have a few minutes.

"You don't need to go through all the details of the crime scene," Max said. "The newspaper accounts were very clear because initially, they believed it was a kidnapping and focused on the search and rescue aspect, which meant giving out as much information to the public as possible."

John nodded.

"Can I see Peter's room?"

John led Max down the hall. Every footstep seemed to physically pain him.

"You don't need to come in with me," she said. "The police must have finished their on-site investigation long ago."

"They took his bedding, a throw rug in front of his bed, made a mess—but I didn't blame them. They were looking for my son. We thought we could find him." *Alive.* John hadn't believed Peter was dead until they found his body. Most parents didn't. Hope always lived.

Max hadn't had that hope with her college roommate Karen. As soon as Karen went missing, she knew the worst had happened. And any glimmer of hope died when the police found the crime scene stained with so much blood no one could have survived such a brutal attack. And though they'd never found Karen's body, Max had never harbored hope that she was still alive. Not then, and not now, ten years later.

"Other than you and Blair," Max asked, "did they find any fingerprints in the room?"

"Jordan, our babysitter. Jane, our housekeeper. She comes in once a week."

"What day does Jane come?"

"Fridays. But not anymore."

"You fired her? She quit?"

"She quit. She came in after—after the police said we could go into Peter's room. She came in to clean up and started crying. Told me she couldn't, that she was heartbroken."

"Was that before or after Blair was arrested?"

"Why is that important?"

"It could factor into why she quit."

"After," he whispered.

She would get Jane's contact information and add her to the list of people to talk to.

"You can leave," she said when they reached Peter's door.

"I'm okay." He stood at the threshold.

Peter's room was spacious and airy like the rest of the house, only this was a room designed with a little boy in mind. Baseball everything— signed balls, photos, a trading card collection that filled a bookshelf. He had a signed poster of some guy from the Arizona Diamondbacks framed over his bed, and a poster of a young Derek Jeter from the Yankees— being a New Yorker for more than a decade, Max would have to be living under a rock not to have recognized him, even though her knowledge of baseball was limited.

The top shelf of Peter's bookshelf held classic children's books like *Tom Sawyer* and *The Swiss Family Robinson*—Max had read many of them, but it was clear these copies had never been touched. On a lower shelf were a collection of worn choose-your-own-adventure and *Goosebumps* books and an extensive collection of equally worn Marvel comics. Peter had a preference for Captain America and Spider-Man. Polar opposites in many ways, Max thought, one handsome and strong and patriotic, the other a quiet geek who wore a mask and kept his identity secret.

From the press reports, Peter had been kidnapped from his bedroom between midnight and 2:00 A.M. The family had an alarm system, but only used it when they weren't home. The monitoring company had confirmed the pattern of use. John and Blair had gone to a party at the clubhouse and the teenage daughter of a neighbor who was also at the party came over to babysit Peter. Jordan Fellows was their regular babysitter and had known the family since they moved in five years before.

According to the public statement, the Caldwells had left the house just after 8:00 P.M. on a Saturday night at the end of April. Because it was the weekend, Peter was allowed to stay up and watch a movie with Jordan. She put him into bed at ten fifteen, and said she'd checked on him just before midnight because she'd heard him use the bathroom, which adjoined his bedroom. She saw him climbing back into his bed half-asleep, so she shut the door and went back to the kitchen where she was studying. John and Blair came home at two in the morning. They'd walked from the clubhouse. Blair had gone to check on Peter and he wasn't in his bed. They searched the house, the backyard, the pool, and called 911.

Jordan had been a high school senior at the time. She was now a freshman at the University of Arizona. Max had reached out to her, but she hadn't returned Max's calls.

Peter had a bathroom off his room. It was functional and the only kid accents were a bath mat shaped as a dinosaur and a matching dinosaur toothbrush holder and cup.

Two large windows connected at the corner and looked out into the side yard as well as a grassy area behind the house. Each was screened and locked from the inside. Jordan had said she hadn't checked the windows and didn't remember if they were cracked open or closed. There was no direct line of sight to the neighbors, and while the golf course backed up to the Caldwell house, the course had closed at sunset.

There was also a sliding-glass door that went out to the patio. Why had the reports said the killer went in through the window? Evidence outside? The door would have been easier, though perhaps harder to get open.

Max crossed the room, unlocked the door, and opened it. A *beep-beep* sounded throughout the house.

"Child safety beeps—even when the alarm is off, the doors that go out to the pool beep." John's voice cracked. Max looked over at him and saw silent tears.

Max had seen enough. She walked out, leading John down the hall. "The public reports said Peter had been taken out of one of the windows, but there was no indication if it was forced or open."

"We live in a safe neighborhood—Scottsdale is one of the safest communities in Arizona. Affluent. We have a gated community. Gated. Safe." He shook his head, as if realizing he was repeating himself. "Peter liked to sleep with his window open."

"Your babysitter couldn't remember if it was open or closed—if it was wide open, wouldn't she have noticed it?"

"Probably, I don't know."

Maybe, maybe not. Especially on a mildly warm night like the night in April when Peter was killed. Max had checked the weather report—the temperature at midnight was seventy-one degrees. The low was at 5:00 A.M., a "crisp" sixty-six degrees.

Max didn't have access to the coroner's report, but the news reports indicated that Peter's body had been found buried in a sand pit on the edge of the golf course. Max had mapped it out based on the written report and the crime scene photos that had been available through both print and television media. The killer would had to have taken Peter—subdued or unconscious or already dead—across the golf course. That suggested they knew the area, at least marginally. But anyone who might have been outside in their backyard could have seen them, and even though it was late, there had been the annual golf membership party at the clubhouse and more people than residents had been in the community.

Yet maybe that was why no one noticed anything suspicious. Because there were more people out that evening in the neighborhood.

Max was pretty certain that the police would have done due diligence and gone through the security logs at the gate. But were there other ways to get onto the property? Did they log all individuals in the car, or just the driver? Could someone have been hiding in a vehicle? Why would a stranger kill Peter? If he'd been abducted from a park or public place, Max could see a stranger abduction. But there was no sexual assault—and that was doubly odd. Most children who were abducted by strangers were sexually assaulted. Not Peter.

And not the other three young male victims.

That connection alone made John's research compelling.

The gated community, however, made it much more difficult for a stranger to sneak in. Not impossible, she'd already had her assistant David talk to the security firm who handled the community. They had surveillance cameras at the two entrances—one was manned 24/7, the other was for residents only and accessed by a card key. There were cameras on the clubhouse, the first and eighteenth holes, the community swimming pools, gym, and playground. Essentially, the public areas.

Individuals could be a member of the golf club with access to the course from 6:00 A.M. through sunset, or the clubhouse during regular hours—6:00 A.M. to 10:00 P.M. The could only come in through the main gate and had to check in.

Golf club membership was expensive, which expanded the suspect pool beyond residents, but it was still a known list.

Or the killer could have stolen the card key and used it to access the back entrance. Highly unlikely, as that would have come out during the investigation. It would also show premeditation, and yet Max couldn't discern a motive for Peter's murder using that theory.

Someone who lived or worked in the community or who had checked in at the gate for the party at the clubhouse had specifically targeted Peter Caldwell. They knew enough to know which bedroom was his, that his window would be open, and that his parents were gone.

How long would it have taken? The walk from the house to the sand pit where he had been buried would have taken approximately ten minutes. He hadn't been discovered until search dogs had been brought in at noon the following day, ten to twelve hours after he went missing. They'd closed the golf course because of the search . . . otherwise he may have been found earlier.

Reports indicated Peter had been suffocated, wrapped in a blanket from his bed, then buried in the sand. No physical evidence had been found on the body—that detail Max had picked up from both John and Blair's lawyer, though neither flat-out said as much. If there was physical evidence, Blair and her attorney wouldn't be so confident they could win.

Why did the police suspect Blair? The only logical explanation was either she'd gone missing from the party and no witness could state that she was there during the window of death, or they had a witness who saw her *not* at the party. If there was a witness, Blair would have taken the plea deal—unless the witness was somehow unreliable.

Why didn't the police suspect John? Did he have a firm alibi? What about someone with a grudge against one or both of the Caldwells?

"Sit, John, I have a few questions."

Max led John to the kitchen, where he sat down at the breakfast table. They were surrounded on three sides by windows.

Max wished she didn't have to do this.

"Did the police interrogate you before or after they found Peter?"

John nodded slowly. "I don't think they ever looked at anyone else. I mean, I don't know. Do you know how it is when you remember some things so vividly, and other things are all fuzzy? I remember the party, and walking home with Blair—it was a beautiful night. And coming home. I walked Jordan home—she told me not to bother, but there were a lot of drunk people coming from the party and I didn't want her to have to deal with someone being rude or reckless. People think that golf carts aren't cars, but you can still hurt someone, you know?"

She nodded, because she wanted him to continue. She wished she could steer him better, but she didn't want to interrupt his train of thought.

"She only lives three blocks away. I watched her go inside, then I walked back home."

"How long did that take?"

"Less than ten minutes. Ten minutes at most." He paused. "That's exactly what the police asked me."

"They just need to establish a timeline." Timelines were crucial. Max lived and breathed her cases on timelines.

"As soon as I walked in, Blair told me she couldn't find Peter. That he wasn't in his bed, he wasn't in the house. I searched the house again. Called for him. I . . . I looked in the pool. Peter is a great—was a great—swimmer, but even good swimmers . . ." His voice trailed off. "He wasn't anywhere. Blair called nine-one-one and I called Jordan. She came back with her dad, and we all looked for him."

"All of you together?"

"Bob and I looked together. Blair and Jordan stayed in the house to wait for the police. Jordan looked everywhere a second time, under beds, closets, cabinets. She was so upset. I wasn't—not then. I was certain there was a logical explanation."

That was so much like John. He was a numbers guy. Everything was orderly. Math had rules. Finance had rules. He would think linearly.

"Peter was always a curious kid—he was a good kid, he didn't get into trouble much, but there were times he'd do kid stuff, you know? Like once he was pretending to drive the golf cart when he was six and accidentally turned it on and it started moving. I was right there watching him but I was listening to music while working on my laptop, and I didn't hear it start. And then he once climbed into the attic—I didn't even know he knew how to pull the ladder down, that he was strong enough—he was only five. But he'd watched me bring in the stepladder, and I used to bring him up there with me and we'd go through old toys and he'd pick what to give to charity. Sometimes, when he did something he knew was wrong—like coloring on the walls—he would hide, not wanting to get into trouble. H-h-he was such a great kid. A normal, wonderful kid." He pinched his eyes.

"Were the windows open when you went into his bedroom?"

"Yes."

"But you didn't actually go into the bedroom when you got home."

He frowned. "No, but Blair said one window was open and the screen was off. That's why we were looking outside. Not just our pool, but all the pools that he might be able to access from the golf course."

25

"When the police interrogated you, did they ask for an accounting of your time at the party?"

"Yes—and that's why this is so frustrating! We were there from eight thirty until nearly two in the morning. It's the big annual ball after the spring tournament. A lot of my clients have a membership, I had to go, talk to people. But I talked to so many people. I don't know if I talked to Kingston at ten thirty and Jim at eleven thirty and Don at midnight—I just know that I talked to them."

"And Blair was asked the same questions."

"Yes, we were both there, together. I don't know why they think she could do something so horrific."

"John, Blair's attorney believes the evidence is all circumstantial, but the prosecution must have a reason for filing these charges. They don't prosecute unless they have something to hang their hat on."

"No—"

She interrupted. "And my guess is that Blair was missing for a period of time at the party—that after they put together all the witness statements and created a timeline, they realized she was missing for a long enough duration to go home and return to the party without you noticing she was missing."

"Why are you doing this, Max? I thought you wanted to help." His voice was anguished. Max had to stay resolute or she would be able to help no one.

"I do, John. But I don't have the information the police have. I can't retrace their steps, interview their witnesses. I don't have access to the coroner's report or the trace evidence report or anything to prove or disprove their theory. I have to go by what people tell me."

John got up and left the kitchen. Max thought for a moment that he was expecting her to follow—or to leave. He returned a minute later with a thick folder. "This is a list of every resident in this community, and the names and ages of everyone living in their houses. It also includes everyone who signed in at the front gate the night of the party and their license plate numbers. I have many friends here, and while the police also have this information, there's nothing prohibiting them from sharing with me—other than privacy laws. And I don't give a damn about privacy laws at this point, not when my son is dead and my wife is being blamed for something she didn't do."

Glancing at the thick file, this was one of the few times Max was grateful that they had a staff at NET who could follow up with all this in short order. She stuffed the folder into her bag.

"This will help," she said. It might only help to pound a nail into Blair's coffin, if none of these people had the motive, means, or opportunity to kill Peter.

"I hope so, but . . . what are you going to do with them?"

"First thing is to run these names and find out if anyone lived near the locations of the three cold cases or is connected to any of those families."

Now for the hard question. The one thing she had uncovered that connected the three cold cases—the one fact that John didn't know, or may not have considered when he read the press reports.

"John, complete disclosure. Have you ever had an affair?"

He stared at her as if he hadn't heard her question.

"John, were you having an affair last April when Peter was killed?"

"How can you ask that? I love my wife."

"I need to know. It's important."

"I've never had an affair. I've never cheated on Blair or any woman I dated."

She didn't know if she believed him. She wanted to believe him, because the John Caldwell she had known in college had been honest. He was a good guy. But she hadn't seen John in years and marriage changed people—sometimes for the better, sometimes for worse.

"What about Blair? Was she having an affair?"

"Blair? No! This is ridiculous, Max. What are you doing?"

"Covering all the bases."

She was more likely to believe that Blair was having an affair than John, but he could have changed. And it's possible John didn't know if his wife was cheating on him. Max didn't want to explain to John why she needed to know—but she might not have a choice.

"This was a mistake," John said. "You really have changed, Max. I didn't think you would come here and use me, use my son, for some

27

exploitive show. Sex? Affairs? My son is dead! You want to drag us through the mud?"

"Never, John," she said, but she didn't think he heard her.

The door leading from the garage into the laundry room adjacent to the kitchen opened. Blair walked in. She stared at Max. "What are you doing here? I said I didn't want you in my house!"

"Blair, honey," John said, taking her hand. "Max is leaving."

"You let her in?"

"She's just trying to help." But by his tone, Max sensed he'd shifted his faith away from her. He hadn't liked her questions, now he was unsure how he felt.

"No, she's not! She can't do anything except create problems with my case. I explained all this to you, John! Charles explained it to you!"

"*Someone* needs to find out who really killed Peter." John's voice was a whisper as Blair's grew in volume. Max had been around grieving families, and they drained her. This was much worse. John was a friend.

"After the trial," Blair said. "After I'm cleared. I just want to move on with our lives. The last nine months have been hell, John. For both of us."

"I'm leaving," Max said. "I'll call later."

Blair burst into tears and ran down the hall.

Tears?

John ran both hands through his hair and stood there as if he was going to collapse. Then he shook his head and straightened his spine, but his eyes were still as haunted as they'd been when Max saw him last night. "She's on edge, Max. Just—I don't know. I don't know anything anymore. Maybe I'm doing everything wrong."

"Finding the truth is never wrong," she said. But sometimes, the truth hurt. Some people needed lies to survive.

Max wasn't one of those people.

"I need to go to her. Please let yourself out."

Chapter Four

By the time Max was done interviewing Peter Caldwell's third-grade teacher, Barbara Pritchard, her staff had located John's housekeeper, Jane Nunez.

She hadn't learned anything she didn't already know from Ms. Pritchard, but it was always helpful to have an outside opinion of individuals involved in any case and to confirm information. According to the teacher, Peter was a good student who enjoyed school and had many friends. John was an attentive father who participated in field trips more often than Blair. In fact, Ms. Pritchard couldn't remember a time that Blair had gone on a field trip with the school. Ms. Pritchard also talked about how John treated his son and wife with love and respect, so much that Max wondered if the teacher was a bit jealous or perhaps simply a romantic.

The main reason Max wanted to talk to the teacher was to have her share what she told the police, without expressly asking her to repeat what she'd told the police. And Ms. Pritchard came through with flying colors—yes, the police had asked if Peter had been abused, and she had never seen any signs of abuse. No bruises, no broken bones, nothing. Peter was a happy child in a loving, wealthy family. The only time he'd ever even missed school was when he was ill with the flu for a week right before Christmas break, but he caught up on his assignments.

Of course the police had asked about child abuse, Max thought, as she drove to Jane Nunez's house in a quiet, established Phoenix neighborhood. They would want any evidence of abuse as a pattern to show the jury habitual violence leading up to murder. Historically, a parent who killed one of their children had been abusing them. But if there was any evidence of abuse, John would have known about it—and he wouldn't have been so quick to think Blair was innocent.

Unless he was in complete denial.

Yet she couldn't see John turning his back on physical abuse. Once might be an accident, but multiple times? Could he be that naïve?

She couldn't legally access Peter's medical records, and she would have to wait until the trial to find out if the prosecution had uncovered any child abuse, but the teacher seemed certain that Peter was healthy and happy. Would she have caught on to the subtleties of abuse? Max couldn't say, but in the thirty minutes she spent with the teacher, she was almost certain Ms. Pritchard would have been aware of any physical or emotional signs of abuse—and that she wouldn't have kept that information to herself.

Max knocked on Jane Nunez's house at two that afternoon; she wasn't home. She drove to a nearby restaurant—a mom-and-pop Mexican diner. While the atmosphere was a far cry from the Biltmore where she'd eaten last night, Max had learned that some of the best food was found in the most nondescript places. She was not wrong in picking this hole-in-the-wall, if the salsa they put in front of her was any indication.

While she ate, Max read the report her staff had prepared on Jane Nunez.

Jane owned her own small business for the past fifteen years, employed more than a dozen housecleaners but also took her own clients. She owned her house, had no outstanding debt, and had only one social media account, a private page that seemed to be reserved for a limited number of friends and family. The business had a public Facebook page, but it was primarily to steer prospective clients to her Web site. There were comments from clients, most of them positive.

After enjoying a surprisingly fresh and spicy shrimp salad, Max relaxed in the booth and called several of Jane's clients—using the excuse that she was checking references—and they all spoke highly of Jane, her staff, and their overall professionalism. She learned from one chatty older woman that Jane was a widow with four children and the "salt of the earth."

Max glanced at her watch. It was three thirty—Jane might be home by now if she picked up her children from school. She seemed too young to have a child old enough to drive, but anything was possible.

Max paid for her meal and left. Jane's house was only five minutes away; she was still not home. Max sat in her rental car under a tree across the street. She was in the middle of proofreading an article Ben wanted to post under her byline to the *Maximum Exposure* Web site when her phone rang.

Nick.

She almost sent him to voice mail. She should. But she *had* left him a message yesterday when she arrived at the Biltmore.

"Hello, Nick."

"Hi, Max. I called you back as soon as I got your message."

She had to give him credit for trying. She knew he was trying to fix what was broken in their relationship, but she didn't know if what they had was worth fixing. Or if it could be fixed. Or if she wanted it to be fixed.

"I was in a meeting."

"In Phoenix?"

"A case I'm looking into."

"I'd love to hear about it."

Max watched a new, generic minivan pull in to the garage. Before the door closed, four kids clamored out of the van and ran into the house.

"And I'd love to share with you, but now isn't a good time. I have another interview in a few minutes."

"I have swing shift this week." For Nick, that meant he worked three until midnight. It was already nearly four; he was likely calling her from his desk.

"Call when you're off duty. If I'm awake, I'll answer."

"Are you okay?"

"I'm always okay, Nick. My interview is here. I'll talk to you tonight." She hung up before he—or she—prolonged the conversation.

She wished she hadn't answered the phone at all. This dance she and Nick had been waltzing for the last four months had drained her. Four months? Maybe it started when they first started seeing each other nine months ago.

Long-distance relationships had always been best for her because she didn't want to give up her independence or her autonomy. Plus, there was a layer of emotional distance that usually suited her. She could enjoy a weekend every month of fabulous sex and conversation and then resume her life when she returned to New York. But with Nick, she'd wanted more—she had shared more of herself with him than she had with nearly every other man she'd dated, yet he didn't share with her. At least not what she felt was important, namely this routine with his ex-wife over the custody of their son. An important part of his life that he told her in no uncertain terms he would not discuss with her.

You should have broken it off months ago.

She should have, but she'd been in an emotional whirlwind and convinced herself that she could enjoy the relationship for what it was and simply pull back emotionally.

It hadn't worked. She'd pulled back, but she wasn't enjoying the relationship. She felt like she was in a perpetual state of mourning, or anger, or both.

Max pulled herself together, finished proofreading the article, sent the corrections to Ben, and left her car. She walked up to Jane's front door and rang the bell.

A moment later she heard pounding footsteps and jostling behind the door. A young boy shouted, "Ouch!" then the door opened.

Two kids, a boy of about six and a girl of about eight, stood there, crowding into the space between the door and the frame. "Hi," the boy said.

"Is your mom home?" Max asked.

"Yes, who are you?"

"Maxine Revere."

They stood there, her name meaning nothing to either kid. "You're not selling anything, are you?" the girl asked.

"No."

"You sure? My mom doesn't like solicitors."

"I'm sure."

"Then who are you?"

"Abby! Robbie! Rooms, *now*."

Jane Nunez came to the door. Her kids scurried off. "I swear, they are impossible. May I help you?"

"I'm Maxine Revere. I'm a friend of John Caldwell's."

Jane didn't say anything, but she straightened her spine and her friendly expression vanished.

"John and I went to college together," Max continued. "He gave me your contact information." Small white lie, but John had told her he *would* give her the information. Blair's arrival prevented it.

"What do you want?"

Slightly suspicious. Why? "I'm an investigative reporter. I primarily investigate cold cases, and John asked me to look at similarities between Peter's murder and that of three young boys in Southern California."

Jane's face fell. "I don't know how I can help you."

"John said you worked for him for several years. You have insight into the family. You may have noticed something odd in the weeks or months leading up to Peter's death."

"A reporter," she said flatly. "I will not gossip about the family, friend or no."

"I don't want gossip." Though gossip often had a ring of truth, if you could weed through the biases of the person sharing the information. "May I come in?"

"No."

Okay, she had to do this another way. Jane Nunez was a mother, a small-business owner, and married—*was* married. Her chatty client said she was a widow. Yet she still wore a simple, classy wedding band on her ring finger. Four kids? Organized. Her kids had obeyed her immediately with only a simple eye roll of protest, meaning she commanded respect. She wouldn't be easy to manipulate.

"Do you think that Blair Caldwell killed her son?"

"I'm not going to dignify that question with an answer."

"John believes she's innocent, and he wants me to prove it. That's not what I do. I investigate cold cases. I've never investigated a murder that was less than a year old. I'm not here to stir the pot, to impede the police investigation or the trial. I'm here because there are similarities between Peter's murder and the murders of three other boys between the ages of seven and nine. I hope Blair is innocent, for John's peace of mind, but I'm not here to prove it."

"Then why are you here?"

"In the three other cases, one of the parents had been having an affair. That information came out in each of the investigations. John told me he wasn't cheating on Blair, Blair isn't talking about her case because of the pending trial. I want to know what you think."

"I have no idea," she said quickly.

"You have no idea if either of the Caldwells were having an affair?"

"I do not pry into the personal lives of my clients. I don't gossip. I need you to leave. It's been a long day, and I have to get dinner ready."

"Mrs. Nunez, did you notice anything odd in the weeks or months leading up to the murder? An unscheduled delivery, telephone hang-ups, anything out of the ordinary?"

"I was at the Caldwells' house every Friday from eight in the morning until two. That's it. If I had noticed anything, I would have told Mr. and Mrs. Caldwell. I would have told the police."

"You must have an opinion. The police arrested Blair Caldwell. That might jog your memory, something that you think she may or may not have done."

"I have the utmost respect for the police, but even the police can make a mistake."

"So you think she's innocent."

"I don't know! I need you to—"

"John told me that you cared a great deal for Peter. That you quit because you were heartbroken."

"I was heartbroken!" Her voice cracked and she cleared her throat. "Peter was a year older than my own son. I couldn't stop thinking that but for the grace of God, it could have been Robbie." She looked down, put her fingers to her eyes. "Ms. Revere," Jane said in a whisper, "I don't know what you want from me. I worked for the Caldwells since Peter was three, when they moved here from New York. I wasn't a nanny, I didn't watch Peter except on rare occasions. But I knew him, he was a wonderful little boy. Smart as a whip and full of energy. I couldn't work for them anymore because I kept seeing Robbie in Peter's photos." Her voice cracked again, and this time it took her several moments before she could speak again. Max assessed her, and her first impression was accurate.

This woman knew something. She might not know what she knew, but in the back of her mind, something was troubling her, over and above the death of a boy much like her own son.

Jane said, "The Caldwells were good clients. They spoiled Peter, but he didn't act spoiled. I feel for the family, and I feel for that little boy. And that is all I have to say on the subject."

"You know something, in the back of your mind, maybe if we could sit down and—" Max barely got the words out before Jane shut the door midsentence.

She walked back to her rental car, frustrated. The last two days had been a complete dead end. What had she expected? A suspect was on trial for murder. Even if someone thought Blair was innocent, would they still think so now? She couldn't talk to witnesses, she couldn't get back to see Blair, and after today John would probably not cooperate.

Time to focus on the other three cases. She hoped her assistant, David Kane, had better news.

On the drive back to the Biltmore, she made flight reservations for San Diego. Whether Andrew Stanton cooperated or not, she was going to investigate his son's murder.

Chapter Five

Max finished her dinner at the exquisite Wright's at the Biltmore—they'd been closed yesterday when she first arrived, so she'd made sure she set aside the time to enjoy a meal Wednesday evening before she left Thursday for San Diego.

She asked for a third glass of wine while she looked over her notes from her conversation with David earlier. He had mixed news—Chris Donovan's father would talk to him tomorrow at Corcoran State Prison, but the Porter family had refused to meet.

David was playing nice, she suspected, so she told him to try again with the Porters after talking to Adam Donovan. She could drive up to Santa Barbara from San Diego if she had to, but she'd rather avoid the trip. She wanted to focus her energy on the first victim—Justin Stanton. In her experience, the first victim would yield the most information. The first victim was almost always personal and the most likely victim to have known the killer.

The hostess approached her. "Ms. Revere, a Mr. and Mrs. Caldwell are at the front desk. They would like to speak with you. May I bring them here or would you like them to wait in the lobby?"

"Bring them here, thank you." She wasn't going to cut short her pleasant working dinner because Blair Caldwell was having a fit.

She'd bet her inheritance that Blair had convinced John to ask Max to back off.

Her wine came at the same time John and Blair were escorted to her table. "Would you like something to drink?" she asked.

"No, thank you," John said. He looked physically drained and didn't make eye contact. Max felt for him, but at the same time, she wasn't going to be manipulated by anyone's emotions.

Blair was pale and her eyes darted about. Was she concerned about being recognized? Confronted? Max had some sympathy. If she were in fact innocent, these charges and trial would shred her. She'd be heartbroken over the death of her son, and shattered that people thought she had done it.

If she were guilty, Max hoped the prosecution could prove it—beyond a shadow of a doubt. Because John didn't believe it and he needed to. If she were innocent, Max hoped the jury was unanimous, otherwise it would weigh heavily on Blair, on John, and on the community.

They held hands. Unified. Showing their strength.

"If you wanted to talk, I would have come to you," Max said.

"You've done so much for us," John said. "I didn't want to bother you."

"I'm in Arizona because you asked me to come. You're not *bothering* me."

"Blair and I had a really good talk this afternoon—in fact, the best talk we've had since . . . well, it's been a difficult nine months for both of us."

Max enjoyed being right—most of the time. Tonight, she was angry and disappointed.

Not that anything John could say would stop her.

"We very much appreciate your help," Blair said. Her comment surprised Max. She assessed John's wife. Tired, drawn, thin. She wore little makeup and appeared far more fragile now than she had been when Max spoke with her at her lawyer's office. "I want you to know that—I may have seemed aloof earlier, but this entire situation . . . and then on top of Petey's death . . ." She took a deep breath. "I just don't always know how to cope. Sometimes, it's easier to keep everyone at arm's length."

"I called you," John said, "because I was desperate for answers . . . and Max, you have always been so good at finding the truth. When we were in college, I'll never forget when you caught that fraternity in a lie about the party where those girls were mickeyed. You didn't let up, even when you were threatened. In fact, that seemed to drive you. You had those responsible expelled, the frat was put on probation, and everyone was stunned and relieved. No one wanted to confront the most powerful student group on campus, but you did, and you haven't changed. I definitely want you to find the truth. *After* the trial. I didn't realize the stress I'd placed on Blair by bringing you into the situation. Once the trial is over—and our attorney believes the prosecution's case is very weak—I want you to come back. The police will be looking at new evidence, finding out who really hurt our son. And then your help will be invaluable."

Max absorbed what John said. She was having a difficult time reconciling the smart man John was with the desperate man sitting here.

Desperation and fear. Desperation for his wife. What was going to happen at the trial. But mostly, it was the fear. Fear and loss and grief.

"John," she said calmly. "Maricopa County has upwards of a ninety percent conviction rate. If a jury comes back with a not guilty verdict, the police aren't going to look at other suspects."

"They'll *have* to!"

"They won't."

"But *you* can," John said. "You can make them. I've read all your books, Max. I know you don't give up, that you'll convince the police to listen to you."

"You must not have read my work carefully. But that's beside the point. You can't expect the police to do anything more than they've already done."

"That's ridiculous," John said. There was a bit of anger there, a bit of fight. Max would need to tap into that before she was through.

"Honey," Blair squeezed his hand, then turned to Max. "Whatever you can do, Maxine, we appreciate. But if you can't—I understand. That you believe in me, in us, means everything to me."

When had Max given Blair the impression that she *believed* in her? Max didn't know if she was guilty or not. And without access to the evidence or investigation, Max wouldn't know if Peter's death was the same as the other three cases.

"All right," Max said.

John and Blair both looked relieved. "Thank you for understanding," John said. "Will you be covering the trial for NET? You said the other day you didn't know."

"I still don't know," she said. But now she wanted to. Something clicked inside, an instinct that had her more than a little curious about what really prompted this impromptu meeting, and she wanted to be here for the trial.

"Well, if you don't, we'll see you after the trial if you decide to come back from New York and help us," Blair said. "We know your time is valuable, and you might not be able to help, but we understand."

"New York?"

"Yes, I assume you're returning soon."

"No."

Blair stared at her. "But you just said—just now—that you weren't going to pursue this. All the conversation and conflict and stress—"

"Shh, dear," John said. "That's not what she meant. Max has other investigations she's working on."

"I'm going to San Diego tomorrow," Max said.

"Why?" Blair asked. "Isn't that"—she turned to her husband—"John."

"Stanton," he said. "The first little boy who died."

Blair looked pained. "You said you weren't going to pursue these cases!"

"No, I said that I wasn't going to investigate Peter's death. Not now, at any rate. But the other three cases are still just as compelling. Justin Stanton, Tommy Porter, and Chris Donovan. Donovan's father was convicted of his murder, but the case had serious problems—I'm surprised he hasn't appealed the conviction." When Max first read the transcript, she immediately thought that Donovan had the worst representation she'd ever seen in a trial. He should never have been convicted, though he didn't do much to help himself. Guilt? Grief? Max didn't know—and she wouldn't until David talked to him.

"Why those other cases?" John asked.

"Because they're cold cases and that's what I do." She sipped her wine. "John, as I explained to you, I don't get involved with active police investigations. But cold cases—they intrigue me. And these three? I haven't been this caught up in an investigation in a long, long time. I'm going to solve them. And I promise, if I find anything that can help Blair, I'll let you know."

"This isn't going to help!" Blair exclaimed. She glanced around, as if she were afraid someone had overheard. But the dining room was almost empty. It was past closing with only a few occupied tables finishing up dessert and coffee.

"I'm not doing this to help or hurt you, Blair. I'm doing it to give three families closure. To find justice for three little boys who had their lives taken too soon. And honestly—I won't know if they're connected until I dig deeper." Though Max's gut told her they were. "But I will dig, and I will at a minimum prove whether the boys were killed by the same person. At that point, I'll turn the information over to law enforcement. If they pursue it, I won't. If they don't? Let's put it this way—I've never shied away from the difficult cases."

"Max," John said, "I know you mean well, but I think it would be best if you just went back to New York."

"How can my investigation into a twenty-year-old murder affect Blair's case?" What had Blair said to John that had him doing a complete one-eighty? Something had happened between the time Max had walked through John's house and now.

Covering trials wasn't Max's favorite part of her job with NET. She found courtroom procedures tedious and uninteresting. But with the trial often came interviews with victims, witnesses, and defendants, and those were far more exciting for Max, who craved to understand the people and world around her.

But now, after this change of focus with John, there was nothing she wanted to do more than cover Blair Caldwell's trial. If she was going to write about these cases, she needed to be there—to hear the testimony, see the evidence, and know in both her heart and her head whether Blair Caldwell had killed her son.

Because right now, she thought the police had the right person. Though for the life of her, she couldn't figure out *why.*

This time last year, Max would have flat out told Blair she thought she was guilty just to see how she would react. But if Max had learned anything over her last few investigations, it was that sometimes being blunt didn't help. If she revealed her thoughts, John would completely cut her out and she wanted access to him. Access to him *without* Blair in the room.

"I can't stop you." John's eyes were damp, and Max didn't think he was faking the emotion. "I just—please—consider how your actions may have a detrimental effect on Blair's case."

She reached out and touched John's hand, partly because she knew it would irritate his wife. "I promise you, John, I will be discreet. There is nothing I care more about than finding justice for victims, whether the case is a year old or twenty years old."

"I know, Max. I know." He squeezed her hand.

If Blair was guilty, Max would skewer her.

Chapter Six

"Andrew? I'm going to put you on speaker. Sean's here, too."

Rookie FBI Agent Lucy Kincaid Rogan put her cell phone down on the island in the kitchen where she and Sean had been eating a late dinner.

"Stanton?" Sean mouthed. Lucy nodded. Her former brother-in-law had never directly called her before, and she'd known him her entire life. She was both suspicious and curious. Why would the DA of San Diego reach out to her? Family or work? She'd last seen him more than a year ago during the Christmas holidays, and that hadn't been under the best of circumstances.

"Hello, Sean," Andrew said.

"Andrew."

"I'm sorry to call so late."

"Nine isn't late for us," Lucy said. "Just tell me that everything's okay."

"Yes—in a manner of speaking. Your family's fine, as far as I know. They don't really talk to me anymore."

Lucy knew why—her sister Nelia was Andrew's ex, and Andrew had cheated on Nelia. There was more—a lot more—but Lucy had been so young when they split up that she didn't truly understand the situation. Andrew had always been kind to her, and when she needed his help last Christmas to get information, he'd come through. She respected that.

Andrew continued, "I don't know exactly how to broach this subject, so I'll get to the point. An investigative reporter is looking into Justin's

42

murder. She claims that she has compelling evidence that Justin's death is connected to two or more homicides in the Southwest. She'll be in San Diego tomorrow."

That was the last thing Lucy expected Andrew to say. She didn't know how to respond—her nephew Justin's murder had haunted her for nearly twenty years, but she'd put it behind her. She'd been seven, the same age as Justin. They'd been best friends and had grown up together until Justin was kidnapped and murdered. It had torn the family apart.

"A reporter?" Sean said, his voice edged with anger. "Why are you calling Lucy?"

"I think there might be something to this woman's theory. Lucy, I don't have a right to ask for your help, but the last time I wanted to re-visit Justin's murder, I ran up against a brick wall known as the Kincaid family."

That didn't surprise Lucy. Her family never wanted to discuss Justin or his death. It had been a dark time in the Kincaid family history. Twenty years was a long time, and most crimes this old would never be solved.

"I didn't know you had wanted to reopen Justin's case."

"As an unsolved homicide, it's never been closed. Eight years ago— you'd just left for Georgetown." He paused. "I never told you this, and I don't want to bring up bad memories."

"I'm a big girl, Andrew."

Sean took her hand, lightly kissed it, and held it. She could feel the tension within him—this was nearly as difficult for him as it was for her. The past. *Her* past.

"After your kidnapping—when you came home—I wanted to be there for you, for your family. Even after everything that has happened, and all the mistakes I've made, I care about you and all the Kincaids. Your parents have always been cordial, but your brothers and sister never forgave me. Especially Connor and Carina, maybe because they still live here and I work with them. They didn't want me around, and I walked away. But I thought maybe—if I could put Justin to rest—they could find peace. Not knowing why someone killed my son . . ." His voice faded away, then he cleared his throat and said, "I approached your father. He was adamant that I stand down. Carina found out I had pulled the case files, and confronted me—it wasn't pretty. At the time, Patrick was still in a coma, I knew your family was suffering, you'd moved cross-country, Dillon—who has always been the diplomat of the family, and the only one who I know forgave me—was living in D.C. I didn't have a buffer, so I shelved it."

"I didn't know any of that." It stunned her. She caught Sean's eye. He was listening closely to Andrew.

Sean said, "Why? If you had something new, why would you shelve it?"

"I didn't have anything new—I just wanted to look at the case with fresh eyes, time, new technology. But I couldn't put your family through a new investigation when they had nearly lost you, Lucy, and Patrick's future was so uncertain."

"I understand," Lucy said, and she did. "But the reporter changed your mind?"

"Yes, she has. But your family isn't going to want to go through this, and I don't want to hurt them."

"Then why do it at all?" Sean asked.

"Because Maxine Revere is going to investigate whether I want her to or not. And honestly, Sean? I want answers. God, I want to know what happened. For years I deferred my pain to your family—Nelia's family. When every lead dried up, they put it behind them. Not completely—I know Justin haunts them as much as he haunts me. But Nelia moved to Idaho, and that was it. They wanted no part of me, no part of my ideas or talking about what happened. But I'm a prosecutor—having any crime unsolved bothers me, but my own son? It's fingernails on the chalkboard, every waking minute. I've looked into this Revere woman. She has a solid track record solving cold cases."

"But what is she going to do after?" Sean asked. He caught Lucy's eye. She knew exactly what he was thinking. "Lucy and I steer clear of reporters."

"She wants my help, and I plan on laying down ground rules. Protecting you is my number one priority, Lucy."

"I don't need your protection, Andrew." Lucy saw the darkness cross

Sean's face. She took his hand. "What do you want from me? Do you want me to talk to my family? Convince them to cooperate? Talk to this reporter?"

"Actually, I want you to listen to what Revere has to say. You're an FBI agent. You have the training and experience to weed through the bullshit and get to the meat. I know you've had a rocky start to your career—but I have friends in high places, Lucy. You have closed some extremely difficult cases."

True, though she hadn't been the only agent involved in those complex cases.

Andrew continued. "In hindsight, I don't think anyone understood the pain you went through when Justin died. He was as close as a brother to you, we all knew that, but after his death everyone seemed to forget that you were grieving. They shielded you from the investigation, from the truth of what happened that night because you were only seven years old. You're probably the only Kincaid who doesn't have a preconceived notion as to what happened. I think you're the only one who can look at the evidence with an unbiased eye. Who doesn't blame me."

"No one blames you, Andrew."

He laughed, but it was filled with anguish and sorrow. "I wish that were true. Connor said it when the truth came out—when your family found out I was having an affair. He said if I'd been there, at home that night and not in bed with my mistress, Justin would be alive. A bit more crudely, but that was his message. There's not been a day that has passed that I haven't thought about that, whether it was true. If I am ultimately, even indirectly, to blame." He took a deep breath. "Nell and I have made peace with each other. I talk to her, once a year, on Justin's birthday. We made a lot of mistakes, but Justin wasn't one of them. She's content now. She has Tom, he's been good for her, and while I don't know if she's happy, I know she's at peace. I don't want to hurt her. I will keep her out of this as best I can, but in the end, she may have information that she doesn't know she has. I know that no one, not even Dillon, will discuss it with her. Except you. I think you would do it."

What did that make Lucy? Cruel? Is that what Andrew thought of her, because she had a reputation for being cold?

"Andrew—"

"I don't know that it'll come to that," he said, interrupting her. "I'd just like you to hear what this woman has to say. If you tell me there's nothing, that going down this path will result in no answers and only heartache for your family, I'll do everything in my power to stop her. But if you see what I see, that we might finally get answers as to why Justin died, that we might find out who killed him . . . I don't have anyone else, Lucy."

"A moment, Andrew," Sean said. He put the phone on mute. "It's your choice, Lucy. Whatever you decide, I'm with you."

The grief Lucy had experienced when Justin was killed nearly twenty years ago had been young and immature, but no less painful. She didn't know what had happened to him, not right away. She didn't know why her mother cried all the time, why her sister Nelia wouldn't talk to her, why there were policemen in her house, why Carina needed a lawyer, why no one would let Andrew come over for dinner anymore. All she knew was that Justin, her best friend since birth, was gone. One day he was there, playing catch with her in the backyard, swimming with her at the community pool, teasing her when she lisped after her two front teeth fell out. Her mother watched Justin during the week because Nelia and Andrew both worked so Lucy spent more waking hours with Justin than any other person her age. They'd even been in the same first-grade class together. And that summer was supposed to be the most fun ever. They were going to go to a sleepover camp for the first time for two whole weeks. It was all Justin could talk about, he was so excited.

But that never happened because he was killed two weeks before they were supposed to leave.

He was gone. One day there, the next not. She'd been gutted, but she didn't talk to anyone about it because everyone was so sad and talking about Justin seemed to make them sadder.

Maybe that was why she'd always kept her emotions deep inside. Partly because of her own kidnapping and rape when she was eighteen . . . but it had started a long time before then. It had started when she grieved for her best friend and couldn't talk to anyone about it.

While she understood death, had faced evil, and knew that bad people did horrific things to innocent people, she didn't always know *why*.

Maybe finding out who killed Justin wasn't as important as finding out *why* he was killed.

And if there were other victims of the same killer, did that mean the killer was still out there? After nearly twenty years? Would he kill again? Destroy another family?

"I have to," Lucy whispered to Sean.

He kissed her hand. "I know."

She would have smiled if she wasn't so melancholy. "I love you."

He winked. "I know."

Now she did smile, because if she didn't, she might cry. And tears weren't productive.

She unmuted the phone. "When is this reporter coming?"

"Tomorrow afternoon. I don't have the exact time."

"Text me the details. I'll be there."

Chapter Seven

Danielle Sharpe didn't like going out with people from work, but it was expected. For every time she declined an invitation, she had to accept one—otherwise people would look at her too closely. She just wanted to do her job and go home, drink a bottle of wine, and try to sleep.

Try being the operative word. Sleep was a rarity for her. When she felt herself being dragged under from exhaustion, she would take a sleeping pill or three. Her body needed the rest, even if her mind couldn't.

There had been a time . . . more than once . . . when she considered taking the entire bottle of prescription sleeping pills with a large glass of wine and recline in her bathtub. Just fall asleep. Slip under. Disappear forever.

But would death end her nightmare? Or would Earth's cruel God force her to relieve the worst day of her life? Over and over and over . . .

Nina Fieldstone poked her head into the bathroom. "Danielle, are you coming?"

"Just touching up my makeup. Two minutes?"

Nina smiled. She was a pretty woman, smart, and one of the few in the office with whom Danielle felt a rapport. Nina was technically her supervisor but had never made Danielle feel stupid or unvalued. Because Nina had been the one to ask her to join the group for their "Wine Wednesday," Danielle had agreed.

"All right, but remember, happy hour is over at seven, so don't be long."

Danielle turned to the mirror and pretended to put on more mascara.

She didn't wear a lot of makeup, but too many sleepless nights required it. She pulled out a tube of concealer and hid the dark circles. Added a little color. Better.

She still felt like a ghost beneath the gloss and glitter.

The bar—called the Gavel because of the proximity to the courthouse—where the legal secretaries hung out every Wednesday night was two blocks from their law office in Glendale. It was a large firm, and anywhere from four to ten women met once a week to let off steam and enjoy company and gossip.

It was the gossip Danielle hated, almost as much as the small talk.

Tonight six of them sat at one of the booths and drank wine. Danielle had to regulate herself. Alone, she would drink an entire bottle. With people, one glass was all she could handle.

Nina put her hand over Danielle's. "I'm so glad you decided to join us tonight, especially after the victory you helped secure."

"I didn't do anything," Danielle said. "Just my job."

"You caught two huge mistakes that saved our client tens of thousands of dollars, and a major embarrassment for our firm. Your drink's on me tonight."

Danielle didn't want the accolades. Yes, she was good at her job. It was all she had. Work or die slowly. Those were her options.

The women all chatted amongst one another. Danielle responded to questions because it was expected. She asked a few of her own—she could play the small talk game when she had to. Half the women at the table were married. Grace had no kids, Natalie had a teenage daughter, and Nina had a son.

An eight-year-old boy named Kevin.

Danielle didn't want to ask, but she couldn't help herself. As the conversation turned to relationships and children, she said, "Is your husband home with Kevin? Does he watch him every Wednesday?"

It was a casual question and fit the conversation, but it was something that had been on Danielle's mind a lot lately. Especially after she saw Tony Fieldstone watching his law partner, Lana Devereaux, at the Christmas party six weeks ago. The way he looked at her. The way he watched her walk. Danielle knew the look.

She knew it well.

Too well.

Nina rolled her eyes. "Sometimes he does—he loves spending time with Kevin, don't get me wrong, but Tony is all work, work, work. And tonight he had a poker game with Judge Carlson and the gang. Third Wednesday of the month. I say, why not Fridays when you don't have to be in court the next morning? But *men*."

Men. Right.

Danielle had worked for Taggert, Fieldstone, Finch, and Devereaux for three years. She knew of the poker game, it was common knowledge just like Wine Wednesdays and the monthly bunco game Grace hosted that she had, thankfully, avoided almost every month. But she wondered how long the game really went. If maybe Tony Fieldstone had someplace else he wanted to be.

A place he wasn't supposed to be.

With a woman he wasn't supposed to be with.

"You okay, Danielle?" Nina asked.

"Sorry, long day. Little headache."

"Another glass of wine? You can Uber home and I'll pick you up in the morning. You don't live too far from me."

"No, I'm fine." She smiled, such a fake smile, but no one knew. "Do you have a regular babysitter for Kevin? He's such a good kid." Nina had brought him into the office a couple of times when there were minimum days in school and she didn't have a sitter. Danielle tried not to pay attention to him, but she couldn't help it. He was a perfect child.

Perfect.

Tony didn't deserve a perfect son like Kevin when he was off screwing another woman.

You don't know that he is having an affair. You only suspect.

She knew. She damn well *knew* and she would prove it.

She always did.

"Tony's mom watches him after school—she lives only a couple blocks from his school, walks over and gets him every day. It's nice, Kevin being able to spend some time with his grandmother."

"It is," Danielle agreed.

But you should be picking him up at school. You should be spending that time with him. Instead you're sitting here laughing and drinking wine with a bunch of selfish, arrogant women.

"We have a regular babysitter when we have to work late—Maggie Crutcher."

There was a lawyer named Wayne Crutcher. Maggie was his daughter. A teenager. Probably brought her boyfriend over to fuck when Kevin went to bed. They all did. They couldn't be trusted.

The talk turned back to the office, and Danielle was relieved. She still needed to get out of here. Forty-five minutes . . . that was long enough, wasn't it? She showed her face, made the small talk, did the dance, she needed to go because she was already on edge.

"You know, I'm really tired after today," Danielle said. She finished her wine and smiled. "I think I'm going to call it a night."

"Do you want to join us Friday for bunco? It's at Shelly's house in Burbank," Grace said. "You had so much fun last time you came."

Danielle barely remembered the last time—it had to be six months ago. She had too much wine, of that she was certain.

"I don't know, my mom is having a hard time getting around and I help her on the weekends. Shopping, fixing things around the house, you know."

"You're so good to your mom," Nina said. Danielle had told her all about her mother years ago, mostly to get out of socializing. "To drive all the way up there."

"Where does she live?" Natalie asked.

"Sacramento," Danielle lied. But it was a lie she told often, so it was one that came out smoothly. "It's only five, six hours depending on traffic. I don't mind, put on a book-on-tape or listen to music. But if she doesn't need me, I'll consider bunco. You know me, I'm not really an extrovert. Too many people makes me antsy." That was the truth.

Nina smiled and patted her hand. "No pressure, but I would love you to come. It's one night a month, a great way to get out and just relax, no work the next day."

"Thanks." She got up, said good-byes—why did it take so long to just tell people *good-bye?* Why more questions, more small talk, more *nothingness?*

Finally, she was free. She walked back to the parking garage and retrieved her car. She intended to drive home where she could open a bottle of wine and maybe eat something, but she found herself outside Judge Carlson's house.

The judge had a private address, but she'd followed Tony Fieldstone here last month, after she suspected he was screwing Lana Devereaux. She saw Tony's car in the driveway of the opulent house in the Glendale hills.

And Lana's car. Did Nina know that Lana played poker with "the boys"? The only female partner . . . is that how it started? The one night a month . . . turning into something more?

For two hours Danielle watched the house from down the street. Then a car left.

Lana.

Five minutes later a second car left.

Tony.

She followed him.

Tony didn't go home. She knew where he lived, because she'd once gone to bunco at Nina's house when she first started the job with the law firm. Instead, Tony went to Lana Devereaux's condo in Los Feliz.

Heart racing, she drove past his car as he got out. He didn't pay any attention to her. Or her common black Honda Accord. It didn't stand out. Just like she didn't stand out.

Danielle went straight home. When she pulled into her garage she turned off the ignition and sat there. Her knuckles were white. Slowly, she peeled her hands off the steering wheel. They were sore from gripping so hard.

She went inside and poured a glass of wine. Drank it quickly, then poured another, and picked up her phone.

"Hello," the familiar voice said. A voice that belonged to a man she had once loved with all her heart and soul . . . and now hated.

"Have you cheated on your wife yet? Because you know you will. You're all the same. All of you. Disgusting."

"Danielle."

"Why did you do it? Why?"

She asked the same question every time she called him. He never had a good answer. Because there wasn't a good answer.

"I was a fool."

"I hate you."

"I know. Is that why you called? To tell me how much you hate me?"

"No." She closed her eyes. "I loved you so much. I loved you so much it hurts. And—" Her voice cracked. The pain was real. Still so very real. Time doesn't heal all wounds. Whoever said that hadn't lost their entire world.

"I'm sorry, Danielle. I truly am sorry."

"It should have been you. I wish you had died instead."

"So do I, Danielle. But you can't—"

She ended the call, unable to listen to her ex-husband anymore. She threw her half-filled wineglass across the room and screamed as it shattered against the wall. She watched the red liquid run down the plaster for several minutes, her mind blank.

Then she walked back to the kitchen, retrieved another wineglass, and poured more wine. She sat at the table and stared straight ahead as she drank.

Thinking.

Planning.

Hating.

It was so much easier to hate than it was to forgive.

Chapter Eight

David left Santa Barbara at dawn for the three-hour drive to Corcoran State Prison. Rising early wasn't a problem for him—he was up before 6:00 A.M. every morning. But he felt that this entire endeavor was an exercise in futility. While Max's analysis was intriguing, when a man is convicted of killing his son, he is most likely guilty. Prisons are full of killers and most are there because they did the crime.

Adam Donovan had been convicted of murder without taking the stand in his own defense. There was no hard evidence against him—even the circumstantial evidence seemed thin when David read the trial transcript. The prosecution had gone for the lighter sentence—they claimed that Donovan had accidentally killed his son and in a panic buried his body only a few miles from their house. According to a conversation Max had had with the public defender who had represented Donovan, she'd urged him to take a plea deal of involuntary manslaughter and five years in prison. He refused.

Either the guy was truly innocent, or he thought he could beat the rap because the evidence was so shaky. His alibi was his mistress—the same alibi that Andrew Stanton used—but unlike the Stanton case, the police didn't find Donovan's mistress reliable. They completely discredited her on the stand, and while she didn't waver from her claim that they'd been together the night that Chris Donovan had been killed, in the end, the jury hadn't believed her.

It didn't help Donovan's case that he initially lied to police about where he was when his son was kidnapped. Only when the police seriously looked at him did he give up his mistress. It also didn't help that Donovan had a prior record—he'd been arrested for assault when he was nineteen, given time served and community service, but the ding was on his record.

David didn't think that information should have been given to the jury twelve years after the fact, because Donovan had kept his nose clean since. David had a couple of dings on his own record before he had enlisted in the army. He'd been an angry teenager, and was still angry much of the time—but he'd learned to temper his darker nature through exercise, working long hours, and his daughter. He didn't want to give his ex-girlfriend any reason to prevent him from seeing Emma.

What seemed particularly odd to David was that the defense hadn't even asked the judge to disallow the assault. After more than a decade? Before he was even married? It seemed like negligence or incompetence.

David didn't have a lot of respect for the legal system. He'd had his own issues when he had to fight for the right to see his daughter. He paid child support, he wanted to be in her life, but because he'd never been married to her mother, he'd had an uphill battle and Brittney constantly held his visitation over his head like a fucking carrot.

Do what I say or you'll never see Emma.

So he jumped through the hoops because there was nothing more important to him than his daughter.

Which is why he was having a difficult time with this investigation Max had launched. Adam Donovan had been convicted in a court of law of murdering his son. Even though the evidence was circumstantial, he had been convicted, he hadn't filed an appeal, and statistics showed that he was most likely guilty. David wanted to punch him more than talk to him.

Not only that, but Max was far better at getting people to talk to her. Often because she irritated them so much, they couldn't shut up. David wasn't a reporter. He wasn't a cop. His claim to fame had been ten years in the U.S. Army, eight of them as a Ranger. He had no college degree, and his only training outside of the military was when he went into private security.

"You're a dad," Max had said. *"You'll know what to say, and you'll know if he's guilty."*

He disagreed, but she didn't budge. Max didn't falter when she believed that she was right. *Ever.* It was enough to drive anyone crazy—especially since she was rarely wrong.

Maybe after his failed attempt to meet with the Porters yesterday, she would understand he wasn't good at this. They wouldn't talk to him and threatened to call the cops when he showed up at their house.

Try again, Max said. Maybe they'll have a change of heart after sleeping on it, she said.

Right.

And that's what Max didn't understand. If David was in the same situation as Doug Porter, he would have done exactly the same thing. Well, not exactly. He wouldn't have threatened to call the cops. He would have slugged the asshole wanting to talk about his dead kid.

But if anything happened to Emma like what happened to these little boys, David wouldn't rest until the killer was dead. These dads, while they grieved, would never take the law into their own hands, which meant David didn't completely understand them. He wasn't like them just because he happened to be a father. Why didn't Max see that?

Because Maxine Revere sees the world through her own glasses, and damn anyone who doesn't get with the program.

So now David was here, at Corcoran State Prison, to interview a man convicted of murdering his son. It took more than thirty minutes before he was cleared through security and taken to the visiting area—a large room with several guards at the doors and along the perimeter watching the group of prisoners and visitors. Tables were set up on one side, a television area on another; toys and puzzles were in another corner. David watched as a burly, tattooed convict played dinosaurs with his daughter who couldn't be more than four. A woman, who David presumed to be the child's mother, sat to the side, tears in her eyes, watching them.

"Wait here," the guard told David and led him to a table in the far corner.

It took several minutes before another guard brought in Adam

Donovan. Donovan sat in the chair across from David and stared without comment.

The man had hardened, lost weight, gained muscle, and his dark hair had turned half gray in the span of five years since his conviction for the murder of his son. He was only thirty-six, but he looked closer to fifty. A long, jagged scar on his neck hadn't been there in the last photo David had of him on the day he'd been sentenced.

"Mr. Donovan, I'm David Kane. I work for Maxine Revere, an investigative reporter with NET television."

David had told Max he wouldn't do well with a man who was convicted of killing his son. All David could think about was his own daughter. If anyone hurt her, he would see red. Anyone who did violence to a child deserved worse than prison.

Yet here David was, facing a convicted killer, because Max insisted.

"You don't like me, so why are you here?" Adam said.

Perceptive.

"Because my partner is investigating a crime similar to your son's murder. Dead boy. Only child. One or both parents a lawyer. Kidnapped from his bedroom and found less than two miles from his house."

Adam didn't look surprised, just sad.

David continued. "There are enough similarities to your son's murder that we wanted to talk to you."

"Well, fuck you. I didn't kill that kid. I've been locked up for five years, three months, and ten days."

"I wanted to talk about Chris."

"The only reason I agreed to meet with you is to tell you to go to hell. I do not want my family to go through this shit again. My ex-wife . . . or my mom." His voice cracked. "My brother and sister, they don't deserve to be hounded by the fucking press like they were five years ago. No one does. So just—fuck off. Leave us alone."

"You pled not guilty."

"Doesn't matter."

"You didn't take the stand. Maxine's attorney thinks your attorney was an incompetent idiot, but you haven't filed an appeal. You would probably be granted a new trial for a half-dozen different reasons."

"You just don't get it. My son is dead." Adam glared at him. "Someone took him from his bed, where he should have been safe, suffocated him, and buried him at the park down the street. Why? Hell if I know. Yet, my ex-wife thinks I killed him. She believes it deep down that I am not only capable of killing a *child*, of killing *my own son*, but that I actually *did* it. My life means nothing. I don't care. Just—go away."

"I have a daughter. I would be moving heaven and earth to find out who hurt her."

"How? I have no money—used it all for the trial. I have no family. No one who believes me except my mother, yet she cries every time she visits. I told her to stop coming because it's going to kill her. And my son is still dead. Finding the killer isn't going to bring him back."

"Let me ask these questions my boss prepared and I'll let you get back to wallowing in self-pity."

"Charmer, aren't you."

David opened his mouth, then closed it when he realized that he had sounded exactly like Max.

"Adam," David said, putting aside all Max's questions, "I'm not going to sit here and lie to you—I came in here believing the jury was right, that even though your trial was fucked, you are exactly where you belong. But when Maxine Revere gets an itch, it has to be satisfied, and if I didn't talk to you in person, she would, and she doesn't take excuses or bullshit. I personally don't care. I don't have a vested interest in this case or any case. I just do my job."

That had begun to change, because David had begun to care about the work he did with Max, but David didn't want to think too much about that right now. He'd only noticed that lately, Max had been . . . different. He couldn't put his finger on it, but she'd put up this wall between them. Last year he would have been grateful to get the space. Now? Not so much.

"Ask," Adam said through clenched teeth.

"Your alibi was your mistress. Two of the other victims we're looking at also had cheating fathers. How long had you been involved with Amy Lovell?"

"Nearly a year."

"She was discredited on the stand."

"Fucking prosecutor."

"You initially lied to police."

"Because I didn't know what happened to Chris, I didn't know he'd been killed . . . I don't know *what* I thought, only I never once thought that he was dead." He took a deep breath. "I cheated on my wife. I'm not proud of it, but it wasn't like we had a perfect marriage. We went through a rough patch and Cindy didn't want a divorce."

"You did?"

"You read the transcript. Don't ask stupid questions."

David bristled. "I'm trying to wrap my head around the fact that if you are innocent, why you're not exercising your right to appeal."

"Because my son is still dead! Back then, I was a borderline alcoholic. I'm clean in here. Not much else good about the place, but I'm sober, and I'm doing my time and trying not to think about anything else."

It was clear that all Adam Donovan thought about was the past.

"Did anyone know about your affair?"

"No."

"No?"

"Cindy didn't know, if that's what you mean."

"Cheating spouses always think that."

"If she'd known, she wouldn't have been so vindictive on the stand. She really believes I killed my son so that I could run off with Amy. Yes, I wanted a divorce because Cindy and I argued every fucking day about every fucking thing. That wasn't good for Chris. I drank too much because I didn't know what else to do. Amy was a distraction and she didn't scream at me. We talked more than we screwed. Cindy wasn't a bad person, she loved Chris, just like I did. Her parents had divorced when she was twelve and she had it in her head that we had to make it work for Chris. We tried . . . God, we tried. We even went to marriage counseling. But it had been a mistake from the beginning. We were just too young and stupid to see it."

"So you and Amy discreetly had an affair for a year."

"Yes."

"You worked together."

"We both worked for the same software company, I was in IT and she was in human resources."

An idea came to David, but he filed it away to follow up on later.

"It came out in the trial that Chris was drugged prior to being suffocated."

Adam flinched, then nodded.

"He was buried in his blanket with one of his stuffed animals."

Adam nodded again, but didn't say anything.

"According to the transcript, the stuffed dinosaur was his favorite animal."

"He had many favorites—Chris couldn't go to the zoo or mall without coming back with another stuffed animal—but he slept with the dinosaur every night." Adam looked down, then whispered, "He said the T. rex would protect him when he slept."

"Who else might have known which was his favorite?"

"Who cares?"

"It might go to motive."

Donovan slammed his fist on the table. "There is *no* fucking motive!"

The guard closest to them came over. "First and only warning, Donovan."

Donovan's jaw tightened. "What do you want from me, Kane?"

"Max wanted me to tell her whether you are guilty or innocent."

Donovan laughed out loud. "You a fucking psychic? Oh, that's good. You come in here, spend thirty minutes talking to me and you can tell if I killed my son? That's rich."

"I told Max I wouldn't be able to do it. She has an uncanny way of reading people. Not a psychic—more like an astute observer of human behavior and emotion."

"So this has been a waste of time. You dragged me in here to talk about my son for no fucking reason. Unbelievable. Leave me alone, Kane. I don't need this. I just want to do my time."

"Don't you want to know who killed Chris?"

"The world knows. The world believes I killed my son. Nothing else matters. I don't live in a fantasy world. Every guy in this joint is guilty, but they'll lie through their teeth to anyone on the outside that they're innocent, then laugh all the way to the yard that they pulled one over on their girlfriend or attorney or the parole board. I'm not getting out of here. And if I appealed, got out on a technicality, the only people in the world I care about will still think I'm guilty. My life is over. Don't come back."

Amy Lovell had never married. She'd visited Donovan only once in prison, the month after he'd been transferred to Corcoran, but never again. She'd moved from Santa Clarita to Pasadena. Not far as the crow flies, but a completely different city, friends, job. Maybe she'd had a difficult time after the trial, maybe she just needed a change. Whatever reason, it wasn't difficult for David to track her down.

David didn't want to believe that Adam Donovan was innocent . . . but he said he didn't kill his son, and when faced with a reporter who could blast the news far and wide, David expected him to. All he had from the trial was the transcripts, and he couldn't tell if Amy was lying based on the written words. He saw why the jury didn't believe her—she hesitated, was asked to constantly repeat herself, and got trapped in a logic problem. Either she wasn't bright, or she was flustered, or she didn't understand what was going on.

"Thank you for meeting with me," David said. Amy was several years younger than Donovan. She had once been pretty—but the years hadn't been kind. Or maybe it was how Amy felt about herself. She was far too skinny to be healthy, her hair was severely styled, and she wore unflattering colors.

"I only agreed to tell you to your face that I will not let you drag me into this again. The press vilified me once, I won't let it happen again."

"I only have one question."

"You drove all the way here to ask me one question?" Her distrust was evident.

"Was Adam Donovan with you the night his son was kidnapped and murdered?"

Tears welled in her eyes. "I don't believe this," she said. "I'm going to call the police. This is harassment. You can't d-d-do this to me."

David softened his tone—difficult for him, because he wasn't a soft guy. Amy might look tough on the outside, but she was mush on the inside.

"Amy," he said in an even tone, "I read the transcript. You became flustered on the stand and backtracked. You lost credibility in the eyes of the jury. I can just imagine how nervous you were."

"I didn't know what to expect—the questions about my life, about things I didn't want to talk about . . . about sex." She whispered the last word.

David was surprised that the defense hadn't prepared Amy for questioning. It seemed pretty basic to David that you needed to prepare your witnesses, but this attorney was slipshod in many ways.

"The answer is important, Amy. There are three other boys who died in the same manner as Chris. If Adam is truly innocent, my employer is ready to fund an Innocence Project campaign on his behalf." That was partly true. But Donovan would have to file an appeal first, and he didn't seem to be inclined to do so.

"I told the court that Adam was with me that night. Through all my embarrassment, through the way the press dragged me through the mud as a slut, home-wrecker, and liar, I was with Adam that night. The prosecutor wanted the jury to believe that *if* I was telling the truth, I had fallen asleep and Adam snuck out. We were more than thirty minutes from his house. How could he have snuck out, killed his son, then snuck back into my bed where we woke up and made love again at five that morning?"

"One thing the jury had a problem with, according to exit interviews, was that Cindy Donovan was working late that night—she was a tax attorney preparing for a major audit. Why wasn't Adam at home with his son?"

"That question haunted Adam. He won't talk to me anymore—I tried. He doesn't hate me. He doesn't love me. He has no feelings at all. I've tried to move on with my life, tried not to blame myself, but I can't help it. Adam hired a babysitter because he was angry with his wife for any number of things. I honestly think he wanted Cindy to find out about our affair because that would give her a reason to divorce him." She rubbed her eyes and took a deep breath, but David didn't interrupt her train of thought. "I didn't have any illusions that Adam loved me, Mr. Kane. We were friends at work, we became lovers, and I cared about him. Yes, I fell in love with him. I wanted him to love me the same way, but I knew he couldn't. Even then, I knew I was lying to myself. He was angry and hurt and frustrated with his marriage and girls like me always try to fix men who are broken. I'm not that girl anymore.

"There's no cell in my body that believes Adam killed his son. Not one. I hate that I was so wishy-washy on the stand, that the jury thought I wasn't credible, that I was a love-struck twenty-year-old sleeping with a man ten years older. But you know what I hate more? That Adam was convicted for murder and he didn't do one thing to help himself. It's like he wanted to be punished. Where's the justice, Mr. Kane? Because neither Adam nor Chris Donovan has seen it."

Chapter Nine

Max reluctantly rented a car at the San Diego airport. She hated the process and hassle and complete *unfairness* of how they treated her. They charged her triple the rates *and* she self-insured. Her minor accidents were rarely her fault—the last time she'd been legally parked when someone rear-ended her and stole a diary she'd uncovered that ultimately helped her solve a cold case. Yet they punished her? Ridiculous.

She read David's notes from his conversation with both Adam Donovan and Donovan's mistress while sitting in the rental car. She made a note to touch base with Stanton's mistress—no assumptions, she told herself. Just because the police did due diligence twenty years ago didn't mean that they didn't miss something.

Once Max was done with her tablet—as well as checking her e-mail—she drove out of the rental lot. On the freeway, she called Stanton and confirmed the time and place of their meeting.

"I've asked my sister-in-law to meet us," Stanton said.

"That's great," Max said. "The more support and information we can get from Justin's family will help. I appreciate your cooperation."

"I haven't decided whether to cooperate, Ms. Revere. I talked to your producer at length. I grant you, your theory is interesting, but I still need more information."

"Fair enough. I'm ready to answer all questions you and Detective Kincaid may have."

He paused. "My sister-in-law Lucy is flying in from Texas. She's an FBI agent and will likely be the only Kincaid willing to talk to you."

"She's coming in from Texas?" Max mentally ran through the Stanton case. The name Lucy Kincaid was familiar, but because she lived out of state and had been a child when Justin was murdered, Max hadn't dug into her background. She didn't think she'd be useful in the investigation. Yet she was an FBI agent? Max couldn't remember that in her notes.

"You will need to convince Lucy of your theory, so bring your A game, Ms. Revere. I don't appreciate being threatened, and I would suggest you avoid playing hardball with Lucy. I'll see you at three."

He hung up.

Max was not pleased with this new development. Not because Stanton was bringing in someone else—she had hoped to talk to Carina Kincaid, not only because she was related to the victim but because she had been a suspect for a brief time. She'd fallen asleep on the couch during the time frame that Justin had been kidnapped. Carina hadn't heard or seen anything, according to her statement. Maybe the years—or different questions—could jog her memory.

But convincing a federal agent of her theory? What was with that? As if she had to ask for permission to work this case? What *bullshit*.

What did Lucy Kincaid know about the murder? Absolutely nothing. She'd never been interviewed, never been part of the investigation even in an ancillary way. And bringing in a federal agent to boot? What did Stanton hope to accomplish? Was he deliberately trying to sabotage Max's investigation? Or perhaps wanting to listen to her theory then have the feds swoop in citing a multistate jurisdiction issue and tell her to back off, that they were reopening the case?

That would infuriate Max. While she'd want their resources, she knew after almost twenty years the FBI wouldn't spend the time and money necessary to find the answers. If they got nothing actionable after a week or two, they'd shelve the case again until something new came up. Been there, done that. It had been one of the biggest recurring arguments in her relationship with her ex-boyfriend, Special Agent Marco Lopez.

Without Max stirring the pot, nothing new would rise to the surface. She rolled her neck, willed herself to relax. She held all the cards here. Law enforcement wasn't interested in an almost twenty-year-old cold case. She had the time and resources to pursue Justin Stanton's murder, but even more important, people would talk to her because she *wasn't* a cop.

Max called her producer, Ben Lawson. He put her immediately on hold—she hated that.

Max wondered if Lucy Kincaid really did hold that much sway with Stanton. Stanton was the district attorney, he could delay access to files that would normally be public. She already had all the files that had been archived online, and had read every press story and watched every archived news program. The one thing she needed was the one thing that Stanton might be able to screw with—access to the retired detective who had led the investigation.

Her research into Stanton told her that he was a hard-nosed prosecutor who first ran for DA ten years ago and won in a tight race. His last two elections had been landslides. He could run for a fourth term in two years—there were no term limits for the district attorney—but California political types said he was considering a bid for attorney general. There was a rumor—a deeply buried rumor, but Max had a good friend who worked on the Judiciary Committee in the U.S. Senate—that Stanton was on the short list for an opening on a federal bench. Was that why he wanted his son's murder solved? Political expediency?

"Hello, Max," Ben finally said.

She looked at the time on her phone. "You kept me on hold for three and a half minutes."

"I'm surprised you waited that long."

So was she.

"Stanton is bringing in his former sister-in-law and she apparently has veto power on his cooperation."

"Which sister?"

"Lucy Kincaid. He said she's an FBI agent."

"I sent you information on the Kincaid family. She's a rookie out of the San Antonio office—been there a year."

"Just terrific," she said. A rookie fed. "She was *seven* when Stanton's son was killed. I don't get it."

"I'll see what we have on her—if I recall, it's not much. It's difficult to get information out of the feds as you know."

She could call Marco, she thought. He was now an SSA out of Miami. But she didn't want to ask her ex-boyfriend for a favor. She'd spoken to him two or three times in the last six months, but she wanted to keep her distance while she tried to work things out with her current boyfriend. Though she hadn't really been trying to work things out with Nick.

"I could call Marco instead," Ben said.

"I didn't say I was going to call him." When had her producer started to read her mind?

"Let me see what I can find out without contacting any of your exlovers."

"Don't be crass. Tell me what you have so far."

"On Agent Kincaid?" She heard him typing on a computer. "She was low priority because she was out of state. We have the basics—Lucia Kincaid, the youngest of seven children—by ten years—was born the same month as her nephew, Justin."

"Geez, how old was her mother?"

"I don't know, but there's twenty-three years between the oldest—Justin Stanton's mother Nelia—and Agent Kincaid."

"I recall that the father was a colonel in the army and the mother was a homemaker."

"Correct. The father, Patrick Kincaid Senior, retired after serving forty years. The mother escaped Cuba, the father met her when he was stationed in Florida. Moved around a lot, the kids are all army brats, in and outside of the U.S., until he took a position in San Diego shortly after the youngest Kincaid—Lucia—was born."

"Everyone in the family is some kind of hero or in law enforcement."

"So it seems. Hold on—"

"Don't—"

Dammit, he put her on hold again.

This time, she only had to wait twenty-six seconds.

"C. J. just handed me a clip from the San Antonio paper. Seems Agent Kincaid married a security expert last October. Sean Rogan. He's a principal in a private security firm based in Sacramento. They also have an office in D.C., but he works out of his house in San Antonio."

"This just gets better and better."

"I don't see your concern."

"Where do I start? The victim's father is the DA of San Diego. And how I find out that he's on board with my investigation unless his former sister-in-law, who happens to be an FBI agent, vetoes my theory. And said sister-in-law is married to some security guy? What do you know about this Rogan? Is he like David? Or more like our IT security guy, what's-his-name?"

"Leo. And I don't have anything else on Kincaid or Rogan, but C. J. is on it. You don't have to remind me that you need all the information you can get before you go into this meeting. But remember, this is a good case. Caldwell's theory makes sense—the story is compelling."

"Now it's compelling? You didn't even want me coming out here."

"I've reconsidered."

"Found a commercial angle to the deaths of four little boys?" she snapped.

"Fuck you, Maxine."

She sighed. "I'm sorry."

"No, you're not."

"Yes, I am. Really, Ben, this whole thing with Kincaid has thrown me for a loop. I don't like surprises."

"Apology accepted—once you return and let me take my pick from your wine cellar."

"You're impossible."

"I just have good taste—and know you do, too. In fact, I'll go over tonight and help myself."

"I should never have given you a key."

"Did you break it off with Nick?"

"No."

"You should. He's turning you into more of a bitch than you already are."

"And here I thought you accepted my apology."

"You hurt me."

"You don't sound hurt."

"My heart is broken. You haven't seen Nick since Thanksgiving, why the hell haven't you just told him to kiss your ass?"

"How do you know I haven't seen him?"

"I know everything about you, Max."

She didn't have a good response to that. Ben did know her better than anyone—part of the curse of working with someone who knew you from college. She and Ben hadn't even liked each other for years, but for their mutual best friend Karen—the mediator, they used to call her—they forced themselves to remain civil. Most of the time.

And after Karen disappeared and was presumed dead, Max didn't have it in her to hate Ben anymore.

But he still annoyed her.

"You're taking your frustrations out on everyone here, and it needs to stop. Stanton's single, I've seen his photo. He's your type. Maybe a little older than you usually go for, but attractive and smart. Screw him and get it out of your system, because God knows Nick isn't giving you what you need."

"Don't be so crude. Since when have I dated anyone over the age of forty?"

"Marco."

"He was thirty-two when I met him. I draw the line at ten years."

"Then maybe you should find a twenty-two-year-old boy toy you can toss back into the pool when you're done."

"Good-bye."

She hung up. Why did Ben think she needed to have sex? She didn't need sex. She needed Nick Santini to stop being an ass.

Maybe he's not worth it.

She was tired of talking about her love life with Ben. He just wouldn't let it go. Maybe because he enjoyed seeing her fail at something. Max succeeded in everything she did, except relationships.

She and Nick should have split after that first weekend they spent together. They'd had fun, they were very compatible in bed, and for a while the coast-to-coast relationship had worked perfectly for her. No commitment because they both had careers and lived three thousand miles apart, yet there was a warmth and contentment she enjoyed in the bicoastal affair.

Except Nick had an off-limits subject—his ex-wife—and Max didn't do off-limits subjects. Secrets were kissing cousins to lies and Max didn't tolerate lying. Especially in her relationships—friend, family, or lover. And Ben was right about one thing: she'd let her relationship impact her work. That had to stop.

She pulled up to the roundabout and checked her rental car in with the hotel's valet service. Max fell in love with the US Grant hotel as soon as she stepped into the lobby. She knew exactly why her grandmother stayed here. The staff was impeccable but discreet, the lobby was stately but subdued—not excessively ostentatious. Eleanor Revere liked quiet money. Flaunting wealth was unbecoming and crass.

The hotel desk clerk knew her by name even though she'd never stayed there.

"Welcome to the US Grant, Ms. Revere. We have your suite ready for your early arrival."

Max appreciated good service, and was happy to pay for it.

Max didn't take the time to unpack her clothes—a chore she rarely put off when she checked into a hotel because she loathed living out of suitcases. But she needed the time to prepare her timeline and read over everything Ben had sent on Lucy Kincaid, as well as refresh herself on the Kincaid family.

Patrick Kincaid, Senior—retired army colonel. Rosa Kincaid was a few years younger, had been a stay-at-home mother. With seven kids, Max supposed you'd have to stay at home. It would drive Max crazy, but she admired women who could keep a house and raise a family. And apparently, Rosa Kincaid had done an exemplary job—all seven of her children had been successful. Considering they lived on one modest government income, they'd managed fairly well, had no outstanding debt, and still lived in a 2600-square-foot house they'd purchased twenty-four years ago when Patrick, Sr., was stationed in San Diego.

That's a lot of people for a house that size.

The oldest, Nelia Kincaid, had been in law school when she married Andrew Stanton and gave birth to Justin four months later. It was pretty clear they married because of the child—not unheard of, especially nearly thirty years ago. After Andrew—who was a year older—graduated, Nelia went back to law school, then took a job as a corporate lawyer for a defense contractor. After her son was killed, she resigned and moved to Idaho. She worked from home for a law firm reviewing contracts, which seemed tame and completely uninteresting, but after losing her son she had never returned to a regular nine-to-five position.

After Nelia, Rosa had twin boys—fraternal, according to Max's research team. Jack Kincaid had enlisted in the army when he turned eighteen, never went to college, then after fourteen years left the service voluntarily and honorably discharged. He had numerous medals and accommodations. He became a mercenary—that was interesting, Max thought. She wished she had more time to delve into his background, but it didn't seem relevant when he'd been deployed in the Middle East when his nephew was murdered.

Now, however, Jack Kincaid was married to an FBI agent in Sacramento—an SSA, same rank as Max's ex-boyfriend Marco—and he was a principal in the security company of Rogan Caruso Kincaid . . . that must be the same company that Agent Kincaid married into.

Dr. Dillon Kincaid was a forensic psychiatrist who lived in Washington, D.C. with his wife, an FBI agent who taught cybercrime at Quantico. Max had hoped to speak with Dr. Kincaid at some point, but he had been in medical school when his nephew was killed, and it didn't seem that he would have any relevant information—except for his expertise working with criminals and the criminal justice system. Max hadn't asked her staff for anything except the basics on Dillon and Jack Kincaid because they hadn't been around during Justin Stanton's murder, but now she wanted to know more. She sent Ben a note to that effect. Interesting that both twins married FBI agents.

Connor Kincaid was the middle child. He was a private investigator, though he had been a cop for ten years first. He resigned after a public trial where he testified against a corrupt cop. Max had to admire him for that—it took a lot of courage to stand up against one of your own, even when one of your own had done something illegal and morally reprehensible. He was married to an assistant DA, the independently wealthy Julia Chandler. Max was familiar with the Chandler Foundation—they were generous in their philanthropy.

Carina Kincaid had been in college when Justin was killed—but afterward she dropped out and joined the police academy. She became a uniformed officer at the age of twenty, then made detective before she was thirty. She'd been married to Nick Thomas—former sheriff of Gallatin County in Montana—for nearly eight years. They had a seven-month-old son, and Nick was now a PI in the same business with his brother-in-law, Connor.

And because it seemed everyone in the Kincaid family—except the oldest, Nelia—was in some sort of law enforcement, Max hadn't been surprised to learn that Patrick Kincaid had also been a cop. Again, he had been lower on her list because he lived in Washington, D.C., but as she reviewed the file on him, her curiosity was piqued. He'd been a detective with San Diego PD until he was injured and in a coma for nearly two years. Nothing in the file said how he was injured—was it on the job? A year after he recovered, he joined Rogan Caruso Kincaid Protective Services.

That company again.

She sent another note off to Ben to dig deeper into Patrick Kincaid. Just because she was curious—his injuries were sustained nearly nine years ago, they had nothing to do with Justin's murder or the investigation—but information was king. It was better to know everything than to make assumptions.

More than ten years after Patrick was born came Lucia "Lucy" Kincaid, born two weeks before her nephew, Justin.

Max quickly did the math . . . Rosa Kincaid would have been forty-three or forty-four when she had Lucy. Not unheard of, but not common.

There wasn't much on Lucy Kincaid. She graduated from George-town University in D.C. with a dual degree in psychology and criminal justice, and then earned her master's in criminal psychology from the same school. She'd served as an intern in several capacities, but the longest stint was thirteen months at the D.C. medical examiner's office. She was a certified assistant pathologist—that seemed odd for a federal agent. Had she considered going into the field? She also held a certification in underwater search and rescue through the Commonwealth of Virginia. It would probably have been updated when she joined the FBI, they had their own underwater training program, but Max couldn't access Kincaid's FBI records.

Max continued to stroll through the original documentation her team had put together.

Lucy would be twenty-seven next month—young to have such a weighty background. Seemed she did a little of everything. Dabbled? Overachiever? Undecided? Flighty? What little Max knew about the Kincaid family told her that they were all overachievers, at least when it came to law enforcement careers. But as the youngest in the bunch, maybe Lucy Kincaid didn't know what she wanted so tried a little of everything.

Max didn't have much time before she needed to meet Stanton and Kincaid, so she checked her e-mail to see if Ben had uncovered anything else. He had sent her an e-mail with several attachments.

Max—

Federal agents rarely make the news, but I've pulled all the articles referencing the San Antonio Field Office over the past year.

Kincaid graduated from the FBI Academy a year ago December and was assigned to the San Antonio Field Office. She and her then-boyfriend Sean Rogan bought a house in an established neighborhood (property records attached).

As you know, most federal agents stay out of the press, and Kincaid is no exception. I learned that she was part of Operation Heatwave (details in the article from the SA Press) and she was part of the task force during the manhunt for escaped prisoner, former DEA Agent

Nicole Rollins. It appears she's been involved in several major cases during her first year as a rookie agent, but according to my friend in the N.Y. office, the San Antonio office has been short-staffed. Maybe an all-hands-on-deck situation?

Now here's the interesting point—when I talked to my contact in N.Y., he told me off-the-record that Kincaid had been involved in at least two investigations in N.Y. before she was a federal agent. She was a consultant for the Cinderella Strangler investigation, which seems odd considering she wasn't even in law enforcement at the time. While she was at the FBI Academy, she consulted on the Rosemary Weber homicide. Both cases were NYPD investigations, but the same FBI agent liaison worked with the police. My contact either wouldn't or couldn't give me more details, but it seems interesting to me that someone prior to graduation—especially a young recruit like Kincaid—was consulting with the FBI on major criminal cases.

I'm reaching out to the liaison to see what else I can learn.

I'm asking C. J. to dig into Kincaid's husband, Sean Rogan. He's a principal with Rogan Caruso Kincaid Protective Services, but everything we know is from their Web site and a few articles. And you'll probably remember from the previous documentation that Jack Kincaid and Patrick Kincaid both work for RCK. It seems they stay well below the media radar. I'm going to reach out to the media contact there and see what I can learn.

If Stanton wants Lucy Kincaid's blessing, it may not be for obvious reasons. Maybe he thinks she's the only one he can convince to help— he made it clear during our conversation yesterday that the Kincaid family would put up a major roadblock in our investigation into Justin Stanton's murder. Stanton's reasons were vague. Emotion? Bad blood?

You never know who might be hiding what. You taught me that—so I'm reminding you to tread carefully. We'll go back further and see what we can learn. I'm copying in David—since David was an Army Ranger, maybe he can get more information on Jack Kincaid. Their service didn't overlap, but maybe David has some inside knowledge or knows where to get it. Hint, hint, David.

—*Ben*

Max didn't have time to review any of the attached articles, but she appreciated Ben's quick analysis and sent him a thank-you. The thank-you would also serve as a second apology for her comment about commercializing the murders of four boys. Ben did overstep the media angle on occasion, but he wasn't an asshole, and he cared about the victims. It wasn't fair of her to snap at him because he was thinking of her show and NET—that was his job.

She quickly changed out of her travel clothes then went downstairs a few minutes early. She wanted to assess the group when they walked in—body language and first impressions were important in how she would handle the conversation. Her goal was simple: she wanted Stanton's help, and if Kincaid had any insight or information, she wanted her help; but she didn't want them involved on the investigative level. Having a federal agent to consult was good; having a fed breathing down her neck was bad. Been there, done that.

When she stepped out of the elevator and into the lobby, she saw Andrew Stanton walking in through the main doors. He looked almost exactly like the photo on the DAs Web site, even wearing a similar gray suit.

But he was alone. Maybe Agent Kincaid couldn't get away from San Antonio. That would be a relief.

Andrew recognized Max a moment later. "Ms. Revere," he said.

"Max," she said and took his hand. "Good to meet you, Counselor."

Conservatively cut light brown hair, pale green eyes, and trim to the point of being on the thin side. But she was surprised he was so tall—at least six foot three—and though she knew he hadn't been a cop or in the military, he had a cautious, suspicious manner about him.

But he'd come alone. Without Agent Kincaid, an assistant, or an entourage. That took guts, in her experience. Politicians didn't like speaking to reporters without a witness or three. And even a DA, who was ostensibly law enforcement, was a politician at heart. She'd known enough of them.

"I wanted to talk to you before Lucy arrived. They're driving in from the airport now, we have a few minutes."

So Kincaid hadn't backed out.

Max led the way into the lounge. Because it was the middle of the afternoon, they had their choice of tables. Max selected one in the far corner, where they would have privacy.

The bartender approached almost immediately. Max wanted wine, but asked instead for coffee. Andrew said, "For me as well, and keep it coming."

When the bartender left, Andrew said, "You didn't sound pleased over the phone when I told you I was bringing in Lucy."

"Right to the point. I like that."

He smiled briefly. "I need a Kincaid on board."

"But I don't." She leaned back, assessed him. "I want your help, but I can and will investigate on my own. Just so we're clear."

"You won't get anywhere."

"You don't know me."

"I know your reputation."

"If that were true, you would know I don't back down. Ever."

"I also know that you don't investigate cold cases when the family doesn't want you involved."

So he had done a bit of research. "Usually. But this case is different. This isn't one crime. This is four separate cases that may be linked."

"Yet, you need my help."

She raised an eyebrow, but didn't say anything as the bartender brought over two cups of coffee, cream, and sugar. When he left, she doctored her coffee and said, "I'm quite resourceful, Counselor."

"So I've heard. But you do not know the Kincaids like I do."

"What, will they destroy evidence? Threaten witnesses?"

"Carina was babysitting the night Justin was taken." Andrew paused, lost briefly in a memory. "She's now a detective with SDPD, is well-liked and has many friends. If she doesn't want you looking at reports, you won't see them."

"That's where you come in."

"The Kincaids don't like me. Lucy is the only one who will talk to me outside of work. Carina has to work with me because I'm the DA, and her brother is married to one of my prosecutors, but it hasn't been an easy nineteen years."

"You'd think a cop family would love a DA in the fold." She sipped her coffee. "What, they're holding your affair against you?"

"You read the articles. I was with another woman the night my son was murdered." He cleared his throat and stared into his coffee.

It bothered him, as well it should. "The police verified your alibi with your mistress, who was a prosecutor from Orange County, correct?"

Andrew nodded curtly. "What wasn't publicized in the newspaper— but the Kincaids know—is that Nelia and I had an understanding. We married because Nell got pregnant. We knew it was a mistake, but we were in law school and were best friends and it just happened. We loved Justin. We didn't love each other. We were friends. And marriage made everything . . . awkward. Nell knew I was seeing someone else. She didn't ask for details, it wasn't spoken, but she knew. And she blames herself as much as me for not being home that night."

"Would being home have changed anything?" Max asked. "Couldn't Justin have been taken while you were there sleeping?" Each of the cases that Max had on her list, the parents weren't home when the child was taken. Another similarity, which suggested that the killer had knowledge of the family schedule.

"I don't know."

"Guilt is a useless emotion, Andrew," Max said. "It clouds judgment, it fuels self-loathing, it makes good people do stupid things. *Someone* killed Justin. And if the research that my staff and I have done is any indication that individual killed four boys over nearly twenty years."

"This is why I need Lucy. She has experience in complicated cases like this. I find it difficult to believe that one person can kill four children over such a length of time with such a long wait in between. Why did no one notice the pattern? I don't want to be grasping at straws. I want answers, but I don't want to live through this and come out with nothing."

"You want the truth. That should be enough."

"I don't know that you can find it."

That bothered Max as well. She had never tackled such a difficult case—twenty years *was* a long time. And while on the surface there appeared to be a connection between the four cases, what if, in fact, they weren't connected and there were four separate killers? How could she solve four separate cases where three of them were so cold?

"I need access to all the cases to see if there is another commonality . . . something that proves that we're looking for one killer. If I can find that, I can open up far more avenues of investigation. I came here for two reasons. One, Justin is the first known victim. It's the beginning for this killer. Second, you can get information from the other jurisdictions easier than I can."

"Max." Andrew leaned forward, his expression borderline hostile. "I didn't want you here, but you said something yesterday on the phone that stuck with me. I am a prosecutor at heart. I'm not always a good person, I wasn't a good husband, but I am a great district attorney. It sickens me that my son's murder is unsolved. That someone killed him and destroyed my wife—my best friend—and tore her family to shreds with grief. It pains me that if you're right, and Justin's murder is connected to others, that the killer is still out there. And I keep asking *why*. Why, dammit! That question keeps me up late at night. It was a senseless murder, but until you contacted me, I never once thought that it was part of a pattern. If you and your resources can find the answers, I can work with you. But if—and only if—Lucy agrees."

"Why is your former sister-in-law the decider for you?" That made no sense to Max, and it bothered her that she couldn't figure it out.

"Lucy is not only good at her job, she has a unique skill set. Experience investigating serial killers—because honestly, if you're right, that is exactly what we're dealing with. And I think she's the only one who might be able to figure out *why*. As I said, she's the only Kincaid who will work with me on this. She's the only one who might be able to convince her family to help. And if she doesn't, then you're back to square one, because I guarantee that the Kincaids will do everything they can to stop you. If you think they can't, you're lying to yourself."

"Why wouldn't they want the truth?"

"That's not the question you should be asking. This isn't about the truth, this is about protecting their family. Nell had an extremely difficult time after Justin's murder. She hated me, hated herself, and I thought—her family thought—that she was going to kill herself. She moved out of our house, filed for divorce, lived with her parents. But I saw her—she wasn't all there. When the police put the case on the back burner for lack of evidence, she moved to Idaho. Disappeared from everyone's lives. The Kincaids will do everything to protect her. Carina went through hell and back during the investigation—she was interrogated, treated as a suspect. The Kincaids have powerful friends. You need a Kincaid on your side or you will get nothing."

"I have two other cold cases."

"But like you said," he said, raising his eyebrows, "Justin was the first victim."

He was right, and he knew he was right.

"If Lucy agrees to help, I'll give you everything you need even if I have to go up against my former in-laws. If Lucy doesn't, you'll be on your own. And don't be surprised if you end up in jail."

"So the Kincaids would abuse the law to stop me from finding the truth."

"The Kincaids would do anything to protect those they love."

"You haven't said a word since we landed."

Sean pulled in to the US Grant parking garage. He turned off the ignition of the rental car and turned to face Lucy.

"Thinking." A lot of thinking.

She reached for the handle but Sean took her hand. "Worrying," he said. "You don't have to do this."

"I do." She looked at Sean, saw the concern in his expression. Just having him here with her meant everything. She touched his face. "Thank you."

"Don't thank me—I would do anything for you. But this is going to hurt you and I don't want to see you hurt."

"I'll get through it."

"Of course you will, you're a survivor. But I know you and I know your family. You're going to tell them."

Sean had suggested that she come to San Diego and work with the reporter without talking to her family—at least initially. She'd seriously considered it, but she didn't think the situation was as awful as both Sean and Andrew thought it might be.

"My family may not be happy with my involvement in this, but they will understand. They want the truth just like I do, just like Andrew. I'm going to listen to what this Maxine Revere has to say first, then we'll decide what to do."

"It's me you're talking to, princess," Sean said.

She leaned over and kissed him. "You know me well."

"That I do. You want to wait until you hear all the facts, but in your heart you know you're going to pursue it. No matter how thin a lead Maxine Revere came up with."

"I read one of her books last night. Her college roommate disappeared over spring break in Miami. Karen Richardson."

"I don't know the case."

"She went out with a group of people and never returned. Blood was found at the suspected crime scene—Karen's blood, they proved later—but her body was never found. Revere hounded the police, the FBI, search and rescue, but the book was not just about the investigation. It was about predators, about knowing someone committed a crime but being unable to prove it. It was also about friendship and victims and survivors. How crime affects everyone." She paused. "After the whole Rosemary Weber situation, I thought the worst. True crime writer? I wanted no part of it."

Weber intended to write a book about the Cinderella Strangler, a case Lucy and Sean had assisted with before she was in the FBI. But Lucy had a great fear that some reporter would uncover her past and write about her. When Andrew first called her, she thought of how it would hurt her . . . which is why she had to read Maxine Revere's books first. To see what she wrote about, how she wrote, whether Lucy could even trust her enough to work alongside her to see if maybe there were clues others had misinterpreted when Justin was killed.

"I think she's different." She *hoped* she was different, but Lucy didn't think she was wrong.

"I did my own research," Sean said. "The jury is still out."

"You're being protective."

"Of course I am." He caressed her cheek. "I'm going to be there when you tell your parents."

Lucy hesitated.

"Lucy, you shouldn't have to face your family alone. Not about this." He frowned. "What's wrong? Do you not want me here?"

"I do, but you have to promise to stand down. I don't want to go through the conversation with everyone separately—I'm going to ask my mom to have everyone over for dinner. Bite the bullet. I think it's going to be okay."

"I can't promise to let your family jump all over you."

"They're not going to jump all over me." Lucy had thought about this all night. She understood why her family would put up a brick wall with Andrew, but not with her—they would understand, she was certain of it.

"What if it doesn't work out the way you think?"

"I know them. Carina is a cop. Connor used to be a cop. They want the truth just as much as I do. As Andrew does. They had a hard time forgiving Andrew for having an affair, I get that. Family is everything and he blew it. So I see why they won't listen to him, but this is different."

She could see that Sean didn't believe her, but he didn't have the same family growing up as she did. And lately, he'd had to reconcile that his family had dark secrets that nearly got them both killed. He was still having a difficult time working through the aftermath.

"I don't have to be in Sacramento until tomorrow morning, and I'm not going to leave you alone tonight. Well shit, not again." Sean pulled out his phone. "My phone has been buzzing my butt for the last five minutes." He frowned.

"Who is it?"

"Suzanne."

Suzanne Madeaux was one of Lucy's closest friends, an FBI agent in New York City. She'd been in their wedding and indirectly helped with one of Lucy's recent cases.

Sean answered the phone. "Suz, what's up?" He listened, his expression turning to stone. He said after a moment, "What else?" A minute later he said, "Keep me in the loop—and thanks, Suz." He hung up.

"Bad news?" Lucy said.

"That fucking bitch," Sean mumbled.

"*Suzanne?*" Lucy had seen Sean angry before, but she couldn't imagine what Suzanne could have said to set him off.

He spat out the name. "Maxine Revere."

"I don't understand." But maybe she did. Maybe her worst fears were coming true.

"Her staff has requested all the files on the Cinderella Strangler case and the Rosemary Weber homicide—both from the FBI and NYPD. Her staff also wants to talk to Suzanne about the use of 'civilian consultants.' That means you, Lucy—you were involved with both cases."

Lucy didn't know what to say. "Maybe it's just background—"

"Maybe she's a chameleon, maybe she found out something about you and is now going to try and write some big story. It will not happen. I will shut her down so fast—"

"Don't jump to conclusions, Sean."

"Would Andrew set you up?"

"No."

"You sound so confident. He's a damn politician, Lucy."

"He wouldn't," she said firmly. "Andrew isn't a bad guy."

"Good people do shitty things. Give me a minute."

He took out his phone again. A moment later he said, "JT, it's Sean. Has RCK received any press inquiries in the last twenty-four hours? . . . Who? . . . Shit. What'd you say? . . . Okay. Hold off on any follow-ups, I'll explain later." He hung up. "Maxine Revere has been a busy little bitch. All press inquiries regarding RCK go through JT, and he had a call two hours ago from NET—that's the network that hosts Revere's television show. The inquiries were general, JT sent the standard press packet, but I'll bet they'll follow up wanting more information about me, Jack, and Patrick."

"Why?"

"Because the media sucks."

She almost laughed, but her stomach felt sick.

Sean took her hand, squeezed it. "I won't let her dig around into your past, Lucy. I won't."

"I'm not going to let her scare me off," Lucy said.

"She already has two strikes against her, Lucy. One more, and I will skewer her."

"Promise me you'll listen to what she has to say."

"That's about all I can promise."

Chapter Ten

Max recognized Sean Rogan and Lucy Kincaid as soon as they entered the lounge. Not only because she was expecting them, nor because the lounge was quiet before happy hour, but because they looked exactly as she expected.

Rogan reminded her not a little of David—the way he stood protectively next to his wife, scanning the room and immediately assessing the people, the layout, identifying the exits. Had he been in the military? Perhaps, that hadn't been in Ben's notes. All she knew was that he was thirty-two—same age as her—and was a principal of RCK who had graduated from MIT and specialized in cybersecurity. When Rogan caught her eye, she had the strong sense he disliked her. She was used to that—reporters often brought out the worst in people—but this was different. It felt more . . . personal, and she wondered what his story was.

She would find out.

Max had wrongfully assumed that since Rogan was a computer security expert, he would appear a bit more . . . *nerdy*, for lack of a better word. He obviously had brains—evident from his educational background and his position in his company—but he was definitely built more like a personal bodyguard. Interesting. She had Rogan pegged pretty quick—he was protective of his wife, he was smart, shrewd, even, and self-confident. It oozed from his every pore to the point that it might become a problem. Perhaps it wasn't a fair assessment because he hadn't even spoken a word, but physical presence plus what she learned about RCK? Rogan wasn't a man to lie to or manipulate.

Which was good for her, because she didn't lie.

Lucy Kincaid Rogan—Max didn't know what name she went by— looked exactly like a federal agent. She, too, scanned the room, but she focused more on the people than the environment. She dressed the part as well—functional clothes, a bit drab Max thought, with the dark slacks and thin off-white sweater. A little color would do wonders for her, a blue scarf, or red—yes, definitely red or a vibrant purple. Lucy was classically attractive, just needed a little brightness. Her half-Cuban ancestry showed in her complexion and thick dark hair. The two made a good-looking couple—in business, they would certainly be known as a power couple, like the owners of NET.

What stuck out the most to Max was the icy exterior—Lucy radiated *stay away* as if she wore a blinking neon sign. Max was a good judge of people, but she made snap judgments—often on first impressions. She'd been trying to break herself from the habit, and Lucy Kincaid was a classic reason why. Lucy's coolness didn't seem to be introversion or arrogance, but something else . . . something so deep-seated that Max would have a hard time figuring it out.

But she would. She always did.

Lucy caught her eye. She didn't change her expression, but there was a subtle shift in her posture, as if she knew Max had been watching her.

Andrew rose from his seat and greeted Lucy with a hug when she approached, then shook Sean's hand. "Thank you, Lucy. Sean. I appreciate you coming out with such short notice." He turned to Max. "Maxine Revere, this is my sister-in-law, Lucy Kincaid Rogan, and her husband Sean. Maxine Revere is an investigative reporter with *Maximum Exposure*, a cold case crime show on NET."

"I'm familiar with the network," Sean said. "It was one of the first to successfully integrate television with the Internet in an interactive way."

"The Crossmans are visionaries," Max said. No one ever commented to her about the network she worked for.

Sean and Lucy sat down. The bartender immediately came over. Lucy asked for coffee; Sean asked for a beer. Definitely not someone who followed conventions.

"I want to make something clear from the beginning," Sean said. He glared at Max. Was he trying to intimidate her?

"By all means, Mr. Rogan."

"If you write one word about Lucy or me without our express permission, I will destroy you."

"My investigation isn't about you or your wife. But I don't like threats."

"I don't believe you."

Max was a lot of things, but a liar wasn't one of them. "You'll have to take my word for it."

"I don't trust you."

"I don't care."

Lucy cleared her throat. "Sean and I are very private people, Ms. Revere. It came to our attention that your staff has been making inquiries about us."

"I need a more discreet staff." If she was going to get anywhere with these people, she was going to have to adjust her strategy. "When I come into any investigation, I research everyone involved. It's standard. I need to know every possible angle, who's important, who isn't, their background, the whole nine yards. But I can assure you that my focus is not on either of you. My focus is on solving the deaths of four little boys."

Though she was intensely curious about what these two people were hiding. People with nothing to hide didn't generally lead with threats.

"My statement stands," Rogan said.

She didn't want to give an inch, especially since Rogan was making her angry—and calling her a liar—but if Andrew needed Lucy Kincaid's blessing before he would get her the information and files she needed, she would relent. Reluctantly. Very, very reluctantly.

"Fair enough," she said as calmly as she could. "I won't mention either of you without your express permission."

"Thank you, Ms. Revere," Lucy said. Her hand was on her husband's arm. Was there something else going on here that she wasn't privy to?

Just because she promised not to write about them, didn't mean she couldn't learn more. And she would.

She always did.

Max said to Lucy, "You're an FBI agent. A rookie?"

She nodded. Didn't offer anything else. Open-ended questions usually resulted in information—either by what they said or how they said it. How people answered such questions gave Max extensive insight into them—primarily to help her figure out how to gain the most information from them.

Lucy Kincaid Rogan wasn't going to be easy. It didn't help that Max had already had a tense exchange with her husband.

"My ex-boyfriend was a federal agent," Max said, attempting to develop a rapport. "It can be a demanding job."

"Marco Lopez?"

Surprise, surprise, she'd read her book. "Yes." Maybe not a surprise. If Andrew had talked to Lucy last night, she would have done research on Max. It's exactly what Max had done, as Rogan pointed out. "He's currently the SSA of Violent Crimes in Miami, though I heard he was up for a promotion. Considering he works his ass off and plays the game well, he'll probably get something juicy."

Again, silence. This was not going to be a fun conversation for Max if she couldn't learn anything about Lucy.

Except—perhaps—she already had. The girl was cautious, she prepared for the meeting by reading Max's most popular true crime book—her first—and suspicious. The cool suspicion oozed from her pores; Max could almost see it.

After the bartender brought coffee for Lucy and refilled the other cups, then placed the beer in front of Sean, who waved away the glass, Andrew said, "I have to get back to the office by five, so let's get to it. I spoke to your producer and he explained your theory about Justin's murder being connected to three other murders over a nearly twenty-year period. State your case."

Right to it. Max wanted more from Lucy first, but maybe if she sparked her curiosity, she'd get the interaction she needed to understand her.

"I'm a visual person, and I have a full timeline in my suite upstairs," Max said, "but I think the correlation is clear. I'm missing some pieces that I'm in the process of getting, but so far, everything has fallen into a pattern.

"Four victims—your son, Justin, Tommy Porter, Chris Donovan, and nine months ago, Peter Caldwell. All between the ages of seven and nine. All kidnapped from their bedrooms in the middle of the night while their parents were out and left them with a babysitter. All were buried in a shallow grave, wrapped in a blanket from their bed, five miles or less from their homes. All were killed relatively quickly in the same manner—suffocation. None had any signs of sexual assault.

"On the surface, connecting these cases seems a stretch because they are roughly five years apart—Justin nearly twenty years ago, Tommy fifteen years ago, Chris six years ago, and Peter last April. My staff is looking hard at missing boys kidnapped from their bedrooms between nine and twelve years ago to see if there is a fifth victim who fits the pattern. We're focusing in Southern California, Nevada, and Arizona, and will expand as necessary. If in fact this is a serial killer, there could be more victims. Or there's a specific trigger that set this person off that is unique to these victims." Max was expecting questions, but no one spoke.

So she continued. "We know from the Porter and Donovan homicides that the victims were drugged and likely unconscious when they were suffocated—no signs of defensive wounds, no restraints other than being wrapped in the blanket. I don't have the autopsy report on Justin because for some reason the ME wouldn't send it to my office upon request—it wasn't until I talked to Andrew that I realized there were family members with the clout to prevent the media from obtaining any information on this case."

Andrew spoke. "I told you it would be an uphill battle."

"Do you know if your son was drugged?"

Andrew nodded. "He was."

"The Porter case didn't have a tox screen report attached to the autopsy report, though there was a note that a narcotic was found in the boy's system. I'm working on finding that report—it's still an open case. The Donovan case is closed—his father went to prison for second degree murder."

"So the cases aren't identical," Lucy said.

"The facts are the same regarding the kidnapping and murders of each of these boys. What isn't the same is that in the Donovan case, the father went to prison. I read the transcripts and he had a really bad attorney. The evidence was circumstantial, Donovan initially lied about his alibi, and when he realized that the police thought he had killed his son, he admitted to having an affair. The prosecution was able to discredit his mistress, though she never wavered that he was with her the night Chris was killed. My associate interviewed her and while he was initially skeptical of Donovan's innocence, he doesn't think she's lying."

"If the case was circumstantial, why hasn't he appealed?" Andrew asked.

"Guilt that he was in bed with his mistress when his son was murdered," she said bluntly.

Andrew bristled, but didn't comment. Max continued. "In the Porter case, the father was also having an affair. He, too, was with his mistress the night his son was killed. That's three."

She was watching Lucy carefully, and the fed saw the same pattern she did. But she didn't flinch. It was simply a subtle change in her posture, a faint leaning forward that told Max she was hanging on every word, processing the information, putting together the patterns.

"And the last victim?" Lucy asked.

"Unconfirmed," Max said. "The victim's father and I were in college together—it's how I became interested in these cases. He denied having an affair. I know him, and in the past I would say he'd never lie about something like this. But when you don't see someone for ten years, you don't know how they might have changed.

"His wife? Another story. But there's a catch. She's pending trial for her son's murder. I can't access the information I need to determine if Peter's case matches the other three. The autopsy report is only available to law enforcement and the defense right now, and the defense doesn't want me involved."

"Why?" Sean asked. "If they think you can help clear their client." It was a valid question, but the tone was skeptical. Accusatory. Max knew she was winning Lucy over with the facts, but now she wondered if Sean had more sway. Did she have to convince both of them?

"Because the evidence is circumstantial. My gut says that the prosecution has a witness that places Blair Caldwell someplace other than where she said she was during her son's murder. She and her husband were at a charity golf fund-raiser in their own neighborhood, a gated community. As the crow flies, she could have crossed the golf course in four minutes if she walked briskly—I timed it—and reached her back-yard, which is accessible through a gate in a wrought-iron fence. Peter's body was found in a sand pit on the portion of the golf course farthest from their house. Assuming about five minutes to climb in through the window, grab the kid, climb out with him. It would have taken eight to ten minutes briskly walking—maybe longer carrying a body. Three minutes to suffocate him, and since he was buried in the sand, maybe another minute or two to conceal the body. He could have also been suffocated in his bed and carried already deceased to the sand pit. From the sand pit back to the party at the club would take four to five min-utes. That's roughly twenty-five minutes, thirty tops. And that's being conservative. I think a determined person could have done it in twenty."

"Forensic evidence?" Lucy asked.

"I can't access what they have. I can't prove that they offered her a plea deal, but my gut says they did and she declined. The defense must know what the prosecution has and they must think it's weak. Or weak enough that they can play on the emotions of the jury—how can a mother kill her own son? What is the reason? Happy family and all that."

"Premeditated," Lucy said quietly.

"Excuse me?" Max said.

"If Blair Caldwell killed her son, it was premeditated. She was at a party in her housing community. She would have known exactly how long it would take to get to her house, kill her son, bury his body, and return to the party. Maybe she had access to a golf cart—which would cut down your timeline quite substantially."

Max couldn't speak. She prided herself on thinking of every possible scenario—it's why she was so good at solving cold cases, because she *didn't* think like a cop—but she hadn't thought about the golf cart. Why was that? Because she thought someone would have seen her? Or some-one would have heard her?

Lucy continued. "Did Blair tell you about these similar cases? Maybe in an attempt to throw suspicion off herself?"

"John uncovered them, but he didn't know all the details. He was going off the gender, age, and circumstances of the kidnapping. Many of the details weren't in national media reports. Many I got from archives and my own personal research. I'm good at uncovering information."

Lucy said, "They could be in it together."

"No."

"No?" Lucy shook her head. "As you said, ten years is a long time. People change."

"Full disclosure—I haven't firmly put Peter Caldwell's murder in with the other three. There are many similarities and the only difference *at this point* is I don't have confirmation as to whether John or Blair were having an affair, though I know for certain that John wasn't with a mistress while his son was killed. He was never a serious suspect because, according to a reporter friend of mine in Scottsdale, the police were able to account for his whereabouts during the entire window, midnight to two A.M. I also don't have access to the autopsy report—at least until the trial."

Max sipped her coffee, waited.

"Is that it?" Lucy asked.

"I need the information from Justin's murder—the autopsy report, the tox screen report, the investigation notes. I need to talk to the lead detective. Once I gather that information, and the few missing pieces from the Donovan and Porter homicides, I'll put together a report showing the pattern."

"And if something doesn't fit, what do you do?" Sean asked. "Ignore it? Make it disappear?"

Max bristled. "I don't lie, Mr. Rogan."

"It seems highly unlikely that a killer would be targeting these boys and waiting years between murders," he countered.

"When children are murdered more than eighty percent are killed by someone they know. Most often, that is a family member or a family friend. When children are murdered, they are more likely to be sexually assaulted. It's also extremely rare that a child is kidnapped from their own home—from their bedroom. That's why cases like Polly Klaas and Danielle van Dam make headlines. And those cases were more than fifteen years ago. Both females, both sexually assaulted, but still, these type of kidnappings are rare.

"Once I can confirm the facts of each case, I will produce a detailed report. Prior to airing the report, I will contact the FBI media relations office and present the information to them and ask for their comments. Two of the three times I've done this, the FBI has reopened cases that resulted in an arrest. I have a good rapport with that particular office. I don't withhold evidence from law enforcement. However, when a case is more than a year old, I've found that it disappears into cold case hell—unless someone like me shines a light. I am good at what I do. I wouldn't be here upsetting the victim's family if I didn't believe that I can find answers. But it starts with Justin. If he's the first victim—the answers are in his investigation. I have the staff and resources to take that information and compare it to the other cases I'm looking at. There will be another common factor we can't see right now—a person, a vehicle, *something* that will lead to the killer. No one has looked at Justin's murder as anything but an isolated tragedy."

Lucy turned to Andrew. "Is that true?"

"Mostly. For the first few years after Justin was killed, anytime a child was found dead, SDPD looked at the evidence in Justin's case to see if there were any similarities. There never were—and eventually those inquiries stopped. When Carina first made detective ten years ago, she looked at Justin's case files—it went nowhere. Because no other boy in San Diego or the surrounding counties had been kidnapped and killed under the same circumstances. I tried to open it again eight years ago and also got nowhere. Partly because I didn't want to upset your family, Lucy."

Lucy looked at her husband. It was like they were telepathically speaking. Though brief, the silence felt weighty.

Then Sean nodded.

Lucy turned to Max. "I'd like to see your timeline. You said you had a visual chart upstairs."

"I do. Why?"

"You want my help."

"No-o-o," Max said slowly. "Andrew said that if I convinced you that there was merit to these murders being the work of the same killer, that he would cooperate and help me get the information that the ME and the police department are holding back in Justin's death."

"Yes," Andrew said, "but I also said you needed the Kincaids' cooperation. I can get the files, but you won't have access to people, the lead detective—anyone—without Lucy."

Max froze. He could not be saying what she thought he was saying.

"Ms. Revere," Lucy said, "I am curious. I want to verify what you've told me, because on the surface it is extremely compelling. But I will not have my family relive this nightmare unless I am positive these crimes were committed by the same person *and* there is a chance that we can identify the killer."

We. She said we.

Max was going to explode. That she didn't was a testament to the patience she had learned from her assistant, David.

"I'm a reporter," Max said bluntly. "I interview cops, I don't work with them."

"There's an exception to everything," Lucy said. "If I'm going to talk to my family, I have to tell them I'm intimately involved in the investigation."

"Lucy—" Andrew began.

"That's not going to work for me," Max said.

"Fine," Lucy said. "You found this information, so can I. I'll look at the cases on my own."

The conversation had gone from bad to worse. "I'm not backing down from this," Max said. "You care about Justin's murder, I care about *all* of the murders."

A flash of anger crossed Lucy's expression—it was the first real, unfiltered emotion Max had seen since the fed sat down.

"Do not presume that you know what I care about," Lucy said coolly.

"I have resources that you do not," Max said. "Time and money at the top of the list."

"I have two things you do not. I am a Kincaid and I have experience."

"Your FBI training last year? Four months at Quantico and a year in the field is what you're going with? I've been investigating cold cases since you were in high school." Truth was, Lucy was only five years younger than Max . . . but she had just graduated from the academy. Hardly enough time to amass a huge level of experience hunting down killers and deciphering old clues, subtle nuances, and faulty memories that were the backbone of working cold cases.

Sean pushed his chair back. "We're done."

How had Max lost control of this meeting? After the initial tension with Sean, she'd had them completely engaged . . . then lost it because Lucy wanted to partner with her.

"I'm not backing down," Max said. "This is my story. It's more than a story. This is about a killer—or two. If Blair Caldwell killed her son, I might be able to prove it if I can prove Peter *wasn't* killed by the same killer as these other boys."

"That's a stretch," Andrew said.

"No, it's not," Max insisted. She noticed that Sean didn't get up—he was still ready to stand, but he was listening. "John believes in his heart that Blair is innocent, but I think a tiny part of his brain is suspicious. It's why he didn't want to wait until after the trial to ask for my help—I think he's scared, based on the fact that his wife has an amazing criminal defense lawyer, that she will be exonerated. Yet, being proven not guilty is not the same as being proven innocent. And if I can't prove that Peter was killed by the same man who killed Justin, Tommy, and Chris, John will never really believe his wife is innocent. Because this specific type of murder is extremely rare."

Lucy said, "Ms. Revere, I will work with you on this. You should accept my help. If you don't, I will learn everything you have and investigate it myself. That's not my first choice. You've done the work, it would take me weeks to duplicate it. And while I'm willing to give up all my free time to find out who killed my nephew—my best friend—I still have a job. You're right about one thing—time is not on my side. But if we do this together, we can find the answers faster. And if that's the case, we can save the next victim."

Max stared at her. She didn't know what to think. There was something in Lucy's personality that she couldn't quite put her finger on, but part of it was definitely obsession. Max was very familiar with the feeling. She'd had it when she investigated Karen's disappearance more than ten years ago. That she had to find the truth at all cost. Max believed every word Lucy said. That Lucy would pursue the case, with or without her. Max had never found herself in this position. She was always in the driver's seat, she always had control in any situation. When she gave up control—even a tiny bit of control—it was a strategic move.

She hated being forced into anything.

She didn't like this. *At all.* She didn't want to work with anyone, but she especially didn't want to work with a federal agent. It never ended well. They had rules they had to follow, rules she didn't have to.

"I have one other thing over you that isn't time," Max said, grasping at her last straw. "I don't have to follow the same rules you do. And sometimes, the only way to get answers is to break the law."

"I'm not hearing this," Andrew said under his breath.

Max continued. "You break the law and you can lose a conviction. A killer can walk."

"I don't plan on breaking the law," Lucy said. "I'll leave that up to you."

That was the last answer Max expected.

"Take it or leave it," Lucy said.

Max hated this. But what choice did she have? She could push and get what she needed, but it would take much longer . . . and she hadn't lied about Blair's trial. John needed to know, in his heart and head, that Blair was innocent. But more than that, if Blair was guilty, Max wanted her to fry.

"Fine." She already regretted her decision.

Lucy smiled, though it didn't reach her eyes. "I'd like to see your visual timeline. I . . . I have a theory."

"About what? I already laid out the theory."

"Theory is the wrong word. I should say profile. Tentative profile. I want to look at the autopsy reports before I say anything. You have the two, Porter and Donovan, correct?"

"Yes."

"And the transcript from Donovan's trial?"

"Yes."

"Great—Andrew, when can you get Justin's autopsy?"

"Tonight or first thing in the morning."

"Good. And you know how to contact the lead detective on Justin's case?"

"Yes, he'll talk to you if I ask him to. We've kept in touch, though he's been retired for seven years."

Max had completely lost control of the investigation. She needed to regroup and figure out how to take charge again. "I'm in room one-four-oh-oh if you'd like to see the timeline."

"I have to get back to my office, but I need a minute with Lucy."

"I'll meet you up there, Agent Kincaid," Max said and walked away.

This was not supposed to happen. How in the world was she going to work with a federal agent? Every time she and Marco crossed paths, it had been a disaster . . . this was going to be worse. She'd been sleeping with Marco, she knew exactly how to push his buttons or calm him down. She could usually get him to do exactly what she wanted . . . and even then, they ended up with an intense on-again, off-again love affair that had been firmly *off* for nearly a year.

She had no idea what Lucy Kincaid's story was.

She called Ben from the elevator. "I need information. Now."

"I don't like her," Sean said. He drained his beer. "Arrogant. Privileged. Know-it-all."

Lucy almost laughed. "Some have called you similar names."

He narrowed his eyes. "Touché."

"You're perfect."

"I know." He took her hand and kissed it.

Lucy ran her fingers over Sean's palm. He was still tense, but he was trying to keep his calm. She appreciated it. "I don't know quite what to make of Max Revere. Her book was emotional on one level—raw and honest, I'd say—and also straightforward, like a good police procedural. Personally, she's more brusque and—" She searched for the word.

"Bitchy?" Sean suggested.

"I wouldn't say that."

"Because you're too nice."

"I have to get to my office, and I want to pull the reports now, not to-morrow," Andrew said.

"It's already after four—tomorrow is fine. They're not going any-where."

"Don't be so sure of that," Andrew said.

"What do you mean?"

"I think you should hold off talking to your family."

"I know you mean well," Lucy said, "but they'll understand. Once they see the pattern, they'll want to help. We're not just talking about Justin. If an innocent man is in prison—unlikely as that may be—we need to help him. I'll be delicate. But Carina is a detective, Connor used to be a cop, they're going to understand and see the same things I do."

"It was a difficult time for your family. You were young, Lucy."

"They tried to shelter me. Do you think I didn't know what had happened? Sometimes, not knowing is worse because I thought some pretty awful things before I learned the truth. Andrew, I know my family. They'll want to protect Nelia, I get that, we don't have to involve her." She didn't completely believe that, but she would cross that bridge later. "Isn't it better if I'm here with some control over what the reporter does and says without her stirring the pot?"

"She's not going to be easy to control," Sean said.

"We got what we wanted," Lucy said. "Equal involvement."

"She won't stick to it."

"Maybe not," Lucy concurred. "I'll keep close tabs on her."

"Tell me the truth," Andrew said, "do you think that Justin's killer is still out there? That he has killed more than one child?"

"If the evidence she claims to have holds up? Yes, I do. And I think the killer—" she stopped herself. "Give me tonight. I'm going to write up an informal profile. I might want to talk to Dillon. Be prepared to answer the hard questions, Andrew."

"I always have been, Lucy." He closed his eyes and sighed. "I've never felt this was over. Justin's murder has been an open wound for nineteen and a half years. It sits there, festering. I wanted so desperately to believe Max, but I knew I wasn't objective, not when it comes to Justin. That's why I called you, Lucy. Truth be told—I called you to make sure I wasn't grasping at a fantasy, or a reporter bent on digging up dirt on me because of the rumors."

"What rumors?"

"I may be up for a bench—California Supreme Court. It's a long shot, but the vultures are circling. I'm too conservative on these issues, too liberal on those issues." He shook his head. "All I can say with complete honesty is that I have always upheld the law."

"You'd make a good judge, Andrew," she said.

"Thank you, but I would give up the opportunity if I can put Justin to rest. If I can just know *why* someone took him from us. It's senseless. Completely senseless."

"Senseless to us," Lucy said, "but not to the killer."

"I know this is hard on you, too. I sincerely appreciate your help."

"I want to do this," Lucy said. "Believe that. Honestly, I'm not doing this for you. I'm doing this for Justin."

He nodded, his eyes damp with emotion. But he gathered himself together quickly. "Tread carefully with your family, Lucy. I wish you luck."

"I don't need luck. This is my family, Andrew. They want closure as much as you and I do."

Chapter Eleven

Lucy stepped into Max's suite—an amazing and elegant space with high ceilings and a wall of windows in the main room. Stairs led to the bedroom. Sean had said Max Revere was independently wealthy, but this was beyond Lucy's idea of how even a wealthy reporter would travel.

Sean was right behind her. Sean was still angry and had made it clear he didn't like or trust Max, but Lucy had calmed him down in the elevator.

"So I get both of you to help me," Max said with a fake smile. "Terrific."

"Just me," Lucy said. "Sean's leaving in the morning."

He didn't want to. He offered to back out of the RCK annual meeting to stay with her and "keep an eye" on Maxine Revere; Lucy told him no. She was confident she could handle the reporter, especially now that she'd met her. Max was surprisingly easy to read. She had a straightforward manner that Lucy respected. Lucy recognized that part of her profile of the reporter was because of the book she'd read. It was clear from the moment Lucy walked in that Max expected to get exactly what she wanted. She had definitely thrown the woman a curveball when she insisted on working with her.

But Justin was her family. Lucy wasn't backing down.

"I'll be back Sunday," Sean said pointedly.

"Wonderful," Max said without hiding the sarcasm. "May I offer you something to drink? Coffee? Water? Another Samuel Adams?" she offered Sean.

"No, thank you," Sean said brusquely.

"I have a dinner at my parents shortly," Lucy said, trying to diffuse the tension between Max and Sean. "I'm interested in your board and timeline. I think it'll help me explain how the cases connect if I see it all laid out."

"I can talk to your family. If you introduce me—"

"Not right now." Lucy wasn't going to let Max near her parents. "My father had a heart attack last year, I don't want anything to upset him. My goal is to get Carina and Connor to have a sit-down with you at some point—after I read the police reports and confirm my suspicion."

It was clear that Max understood exactly what Lucy had said. "You have a suspect in mind? How?"

"Not an individual, a profile. But if I'm right, asking specific questions to each witness, in particular Andrew"—and Nelia, but Lucy didn't say that—"will yield a suspect."

Max walked over to the bar and poured herself a glass of white wine. "This way," she said, gesturing to a wall in the living room. She'd removed the picture that hung on the wall and put up a horizontal timeline starting with Justin's murder—twenty years ago this June.

"It's clear that we'll never solve these murders without knowing the motive," Lucy said. "We need to find out why Justin was targeted. Why these other boys were targeted. What was the motive for Adam Donovan?"

"He had none."

"In the trial, what did the prosecution say that convinced the jury that he was guilty? You said he didn't take the stand, correct?"

Max nodded. "In closing statements, the prosecutor said that while the world may never know why Adam killed his son, it's clear that he wanted out of his marriage. His wife had made it clear that she didn't want a divorce because she had a miserable childhood with divorced parents who fought all the time, so Adam may have killed his son so he could leave his wife."

"It would be more likely he'd kill his wife, if that was his mind-set," Lucy said. "But I'd have to read his statement, talk to him."

"My associate spoke to him this morning."

Lucy wanted more information about that, but first she focused on the timeline.

Max had divided the timeline into twenty columns, starting with the year Justin was murdered. The columns between murders were narrower. Then she'd listed the facts of each case under the name of the victim.

The similarities among all four murders were even more obvious when they were laid out in the grid.

The boys were all between the ages of seven and nine.

They'd all been kidnapped from their bedroom within two hours of midnight.

They'd all had a sedative in their systems—now that Andrew had confirmed that Justin had a narcotic in his system.

They'd all been suffocated and buried in shallow graves, wrapped in a blanket from their own bed.

Sedative . . . it seemed so obvious to her, but maybe she was jumping the gun. She wished her brother Dillon was here. Someone to bounce the idea off of, someone to work the back-and-forth.

She acutely felt Sean watching her. His fear for her—that she would get so emotionally involved in the case it would physically hurt—was clouding her judgment. She walked over to him and kissed him. "Do you think you can get our bags and meet me in the room in thirty minutes? That'll give us enough time to change before dinner."

He stared at her intently, concern in his eyes. "Are you sure?"

"Your concern for me is clouding my perception. I just need a few minutes without worrying about you worrying about me." She smiled, touched his lips. "I love you."

He rubbed her chin, kissed her, and left without a word to Max.

"What was that?" Max asked.

Lucy didn't know how much she'd heard, but she didn't feel the need to explain herself. "Sean's going to get our bags from the car. We didn't check in before the meeting."

Sean was everything she could have hoped for in a lover, a friend, a husband. And he got that she needed to sometimes look at crimes alone. She was sensitive to his emotions, and sometimes that clouded her ability to get inside the killer's mind-set. But knowing he would be there for her tonight made all the difference.

Lucy turned around and faced the board, looking at each case. "The Porters also had an affair?"

"Yes. The husband was with his mistress. It was a short-term thing, but it wasn't his first affair. Tommy's parents separated for a while after his death, but got back together and now have twin daughters, age six."

Lucy nodded. So often, when a child was killed, the parents couldn't withstand the pain, guilt, and grief. Divorce was all too common.

"You mentioned that Adam Donovan's mistress had been discredited. Do you have a sense as to why?"

"I wasn't on the jury, and reading the transcript is different than hearing and seeing the testimony."

Max was perceptive, though Lucy had already noted that from her writing.

"However," Max continued, "I suspect it was more to do with her image. Young, impressionable, attractive. She became flustered at questions about her sex life, about where they had sex—and at first the defense attorney didn't object, which I thought was odd. Her sex life wasn't material as to whether Adam Donovan was with her or not with her during the time in question. Then the prosecutor got her to contradict herself on the time frame. When she clarified in the recross, she was consistent with her original statement. Yet he still hammered home the fact that she was asleep during part of the time-of-death window—which for the jury was enough to think that Donovan snuck out on his mistress, drove thirty minutes home, kidnapped and killed his son, and snuck back in. There was no physical evidence that he left her apartment and no witnesses." She shook her head. "It's a stretch. Like I said, the defense was pathetic."

"I'll read the transcript tonight."

"I thought you were meeting your family."

"I'll come back after dinner, if that's okay. I want to be caught up to speed before tomorrow."

"And what is tomorrow?"

"We'll talk to the detective in charge."

"That was my plan. I just intended to do it alone."

"Sometimes, having a partner is not a bad thing."

Max clearly didn't agree. Lucy focused again on the timeline in front of her. She came back to the sedative. Was that solely to make the child compliant? Or because the killer didn't want to make the victim suffer?

No sexual assault. Sedative. Wrapped in a blanket. Comfort. An easy death . . .

"The killer is a woman," Lucy said.

Max almost spit out her wine. She swallowed and stared at Lucy. "That's a leap."

"It's the manner of death. The care given to the bodies. The personal touch—the blanket. And I'll bet my badge that there was one more thing in the graves. Likely a stuffed animal or toy that the child slept with. I would have to look at the autopsy reports to be certain, but I also think that the killer suffocated the boys after they were unconscious. That should be easy to determine based on the tox screen and physical evidence on the victim—whether they fought back or struggled. The killer didn't want the child to know he was dying. That's a mercy killing. Mercy killers are almost exclusively female." She wrote a few notes on her cell phone so she'd remember to look at some specifics on these type of crimes and what she needed to learn from the reports. "We need to find out exactly what kind of sedative was used and how easy it is to purchase and administer. Why drug them? So they're quiet, compliant, and don't feel pain. They won't know they'll never wake up. She didn't want them to be scared."

For a minute, she almost felt Sean's presence and it was comforting. Maybe she shouldn't have sent him away. But she had to be sure. She had to focus on the clinical, the psychology, the forensics . . . not her emotions or Sean's or the fact that Justin had been her best friend.

To solve his murder, she had to keep her emotions in check.

"With this evidence, I really think I can convince my family to help."

"That would be ideal," Max said, "but I already don't like the fact that you're jumping in. I can't have a half-dozen people messing around with my investigation, my evidence, my organization. I simply want to talk to them. They might know something they don't realize is important."

It was clear Max was still angry that Lucy had insisted on being involved. Lucy continued. "You're missing something."

"I'm missing a lot of things. I have no proof that either John or Blair were having an affair—though I'm working on it. That's another common thread—each of the fathers of the first three victims had been with their mistress during the murder. I know for a fact that John couldn't have been because he had a solid alibi during his son's death, and numerous witnesses at the party. I'm also missing details from the crime scene, because the police notoriously hold back, but I'm good at getting information. With Stanton on board, we can get that intel."

"You're missing the most important piece of the puzzle."

"What?"

"I'll tell you if you agree to keep nothing from me. I have a sense that you're already trying to figure out how to lose me, and that won't go over well—trust me on that. We're full partners in this, Maxine."

Lucy watched the reporter wage an internal battle. She didn't want to work with Lucy, but she would . . . her curiosity and need for answers was greater than her lone wolf approach.

"I said I'd work with you, I keep my word," Max said with a sigh. "What am I missing?"

She stared at her timeline. Lucy had to admit she liked the format—she usually put index cards into a vertical timeline, but this approach was more linear and everything far easier to see in one big picture.

"First, you were right to think there may be another victim between Chris Donovan and Tommy Porter." She walked over to the desk and wrote on a Post-It note.

Unknown victim.

She stuck it between Donovan and Porter. "A serial killer can wait long stretches—even years—between murders. But there is a distinct pattern here, and I suspect five years is the longest she can go. Why five? I don't know." *Yet.*

She then wrote on another Post-it note, and stuck it at the beginning of the timeline.

Victim—0
Unknown male under ten

Max stared. "You think there's another victim."

"Victim might be the wrong word. But—"

"How the hell can you make that statement? You're guessing."

"It's an educated guess. It goes to motive—there is no motive for any of these crimes. *None.* The first victim may not even have been found—he may be a missing person. But the first victim will lead directly to the killer. I'm almost certain of it."

"It makes no sense. I'm not saying it's not possible, only that you can't be certain."

Max was right, but Lucy couldn't shake the feeling. Justin's murder was too well-planned. No trace evidence. Though Lucy didn't know the *why,* she was certain that Max was correct that adultery played a part in the motive.

"Don't think of Victim Zero as a victim per se . . . think of the killer as suffering a grave loss. There was an inciting incident that started her on the road of murder. She could have killed her own son, or he was taken from her by her husband or someone else, or her son could have been a victim of another crime. Consider that there is a lawyer in each of these families—Andrew and Nelia, Mr. Porter, Mrs. Donovan, Mrs. Caldwell. It could be she lost her son to the system."

"And she wants to spread the misery?" Max said.

Lucy had some ideas, but she needed to confirm facts before she would theorize further.

"I have a good friend with the National Center for Missing and Exploited Children. I'm going to write some parameters and see if he can give me a list of missing children and unsolved crimes that fit the victim profile, plus a list of crimes against boys under ten during that window that were solved. It may give us a direction."

"I'll have my staff work on that angle as well."

"You don't have access to the same database. Have your staff continue to look at similar crimes post-Justin—perhaps if we identify this victim between Chris and Tommy we'll gain additional information and narrow our suspect pool. We'll get more done if we focus on different parts of the whole."

Lucy rubbed her eyes. "I need to see my family. Will you be awake around ten if I return? I'd like to bring Sean as well—I know you didn't hit it off, but he's sharp—he sees things other people don't see."

"He called me a liar."

"He's protective."

Max raised her eyebrow. "I noticed."

She wanted more information, Lucy could tell by her expression. Lucy had no intention of sharing anything about herself with the reporter.

"Ten?" she repeated.

"I'll be awake," Max said. "Sleep is not my friend."

Lucy smiled. "See, we already have something in common."

Chapter Twelve

Danielle left work at 2:00 P.M. Thursday, feigning a doctor's appointment. Because she rarely took time off and always did a good job, no one questioned her.

She drove to Kevin Fieldstone's school. Perhaps ironically—or because of fate—Danielle's house was in this school district. She lived only four blocks away. There had been times—rare though they were—when she called in sick and she'd sit in her living room and watch the children walk by her window.

Children that weren't hers.

Today she waited along with mothers and fathers; grandmothers and grandfathers; aunts, babysitters, and older siblings. She waited in her car, down the block, for school to let out. She didn't know what Kevin's grandmother looked like; she did, however, know what Kevin looked like from meeting him in the office and the picture she'd stolen from Nina's office this morning. One of many pictures Nina had of her son on a bulletin board behind her desk.

She wouldn't notice it was gone. If she did, she would assume it had been knocked off and swept away with the trash.

No one would think that Danielle had taken it.

"You are perfect," she whispered to the photo before putting it in her pocket. Too perfect to have such miserable parents. A father who would rather be screwing his mistress than home with his son; a mother who worked long hours and would rather be out with friends and colleagues than home with her son.

Kevin was perfect; his parents didn't deserve him.

Even before the bell rang, children trickled out of the school. Teachers or aides stood at the gates, watching the kids, the buses, the parents. Saying hello to who they knew, and maybe who they didn't. Boys and girls of all shapes and sizes, every color and ethnicity.

She was looking for a blond boy with hair that was always a little too long, always seemed to hang in his eyes. A blond boy with dimples and a light smattering of freckles who was just a little shorter than an average eight-year-old.

The crowd was thickening and she feared she would miss him. Her heart raced as she scanned back and forth. What was the urgency? She could come back. She didn't have to do this now. She could wait.

Wait? Wait for his parents to fail him?

She thought she'd missed him as the crowd thinned. Her hands tightened around her steering wheel. Her vision began to fade.

No, no, no!

She watched as an older woman in blue walked to the gate. A moment later a little blond boy ran out and took her hand. He was jumping up and down and talking, then he waved to someone Danielle couldn't see. He bounced as he walked with his grandmother, chatting freely.

Carefree.

Kevin.

Danielle watched as they reached the corner. When the light turned green, they crossed the street and turned right. Danielle waited a beat, then followed.

She lost them for a moment and nearly panicked, then she turned around and saw them down a side street. She drove down the street at the legal limit and passed them. She turned down the next street, then watched through her rearview mirror.

They, too, turned down this street. Walked right by her car.

"And Daddy said I can play baseball! Sign-ups are this weekend, I'm going to sign up. I want to be a pitcher, Grandma! I want to pitch like Clayton Kershaw! He's with the Dodgers. You know the Dodgers, right? Daddy took . . ."

And then she couldn't hear them anymore.

She watched as they walked up the short walkway to a house halfway down the street. She waited five minutes.

Then she drove by the house before she left.

I hope I'm wrong. I hope Tony Fieldstone isn't the bastard I think he is.

She knew she wasn't wrong. She'd never been wrong before.

It pained her greatly that Tony's son was going to suffer for his sins. But she took some comfort in knowing Tony would suffer for the rest of his life.

She drove home. As she pulled in to the driveway, her phone rang.

Nina.

"Hello?" she answered.

"Hi, Danielle, sorry to bother you. Can you come back to the office after your appointment? I know I said you can have the afternoon off, but we have an emergency briefing to take care of, and then—"

"It's fine. I'm just leaving now. I can be there in twenty minutes or so?"

"Thank you *so* much. You're a godsend!"

Danielle sat in her driveway for a long minute. She picked up her phone and dialed her ex-husband's number.

It rang. And rang. Voice mail picked up.

"I miss Matthew," she whispered. "I miss him so much."

She stared at the phone for another long minute, until it automatically disconnected the call.

She pressed redial.

"I hate you," she said when voice mail picked up again.

Then she backed her car out of the driveway and went back to work.

Chapter Thirteen

Rosa Kincaid flung open the door Thursday evening, beaming. "Lucia! Sean! This is the best surprise."

Lucy hugged her mother. "It's so good to see you, Ma."

"Let me look at you—you are good." Rosa smiled at Sean and hugged him. "You make her happy."

"That's my job." Sean kissed Rosa on the cheek. "I'm sorry we called last minute."

She waved off his comment with a frown. "Family is always welcome, anytime. Did you ask the FBI to transfer you home?"

"Mama," Lucy said. "I told you, that's not how it works."

"But you know important people. Dillon told me that you've done a good job, can't you pick where you work?"

"No, I can't. Please don't talk to Dillon about my work."

"I don't—just making sure you're okay. I worry. But no details. I don't need details."

Lucy had done everything she could before her wedding to hide the bruises and injuries she'd sustained the week before she married Sean, but her mother had seen some of them. Now, she was worried all the time—even more than before.

On the day of Lucy's high school graduation, she'd been kidnapped and raped. She nearly died at the hands of a psychopath. Her brothers had found her, but in the process Patrick had been seriously injured, resulting in a long coma. Lucy couldn't bear the guilt and pain of what happened to Patrick, on top of the grief she saw in her mother's eyes. She moved three thousand miles away to Washington, D.C. and lived with her brother Dillon while attending Georgetown University. It had taken Lucy years to put the past behind her, and unfortunately, sometimes her job brought her past to the forefront.

Back then, her mother had called her all the time, but they'd worked through the trauma and for years enjoyed a pleasant weekly conversation that wasn't tainted with Rosa's fear and worry for Lucy. But now, since Rosa had seen Lucy's injuries and scars and learned that her job was dangerous—more dangerous, according to Rosa, than Carina's job because Carina never came home with bruises and cuts and had never been shot—she called or e-mailed her almost every day. Lucy had to respond or her mother would worry about her safety. And now, apparently, Rosa was talking to Dillon about her.

That couldn't continue, but Lucy didn't know how to make it stop. She loved her mother and didn't want to hurt her feelings. Yet . . . how could she tell her that this was her chosen life? That while she didn't seek out dangerous situations, they often found her?

Lucy didn't want to work out of the San Diego Field Office. She loved her family, but there were some things she wanted to keep from them. Dillon was different—not only was he married to Lucy's best friend, Kate, but he was a forensic psychiatrist. Lucy could talk to him when no one else would understand. She'd lived with Dillon and Kate for six years and there was a comfort and trust there that she didn't really have with anyone else. If Lucy lived here in San Diego, she didn't think she'd be able to keep anything from her family.

Sometimes, ignorance was better. Safer.

"Who's here?" she asked.

"No one yet, except John Patrick. I'm so blessed, I watch him when both Nick and Carina have to work. They'll be here any minute."

Lucy felt a pang she hadn't expected . . . her mother had also watched Justin all those years ago. That's why Lucy felt so close to her nephew, she was practically raised with him. Like a brother. A twin. Lucy had wanted Justin to be her brother because her real brothers and sisters were all so much older than she was. In fact, they'd often pretended they were twins—though they were born ten days apart, they always had a joint birthday party.

Justin would forever be seven to Lucy. He should have been here with her. He should have graduated from high school with her. Gone to college. Fallen in love. He should have had a full life with friends and family, but it was stolen from him.

Sean rubbed her back, then kept his hand on her. She leaned into him, grateful beyond all measure that she had Sean not only here tonight, but in her life.

"Where's J. P.?" she asked, hoping her mother didn't sense her melancholy.

"Your father is spoiling him, I'm sure."

Pat Kincaid walked in carrying the seven-month-old boy in one arm. "Here's the little bruiser." They were both grinning—though J. P. was drooling profusely. Her mother reached over and wiped his chin with a tissue, then kissed J. P. on the head.

Lucy smiled, though she felt that all-too-familiar pang of loss because she was sterile. She didn't think it would ever go away, but it was a little better now than it had been the first time she saw J. P. after his birth.

Sean entwined his hand in hers. "Let us help you in the kitchen," he said to Rosa.

"You can set the table—don't let my daughter touch the stove or we'll be ordering out for pizza. Why is it none of my daughters can cook? I don't understand it. My boys, they cook. My girls?" She shook her head and mumbled rapidly in Spanish that Lucy decided not to translate for Sean.

Nothing had changed in the kitchen. The dishes were in the same cabinet they had been in when Lucy was growing up, the napkins in a drawer, the place mats in the dining-room hutch. She brought everything out to the table and let Sean set the places. Eight—there was a high chair in the corner.

"Lucy," Sean whispered, "what's wrong?"

"Nostalgia," she said.

"Your mom's right—you could request a transfer at the end of the year."

"Sean, would you really want to live in the same town as my family?"

"I like your family. You love them."

Sean had a large family as well, but they were wholly different than the Kincaids. Not as close. And he'd recently faced the truth that he didn't know all of them as well as he'd thought.

"Or," Sean said, "maybe we can just stay in San Antonio and visit more often."

"That would be perfect." She leaned up and kissed him.

"I could buy a house here—a beach house."

"Don't spend that kind of money for a place we might visit once a month."

"I want to."

"You just bought the house in Vail."

"I could sell it."

She must have looked panicked, because he laughed and kissed her again. "I won't sell it."

"Good. We have memories there. Great memories." They'd spent their honeymoon in Vail, and Lucy hadn't wanted to leave.

"I would never sell the house. Maybe we'll retire there." He kissed her. "Celebrate every anniversary alone."

She smiled. "I miss the hot tub on the deck."

"We have a Jacuzzi at home."

"Not the same." She wove her fingers in the hair that curled at Sean's collar and pulled him down for another kiss.

The front door opened and Connor and Nick walked in together.

"What, the honeymoon isn't over yet?" Connor said. He came over and gave Lucy a hug, then shook Sean's hand. "What a great surprise, sis," Connor said. "When Mom called this afternoon and said you were coming for dinner, I thought it was a ruse to get me over to fix something."

"Connor Kincaid," Rosa said as she came in with a basket of freshly made tortillas. "If I want you to fix something, I would tell you so. I don't need to lie."

"I was joking, Ma," Connor said and kissed her on the cheek.

"Nick, Pat has John Patrick, took him out back to watch the sunset. Don't think J. P. knows what he's seeing." But she smiled. Rosa loved having her grandson here as often as possible. Lucy was so happy her mother was finding peace. She'd be seventy at the end of the year . . . Lucy was used to having older parents—older than her friends at any rate—but seventy was a turning point.

"Thanks." Nick nodded to the group and went out to the backyard.

"Where's Julia?" her mother asked Connor.

"On her way, she had a late meeting. Stanton took the afternoon off, dumped a shitload of—um, a bunch of work—on her desk."

"Go toss the salad, then dish up the carnitas. Use the brown bowl, with the lid, not the blue one. Check the rice—it should be done by the time you're finished with the salad."

"Yes, Ma." Connor winked at Lucy, then followed their mother into the kitchen.

"I hope Andrew didn't say anything," Lucy said. "I want to be the one to tell my family."

"Why would he? He didn't even want you talking to them."

"That simply isn't an option." She paused. "Max wanted to come."

Sean snorted. "You know what I would have enjoyed? Putting Max in the same room with Jack. Now *that* would be fun."

"You're impossible."

"Your brother would take her down a peg or two."

"She's very smart. She thinks like a cop."

"You *like her?*"

"I don't know her, not yet. I just think she's more complex than she seems on the surface. She's very straightforward, she's obviously driven—and she doesn't have much tolerance for people who get in her way. As long as she doesn't think I'm hindering her, the temporary partnership should work." Might be wishful thinking on Lucy's part.

"I meant it, Luce, if she starts digging around again, I'll retaliate." He kissed her. "I'm not going to have either of us the subject of a news program."

"I sense she's someone of her word."

"She didn't promise not to dig around, Lucy, she only promised she wouldn't write about us. What if she changes her mind if she thinks there's a juicy story?"

Her stomach tightened, but she said, "With you, I can handle anything."

"I don't want you to have to."

"Isn't the table done yet?" Rosa walked in with a bowl of jalapeño corn bread.

"My favorite," Lucy said and reached for a piece, glad for the distraction from her conversation with Sean.

Rosa slapped her hand. "You wait, Lucia," she said. "You're the absolute worst at nibbling before dinner. Remember the Christmas dinner when you ate the entire basket of corn bread?"

Lucy put her hand to her stomach. "Ugh. I was sick all night."

"That's right. Too much of a good thing."

Rosa left and Sean kissed Lucy. "I love you."

Lucy put her hands around his neck. "Right back at you."

"We'd better finish the table before your mom slaps my hand, too."

"Geez, get a room."

Lucy jumped. "Carina, I didn't hear you come in."

"I came around back. Saw Nick and Dad out there with J. P." Carina hugged Lucy, then Sean. "What a surprise, and you hate surprises."

"Last minute. Sean has business in Sacramento, so I took a couple of days off."

She was lying. Sort of. Sean did have business in Sacramento—a meeting of the principals of RCK starting Friday, but it would likely last all weekend. Lucy had planned to stay home and catch up on work—her new boss, who replaced the last SSA, took over while Lucy was on her honeymoon, and Lucy had felt like she was playing catch-up ever since. Things were very awkward. She supposed that was to be expected, but she hadn't wanted to take the time off until the adjustment period was over. *If* it ever ended.

And yet here she was, because of Justin.

Not Justin specifically—because of Maxine Revere, the reporter, who was positive that she could solve Justin's murder. Her confidence was contagious. Lucy believed it, too. Now she had to convince her family.

"Patrick mentioned that he would be in Sac, said he might stop by on Sunday."

Lucy hadn't known. She should have talked to Patrick . . . or maybe not. She and Patrick were close—Patrick had been Sean's best man at their wedding—but Patrick and Carina had been best friends since childhood. Patrick may have told Carina before Lucy had a chance to.

Didn't matter, she was doing this her way. But she made a mental note to call Patrick tonight.

Sean had his arm around her shoulders. Though he and Carina had a cordial relationship, they weren't close. Lucy wasn't quite sure why . . . part of it had to do with the first time they'd met they had a major disagreement, and another part of it had to do with their personalities. And Lucy suspected Carina was a little hurt that Sean and Patrick had become so close after Patrick came out of his coma and started working for RCK. Carina and Patrick used to be inseparable, and now they lived three thousand miles apart.

Connor and Rosa came in with the rest of the food. "Go fetch your father and Nick," Rosa told Carina. "They're talking to J. P. about baseball. J. P. can't even walk yet, but they're showing him how to throw a ball."

Carina grinned and went outside. Julia walked in, flushed. She was always impeccable with stylish, feminine suits and long hair she wore up in complex twists that Lucy was envious of. She could french braid her hair—that was the extent of her fancy.

Julia glanced at Lucy and Lucy thought she knew or suspected. Maybe Andrew had said something. Even if Andrew had simply said he'd seen Lucy, that would make Julia suspicious. Because why would Lucy see Andrew before her family?

"I'm sorry I'm late, Mrs. Kincaid."

"Rosa. Rosa. It's been five years since you became my daughter-in-law. Rosa, or Mom, or Mama. Go wash up, dinner is ready. Sit, Lucy."

Connor slipped off with Julia and Sean and Lucy sat down.

Soon, everyone was sitting down and eating. J. P. was in his high chair munching on a tortilla he held between two chubby hands, his large brown eyes watching everyone with great interest, sitting between Nick and Carina. Rosa had a rule—babies ate at the table with everyone else once they could sit in the high chair. They were family, not relegated to another room or early dining hours.

Rosa sat between their dad at the head of the table with Carina on the other side. Connor—the oldest son tonight—was at the other end.

Lucy was sitting between Julia and Sean. They talked about family— J. P. had pulled himself to standing last weekend; Nick and Connor's PI business was in the black; and of course Sean and Lucy's honeymoon.

"You actually *bought* the house in Vail?" Carina said.

"Wedding present to my beautiful bride," Sean said.

"It was bliss," Lucy said honestly. "I don't think I've spent that much time doing nothing in my entire life."

"Nothing?" Sean said. "We hiked almost every day. We went to an art festival. Found an amazing Italian restaurant where the owner gave me the recipe for her gazpacho."

"Sean can sweet-talk anyone into anything," Lucy teased.

"She liked us, what can I say?" Sean winked. "We also helped the local police with a situation."

"Shh," Lucy said, avoiding her mom's concerned glance.

"Why am I not surprised?" Carina rolled her eyes.

"It was a perfect honeymoon. We needed it," Lucy said.

"And you got a dog?" Connor said. "I saw the pictures you e-mailed around. Beautiful retriever."

"Bandit," Sean said. "He's almost two. I'm still working on training him. He has a mind of his own, but he's a great dog."

Though the circumstances surrounding their adoption of Bandit were sad, the golden retriever was a welcome addition to their family. Sean had told Lucy his childhood dog had died the year before his parents were killed, and he'd loved the mutt so much he didn't know if he could ever raise another. Watching Sean with Bandit was a joy, and the dog had brought a sense of peace and contentment to their lives that Lucy had never realized a pet could bring.

"Have you talked to Nate?" Lucy asked. To her family, she added, "Nate Dunning—you met him at the wedding. He's watching Bandit while we're gone."

"Bandit, Nate, and the house are all in order," Sean said.

"And you found him on your honeymoon?" Carina asked. "In Colorado?"

They finished eating, and Sean entertained the group with a sanitized version of the events in Vail and how they ended up with a new dog. Everyone enjoyed the story, except her mom, who kept looking at Lucy with worry in her eyes.

Great. She was worrying her mother. Again.

Lucy kept trying to find a way to bring up the reporter and investigation into Justin's death, but there didn't seem to be any good moment. Lucy had been so confident walking in here, then Andrew's words of warning started to worry her. Before she knew it, dinner was over and she and Sean were clearing the table.

"Dinner was great, Mom, but we'd better get J. P. home. He's practically falling asleep in his high chair." Carina balanced J. P. on her hip. "You and Dad wear him out—not that I'm complaining. He's finally sleeping through the night."

Lucy knew she had to do this now. "Um, I need to talk to you before you leave, if you have a few minutes?"

Nick said, "I'll take him home and give him his bath, you stay as long as you want."

"You sure?" Carina asked.

He raised an eyebrow. "Of course I'm sure." He took J. P. from Carina.

"I won't be long," Carina said. "Try to keep him up for me, okay?"

Nick kissed her, said his good-byes, and left.

They all migrated to the kitchen, where Rosa and Connor began to put away the leftovers. Connor handed Sean another beer, which he took but didn't open. He offered one to Lucy, but she shook her head.

"Andrew called me last night," Lucy said. "That's why I'm here in San Diego."

"Stanton?" Connor opened the refrigerator and put in the plastic container of leftover carnitas. "Why?"

"An investigative reporter has uncovered evidence that connects Justin's murder with three, possibly more, crimes. Andrew asked me to assess the evidence and advise him if we should cooperate with her investigation."

"So the whole thing about Sean's meeting in Sacramento is a lie?" Carina said.

"No." Sean tensed next to her; Lucy had to preempt any conflict. "We just left San Antonio early, to meet with the reporter."

"Why did Stanton call you?" Carina asked bluntly. "He should have talked to us first."

"Because he didn't think either of you," Lucy said, looking from Carina to Connor, "would come into the meeting with an open mind."

"Open mind? Because some asshole wants to drag our family through an ordeal? Exploit Justin? Exploit our family?" Connor was livid. Over-the-top angry.

"Connor," Pat Kincaid said quietly.

"No, Dad, don't silence me. Stanton damn well knows that no Kincaid will stand by while he opens these old wounds. So he goes to Lucy, thinking because she's a young rookie that she's going to cave into his pressure."

Sean opened his mouth, but Lucy squeezed his bicep to keep him quiet. "Connor," Lucy said quietly but firmly, "Andrew left the decision to me. I listened to the reporter—Maxine Revere—and her evidence is solid. I don't want to detail it here." She glanced at her mother, who looked pale and older than her years. *Damn, damn, damn!* The person she least wanted to hurt was her mother. "I think she's onto something, and I'm going to work with her."

"No," Carina said. "You have no right, Lucy. You have no idea what we went through—you want to drag Mom and Dad through this again? Me? Nelia?"

"I know what you went through," Lucy said calmly. It seemed the more worked up Carina and Connor got, the calmer she became. "Just because I was seven, doesn't mean I don't know exactly what happened to Justin. I know you want the truth, just as much as I do. You want to know who killed him and why."

Rosa gasped.

"Why isn't going to bring him back," Connor said. He glanced at Julia. "Did you know about this?"

Julia shook her head, then said quietly, "Andrew has been preoccupied for the last couple of days. I asked him why, but he wasn't chatty. He let it slip that he'd seen Lucy this afternoon, but it wasn't my place to ask for details."

This was spiraling out of control. Lucy had to get a handle on it. She spoke clearly, professionally. "I know this is hard for us to talk about, but there's more at stake than solving Justin's murder. Everyone believed it was isolated, but it's not. Other boys have been taken from their bedrooms and killed. Other families have been shattered with grief. Their killer is still out there and will do it again if we don't do something. Your help, your recollections, are irreplaceable. You were there, and Andrew is—"

"A bastard," Connor said. "He cheated on our sister when he should have been home!"

"Connor Joseph!" their father said.

"Dad, you can't condone this."

"I don't," he said. Lucy's heart fell. "But you're going to respect your sister and hear her out."

Connor glared at Lucy.

Lucy was growing increasingly nervous. "I've looked over the evidence that Maxine compiled and she connected two, possibly three, other murders to Justin's. I won't go into the details now, but if you want to see the facts, I can arrange—"

"You are *not* doing this," Connor snapped.

Lucy hated confrontation, especially with her family, but Connor had no right to order her to do or not do anything. "I *am* doing this," she said. "I'd like your help. Both you and Carina." She turned to her sister, hoping to see agreement, and was stunned to see tears.

"I can't go through this again," Carina whispered. Her voice cracked, she cleared her throat. "I'm a cop, I've seen the worst that people can do to each other, but when it's your family . . . when it's someone you love . . . I can't do it. It's been nearly twenty years. When I first became a cop I read Justin's case file, and there's *nothing*. No evidence. No suspects. No damn *reason*. I had nightmares for years. When J. P. was born, I started having nightmares again. What if something happened to him . . ."

Connor put his arm around Carina. They stood there, united against her.

"Whatever this reporter is doing, it's not for good." Carina wiped her tears away and took a deep breath. "She can't possibly have evidence that the police didn't have. She's going to exploit Justin, exploit our family, dig up dirt that will hurt Nelia, Mom, Dad, me . . . and you want to be part of that?"

"I'm not going to let her exploit anyone," Lucy said. "Someone killed Justin. And I believe the same person has killed another child every five years since. If I do nothing, and another child dies, that's on me."

"Bullshit," Connor said.

"Connor!" Pat said. He turned to Lucy. "Lucy, may I have a word? Alone?"

Everyone turned to her father. He had always been the rock of their family. Honorable and noble, a hero in every sense of the word. There was no one Lucy respected more than her father. Lucy had no idea what he was thinking, though he looked terribly sad.

Sean started to follow her and her father, and Pat turned and said, "Just Lucy."

Lucy nodded to Sean—this might be a difficult conversation, but maybe alone she could convince her dad that this was the right thing to do.

Sean was reluctant, but stayed in the kitchen. As Lucy closed the door of her father's office, she heard Carina and Connor talking to Sean— accusing him, in a not-so-subtle way, of encouraging this "insane" idea.

They hadn't even let her explain. Or maybe she didn't explain it well enough. But her dad would understand. He was retired military. He would understand that she couldn't do *nothing*.

Her father's office wasn't large. On one wall were family photos, dozens of framed portraits and favorite candid shots through the years. One of Lucy's favorites was of her and Justin when they were six. They were each holding up a fish—their first catches. She remembered that camping trip—just bits and pieces, as often happens with favorite childhood memories—of her and Justin swimming in the lake, and her dad teaching them, together, how to fish. That Justin caught fish after fish, but Lucy couldn't catch any. She'd been so upset, but Justin hadn't teased her about it. Instead, they traded poles, and five minutes later she caught her first—and last—fish.

Another wall was Pat Kincaid's military awards and commissions. He'd been a decorated U.S. Army colonel and served his country for forty years.

"Lucy, close the door, sit down," he said.

She obeyed.

He sat behind his desk, not so much to take control—though it had that effect—but because his office was so small.

"Dad, I don't want to upset you or Mom."

"But you have. You knew this would upset everyone."

"No, I mean, I know talking about Justin is difficult, which is why everyone has always avoided the subject. But I thought everyone would be *relieved* that we have a lead."

"Who is this reporter?"

Of course he'd want to know. She should have led with that—eased into the investigation.

"Maxine Revere is an investigative reporter out of New York. She's written several books, has a television show—I don't watch much TV, so I haven't seen it, but I read one of her books last night. She's extremely respectful of the victims, smart, methodical. She primarily investigates cold cases, and has an impressive track record. But that's not why I agreed to help. She laid out the information she's found, and I'm in the process of verifying everything she's uncovered. My gut tells me she's onto something. I had her commit to working *with* me—so I will be privy to *everything* she knows. I'll protect the family. This is hard, Dad, for both of us," she added when he didn't comment immediately. "I've never talked to you about my work, what I do every day. I always had a feeling I disappointed you when I became an FBI agent."

"It's hard for me as well, but you didn't disappoint me, Lucy. I've always been proud of you. I was simply sad that you didn't pursue your dream."

It took Lucy a moment to realize that her dad was talking about her original career goals. In high school, because she had a knack for languages—especially after growing up in a bilingual home—she'd wanted to go to Georgetown and major in international relations. She wanted to be a diplomat, or work in an embassy. She loved different cultures, people, and traveling. At least, at one time that's what she had wanted.

Her eyes drifted back to her dad's wall of pictures. They settled on one of her in high school, standing with her mom after she won first place in the 500-meter swim competition. She'd loved swimming competitively. She still loved swimming. Water gave her peace that little else did.

Yet.

Everything ended—her idea of international relations, of competitive swimming—the day she was kidnapped and raped when she should have been graduating from high school. There was no going back to her childhood dreams. Just like there was no going back to being six and fishing with Justin. For her, solving crimes and finding justice for victims was the only way she could reclaim her life. Hard as it was at times, she couldn't see herself doing anything else.

"Trust me, Dad." She had one shot here. If her dad was on her side, Connor and Carina would follow, if reluctantly. She leaned forward. "Max has been researching Justin's murder and that of three other young boys. There are several similarities, but two facts are particularly compelling. Statistically, when prepubescent boys are kidnapped and murdered, there's a sexual component. There was no sexual crime in these cases. Secondly, they were each buried in a shallow grave less than five miles from their home, wrapped in a blanket from their bed. I speculate that law enforcement didn't connect the murders because they were five or more years apart and in different counties, but when you look at them together, it's a clear pattern. That means that one person—it's most likely a lone individual—has killed multiple times and will continue to kill until she is stopped."

The killer had begun to solidify in Lucy's mind. She'd believed the killer was a woman as soon as she saw the facts together, now she was positive.

She still didn't know why. But she would figure it out. It's what she was good at.

Her father stared at her, his face long. "It took Nelia years to accept that her son was gone. She rarely comes home. Tom has been good for her, but she'll never be fully healed. The loss of a child is overwhelming . . . for everyone. If you dredge this up . . . it's going to hurt a lot of people. Nelia. Carina. Your mother. Even Andrew—he's not thinking straight."

"That's why he left the decision to me," Lucy said.

"Then you're not thinking straight! There is no good that can come from this. Only sorrow and heartache."

"But we can stop a killer. Save another little boy."

"After nearly twenty years? You don't have any proof—only some vague similarities—that the same person is responsible for these horrific crimes. The chances are slim to none you will identify and stop him, and you're foolish to think otherwise. So you're going to stir the pot, bring all this out in the press, bring other reporters here. To my family. To my home. Do you know that a week after Justin's funeral, your mother was at the grocery store and accosted by a reporter? Asked how she felt about her grandson's murder? Wanting to know if she thought her daughter could have killed her own son? Your mother is a strong woman, but Justin's murder nearly destroyed her. You were a little girl, we protected you from the horrors of the time. And now, you want to bring those horrors back into our lives. And do you think you're going to walk away unscathed? We've all done a good job protecting your privacy for the last eight years, Lucia. But someone could still dig up what happened to you. Do *you* want to live through that again? Do you want your *mother* to live through that again? Do you want all of us to remember *how* we almost lost you, too?"

Lucy was stunned into silence. Frozen, unable to move, unable to cry. Her chest tightened and she wasn't breathing. How could her father bring up her rape? As if she would hide forever for fear someone would find out? It wasn't a secret considering her kidnapper posted her rape—not just one, but multiple rapes—on the Internet. It had been her cross to bear, but she had overcome it. She had to or she would have imploded.

She found her voice and, as calmly as she could, said, "I want justice, D-Dad." She wanted to be strong, but her resolve was beginning to crumble.

"Justice." He shook his head. "I don't know you anymore, Lucy. I don't understand you. At first I was desperate for answers, but now we have peace. Real peace. Don't destroy it."

"I made my decision, Dad. I'm sorry you don't agree, but I have to do this."

"You don't have to do anything. This is family, Lucy. *Your* family. Maybe you've forgotten . . . you rarely visit, you live your own life. I understand, you needed to get away after . . . after everything. But you're not the little girl I raised. How you can talk to me about murder so . . . *coldly*. You're acting like this is a job, not our lives. Justin was family. *Your* family. My grandson was not a victim, not a number, but our flesh and blood." Tears clouded her father's blue eyes. Tears she had put there.

Do not cry. Do not cry.

"For me—for your mother—I'm asking you. Do not do this. Let Justin rest in peace."

He wasn't asking. He was telling her.

"I'm sorry, Daddy." She could barely speak. She had never seen her father like this . . . broken, tortured, angry, and so deeply sad.

She stood up, she didn't have anything else to say.

"If you go through with this, Lucy, you can't come back here. I have to protect my family as best I can."

Protect my family. Am I not your family, too?

"You're disowning me like you disowned Jack?"

"That's not fair. These are completely different situations. I'm not disowning you. That's ridiculous—I love you, you're my daughter. But I don't want to hear anything about Justin or his murder, I don't want you talking to your mother about it. Carina or Connor are not going to help you. I don't understand how you can hurt your family like this. We've stood by you no matter what, and that counts for nothing?"

"I understand." Her voice was unnatural and stiff. "Good-bye."

She walked out.

Her father didn't try to stop her.

Sean was still in the kitchen with Connor, Julia, and Carina, though no one was talking. Her mother was nowhere she could see, but Lucy couldn't look for her now. As soon as Sean saw her, he was at her side.

"Let's go," she said.

Sean took her arm and they left.

Carina and Connor didn't say a word.

"Lucy," Sean said as he pulled away in the rental car, "what happened?"

"I'm not welcome home as long as I'm investigating Justin's murder."

They drove in silence for several minutes. Then Lucy said, "Why am I doing this, Sean? Three hours ago when I left Maxine's hotel room, I couldn't imagine *not* finding this killer. I feel like I already know her, at least on the surface."

"You're better than me—I don't know that anyone really knows Max."

"No, I meant the killer. I'm getting there, I'm getting into her head."

"You said her—you think the killer is a woman?"

"I need to talk to Dillon, I don't know how he's going to feel about what I'm doing here, he might have the same reaction as everyone else. But Dillon, more than anyone, will see the big picture—I'll make him see it." She needed someone on her side. Someone who didn't look at her with such pain and heartache. "Dillon will see that another little boy will die if we don't find this killer. And they will continue to die, every few years, until we stop her or she's dead. But . . . I might lose my family."

"You won't, Lucy."

"Jack didn't talk to our dad for more than a decade after their . . . disagreement." Such a light word for what had happened. "Jack told me about it, though I don't think he's discussed it in detail with anyone else. It's complicated, but in a nutshell . . . Jack disobeyed orders for what he believed was a moral reason. My dad covered it up, thinking he was helping Jack avoid a court-martial, and reversed Jack's actions. People died, Jack blamed my father, and my father blamed Jack. They couldn't forgive each other for a long time. Their relationship has never been the same."

"Jack's a grown man. They're both stubborn. You're not."

"If I'm not stubborn, why can't I just walk away?"

"Because some psychobitch is killing children and destroying people's lives. If she kills again, it's not on you. I know that, you know that, the world knows that, but I also know *you*—and you won't be able to sleep if you don't do everything in your power to stop her. To prevent another family from suffering like your family."

Sean understood. That gave her the strength she needed to finish what Max Revere started.

"Your family may never agree with this decision, but when you find the killer, they'll understand."

"I hope you're right." She paused. "You said when I find the killer."

"Lucy, if there's one thing I know about you is that you don't give up. You don't back down when things become difficult or dangerous. If anyone can figure out who killed Justin and those other boys, it's you."

She took Sean's hand. "I love you so much."

"Right back at you. No matter what, Lucy—if you need me here, I'll be here. You will tell me, right? No secrets. No trying to hide what's bothering you. I will jump in my plane and fly back, day or night."

"Knowing you would do that gives me strength." She kissed his hand. "And I promise, Sean, no secrets. If I need you, I will call."

Chapter Fourteen

Lucy woke up when Sean slid out of bed. She moaned. She hadn't slept well. Surprise, surprise.

"Go back to sleep," Sean said.

She looked at the clock. "It's seven. I need to get up. We're not on our honeymoon anymore." She rose at six in the morning when she was working. Seven was almost decadent.

"We're going to honeymoon for the rest of our lives," Sean said and kissed her.

She sat up in bed and stretched. "Andrew arranged for Max and I to interview retired detective Don Katella this morning. I still have more reading to do."

"Think she'll play by the rules?"

"We'll see. She was quiet last night when I saw her, which was fine with me—I didn't want to talk about what happened with my family."

"What did you tell her?"

"The truth, they don't want to be involved. I didn't need to share details."

Sean sat next to her. "If Carina and Connor give you a hard time, let me know."

"I can handle them." Sean was protective, and he was much closer to Jack and Patrick than he was to Carina and Connor. She didn't want any more conflict in her family—she'd created enough. Something like this could divide the family. She didn't want anyone to have to choose sides.

She considered what had really been bothering her when she couldn't get to sleep. "I lied last night."

"About what?"

"I told my dad we could keep Nelia out of it, but we can't. The killer must have stalked the families she targeted. I've thought about this half the night." One of the many reasons she couldn't sleep. "All four boys were taken when they had babysitters. All four boys had been sleeping at the time of the abduction and taken through a window. The killer had to know which bedroom was which."

Lucy got up and began to pace, but Sean took her hand. "Sit."

"I'm antsy. I need to be doing something."

"Talk it out." He kissed her hand.

He was right. It was always better when she could talk through her train of thought. "I think Nelia or Andrew knew the killer—at least casually. So did the Porters and the Donovans. And if Peter Caldwell fits the victim profile, then the Caldwells must have met the killer as well. At least one of the parents interacted with the killer. Otherwise, how would she know which bedroom belonged to her victim?"

"Casing the house. If there was no external security, someone could look through windows to get the layout."

"I suppose you're right."

"But you don't agree."

"My gut tells me these boys were specifically targeted because their fathers were having an extramarital affair. I don't think the infidelity is a coincidence. That means that the boys themselves were stalked as well as their fathers. The killer *knew* about the affair."

"Maybe the killer—if you're right and it's a woman—had been a previous lover."

She hadn't considered that option. "Possibly . . . but wouldn't she then target the new mistress? Or the adulterer? And why kill the boys? It wasn't in rage—the deaths weren't violent. They were quiet. But it's a question we need to ask Andrew." That wouldn't be fun, but Andrew had to know that reopening Justin's case meant he would have to talk about everything, including his personal life. "A crime like this isn't random. If Justin was the only victim, maybe. Maybe random." She didn't believe that, either. "I don't know *why*. Once we know why, we'll know who, or at least have a clear direction. I wish I could put all the parents in a room together and have them talk to one another and find out if they know someone in common."

"Are you going to call Dillon?"

"Yes. Though if I had to guess, my phone will ring at eight."

"You think someone already called him."

"My dad, most likely."

"Why do you think your dad, Carina, and Connor are so opposed to you reopening this investigation?"

"I don't know if it's just because they're trying to protect Nelia from reliving the pain, or not have my mom worried about all of us, or what. Justin's murder was hard on everyone, but Carina is a cop. She should understand better than anyone that the killer isn't going to stop. In hindsight, I should have talked to her alone."

"Why Carina?"

"Because Carina was babysitting when Justin was kidnapped. She knows the case—both because she was there and because she read the files. Without the family audience, I might have been able to have a heart-to-heart with her. Convince her. I messed up."

"You did not," Sean said. "But I know how to get your mind off everything, at least for a few minutes." He pulled her up off the bed.

"A few minutes?"

"Fifteen minutes . . . twenty minutes . . . I have all the time in the world for you. RCK can't start the meeting without me." He kissed her. "I'm taking a shower. Join me."

She smiled. "So you really meant it when you said the honeymoon will never end."

They were halfway to the bathroom when Lucy's cell phone rang. She groaned. "I have to—"

Sean pulled the phone off the charger. "It's Dillon."

Lucy took the call and waved Sean into the bathroom alone. So much for a romantic morning before Sean left for the weekend. But she had to talk to her brother, sooner rather than later.

"Hello."

"It's good to hear your voice," Dillon said.

"I was expecting your call. Dad called you."

"First Dad, then Carina. Why didn't you talk to me first?"

"I didn't think. Andrew called me Wednesday night. Sean and I flew out yesterday to hear what the reporter had to say, what she learned, and then I just thought I should be the one to tell the family. Believe me, Dillon, I wish I had called you first."

"I know you, Lucy—you were going to investigate Justin's murder as soon as you got the call from Andrew. Hearing the evidence, even if it was weak, would have drawn you in."

"So Carina told you what I said."

"Carina was upset when I talked to her, I got more details from Dad. I would have flown out and talked to the family with you."

"With me or against me?"

"What does that mean?" He sounded confused.

"No one listened to what I said, Dillon. Carina is a cop. I expected her to be more impartial . . . or be able to distance herself from the past."

"Not everyone has the same skills we have, Lucy. Carina is emotionally involved. She's now a mother. That changes people. But more than that, she went through the wringer after Justin disappeared. Interviewed both as a witness and as a suspect."

"I didn't know that." Carina had been a *suspect?* How could that have happened?

"She was alone with Justin in the house when he disappeared. For a time, the detective thought that there was an accident and she panicked, tried to cover it up. She was cleared, but it had a huge impact on her."

Lucy had once been suspected of a crime she hadn't committed. She knew exactly how Carina felt. Why hadn't Carina talked to her about it? Because she was so much younger? She wasn't a child anymore.

"I hope I can turn Carina around," Lucy said, "but Dad isn't going to budge. It wasn't a good conversation." Understatement of the year.

"Dad is trying to protect his family. He looks at the world differently."

"It's not that, Dillon. He looks at me and sees my past. I don't think he can ever look at me and not think about what happened on my graduation."

"He loves you, Lucy."

She knew that in her heart, but it had hurt deep down that her father still thought about her kidnapping and rape. "This isn't about love. It's about pain. And—" She didn't want to talk about it. "Anyway—"

Dillon cut her off. "Don't avoid your feelings. You're hurt."

"Yes." Admitting it was hard.

"Dad didn't want to hurt you. He doesn't understand why you do what you do."

"I get that. Maybe I never did before, but I get it now."

"I can talk to him—"

"No. Please, it's not going to fix anything, at least now. He thinks that if I do this, the reporter will exploit Justin's murder, drag the family into it, and bring up my past."

"What do you think?"

"I don't think that's her intention. She will air a program on the murders, of that I'm sure. And de facto that means she'll be talking about Justin, Andrew, Nelia. But what if exposing the pattern helps us find and stop the killer before she kills again?"

"She?"

"I have a rough profile. I'd like to discuss it with you."

Dillon didn't respond for a long minute. Lucy's heart tightened. Was everyone going to be against her?

"You already believe the killer is a woman. This reporter must have something no one else has."

"Not so much what no one has, it's how she connected the crimes, the pattern, and the way the victims were killed. And yes, I'm certain the killer is a woman. I'm going to write up a summary—I want to send it to you. See if I'm missing anything. I think she considered killing these boys a form of mercy killing, though the why I can't figure out yet. There doesn't appear to be a motive. The only thing these families have in common—other than they had one son—was that the fathers were having an affair. They live in different areas of the Southwest—California and Arizona—and neither parent was home during the time their son was abducted. Andrew is going to work on getting me a copy of the forensic reports and determine if the sedatives used in all cases are the same."

"Send me what you have," Dillon said. He didn't sound happy about it.

"I can do this without you."

"Justin was my nephew too, Lucy." He paused. "Are you going to talk to Nelia?"

"I don't want to," she admitted, "but I don't see how I can avoid it. If I'm right and the killer stalked the families, Nelia may very well have met her. If I can narrow down the profile enough to where I can describe the killer's personality that might trigger her memory."

"You're right, but I'll do it. Nelia may not be able to help. Losing a child, especially to violence, is the worst grief that can befall someone. Nelia didn't handle it well—no one expected her to—but she couldn't get out of the pit of despair for years. She's better now, but talking about Justin will destroy that peace."

"Even if we find out who killed him."

"Justin will still be dead."

"This woman is going to kill again. I don't want to hurt Nelia, but I want to save another woman from suffering her fate."

"I understand, Lucy, I do. But this is a delicate situation. When you need to talk to Nelia, call me first. Let me facilitate it. She'll talk to me. I can get the information out of her. I don't know that she'll give you the same."

It might be the best she could get at this point. And if anyone could get Nelia to open up, it was Dillon. "Thank you."

"This is a tough road you've chosen."

"Do you really think I chose this road?"

He sighed. "I wouldn't expect anything else from you. I love you, Luce. Be careful."

She hung up, feeling much more confident about her position. Dillon didn't tell her she was wrong or that she should reconsider. She didn't know how she would feel if everyone in her family opposed her. She didn't want to lose her family. She loved them, but she wasn't backing down.

Sean came out with a towel wrapped around his waist. He had scars he hadn't had when they first met. Some more recent than others. She had led a sheltered existence until she was eighteen . . . and then her life had spiraled out of control.

She had rebuilt her life, slowly and methodically, with no small effort by Sean to help her. In doing so, a path had been forged for her. Maybe she *had* chosen a violent, destructive road. But after she had faced evil and survived against all odds, how could she forget that evil existed? How could she allow innocent people to suffer? Once you knew the truth about human nature—the good and the bad—you couldn't forget, ignore the bad and only see the good.

"Come here," Lucy said and met Sean halfway with a kiss. "When do you have to go?"

"It's my plane, I can leave when I want."

She took him back to bed. She had to remember the good, remember the light, to sustain her in the dark times.

Sean was the brightest light in her life.

Chapter Fifteen

When Carina Kincaid called Max from the lobby and asked to meet with her, Max didn't hesitate to agree. Lucy had thought her family wouldn't cooperate; maybe they had a change of heart or Lucy wasn't as perceptive as she appeared.

But when Carina knocked on the door and walked in with her brother, Connor Kincaid, Max suspected an ambush.

They didn't disappoint her.

Max took them to the balcony to talk—she didn't want to show them her evidence. If they wanted to cooperate, that was a different story, but she couldn't give them any information by which they might be able to sabotage her investigation.

She'd learned the hard way that even innocent people sometimes didn't want the truth to come out.

"Why do I think you're not here to offer your assistance?" Max said, offering them both seats.

Neither Carina nor Connor sat down. They looked like brother and sister. Dark hair, slightly dark complexion. They both looked like cops. United.

"We want to know why you're really here," Connor said.

"I'm an investigative reporter. I specialize in cold cases."

"Why are you *here?*"

"I like the US Grant. It's one of the finest hotels in the country."

"You know what I mean!"

Less than a minute and Max was fully irritated. Was that a record?

She said, "Justin Stanton was murdered. His case is unsolved. I'm going to solve it."

"Bullshit. There's another reason."

"I don't have a hidden agenda. You're welcome to talk to my producer."

"You want to exploit our family."

Max really hated that word. She'd been accused of *exploiting* people when all she did was find the truth. "I'm happy to talk about my investigation with you if you would be willing to listen. But you don't seem to have an open mind."

Carina spoke for the first time. She looked tired, as if she hadn't slept the night before. Max wondered why—what in the past gave her sleepless nights? What about Justin's murder made her fear the truth?

"Nothing good can come from this," she said. "Justin has been dead for nearly twenty years. I've looked into this case. There were no viable suspects. No evidence. Nothing that even points to a suspect. You can't find anything because there *is* nothing to find."

"Tommy Porter has been dead for fifteen years. Chris Donovan for six years. Peter Caldwell for nine months."

"This is where you've gone off the deep end," Connor said. "Donovan's father was found guilty of murder. Caldwell's mother is on trial for his murder. Only the Porter case is unsolved, and it's nearly as old as Justin's murder. Is that why you're here? Did Donovan get you to find some thread of nothing to get him out of prison? Or maybe because you're friends with Caldwell's mother—you want to give the jury doubt that she did it."

Max didn't even respond to that ridiculous accusation.

"If you're not here to help, I need you to leave."

"You won't get anything. This is our town, our people. San Diego isn't as big as you think. You step out of line, we'll take you down."

She laughed. Because if she didn't laugh, she'd lose her temper, and that wouldn't end well for her—or for the Kincaids. She needed Lucy Kincaid's help, at least until Andrew Stanton turned over all the documentation he promised. But once she had what she needed, she'd ice Lucy out of the investigation, because it was clear that the Kincaids were trouble.

"Good-bye, Mr. Kincaid," she said.

"Please," Carina said quietly. "This will destroy our family. My dad had a heart attack last year. My mom is very sensitive. She cried last night. My sister Nelia—losing Justin gutted her. It took her more than a decade to start living again. If you dredge up the past, the violence and death, you're going to hurt everyone I love. Do you think it's easy for me to come here and talk about this? I was *there*—I fell asleep on the couch and my nephew, who I loved with my whole heart, was taken out of his bed and killed. It took me years before I could forgive myself."

It didn't sound like she really had. Max's lost a bit of her temper. She understood guilt; she understood grief.

What she didn't understand was willful ignorance.

"I would tell you to please trust me, but neither of you seem very trusting. So trust your sister. Lucy seems to have a good head on her shoulders."

"Leave Lucy out of this," Carina said. "She was a little girl when Justin was killed."

"She's not a little girl now. She's a rather exemplary FBI agent, according to my sources." She had read all the articles Ben had sent her, and she really wanted to know more about Agent Kincaid. Ben promised to get her more information, but if he couldn't, Max had her own sources.

Connor clenched his fists. "Leave Lucy alone. I swear if you do or say anything to hurt her—"

"Enough," Max said. "You obviously have no intention of listening to anything I might say, and I've already had it up to *here* with threats from Lucy's husband. I will solve Justin Stanton's murder and the murder of three other little boys. Help or hinder, frankly, I don't give a damn. I *will* get the answers. I always do."

Most of the time.

You know who killed Karen, you just can't prove it.

You have no idea who your father is.

You don't know what happened to your mother.

Shit, why was her mother on her mind now? Of all times? Her mother had walked out on her twenty-two years ago, she wasn't coming back now.

But you think if you can solve a nearly twenty-year-old murder you can find out what happened to your mother. Time will no longer be an obstacle.

She stared from Connor to Carina. "Good-bye."

Connor wanted to argue and Max wasn't above calling hotel security, but Carina put her hand on her brother's arm and they looked at each other, exchanged that unspoken conversation that infused Max with a jealousy she didn't understand. Sean and Lucy, Connor and Carina, others in her life who had a deep, intimate understanding of another person.

Max wanted that. She was an only child raised by older grandparents, she had been in and out of many relationships. She didn't have that unspoken connection with anyone—someone who knew what she was thinking and how she felt. Where she didn't have to explain herself. Where she had the same connection with them, not a friend, family member, or lover.

You thought Nick was the one.

No, that's ridiculous. Nick was a cop on a case and Max was attracted to him. Sexual tension and all that.

You hoped. Because you're tired of playing the game.

Maybe it was just better to be alone. Being alone didn't scare her.

It just made her very, very sad.

Connor finally turned and walked out, Carina behind him. Carina stopped for a moment, looked at Max. "I hope you realize you're doing more harm than good."

Max didn't comment. Nothing she said was going to convince Carina. Max could hope that finding the truth would make all the difference . . . but sometimes, people really didn't want the truth. They would rather live in their own fantasy than confront what could be dark answers to difficult questions.

For Max, the truth was always better than the unknown.

She closed the doors behind the Kincaids.

Max was tired of this family. Having Lucy forced on her. What had she been thinking yesterday when she agreed to work with her? Though the rookie fed had been helpful, Max would talk to her own FBI expert before she concurred that the killer was a woman, or that there were more victims than those she'd already identified. Last night she'd put in a call to Dr. Arthur Ullman—he was a retired FBI profiler who taught a seminar at NYU. His last case had been Karen's disappearance ten years ago. He and Max had become friends, and he often consulted with her when she needed a psychological profile or perspective. A different way of seeing the evidence.

Max finished getting ready. She didn't need Lucy to talk to Detective Katella, and she honestly didn't need her for the investigation. She couldn't convince her family to help and instead seemed to have created even more of a problem for Max. What had Lucy said last night when she came by the suite? Something about how she'd approached her family wrong. Then she read over Max's evidence in silence, barely uttering two words before she left just before midnight. Well, that misstep had been major, and now Max walked a tougher road.

She called the detective at the number Stanton gave her. "Detective, it's Maxine Revere. We're meeting at ten this morning—I was wondering if I could push it up to nine?"

"I'll be here. I still don't see what I can tell you that the police reports can't, but anything I can do to find out who killed that little boy, I'll do."

"Thank you." Max hung up and called the valet to bring her car around. She put together her briefcase and made sure her timeline was in order. She hoped to have more information to plug in, and she hoped David was making some headway with the Porters. She knew he didn't want to talk to them, but he'd find a way.

He was dependable that way. Unlike most of the people in her life.

But even David couldn't read her mind.

Chapter Sixteen

Lucy sat in the lobby of the US Grant with two cups of coffee, her eyes on the elevator bank. It was an hour earlier than she and Max had planned on meeting.

But her gut told her Max was going to attempt to meet with Don Katella solo.

Max used valet parking, which meant she would need to come through the lobby to retrieve her car out front.

Sean would be gone before Lucy returned, but that was okay—he needed to be part of the reorganization at RCK. They had several things to address, and since Sean had started working for them again full-time after the honeymoon, he needed to be an integral player. Lucy had suggested that next year she apply to transfer to Sacramento—she had one more rookie year to complete in San Antonio before she could request a transfer. She might not get it and she might not get Sacramento even if they moved her.

Sean didn't want to move back to his hometown, and Lucy respected that. Besides, she would end up working for her sister-in-law. She liked Jack's wife, but what happened when they inevitably butted heads? She didn't want to put Jack in that position, and from what Lucy had heard, Megan intentionally didn't want to know details about Jack's work at RCK. Lucy couldn't live like that, she and Sean had been through hell and back, and honesty—in all things—was the only way their relationship would survive.

They both talked about going back to D.C. There were pros and cons. The pros? Being close to her brothers Patrick and Dillon, as well as Dillon's wife, Kate, who was Lucy's close friend and confidante. They liked D.C., and Patrick and Sean worked well together. The cons? Both Sean and Lucy loved San Antonio, they loved their house, and while they missed their family in D.C., they also enjoyed being on their own. For both of them, it was the first time they weren't under their respective family thumbs.

They agreed to shelve the discussion until next year. And ultimately, if Lucy requested a transfer, she may not have any say in where she went. She'd rather stay in San Antonio than move to an unknown location.

Except for the fact that she was working for a new boss who was prickly and difficult. Maybe it would get better. She didn't want to leave just because her working environment was uncomfortable.

The elevator opened and Max Revere walked out, her long dark red hair pulled up in a twist. She wore heeled black boots and a calf-length royal blue cashmere dress. A black jacket was slung over her arm. She was a stunning woman with an air of confidence that Lucy both admired and envied.

Max saw Lucy three strides into the lobby. Her lips curved, just a bit. "Better than most feds I've known."

"Nonfat latte," Lucy said and handed her the drink.

"Who ratted me out?"

"You had a to-go cup in your room last night and I saw what the barista had written."

"I meant who did you bribe to find out when I summoned my car."

"No one."

"Hmm."

Max walked past her to the door.

"Max," Lucy said without moving.

Max turned around. "Aren't you coming?"

"Don't attempt to ditch me again."

"I don't like this arrangement."

"Neither do I. But if you go this alone, I guarantee, I won't be waiting for you with coffee. I'll cut you out. No one in San Diego will talk to you. Andrew will not cooperate."

"Going to sic your husband on me as well?" she said dryly. "Or maybe your brother and sister?"

Something flashed in Max's eyes and Lucy feared the worst. "Did Carina or Connor come by?"

"Both. Lucky me."

"And?"

"They made it clear they don't want me digging around. So I ask myself, why?"

"I don't think they know why."

"Because they fear the truth will hurt more than not knowing."

"I have no idea what you're talking about."

"A few months ago, I worked a cold case where a mother concealed evidence about her son's whereabouts the night his stepsister was killed. While she professed that he couldn't have killed her, she thought it looked bad that he wasn't at home. That no one would believe her son about where he was or what he was doing. She may have been right, but had the police known the truth, they could have pursued other lines of inquiry. Another person lied in the same investigation and ended up dead because of what he knew about the killer. He was protecting his reputation, but he didn't realize that he was also protecting a killer. So trust me—I know exactly what they're thinking. They'll never admit it, but deep down they think they know who might have killed Justin and they can't accept it."

"No one in my family could have killed him. No one."

"I believe you. Except . . . why don't they want to know the truth?"

"The pain of the investigation," Lucy offered. "The memories of the past."

"And you're immune?"

"Not immune. I have a higher pain threshold than most."

Max turned and walked out to the car that had pulled up. She tipped the valet and slid into the driver's seat. Lucy sat in the passenger's seat.

"It took Marco months before he ever caught me going off without him," Max said as she pulled away from the hotel, too fast for Lucy's comfort. Max typed into the GPS while she drove, further stressing Lucy.

"Marco Lopez?"

"You know him?"

"Like I said yesterday, I read your book."

Max didn't say anything.

"I looked up the status of the investigation last night. It's still unsolved."

"It's solved—I know who killed her." Max's hands tightened around the steering wheel. "But he fled the country, there's no body, no evidence."

"How are you so certain?"

"Circumstantial evidence. And I met him. I had a bad feeling about him from the beginning, but Karen didn't listen to me. I was more worried about him drugging and raping her. I didn't think he'd kill her."

"The same type of evidence against your friend Blair Caldwell. Circumstantial."

"Blair is not my friend. I dated John, her husband, in college."

"You don't like her."

"No, I don't, but I didn't say that."

"You're an open book."

Max laughed. "Most people don't think so."

"I'm not most people."

"I'm beginning to realize that."

Don Katella had retired to an active, over fifty-five community on the beach not far from downtown. He introduced his wife, who was walking out of the house with a briefcase. "Natalie still works, though I'm trying to get her to quit."

Natalie laughed. "Work? Hardly. I teach one graduate class at USD. That's part-time, teaching something I love."

"History," Don said, beaming. He kissed her. "Don't forget we have dinner with the kids tonight."

"Here or there?"

"Here. I'm cooking."

"Thank God." She smiled. "Don couldn't cook for the first thirty years of our marriage. He retires and wham, he's surpassed me."

"I have to do something so I'm not bored witless."

Natalie said her good-byes, and Don offered Lucy and Max coffee. Max declined, but Lucy nodded. "Thank you. Cream and sugar."

Don led them into the kitchen and motioned for them to sit at a round table for four in the breakfast nook. He poured coffee and brought out a carton of milk and sugar to the table. "None of that fake sugar," he said.

"I love the real stuff," Lucy said and put in a hefty spoonful. "I appreciate you taking the time to talk to us.

Don sat down. He added milk to his coffee. "I was surprised when Stanton called me last night." He looked pointedly at Max. "More surprised that he was sending out a reporter."

Lucy only vaguely remembered Don Katella. He'd retired ten years after Justin's murder and was now in his late sixties. She didn't remember much about the investigation, except she'd seen Don at her house, talking to her parents, to Nelia, and to Carina.

"Both Max and I have read the files," Lucy said, "but the reports are basic. I'd like your impression of the crime, your theory."

"First, tell me why after nearly twenty years someone starts nosing around in that poor boy's murder."

Lucy was going to respond, but Max beat her to it. "I would tell you, but I don't want to cloud your perception. Your gut reaction is more valuable to me." She paused. "To both of us."

"Why are you doing this?"

"I investigate cold cases."

"I know who you are. Why Justin Stanton?"

Max hesitated, just a beat, then said, "I don't believe his killer stopped with him."

"Serial killer," Don said flatly and shook his head.

"That's why I didn't want to cloud your judgment."

Don turned to Lucy. "And your family is okay with this?"

"Justin is my family."

"You're a fed though, right? Andrew said you're in the FBI, out of Texas."

"Yes, San Antonio Field Office. I'm on my own time today. However, if I can prove anything that Max has already uncovered, I plan on opening a federal investigation." She couldn't do it herself, but she could make it happen. What was the benefit of having family in the FBI as well as friends in high places if she couldn't use them to solve a two-decade-old murder? Especially when other lives were at stake.

"You read the reports," Don said, leaning back in his chair. "There was little evidence."

"Go back to the beginning," Max said. "When you caught the case."

"I wasn't called in until after search and rescue found Justin's body and it was clear he'd been murdered. I knew about his kidnapping—Andrew Stanton was a prosecutor, we all knew he was going places. So when a prosecutor's kid goes missing, you automatically think it's a perp getting revenge."

"Yet you weren't involved in the investigation until his body was found."

"The scene was fucked up to begin with," Don said. "Excuse the colorful language. Guess I'm still a cop at heart, though my wife would skin me alive for using such language in the house."

Katella sipped his coffee as he collected his thoughts. "From the beginning, we knew someone had come in through the window and taken the kid. The screen was bent, but the suspect wore gloves—no prints. But if the killer left footprints, we couldn't differentiate them from a dozen others—including Stanton, his wife, his sister-in-law—that would be your sister Carina, Lucy—and every other Kincaid and friend of the Kincaids and friends of Andrew and cops who came over to search for Justin. We don't know if he was carried to the park or driven to the park. His body was buried in a shallow grave, wrapped in his own blanket, a stuffed giraffe tucked under his arm."

Lucy leaned forward. "That wasn't in the reports."

"It was a detail we didn't want getting out. I never forgot it. And I guess after all this time, it doesn't matter if it's leaked."

"We'll keep the information private until absolutely necessary," Max said.

"Andrew sent me the full autopsy report, not the summary released to the press," Lucy said. "Justin had a sedative in his system. Some sort of narcotic, though it wasn't specified."

"Correct. Possibly chloral hydrate, a children's sedative, but the tests were inconclusive. The coroner indicated that he was either unconscious or lethargic when he was suffocated."

"Fibers from his blanket were found in his lungs," Lucy said. "Indicating that the killer put the blanket over his face before she suffocated him."

Don leaned forward. "She? Do you have a suspect? Are you screwing with me?"

"No suspect. Just a theory."

"You working with your brother? I heard Dr. Kincaid works for the feds now."

"He's a civilian consultant. But I haven't talked to Dillon in depth about this."

"We had no reason to believe the killer was a woman or a man. We didn't know what to believe. We looked hard at Andrew and his wife. When a kid is killed . . . well, hell, you know this as well as I do. It's almost always someone they know. Especially since there was no sexual assault. We'd considered Carina for a time . . . kills me now that she was a suspect. She's a great cop."

"Dillon told me. But she was ruled out."

Max shot Lucy a glance, but she ignored it. Max had intended to go behind Lucy's back and interview Katella alone, Lucy didn't have any qualms about holding back her conversation with Dillon, at least initially. She was still trying to process everything Dillon had said and how she was going to convince Carina to help.

"I never publicized the theory, but there's a transcript of my interview with her. Remember, she was practically a kid. Nineteen, I think. College student. I wondered if maybe it was an accident. Justin accidentally poisoned himself, she thought he was dead, panicked, buried him, and came up with the story that he had been kidnapped."

Dillon had said nothing about the details of Carina as a suspect, but no wonder she was sensitive about Lucy looking into the murder. To have to relive that again . . . the interrogation, the accusations. She would have been terrified and horrified that anyone could consider that she would hurt her own nephew.

Lucy had once been suspected of a murder she didn't commit. It had been hell going through the interview process—even though she knew she was innocent.

"Truthfully, until we got back the tox screens and determined that the narcotic in Justin's bloodstream was not found in any medicines or chemicals in the house—either the Stanton house or the Kincaid house—Carina was the most logical suspect. Nelia had a solid alibi. She worked for a defense contractor, they have to sign in and out and the log and desk are manned by military security. Andrew's was a little flimsier—with his mistress—but he never tried to hide that fact. His mistress was a prosecutor in Orange County with no reason to lie for him. And they were at a hotel where they were both seen on security cameras. But Carina was alone in the house with Justin."

"And after you received the drug analysis?"

"We looked at every criminal that Andrew Stanton put away. He'd only been a prosecutor for three, four years at the time, most everyone he convicted was still in prison. The few we did interview had alibis. No relative or accomplice seemed to have the means or opportunity. We exhausted everyone, even the most asinine possibilities. And none of them gave me the vibe. I considered that maybe Stanton or the wife hired someone to kill the kid, but that didn't bear out in their financials. And except for the infidelity—which according to Nelia Stanton's statement, she knew about, and Andrew's statement said his wife knew about the affair as well—everyone we spoke to said they were great parents. Justin played soccer, they went to his games, socialized, his teacher said both parents were completely engaged in Justin's schooling. They came together to parent-teacher conferences, they came together to school events. No one suspected they didn't have a picture-perfect marriage.

"By this time, three weeks had passed. Twenty years ago forensics weren't what they are today, but we had decent tools. We collected trace evidence, but found nothing that didn't belong in the bedroom. No foreign DNA at the grave site, but he hadn't been found for twenty-four hours and evidence could have been lost. No witnesses came forward. We canvassed every house between the Stanton's house and the park where Justin's body was found. We talked to every resident, many two or three times. Talked to everyone who knew the family. Teachers. Family. Friends. Colleagues. Dozens of people. The case haunted me . . . because there was next to nothing."

Max said, "I have three cases almost identical to Justin's murder. At least two of them have another common factor—the father was having an affair and was with his mistress the night his son was killed."

Don stared at her. "Why haven't I heard about this?"

"They're all cold cases outside of San Diego."

Lucy glanced over, wondering why Max didn't share the other details—that one parent had been convicted of murder.

"My associate interviewed one of the families, and learned that their son was buried with his favorite stuffed animal. He's working on the other case today."

Lucy said, "I'm not a criminal profiler, but I have worked in the area. This profile is so clear to me, Don. These boys were all killed by a woman. Someone who knew that their fathers were having an affair."

Don shook his head. "That makes no fucking sense. Why kill a kid?"

"I don't know."

Max glanced at her, but Lucy didn't want to give too much away, not yet.

"Don," Lucy said, "Justin is most likely the first of three or more like-crimes, spanning almost twenty years. That tells me that you most likely interviewed the killer, but didn't know it . . . didn't know what to ask because you had no idea why Justin was killed."

"And you do? Because right now it sounds like you're pulling a rabbit out of your ass on this." Don shook his head. "This case was nearly twenty years ago. And while I remember it—I couldn't forget if I wanted to—I don't know what you're looking for. I interviewed a lot of people. So did the beat cops."

"Andrew is getting me a copy of the entire file, including all the notes from the interviews," Lucy said. "What would help us most of all is if you could go through each interview you and your team conducted and look at it again, going under the assumption that the killer is a woman who knew of Andrew's affair."

"This makes no fucking sense," Katella mumbled, then repeated, "Why kill a kid?"

"The killer is likely a high-functioning psychopath. To her, it makes complete sense. Maybe a punishment of sorts—"

As she spoke, Lucy realized she already had a working profile. It was still forming in her head, she was still fleshing out the details, but there seemed to be a retribution feeling to the murders, a way of punishing the family. Why kill the child? Because it would destroy the family. It would destroy the marriage. The pain of losing a child would never go away. Statistically, when a child was murdered, the family disintegrated. Did she kill to punish the father for the affair? The mistress for her culpability? The mother for her ignorance?

It was a direction to look, but Lucy was having a hard time grasping the *why*. Because the killer would still have to look a little boy in his eyes while she killed him.

Except she didn't. She suffocated him with a blanket. Wrapped him tight when he was unconscious.

Max asked, "Why would punishing Justin hurt his parents?" She was looking at Lucy oddly. Had she been lost in her thoughts for too long?

"You're looking at this wrong—the killer wasn't punishing Justin, she was punishing Andrew. And, perhaps, Nelia. Or both."

Don said, "That's fucked, Kincaid. Totally and completely screwball."

"To us, but not to the killer. It makes sense to her. We just have to figure out why, then we will find her. Did she lose a child? Or maybe she can't have a child and doesn't think that Andrew and Nelia deserved theirs?" Lucy hesitated . . . she understood the pain of being barren far too well. But to deny others happiness because of her own sorrow over not being about to conceive? That would never have crossed her mind.

Yet she understood the deep and complex feelings. If someone was psychotic, they might twist that around, punish those who didn't appreciate what they had. A father cheating on his wife, not being home for the family . . . it would fit. But wouldn't that also punish the mother? Except, the mothers were all out the same night. Working late. Not home with their child. Were these crimes also a form of self-loathing? That the killer wants to punish herself over and over through the pain and suffering of the mother who also lost a child?

Did the killer run away from the crime scene . . . or return to absorb the pain of those who suffered? Did that suffering sustain her for years before she felt the need to kill again? To punish again?

"Lucy," Max said, snapping her fingers. "What are you thinking?"

"Nothing," she said. The emotions and impressions were too raw right now for her to make sense of it. She, too, needed to read the transcripts, run background checks on all the women between the ages of twenty and forty—forty because if the same killer killed Justin and Peter Caldwell, that would put her at around sixty now . . . not impossible, but highly unlikely.

She also needed to find out if there were any other similarities among the Stantons, Porters, Donovans, and Caldwells. Was there something they weren't seeing?

"If you think it'll help," Don Katella said slowly, "I'll review the transcripts again."

"Thank you," Lucy said. "I'll have Andrew send them over this morning. I'm going to read everything as well, and may call you if I have questions. We *will* solve Justin's murder."

"I sincerely hope you're right. I don't like unfinished business, and this case has bugged me from the beginning."

Max didn't say anything for nearly the entire drive back to the hotel. She was both angry and impressed. Okay, *mostly* she was furious at Kincaid for holding back on her. For taking over the conversation with the detective. Max had her own questions, but they were slightly altered versions of what Lucy had already asked. Max was used to doing things her own way and while she didn't object to anything Lucy had said or done, it was different. And Max didn't have anything actionable to follow up on. One of her interview rules was to never leave an interview with someone who had information—like Katella—without a thread for her to follow. Giving him this assignment of reading the interviews might be productive, but left Max twiddling her fingers.

She did not twiddle well.

"You didn't tell me about the conversation with your brother the shrink," Max said bluntly.

"It's not over. When I have something relevant to share, I will."

"This isn't a partnership," Max said.

"I thought you didn't want a partnership."

"It was forced on me."

"You planned to interview Don Katella without me."

"As it turned out, you interviewed him without me."

Lucy glanced at Max. Was she actually *bemused* at Max's frustration?

"I'm used to being in charge, Lucy. I'm used to asking the questions."

"Did you have questions I didn't ask?"

"That's not the point. I have a process, a system that works for me. You have a different process. I may have yielded different information, to give us another path to follow. Now we're waiting on a retired cop to read hundreds of pages of interviews? And we have nothing."

"We're not waiting for anything," Lucy said. "Andrew is sending me a copy of the interviews as well, of course we need to review them. But Katella was there twenty years ago. Rereading the statements may spark something in his memory."

She was right, Max admitted, but she felt like she wasn't in control. Max didn't like not being in control.

"I don't see how this is going to work," she mumbled.

"Have you heard back from your assistant?"

Max narrowed her gaze at Lucy as she stopped at a red light. "Excuse me?"

"You mentioned last night that your assistant was following up with the Porter family."

She'd forgotten that she'd told Lucy.

"He'll call when he has something," Max said. "So what now?"

"This is your case," Lucy said. "I just got a text from Andrew—copies of all statements will be delivered to the hotel by one. We have nearly three hours."

"My case." Max laughed. *Really.* "I'd like to visit the crime scene. Get a sense of the neighborhood, the park where Justin was buried, so I can visualize the scene when we read the statements."

Lucy didn't say anything for a long minute. Max could be insensitive, and perhaps she had been on purpose. Justin was Lucy's nephew. What had she said yesterday?

Justin was my best friend.

Max understood loss as much as anyone. That she and Lucy had that in common didn't surprise her; what surprised her was that the anger she had felt earlier when Lucy took over the interview of Katella disappeared.

"Are you okay with that?" Max asked.

"Yes," she said, and remained silent as Max typed the address into her GPS.

Chapter Seventeen

David stood when Tommy Porter's uncle, Grant McKnight, approached him at the coffee shop near the beach in Santa Barbara. It was before the lunch hour, but the place was beginning to fill.

"Officer McKnight, thank you for meeting with me."

Grant shook David's hand once firmly, then sat in the booth across from David. David sat back down.

The waitress approached immediately. "Hello, Grant. The usual?"

"To go, I don't have a lot of time," Grant said. "Coffee now. Thanks, Ann." He waited until she left. "This is my usual lunch spot."

"I was surprised to get your call."

"Jamie, Doug, and I had a long talk about your visit last night. Originally, they'd called me over to find out if they could have you arrested. I was ready to hunt you down, to be honest. Then I read the e-mail you sent last night. Bold, but to the point. I like that."

"I don't want to hurt your family, Grant. Let me make that clear."

"You think Tommy's killer is still out there."

"I do." Max had called him last night after Agent Kincaid left and told him that Kincaid thought the killer was a woman. She had a few other things to say—both good and bad about the federal agent—but David had a strong sense that Max liked her. Which was a feat considering how angry Max had been when she felt forced to work with Kincaid.

David wished he'd been there to see that.

Ann the waitress came over with coffee for Grant and refilled David's mug. When she left, Grant said, "I need more. Look, I want to help, but

Doug and Jamie are my family. They put Tommy's murder behind them. They had to, or they wouldn't have survived. They have two little girls they need to protect. But now they're thinking . . . and that's going to bring back the old memories and pain. Yet they want to help as much as they can. We felt that if I was the go-between, it would cushion the pain somewhat. You understand?"

"Yes."

"Fifteen years is a long time. Do you really—I mean, is there a chance the bastard who killed my nephew is still out there?"

"It seems like a long shot, but so far there are four murders over twenty years that are identical on the surface. The first murder was almost twenty years ago. Maxine Revere, my associate, is in San Diego working the case."

Grant shook his head in disbelief. "Twenty years. How certain are you that this boy and Tommy were killed by the same man?"

"Max is one hundred percent certain. So is the FBI agent who is assisting on the case."

"The feds are involved?"

"Not yet. The agent is on her own time. She's related to the first victim, Justin Stanton. They were both children when he was killed."

"It's awful. There is no hell worse than losing a child."

"I hope I never find out," David said. His daughter was the brightest spot in his life. "I have some questions, and if you can answer them, I won't need to talk to your sister. However, as we move forward, there may be additional questions, and Max will likely want to talk to both of them."

"Meaning, if you get closer to finding out who did this."

"Yes."

"If I see that you're making progress and my sister and brother-in-law are the only people who can answer the questions, I'll go to them. I can convince them to help, but I refuse to get their hopes up. My sister—it was a dark time for all of us, but Tommy was her baby."

"Fair enough. The first question is pivotal—the police often hold back information, and because there was no suspect and the case is still open, I haven't been able to find out a specific detail."

"I don't know that I can—or should—tell you details about the investigation. If the police held something back—I was eighteen and in the navy when Tommy was killed, not on the force—they had a reason."

"We know that the first and third victims were both buried by the killer wrapped in a blanket from their bed, along with a favorite stuffed animal. It's public that the boys were taken from their beds, drugged, wrapped in their own blanket, and suffocated. What is not public is if anything else was found on the body. The fourth potential victim is currently under investigation in Arizona, and we're working on finding out if he was buried with a toy or stuffed animal. What about Tommy? Was there anything buried with him?"

David didn't have to wait for an answer. Grant McKnight's eyes widened, then watered. He cleared his throat. "Yes. Tommy had a bear when he was found." His eyes watered. "I'd given it to him when he was born. He started sleeping with it when I was deployed. He told me at Christmas—the last time I saw him alive—that the bear reminded him of the fun we had together."

Chapter Eighteen

An odd mix of nostalgia and deep sorrow washed over Lucy as she stood in the small park where Justin's body had been found.

The park was a mile from Justin's house, but she remembered her mother taking them there every week for as long as Lucy remembered.

Until Justin was killed.

The playground had seemed so big when she was little. She remembered the swings—her favorite—and the twisty slide, which was Justin's favorite. And the little rocking horses that they'd outgrown by the time they started school, but loved to play on anyway. Pretending they were on the Pony Express. Or racing in the Kentucky Derby. Or riding mules down to the Grand Canyon like they'd watched on *Brady Bunch* reruns.

Justin had been buried in the trees along the far perimeter of the park. At the time, everything south of the park had been an open field. Now new homes filled the acreage, large square boxes oblivious to the young boy who had died there.

The park had been renamed. Lucy didn't know who'd done it, possibly Andrew. Or maybe it was a family decision, one she was too young to remember or her family thought she was too young to be part of.

Justin Stanton Memorial Park.

A tree had been planted nearly nineteen years ago, on the one-year anniversary of Justin's murder. Lucy remembered that day because she had cried—cried that her parents wouldn't take her to the ceremony. Their priest had gone, blessed the tree, spoken to the group there, but

Lucy was excluded. It was the first time and only time she had screamed at her parents. She remembered yelling at them, that she had to go, that she had to say good-bye, but they didn't budge. She ran upstairs and slammed her door—breaking yet another house rule. But they hadn't punished her like they had Carina when she slammed her door in anger when she was sixteen and grounded for breaking curfew.

Her dad had taken Carina's door off for a full month.

But the week after the ceremony, Patrick had brought her to the tree. *"Don't tell Mom and Dad."*

She hated lying, especially to her parents, but she had never told them. And she had worshipped Patrick from that day forward because he was the only one who talked to her about Justin. He explained what had happened—she only knew Justin had died. Patrick hadn't told her the details, but he explained that someone had taken Justin from his house and killed him. She didn't think Patrick had said Justin was murdered. She didn't remember the words he used, except for three short sentences.

"Justin was suffocated. He didn't know he was dying. It didn't hurt."

But the pain to Lucy was real, and it had been from the beginning.

Lucy didn't want to talk to anyone right now. Maybe Max sensed her sorrow, because she left Lucy alone. She walked the perimeter of the park and took pictures, wrote in a notepad, and even took a phone call. Max was a busy woman. Driven, dedicated, abrasive, but surprisingly astute. She gave Lucy the space she needed.

Lucy had an overwhelming urge to call her brother. The RCK meeting would be starting any minute, but Patrick would pick up. She was pretty sure Sean would have told him everything, including what happened last night at the house.

Patrick picked up immediately.

"Hey," she said.

"Hey, yourself."

"Am I interrupting the meeting?"

"JT hasn't locked us in yet."

"I thought Sean was joking about that."

"Nope. No cell phones, no computers, no electronics whatsoever for however long it takes us to get through business. Last year—when Sean wasn't here—we didn't get out until after midnight."

"I'm at Justin's park. No one told me about the name. Did the family do it?"

"No, it wasn't us. Carina told me about it, thought Andrew had it renamed, but she doesn't talk to him. I doubt she even mentioned it to him."

"When I was little, you took me here to say a prayer at Justin's tree."

"I remember. I took you a few times."

"No one else would. I never thanked you for that."

"You don't need to thank me, Lucy. Justin was our family."

"Well. I just wanted you to know I appreciate that you were honest with me. You always have been, and that means so much to me, especially now when I realize it must have been just as hard for you. I'm really sorry I didn't call you when I decided to investigate Justin's murder."

"I wish you had, but I get it. I'm not angry about it. I'm here if you need me."

"Thanks."

"Sean told me about the reporter. He doesn't like her."

"He made that very clear. I do. She's very interesting."

"He also told me what happened last night. Are you sure you didn't hear Dad wrong?"

"I know what he said, Patrick. It's okay."

"It's not okay. I'll come down with Sean on Sunday, smooth things over."

"No, I don't want you in the middle of this." Her voice cracked. She didn't want to cry, she didn't want to get so emotional, but maybe she didn't have a choice. Being here, at Justin's park, remembering her early childhood, her family, the sadness that she grew up with. A deep, almost unbearable sadness that touched everyone she loved. It did get better over time. But it had shaped her. Maybe she didn't realize how much until the last two days.

"We're family, Lucy."

"And I don't want our family divided because of a decision *I* made. I handled the dinner completely wrong—I thought it would be better if I talked to everyone together, but I realized too late that I was dumping a huge amount of information on the family all at once about an extremely painful subject. Sometimes, I don't think—I forget people don't see the world as I do. In hindsight, I wish I'd talked to Carina alone."

"Why Carina?"

"Because she's the one most affected. She was a suspect, she went through questioning, she's still harboring so much pain and guilt and regret. One on one, it would have gone much better."

"Maybe you're right, but you can't put the cat back into the bag."

"I'm going to try and fix this. If you come, Carina is going to feel like we're ganging up on her."

"I don't think so, but I'll do whatever you want. Call me. Anytime. JT will give us a short break at some point."

"Thanks."

"JT is staring at me with his laser eyes." Lucy heard Jack say something in the background, then laughter. "But Sean's here. He wants to talk to you."

"Okay. And Patrick? I just—well, I love you."

"I love you too, Luce."

Lucy gave Sean a brief update, then let him go too. They both had a job to do, and for the next couple of days, they would have to work alone.

Lucy looked around for Max Revere, but didn't see her. Where had she gone? Lucy glanced down at her phone. She hadn't thought she'd been talking long, but fifteen minutes had passed.

It was nearing the end of the school day for younger children, and Lucy watched as three mothers walked into the park with preschool-aged children. They let the kids run and play on the same playground Lucy and Justin had once enjoyed. Some of the equipment had been replaced, bark lined the foundation instead of sand, the trees had all grown and flourished, but the park was still the same.

She saw Max walking toward her from where she'd parked on the street. She met up with Lucy next to Justin's tree. "I'm right."

"About?"

Max opened her iPad and flipped to a mapping program. "I had my staff research the area at the time Justin was killed compared to now.

These houses were all put in ten to twelve years ago." She waved to the backside of the park.

"I could have told you that."

"*But,*" Max continued, "the houses in front of the park were all here. Justin was buried . . ." She started walking, barely looking where she was going, her eyes focused on the map. Max was also wearing heels—how in the world did she walk across the grass without her heels sinking into the soil?

Lucy had to follow. She didn't want to, but she had to.

Max stopped between two elm trees. "Here. And if you turn and look, this is the *only* place that has complete and total privacy."

Lucy did look. Max was right. The park wasn't large—the trees that framed the perimeter, where Justin had been buried, were only two deep, but they'd been growing here since before Lucy was born. A large grass area, perhaps large enough for a little kid's soccer game, separated the trees from the playground. Beyond the playground was the corner and a four-way stop. The houses there were older, post-WWII-style bungalows, similar to the house that the Stantons had lived in when Justin was killed. But none of them were clearly visible from this angle, blocked by either the trees or the play structure.

Max showed her the map. "This is a satellite image taken only a few months before Justin died. These same trees were here, only a little smaller. But my staff says based on the angle, this is still the only truly private spot in the park."

"It was the middle of the night—no one would be out."

"But in case someone was walking their dog, or a car drove by, she wanted to make sure she wasn't seen. The grave was shallow, but she still needed time to bury the body."

Max was right. "It's one more factor pointing to premeditated murder," Lucy said. But right now, it didn't help.

"Maybe she lived in the neighborhood," Max said. "Would people here notice someone new? Maybe not now, but it was a much smaller neighborhood twenty years ago. And it's a park—wouldn't someone be suspicious if an adult was hanging out at a park without a child?"

"It's possible. But she could have been a jogger, she visited after hours, or lived nearby. If she lived anywhere between Justin's house and the park, the police would have spoken to her at least once. Or noted if no one was home and followed up." Lucy pinched the bridge of her nose. The headache had been slowing coming on all morning, a combination of stress and lack of sleep and drinking only coffee this morning. "I'm blanking on your timeline for a minute—the other boys were found in similar parks?"

Max said, "Tommy Porter was found in a neighborhood park. Much larger than this one, with a baseball diamond and a soccer field as well as a playground. It was approximately one and a half miles from his house. Chris Donovan was found in a nature preserve less than two miles from his house. But there was a playground right down the street. Does that mean Chris wasn't killed by the same person?"

"No, look up where Tommy was buried."

"I just said—"

"I mean, exactly *where* in the park he was buried."

Staring at the trees reminded Lucy of a game she and Justin used to play, sort of a weird version of Simon Says meets Truth or Dare. Because the trees were two deep, they would start at one end then ask a question of the other. Sometimes trivia about their favorite television shows—*Full House* and *The Magic School Bus*. Sometimes about what happened at Sunday dinner at Lucy's house—she and Justin were both curious, and tried to learn everything they could about Lucy's older siblings. Like when they hid in the back of Connor's car when they were five and he was twenty. He still lived at home while attending the police academy. They really wanted to see his new girlfriend because Patrick kept teasing him about a girl named Darlene. But they didn't realize that Connor was going to a party after Sunday dinner, and he drove all the way to La Jolla before realizing they were on the floor in the backseat. He had been livid with them for a week. Patrick had thought it was hilarious.

It was within the confines, the safe zone, of the trees where Lucy had once asked Justin why his parents never kissed each other—she'd seen her own mom and dad kissing, usually in the kitchen when they didn't think anyone was around. It used to make Lucy smile *and* scrunch up her nose—it had grossed her out, but she thought it was funny how her mom would blush. There was never a doubt in her mind that her mom and dad loved each other. It wasn't just that they said, "I love you," usually in the morning when her dad went to work, but more than words, they showed it every day. The kisses. The way her mom would touch her dad's hand when she gave him coffee in the morning. The way her dad would open a jar for her mom, then demand a kiss for his hard labor. Or the way he looked at her when she stepped into the room, as if she was the only person in the world in that moment of time.

These weren't things Lucy could articulate when she was younger, they were things she'd simply grown up knowing, and now, looking back, she realized how good she'd had it. She knew what love was because her parents were deeply in love. So when she and Sean found each other, she knew it was real.

"I dunno," Justin had said with a shrug. "Maybe because kissing is gross."

They had spent as much time among the trees as they had in the actual playground.

Max turned her iPad to Lucy. "Here, this is a map of the Tommy Porter crime scene that my staff re-created."

Tommy had been buried among the trees as well, but the trees framed the baseball diamond.

"Did Tommy like baseball?"

"I don't know."

"And Chris Donovan? Was the preserve important to him? Did he spend more time there than at the park?"

"I don't see what you're getting at."

She didn't know. Her head ached and she felt sick, and not just from lack of food and too much coffee. Her heart ached for what could have been had Justin lived.

"I might be too close to this," she said.

"Maybe, or you might just be starving. I know I am, it's after one and your brother and sister interrupted my breakfast. I never finished it, and I'm more of a bitch if I don't eat regularly."

Lucy almost smiled. "I don't think you're a bitch."

Max laughed. "Then you're in an elite crowd of one." They crossed the park. "Tell me, what were you thinking back there?"

Lucy didn't like sharing her theories until she fully developed them and could back them up with something more tangible than her gut instincts or the vague patterns she saw. "We need to find out if Tommy played baseball or if Chris hiked in the nature preserve."

"Okay. I'll do that—my associate David has been building a rapport with the families, he can get the information. Why?"

"Justin and I played in those trees more than at the playground. We made up games. Some of my happiest childhood memories were here. Justin loved climbing trees. He was so much better at it than me. I'm not afraid of heights, but I was always nervous. Justin would go as high as he could, and if he slipped or fell he didn't care. He got right back up and did it again."

She looked back at the trees. She could almost see Justin climbing the tallest tree. The happy Justin, the carefree Justin.

"I think," Lucy continued, "that the killer buried her victims in a place they found joy. A child's joy. A special place. And that means that she had been watching these boys for a long, long time."

Chapter Nineteen

David was waiting for the detective who had been in charge of the Tommy Porter homicide investigation—who was now the assistant chief of police—when he received a message from Max.

> Find out if Tommy played baseball. Plus, the print newspaper archives are not available online. Staff put in a request for print-outs, they'll be ready for you at the paper before five.

No *please*. No *thank you*. Par for the course when dealing with Max, but he'd thought they'd gotten beyond the employer-employee relationship. They'd become friends. But ever since they'd returned from investigating the Ivy Lake cold case in Corte Madera, Max hadn't shared much with him. Four months? Yeah, four months and he had the distinct impression she was giving him the cold shoulder.

A year ago he dreaded her opinion—because Max had an opinion on everything—now, he missed her commentary. Because while Max might lack tact—especially when irritated—her perception of human nature and behavior was both sharp and insightful. Her producer Ben often called her a human lie detector.

David wasn't one for talking, especially about anything personal, but he might have to deal with this Max situation because *something* had happened, and he had the distinct impression she was angry with him. Which was odd, because when Max was mad, she never held back. Maybe he was wrong. But he didn't think so.

A young female officer approached him. "Mr. Kane? Chief Carney can see you now."

David followed the officer through a security door, then through the bullpen. He'd been in enough cop shops to recognize the buzz, though this building was nicer than most he'd been in.

Carney motioned for David to have a seat, then closed the door to his office. He was a large man with a shiny black scalp. David knew his record—Carney was fifty-three, had been a cop for thirty years after serving three years in the marines and completing two years of community college with his AA in business administration. He started as a beat cop in South Central L.A.—a dangerous territory even thirty years ago. He moved to Santa Barbara five years after, also as an officer, took his detective exam at the age of thirty, and was a detective for twenty years until the assistant chief retired and Carney was appointed.

Behind him were photos of family—lots of family. It appeared that he had four or five kids and at least one of them was married with children.

"You don't look much like a reporter," Carney said bluntly.

"I'm not. I just work for one."

Carney grunted a laugh. "I wasn't going to talk to you, but Officer McKnight called me direct. Said you were on the up-and-up and that he wanted to help if he could. Which means me talking about the Porter boy."

"Yes, sir. Did Grant give you the details?"

"He did. The words 'serial killer' were used."

David didn't blame him for sounding skeptical.

"Do you know Andrew Stanton, the district attorney of San Diego?"

"Not personally, but I know of him." He paused, as if accessing his memories. "He lost his son as well."

"Yes, five years before Tommy Porter. There are more than a few similarities. Grant confirmed that Tommy was found with a stuffed animal."

"He was."

"So was Justin Stanton and at least one other victim we're looking at. Max is working with the detective who investigated the Stanton case. He's reviewing witness statements and interviews. I was hoping I could get a copy of the statements and interviews from the Porter case."

"All public information has been released to the media. I checked with our PIO, and she indicated that NET had already received requested information."

"Yes, the public information. The press packets. But the witness statements are key and those aren't public. Max and a federal agent she's working with believe that the killer knew her victims, either through the parents or through the victim. They also believe that she may have been interviewed because she lived near the victims or worked with one of the parents."

"She. What evidence do you have that Tommy's killer is a woman?"

"None."

"Then—?"

"I'm going off what Max told me last night. We're working different angles of the case, but the federal agent surmised that because of the manner of death—the victims were all drugged and unconscious prior to being suffocated while wrapped in a blanket; they were not sexually assaulted; they were buried with their favorite stuffed animal; and they were buried in a place close to home—that the killer is a woman."

"A federal agent is working with a reporter?"

"I'm as surprised as you, sir." More than a little surprised, but Max wanted this investigation and working with Agent Kincaid was the only way she was getting the access.

Carney stared at him for quite some time. David would have been nervous if he was guilty of something—a good tactic, he supposed.

"Tommy Porter was a difficult case for me," Carney said. "I had young children back then—four kids, between the ages of five and sixteen—when Tommy was killed. Any case involving a child was always hard on me, hell, it's hard on most cops, but Tommy stuck with me because it made no sense. Not then, not now. I was positive one of the parents must have killed him. I believed it for a long time, in fact, even after we verified and reverified their alibis. I interviewed them multiple times, and neither gave me any indication that they had the capacity to kill. I didn't want to believe that this was another Polly Klaas, that a stranger can just walk into a person's house and steal their child. Now you're telling me that the killer wasn't a stranger, that it's someone I could have spoken with."

"I'm not a psychologist, but I've read that criminals often return to the crime scene, sometimes trying to put themselves into the middle of the investigation."

Carney nodded. "It happens. Not as often as it's portrayed on television, but it happens. I caught a serial arsonist that way a few years back. Couldn't stay away, wanted to see the results of his handiwork."

"Max Revere already has the list of witnesses from the Justin Stanton homicide and the Chris Donovan homicide. Our staff is inputting them into a database in order to expedite any similarities between anyone involved, even on the periphery. It would help if we had your case files as well."

"I need to talk to the chief about this," Carney said. "Give me your contact information and I'll get back to you."

David didn't know if this was Carney giving him the brush-off or if he was genuinely going to consider the idea. He pulled a business card out of his wallet and put it on Carney's desk. "I appreciate your time. One more question: do you know if Tommy was on a baseball team? Or if he enjoyed baseball?"

"Why?"

"Max wants to know. I would have asked Grant when I met with him if I'd known she needed the information, and now he's on duty." He didn't tell Carney why, but he would if pressed.

Carney looked skeptical, but nodded. "Played since T-ball when he was four. Was a good little player, apparently. He was nine when he died, but played up with the twelve-year-olds. The kids he played with—they were really shaken by what happened. They all came to his funeral in their uniforms. Broke my heart."

"Thank you, sir."

"Did you say that the feds were involved? They can ask for any information without any problem. I don't have a problem with the feds. I have a good rapport with the local ASAC, we have lunch once a month, keep each other in the loop."

"Max is working with a federal agent, but it's not an official investigation."

"How does that work?"

"To be honest? I have no friggin' idea."

Chapter Twenty

Max and Lucy had a pleasant late lunch at a quaint restaurant close to the hotel. Lucy asked questions—smart questions—about Karen's disappearance and some of the other cases Max had worked on over the years. So when they arrived back at Max's hotel room, she was surprised when Lucy said she was going to her room to call her brother, the forensic psychiatrist.

"I'll let you know if he has additional insight," Lucy said as she was about to walk out.

Max had no intention of being shut out by little miss agent Lucy Kincaid, and that's exactly what this felt like.

"This is one of the few times I think more heads are better," Max said. "We should have a four-way conference call."

"Four-way?"

"I have a forensic psychiatrist—retired FBI—who I often consult. I've already reached out to him and he has time tonight."

Lucy didn't say anything. It was quite obvious, to Max at any rate, that Lucy thought this was the one area where Max was a complete novice.

Lucy seemed to be a good cop, but she was still a cop. She would give Max the information she *thought* was important without the nuances that Max needed to put the whole story together.

It was clear that Lucy wanted to argue with her. It surprised Max that she relented—however reluctantly—without further comment. Max picked up the room phone.

"Who else are you calling?" Lucy asked.

"I'm going to have the hotel's IT department set up a video conference."

"I can do that."

"It's a tech thing."

"It's not a problem. I was tech-savvy even before I married a genius."

Max hung up. She'd give Lucy a chance, though Max always believed that when you wanted something done right, you bring in an expert. She didn't like delays, especially when trying to cut corners or because of incompetence.

"Arthur is in New York," Max said. "He teaches at NYU and said to call after seven." She glanced at her watch, adjusted for the time difference. "He should be home now; I'll send him a message. Can your brother talk at five our time?"

"Yes." Lucy typed on her laptop and opened up a video conferencing program that Max had never seen before. Then Lucy opened the cabinet to the large screen television and hooked up a cable. The program was reflected on the TV.

"My tech guys in New York have a similar setup in the conference room."

"We're ready to go."

"That was fast."

"It's not difficult," Lucy said. "I have to call my office, but I'll be back before five."

Max wondered if that was an excuse to talk to her brother alone first. But truth was, she had calls to make as well. She walked Lucy to the door, then pulled out her cell phone and called David.

"Have you heard back from Carney?"

"No."

"We need those files."

He didn't comment. Of course he knew what she needed. "I sent you photos from the crime scene like you asked," he said instead. "I don't know what specifically you were looking for, so I took a little of everything."

Max sat down at her own computer and pulled up her e-mail. She scanned through all the photos. "This is good. Did you find out about baseball?"

"Carney said Tommy played on a Little League team."

"Do you know which one?"

"Is that important?"

"I don't know yet. Just trying to piece together all the information I can before we talk to the shrinks."

"I'm having coffee with Grant in the morning. I'll ask him."

"Why? Does he have more information?"

"I promised to keep him in the loop. He's the one who got me the meeting with Carney in the first place."

"Fine, just be cautious in what you reveal."

"I'm not keeping secrets from the family."

"Not secrets. I don't want any of this leaked out."

"You want the story."

Max bristled. He made it sound like a sin. "Yes, I want the damn story. If a lesser reporter gets wind of this, they'll blow it. The entire investigation. It's happened to me before you joined my team. I'm not going to ruin this, not when it's at a sensitive stage. What if Lucy is right and the killer is out there, looking for another victim? Right now we have time on our side. We don't want to tip this woman off."

"Hold on, I have a call coming in from the eight-oh-five area code."

David put her on hold. She would have been angry, except 805 was Santa Barbara, and that could mean that Carney was giving him good— or bad—news.

She put her phone on speaker and read over her other messages. Her staff had come through with a rather short list of articles about Rogan Caruso Kincaid Protective Services, which she put aside to read tonight. Ben sent her an e-mail that RCK hadn't responded to his inquiry, over and above the press packet, and did she want him to press. She told him to hold off for now, but that she might change her mind.

She still wanted to know about Lucy Kincaid and her husband, but decided that she'd stand down for the next day or two. She didn't want to give Kincaid any reason to pull out her badge and assume authority.

Though somehow, Max didn't think she'd do that. There was something else going on with Lucy, and Max hadn't quite figured it out.

Instead, she sent Ben a message.

> I read the brief info you sent on Dillon Kincaid—I'm having a conference call with him in less than an hour, have you learned anything I need to know?

David said, "Max?"

"Still here."

"Carney wants Agent Kincaid to request the files."

"*What?* Doesn't he know this isn't a federal investigation?"

"He knows. His chief won't give the witness statements to the press. It's a back door he's taking, Max. He wants to help, but is stuck. He's already requested the files from archives—it's a fifteen-year-old case, it may take a day or two."

"Dammit," she mumbled. "Fine. I'll make it happen." She hoped, because Lucy wasn't here as an FBI agent. "Wait, it's Friday afternoon. Do we have to wait until *Monday*?"

"Possibly, but Carney may have pull. The archive is attached to police headquarters, so he may be able to grant access over the weekend."

"Road trip—not my favorite thing, but I suppose it wouldn't save much time if we chartered a plane to Santa Barbara."

"Driving through L.A. traffic?"

Max groaned. She hated traffic. "I'll let you know. Thanks, David." She ended the call and read a message that had just come in from Ben.

> Max—I don't have much on Dillon Kincaid. We've spread our research staff thin this week, piling on more assignments while they still have work on their desks. We have to prioritize, and this wasn't a priority. He's a forensic psychiatrist. He works from home, but doesn't see patients there. He consults for the Federal Bureau of Prisons and has served as an expert witness in more than two dozen trials over the last eight years, when he opened his practice in D.C. Prior to that, he was in private practice in San Diego. He's married to an FBI agent, Kate Donovan, who's an instructor in cyberterrorism at the FBI Academy in Quantico. If you need more, you're

going to have to wait. I'm off to dinner with the Crossmans and some of our key investors. Don't call me; I won't answer.—Ben

Max was supposed to be at that dinner. She felt marginally guilty—the Crossmans gave her a lot of leeway in her position at NET and asked little in return. They had planned to show her off, in a way, let the money people pick her brain. Max didn't care much for money people, perhaps because she was one of them and knew more than her fair share of philanthropists and sharks.

She sent Ben a text message—knowing he might not read his e-mail, but he would always read a text.

If you want me to do a call-in or video chat at the end of dinner, I should be done with Arthur by nine ET.

Ben responded with a dancing happy face emoji. She rolled her eyes.

It was close to five before Lucy returned. She'd showered and changed—Max supposed she should have taken the opportunity to relax, but she would relax with a bottle of wine in the Jacuzzi bathtub tonight or perhaps go down to the hotel's spa and soak in the hot tub.

"You look refreshed," Max said.

"I think better in the shower."

"And?"

"And what?"

"What were you thinking about?"

Lucy was surprised by the question. "Well, I guess I was formulating my presentation."

"What presentation?"

"To Dillon and Dr. Ullman. I know how they think, I want to present our case to them clearly."

"You know Arthur?"

"No, but I know people like him. And I read your book."

Max hadn't considered that. "It's eight on the East Coast, they should be waiting for us. I have some news."

"Good, I hope."

"Neutral. Carney from Santa Barbara said his boss will only give us the files if you request them."

"Me? Why?"

"You're FBI."

"No. I can't—I'm not here officially."

"Carney is just covering his butt. We can go up there, you show your badge, and we get them. You can even go up without me." Max was trying to make light of the situation, but Lucy looked more than a little nervous. Max didn't understand why . . . and she became suspicious.

Was there something Lucy wasn't telling her?

"Look, this may be the only way we can get the files because techni-cally the Porter case is still open. If I were there, I'd get them—David plays too nice with cops. I don't."

"How would you get them?"

"The power of the press—no police chief wants me going on the air and stating that he or she refused to give me access to files that could bring a killer to justice. I remind them of that. I play hardball when nec-essary. David isn't me."

"And you usually get what you want?"

"Always." She backtracked a bit. "Say, nine times out of ten. Last case I worked I wasn't allowed to take the files from the police station, but I had full access to everything the police had, and in the end, that made the difference in solving two murders."

"Maybe we won't need them," Lucy said.

"You don't believe that."

Lucy started typing on the computer and ignored Max. She fumed. She didn't like being ignored, and she didn't like not knowing what was going on. Lucy was keeping something from her, what? Why wouldn't she want to get the files from Santa Barbara when she'd made a point that comparing the interview list in all four cases could be the key dif-ference in finding her nephew's killer?

It took Lucy less than five minutes to bring in both Dillon Kincaid and Arthur Ullman to the video conference. She spent a moment adjust-ing sound and settings, then sat back. "Thank you, Dillon, Dr. Ullman," Lucy said.

"No formalities," Arthur said. "Call me Arthur, please."

"Agreed," Dillon said. "Your reputation precedes you, Arthur, and I'm pleased we're able to consult together on this case. Hans Vigo speaks highly of you."

"You know Hans? I haven't seen him since I retired—well, about two years after I retired he came to a seminar I was teaching at Quantico. We never worked together on a case, but he's consulted with me from time to time."

"Hans is a good friend," Dillon said.

"Please give him my best when you see him."

Max watched the exchange. Probably good that they were building rapport with each other, a sense of trust. She would much have preferred dealing with one shrink instead of two, but it had been a compromise. Something she didn't particularly like, but did when necessary.

"Dillon, I'm Maxine Revere. Lucy probably told you I'm an investigative reporter with NET and host the show *Maximum Exposure*."

"Yes," he replied rather icily. "I'm aware."

"And, Arthur, this is FBI Agent Lucy Kincaid. She's out of the San Antonio Field Office, but she's assisting on her own time. She has a personal stake in the case—as well as Dr. Kincaid. The first victim was their nephew."

"I familiarized myself with the case after you e-mailed me yesterday," Arthur said. "And I also reviewed your notes. I'm happy to help, though I don't know that two of us will be any better than one."

"Lucy trusts her brother, I trust you. Hopefully by the end of this conversation, we have a clear direction." Max hesitated, then added, "I'll admit, though I didn't like the idea of working with a federal agent, Lucy has provided some interesting insight and a compelling profile of the killer, but I still don't see the big picture."

"We have additional information from our research today," Lucy said. "We've confirmed that the second known victim, Tommy Porter, was also buried with his favorite stuffed animal. That's three of the potential four known victims."

"Known?" Arthur asked.

"Lucy modified my timeline. She put Victim Zero before Justin Stanton."

Dillon said, "What makes you say that?"

"I put a question mark next to it," Lucy clarified. "I don't see at this point how or why Justin was the trigger. I think the trigger came before Justin, but again, I can't be certain without more information."

Arthur said, "You mentioned in your message, Max, that the killer is most likely female. Did you come to that conclusion, Dr. Kincaid?"

"No, that was Lucy," Dillon said. "She has a master's degree in criminal psychology from Georgetown and is well-versed in profiling. Don't let her rookie status deceive you."

Max glanced at Lucy. Was she actually *blushing*? That would be hard to fake. Max said, "Lucy, tell Arthur why you think the killer is a woman."

"First," Lucy said, "we should backtrack a bit. Did you familiarize yourself with the commonalities of each case?"

"Yes," Arthur said, "though there are a few holes because of the pending trial of Mrs. Caldwell, correct?"

"I can't access any of those records," Max said. But after David's conversation with Carney, she wondered if Lucy might have a better chance. In fact, if the FBI wanted to take a peek, would the DA say no? It was worth a shot, if Lucy was willing. And why wouldn't she be? She wanted to solve these murders as much as Max. And Max didn't say that lightly— she rarely found anyone as invested in any of her investigations as she was. Yet Lucy wanted answers, maybe even more than Max, and that was saying something.

"I filled Dillon in last night," Lucy said, "so we're all on the same page. The manner of death—it was set up as a mercy killing. No sexual assault, no violence, a quiet death. I suspect the boys were all unconscious from the sedatives in their system before they were suffocated. She also couldn't look at them while they died—she wrapped them completely in their blankets. The other details are all similar. But the trigger eluded me until this afternoon when we visited the park where Justin was buried."

Max was watching Dillon Kincaid closely. He was much older than Lucy, almost old enough to be her father. His expression was more than a little protective and he had a tense jaw. It was clear he hadn't known she'd gone to the park. Was he worried about her? Or angry? Why?

"Justin was buried in a park where he often played—in fact, it was a favorite spot of his. Max's assistant followed up with the Porter family—Tommy was also buried in a park. But he was buried at the edge of the baseball field, and he loved the sport—he was on a Little League team. Max asked her assistant to find out if Chris Donovan spent time in the nature preserve where he was found—I suspect yes, he did. I suspect it was a favorite spot."

"Excuse my interruption," Arthur said, "but weren't all these locations close to the victim's home? Possibly chosen because of proximity?"

"That was part of it, she didn't want to be with the dead child long. But there was a playground closer to the Donovan house than the nature preserve. It was only two miles away, but the park was much closer. Alone, this information may not seem important, but in context it is absolutely imperative that we understand she buried her victims in these locations on purpose.

"The context is this: the killer knew that the father was having an affair. The killer knew where the family lived. She knew where the children played. She knew when the parents were not home and what bedroom the child slept in. She stalked the families for weeks, if not months. She had intimate knowledge of their lives. *How?* That is the question we need to answer. *How* did she know that the fathers were having an affair? We know Nelia was privy to Andrew's affair, but it wasn't discussed between them. Andrew *claimed* that no one else knew, other than his mistress. But cheaters often think that they are being discreet when, in fact, those closest to them know the truth. Adam Donovan told Max's assistant that he 'almost wanted' his wife to find out so that she would divorce him. That tells me he wasn't being discreet. Porter was a repeat cheater. But still, while adultery doesn't have the stigma that it once did, people don't generally talk about their affairs openly."

"You think that the killer followed the husbands," Dillon said.

How the *hell* did he come to that conclusion? Max wondered if having a sibling made you somehow psychic.

"Yes, I do," Lucy said. "Maybe she overheard something or saw something, I don't know, but she followed the husband until she confirmed that he was having an affair. That was the trigger. That's what told her that he didn't deserve a family."

Arthur said, "That's a big leap. Why not kill the cheater? Or the mistress?"

"Because she doesn't view death as punishment. She views suffering as punishment. And what better way to make someone suffer than to take away the one thing they love more than anything else?"

Max felt ill. She'd heard and seen a lot—mostly by choice in her profession—but she couldn't begin to understand what would make a person kill a child to punish a parent. And Lucy . . . she was so matter-of-fact about it. As if she had conversations like this every day.

Maybe she did. What had Dillon said earlier? *Don't let her rookie status fool you.*

There was far, far more to Lucy Kincaid Rogan than met the eye.

Lucy continued. "It's clear she didn't want the boys to suffer. That's why they were drugged and suffocated. She also didn't want them to suffer in the afterlife, which is why she buried them in a place they had been happy in while alive, it's why she buried them with a stuffed animal."

"And in their own bedding," Dillon said.

"Perhaps not," Arthur said. "Perhaps she couldn't look at them, as Lucy said earlier."

Lucy nodded. "Exactly, she couldn't watch them die. She covered their faces—they were all suffocated with their own bedding, and I suspect she didn't remove it when she buried them. She couldn't watch them die, she couldn't look at them after she killed them. My guess is that when she came into their bedroom, she injected them."

"And they didn't wake up?" Dillon said.

"We know there were no drugs found in any of the houses that matched the drugs found during autopsy. She must have brought them with her. The only autopsy that showed an injection site was on Chris Donovan—it was a huge problem with the prosecution of Chris's father because no syringe or drugs were found at his house, his office, his car, his mistress. The prosecution claimed he threw everything away and the defense didn't counter."

Lucy must have spent all night reading the transcript Max had given her, because they hadn't even discussed the case.

"It's still odd that none of these children cried out after being stung by a needle," Arthur said. "But it does sound more like a mercy killing."

"It is," Dillon agreed. "Each step of the killer's process suggests mercy killing. Except that she's not putting the child out of suffering from an illness, she's creating misery."

"She's methodical," Lucy said. "She has to know the families—maybe not well, but well enough that she can get all the information she needs. She's either a neighbor or a colleague."

"Colleague?" Dillon asked. "Wouldn't that be easy to confirm?"

Max spoke up. "I'm going with colleague here. One or both parents are lawyers. While lawyers may be a dime a dozen, it seems too coincidental. That makes me think that the killer is a lawyer or works with lawyers—legal secretary, paralegal, something like that. My staff is doing the research on employees who worked with each parent, but it hasn't been easy. First, Adam Donovan was convicted for his son's murder and the police only interviewed his direct supervisor and his mistress. We have been trying to get an employee list out of the company and they cite privacy records. Donovan's wife worked at a small law firm and they haven't cooperated at all. The Porters, though initially opposed to helping, have been persuaded to assist us. My associate is in Santa Barbara working with them, and the police are cooperating as well, so I hope we'll get a list of witnesses as well as colleagues. The Porters themselves may be able to give us names. Neighbors for both cases were easier because they are part of the official record—the neighborhoods were canvassed and everyone who was interviewed documented. So far, no name has been duplicated. I e-mailed Andrew Stanton and he's creating a list of every female employee he worked with and I'd like to do the same with his ex-wife."

"Absolutely not," Dillon said.

"Dillon," Lucy began, but Max interrupted.

"It's the single best lead we have."

"It's not a lead. It's fishing and I'm not putting my sister through that."

"That's not your call," Max said.

Lucy said, "Dillon, we can talk about this later—"

"You told me last night that you would leave Nelia alone."

"And you said," Lucy added, "that if we needed it, you would talk to her."

"You don't need it."

"What about my profile is off?"

"It's not a profile," Dillon said.

Lucy frowned. "I wasn't finished."

"Well?"

Lucy was flustered, maybe because her brother was being a jerk. What was it with these Kincaids? Did they really not care who killed Justin? Max said, "Lucy already concluded that the killer is a woman, and neither of you objected."

"Identifying the gender of the killer isn't a profile," Dillon snapped.

Lucy raised her voice, "No, it's not." She cleared her throat. "The killer was a mother. She lost her only son to violence, and her husband was having an affair—not only having an affair, but he was with his mistress when their son was kidnapped or killed. I also think she wasn't home, most likely working late. She never forgave him, she never forgave herself, and she cracked. She left her husband, moved as far away from him as possible because she hates him and blames him for her son's death. He should have been there with his son, not with another woman. She also harbors intense guilt, because she also wasn't there. Possibly she worked, or was at a book club, or *somewhere* other than in her house. She'd left her son with a babysitter to do something for herself or her family and when she got home, he was dead. And through the investigation into her son's death, she learned about her husband's affair."

Little impressed Max, but Lucy impressed her. She'd talked loosely about the killer, the victims, the situation—but hearing it laid out as if Lucy had actually spoken to the killer was a little unnerving.

No one spoke, but Max had a hundred questions. "Why do you think she moved far from her husband?"

"Because she can't fathom being near him or anywhere near where her son lived or played. It's a guess, but they probably lived east of the Mississippi."

"Lucy," Arthur said, "I am very intrigued by your profile. Yet if you're right and the killer lost her own son, how would she justify to herself to take another woman's child?"

"They don't deserve a child. They were all working mothers. All in professional jobs. They weren't home when they should be, they don't deserve him any more than their cheating husbands."

Max shot Lucy a glance. She was tense, not a little bit angry, but she held it back far better than Max would have been able to. Yet part of the anger wasn't directed at her brother—though honestly, Max felt he deserved it after that last exchange—but almost as if it was directed inward. Or as if Lucy was projecting the emotions of the killer herself.

Max understood the importance of understanding the motives of the killer, as well as victimology. It was crucial in any criminal investigation, but doubly important—and harder to understand—in a cold case, where time and distance created a layer of distorted memories.

Yet Lucy took profiling—which was exactly what she was doing, Max realized—to another level. She personalized it, which couldn't be easy considering that one of the victims was her nephew. She compartmentalized as well as any cop Max had met. Maybe too well. Is that why she'd seemed so cool and distant? Even after they'd spent the day together, Lucy hadn't warmed up. She was polite, professional, cordial, but Max knew the only way she'd ever understand Lucy was to observe her. She certainly wasn't someone who shared much about herself. Max could get anyone to talk—either because they wanted to or became so irritated with Max that they talked just to make Max go away. Few people were as close-lipped as Lucy Kincaid. The closest she'd come to was her assistant, David, but even he wasn't this complex.

Interesting.

Arthur said, "Agent Kincaid, it sounds like you have a good foundation on a profile. You certainly don't need my input. I would concur with your assessment, but I have one thing to add. Did you note that all of the mothers were in the legal profession? Two were lawyers—Nelia Stanton and the most recent, Blair Caldwell; Mrs. Porter was a court reporter and Mrs. Donovan was a paralegal."

"I didn't quite make that connection," Lucy said. "We knew that one or both parents were lawyers."

Dillon spoke. "Arthur, are you thinking that the killer is also in the legal profession?"

"I'm connecting the dots that Lucy already put on the map. I concur that the killer has some connection to each family, and probably the strongest connection to the first victim, Justin Stanton. I don't know that he wasn't the first victim, however—if there was another three to five years before him, you're looking at a woman who could easily be in her sixties. Justin may have been the first after the loss of her own son, so it took her time to build up to it—and in taking that time, with her own professional background, she was able to come up with a plan that protected her. Victim Zero, for example, may simply be her own son, the trigger of her psychotic break."

"I see what you mean," Lucy said. "And if she has the intelligence coupled with the psychosis, she could plan out the entire murder, beginning to end."

"Psychotic?" Max said. "What exactly do you mean, Arthur? How can someone this looney tunes function in a professional job for the last two decades and continue to commit such cold-blooded murder?"

"Psychology is not a hard science," Arthur said. "It's more complex because while we have certain standards and rules, we don't have absolutes like in physics or chemistry. What we have is a wealth of information and experience from life, and an analysis of like crimes. When dealing with a female killer, we have a more finite set of data because females historically don't become serial killers. Females are passion killers. A cheating spouse. A boyfriend who left them. Mercy killings. Poison is the primary method because it separates the killer from the murder."

Arthur took a sip from his coffee mug, then cleared his throat, and continued. "Severe depression plays a bigger part in the makeup of lone female killers—meaning those who do not have a killing partner—especially those who target their family, like Andrea Yates. Women also tend to focus in the world they know. A nurse who thinks she's saving someone a lifetime of pain and suffering—that is her justification—but in fact her psychosis is often much darker than that. She justifies it to herself—that she is noble or doing society a great service or ending the pain of another—but that's her logical answer to her darker need to take a human life as punishment and the sense of power it gives her. A sense of . . . playing God. The killer we're looking at has completely separated herself from the act of murder. She's *only* looking at the outcome—making the family suffer—not the act itself. I suspect she takes so long between crimes for two reasons. First and foremost, she needs to relocate. She has a powerful self-preservation drive, and knows that the longer she stays, the more likely someone will look to her for murder—possibly because of her own guilt and obsession and inability to stay out of the investigation. Essentially, she doesn't completely trust herself. Second, she doesn't have a specific target initially. It takes time to develop this pattern. To find a cheating spouse who has one son and fits the profile of her own past."

Dillon said, "Do you think that the killer was working with my sister Nelia—she was a lawyer for a defense contractor, she didn't work in a law office—or with my brother-in-law, Stanton? Stanton was a prosecutor at the time, he had many more colleagues. Nelia worked for the legal counsel, who was a man and much older. I may be able to find out if there was anyone else with a legal background at her company, but it'll be difficult."

"I couldn't say," Arthur said. "I suppose I would be inclined to think that she'd work with the wife, only because she has some sympathy toward the female in the partnership, but the Stanton case is unusual because both parents were lawyers."

"What we should be looking for then," Dillon said, "is a list of female lawyers, paralegals, court reporters—anyone who worked for the County of San Diego or for the defense contractor, who came from out of state and then left employment within a year of Justin's murder."

"And moved to Santa Barbara," Max said. "Because the Porters lived in Santa Barbara."

"Employee records are generally private," Arthur said. "It may be difficult to get any viable list."

"I'll talk to Andrew," Lucy said.

"You may need to consider turning this over to the local field office, Lucy," Dillon said.

"No," Max interrupted. "Absolutely not. While I appreciate Lucy's help on this, I've worked with law enforcement on many cold cases over the last decade. If we don't give them something solid, they will shelve the entire investigation. I can't go to them with this theory and expect them to expend resources when one of the crimes is ostensibly solved—Donovan—and one of the crimes is currently pending trial. They'll laugh as they slam the door in my face if I suggest a grieving mother is going around killing little boys to force other mothers to grieve. Oh, and I only have evidence of crimes committed more than fifteen years ago."

"Max is right," Lucy said. "Every FBI office is spread thin right now, and has been for years. Violent crimes goes to the bottom each and every time."

"We have friends, Lucy," Dillon said.

"And when I have something actionable, I will call in every favor. But we don't have it now."

The room was silent for a long minute. Max wondered if they'd lost the feed, and she said, "I can file a Freedom of Information Act request and Andrew can expedite it—I've done it before when I had someone working with me. It's a way to cover all bases in case there's a legal challenge later."

Arthur said, "Max, Lucy, I'm happy to consult further if you need advice, but I think you're on the right path here. I'll review the evidence and timeline again, if I see anything we haven't discussed or have additional insight, I'll send you an e-mail."

"I appreciate your time, Arthur," Max said. "Dr. Kincaid? Anything else from you?"

It was clear he wanted to talk to Lucy alone, but before that happened, Max needed a conversation with her. They had to be on the same page before Lucy started making promises to her family.

"No," Dillon said. "Just—um, Lucy, tread carefully."

Lucy thanked Arthur and her brother, then shut down the conferencing program.

"That was enlightening," Max said. "You earned Arthur's respect. He's a good man, one of the brightest in his field. It's hard to impress him."

"He reminds me of someone," Lucy said.

She was off in her own thoughts, Max realized. Now would be the best time to get more information from her. Out of curiosity.

"Your friend Hans Vigo?"

Lucy nodded, but didn't elaborate. Max wondered if there was more to the story—Lucy was a difficult woman to read, but Max was learning. There was definitely something here.

"I need to call Dillon," Lucy said. "It's personal," she added quickly. "We have to work through how we're going to contact Nelia. I'll let you know what we decide. I'm not cutting you out, Max, I just need to handle this delicately."

"Your family is overprotective of everyone."

"They're my family. I've already damaged my relationship, but I'm not going to let the family take sides on this. I'm not going to destroy their relationships with one another because they don't like the path I'm on."

"That would be their choice, not yours."

"Max, you're astute, and a good study of human behavior. It's why you've been so successful in your career. But some things you can't learn from observation. Some things you can only understand through living them. I love my family. They have been to hell and back, and not just what happened to Justin. Standing against them on something so fundamental to who we have all become is one of the hardest things I've ever had to do. I understand their pain because I lived it. I don't want to lose them, but I made my decision. I've made tough decisions before and lived with the consequences. But I will be damned before I allow any of my brothers or sisters to take sides and divide us or further damage their own relationships. So I'm going to talk to Dillon and tell him I appreciate his assistance but he needs to stand down, you work on the FOIA, then we'll talk to Andrew and I'll delineate exactly what we need and he'll figure out if he can get it. I will tell you what we decide, and honestly, you're just going to have to live with it."

Lucy stood up and Max had a snide comeback, but something in Lucy's expression stopped her from commenting.

"Fine," Max said. "I'll meet you at the restaurant downstairs at eight—you can tell me then what we're going to do next."

Lucy started to walk out. She then turned and said, "Is there any way you can find out if Peter Caldwell was buried with a stuffed animal?"

Max wasn't certain John would even take her call. "I will most certainly try."

Chapter Twenty-one

"I was expecting your call," Dillon said as soon as he picked up the phone.

Lucy wasn't surprised. "I don't like it when we argue."

"Argue? That's kind of strong, don't you think?"

"I need to talk to Nelia."

"No."

"I'm not going to let you damage your relationship with Nelia or with everyone else."

"Why do you think this is you against the family?"

"You weren't there!" Lucy rarely lost her temper, but it had been a really awful two days. She pinched the bridge of her nose and willed herself to be calm.

"Luce," Dillon said softly, "I know this is difficult for you and for our family. You've never chosen the easy path. It's one reason I love you so much. Let me be a buffer. It's something I'm very good at."

"It's too late."

"It's never too late."

Lucy didn't want to tell Dillon exactly what their father had said. She didn't want to dump her frustration on her brother. Instead she said, "I guess I was expecting a different response. In hindsight, I screwed up. Why did I think having a nice family dinner would soften the blow?"

"You're probably right, though I can see why you did it—you were expediting."

"Exactly. But I was too blunt. I should have considered all the ramifications first, especially on Carina."

"Did you read her interview?"

"I haven't had the chance. I will after dinner tonight. Then I'll talk to her. One-on-one."

"I think that's smart."

Lucy was relieved.

"Just like it's not smart for you to contact Nelia. I will do it, and I will accept any fallout. She needs to know—even if this reporter you're working with doesn't reach out to her, someone will. She'll hear about it and it'll be far worse if she hears about it from anyone other than family."

Lucy hadn't thought that far ahead. She hadn't thought about what happened after they found the killer and when the news became public. "Thank you, Dillon."

"I recognized your focus on the video conference—you're not going back, are you?"

"What do you mean?"

"You're not going back to San Antonio until you solve this."

"I don't know that I'll be able to take that much time off."

"But."

Dillon was right. "I can't walk away. I don't want to lose my job, but this might be my stand. I'll accept the consequences."

"You always do."

"My new boss already doesn't like me." She rolled her eyes. "That sounds so junior high."

"Yet."

"She started while I was on my honeymoon. I met her the Monday I returned and it was extremely uncomfortable—I can't pinpoint it exactly. But I'm not comfortable with her knowing so much about me, and I know she has read my files, and talked to Juan as well. I'm sure she talked to Noah, but she knows that Noah and I are friends. She made a comment about it, and maybe I'm reading into the subtext, but it seemed that because Noah and I had been friends, she doesn't believe anything he says about me. Not to mention that everything that happened in

Mexico last October is sealed. No one in my office knows, except for Nate, and I think that bugs her. Because she doesn't know what happened."

"It's difficult for a supervisor to have a staff member who has, for lack of a better word, protection from on high."

"I don't want that kind of protection."

"But it's there. It's not something you can turn on and off. Just recognize that her perception is tainted. But also recognize your own motives."

"I want to find Justin's killer. That's my sole motive."

"Motive was the wrong word. Motivation, because you have been given a lot of leeway in pursuing cases, both on and off book, that in the back of your mind I'm pretty certain you think that you'll get a pass no matter how long this takes."

She was about to object, but maybe Dillon was right. "That would make me a total prima donna."

Dillon laughed. "You're hardly a prima donna, but you have a certain confidence. How do I explain it? You have an intuitive understanding of how the system works. That there are give-and-takes and some people are treated differently than others. While the FBI is a bureaucracy, it's still run by human beings, and there is always a level of friendships and trust that supersedes certain situations."

"I don't expect Rick to swoop in and rescue my career," Lucy said. Rick Stockton was the second-highest-ranking director in national headquarters.

"I know, but—"

"I see what you're saying, and you might be right—except my excuse is that I *will* find Justin's killer. I have to. Knowing that we're this close—I wouldn't be able to sleep at night if I walked away and another little boy died. If I lose my job over it, I can live with that." She didn't want to lose her job, but she'd resolved that sometimes her decisions didn't fit into the structure of her chosen profession. She just had to take each situation as it arose.

"Are you sleeping?" Dillon asked.

"Enough."

"I'll call you after I reach out to Nelia. Tread lightly with Carina, but

I think you're doing the right thing. She needs to hear from you what you're doing and why. She's a cop at heart, but she's also a mother."

"Thanks, Dillon. Tell Kate I said hi."

Lucy hung up.

She still had a hour before she needed to meet Max for dinner. She took a deep breath, considered what Dillon had said. He was right—she did have confidence about her job. Not that she could "do no wrong" per se, but that she could justify her actions.

She considered the situation—would she be willing to walk away if quitting was the only way to solve Justin's murder?

She wanted to make a flip answer—yes—yet she loved her job. She was good at it. She'd saved people. Last September she had worked on a particularly emotional case involving black-market babies. She'd not only saved several of the women who had been used as breeders, she and her partners in the San Antonio office—in fact, FBI agents across the country—had located nearly every baby who had been sold.

She did good. She didn't want to quit. She didn't want to be fired. She would fight it.

Yet.

It all began with Justin.

Her dad thought that she'd given up on her dream of majoring in linguistics and international relations because she'd been kidnapped. But she'd begun to wonder if maybe, just maybe, that had been a false dream. One she told her parents to protect them over the years, because after Justin was killed, everything changed.

Her dad thought she joined the FBI as some sort of . . . what? Justice after what happened to her? Penance because she'd killed the man who destroyed her life? Yet she had known for a long time that righting wrongs was the only way she could find peace. Even before her rape. Because Justin's murder had never been solved.

Patrick had an opportunity to be drafted into major league baseball, yet he'd pursued a career in law enforcement. Carina had dropped out of college to join the police academy. Dillon had given up his plan to specialize in sports medicine and turned instead to criminal psychiatry. And Lucy . . . maybe she knew, back when she was seven and her best friend was suddenly not there, that she had to do *something* to stop the pain.

She couldn't prevent her own. But she could prevent other people from suffering as she and her family had.

Lucy sat on the balcony of her hotel room, even though it was getting chilly. The light was good and she enjoyed the fresh sea air. She couldn't see the ocean, but she could feel it around her, and there was a sense of peace at being home . . . even if San Diego was no longer her home.

She had the copies that Andrew had given her of the investigation into Justin's murder. She'd already read all the forensic, autopsy, and police reports. Notes weren't in the file, which was another reason Katella reviewing the files again was so important. He might remember things they couldn't know based on what *wasn't* written down.

But she hadn't read the transcript of Carina's interview with police. Partly because she had so much information to digest and partly because she was a little nervous about it.

But Dillon was right: she needed to know what Carina had gone through. She'd been a nineteen-year-old college student. Not much older than a kid. She'd only lived in San Diego for a few years because she, like every Kincaid except Lucy, had been raised an army brat.

Her nephew had been kidnapped from his bedroom while she was babysitting. The guilt would have eaten her up—a lesser person may never have recovered. Nelia had treated Carina poorly after that, but Nelia had treated everyone that way, including herself. She'd lost her son, her marriage was over, and she felt like she'd lost everything. There were likely many psychological issues with guilt, grief, regret—things Lucy understood on one level, but she'd never lost a child. She'd lost people she cared about, people she loved, but a child was a deep part of a parent, part of the soul of the people who created it. And to be the mother—nine months of sharing space, of feeling a new life grow and move, of holding the infant you had helped create, and nurturing and protecting the young life.

Until violence walked in and everything was destroyed.

Lucy understood violence. She dreaded getting into the mind of

Justin's murderer. It would hurt, it would tear her up inside, but it wasn't her son who'd been killed. Didn't she owe it to Nelia—to her family—but most of all to Justin and the other boys this woman killed? Lucy could withstand the emotional pain because if she didn't, who else would?

It was a cause that drove her, one she barely understood and tried not to think about too much. But in the end, she did what she felt she had to do.

Carina would feel the same. As Dillon said, she was a cop at heart. But what she'd endured those days after Justin's disappearance had affected her, not only at the time, not only in who she had become, but had instilled a deep-seated angst and unresolved grief.

It became all too clear as Lucy read the transcript.

DET. KATELLA: We found Justin.

CARINA KINCAID: Thank God, thank God, is he okay? I need to see my sister.

KATELLA: Justin's dead.

CK: No, you said you found him. He's not dead. He's not.

KATELLA: He was found in a shallow grave in the park on East Street. Less than a mile from his house.

CK: How? No . . . please, I need to see my sister. My mom . . . oh, God, no.

KATELLA: I have a few more questions, Carina.

CK: I just want to go home.

KATELLA: If you tell me the truth, you can go home.

CK: I told you everything I know. Everything.

KATELLA: Let's go over it again. Last night, you went to your sister's house to babysit Justin. You told me you hadn't wanted to go because you cancelled a date.

CK: No I didn't, I mean—

KATELLA: I can read you back what you said yester-day.

CK: I said I had a study date. I have finals.

KATELLA: Still, a date.

CK: What? I don't understand.

KATELLA: Your study date was with Ben Jordan, right? He's your boyfriend.

CK: Yeah, so?

KATELLA: But you had to babysit last minute. Justin was going to be at your mother's house, but your little sister was sick and so you were stuck babysitting.

CK: I wasn't stuck. I always babysit.

KATELLA: Not something most nineteen-year-old college students want to be doing on a Friday night.

CK: It's not like that.

KATELLA: And your sister said you couldn't have Ben over to study because she didn't feel comfortable with someone she didn't know in the house with Justin.

CK: You make it sound bad. It's not bad. Nelia has always been overprotective. She loves Justin, I get it. He's a little kid.

KATELLA: You resented her.

CK: No—I don't understand—why are you doing this?

KATELLA: I just want the truth.

CK: I told you the truth!

KATELLA: Tell me again. What time did you arrive at the Stanton residence?

CK: Five or so—Lucy got sick, and Nelia was panicked, asked me to take him home.

KATELLA: But she was supposed to be home by seven, right?

CK: I thought—I didn't know that she was preparing for a big presentation. I called her at eight, she told me.

KATELLA: You must have been angry.

CK: No. Irritated, not angry. I wasn't mad—I wish she'd told me earlier, but really, it . . . what happened to Justin? What happened to him? Are you sure he's dead? He can't be. He just . . .

KATELLA: And what did you and Justin do?

CK: I ordered pizza and we ate and he watched a movie while I studied. Why won't you tell me what happened to Justin?

KATELLA: What movie?

CK: I, uh—I don't remember. I wasn't paying attention.

KATELLA: Justin watched a movie for two hours and you don't remember what it was?

CK: I-I was studying at the dining-room table. I wasn't paying attention. It wasn't a cartoon. It was one of his tapes, he can watch anything on the bottom two shelves. I didn't care what he watched—I needed to study.

KATELLA: And after the movie?

CK: He went to bed.

KATELLA: Just like that.

CK: Justin's a good kid. It was ten, past his bedtime . . . he's a good kid. A good . . .

KATELLA: Here.

CK: I-I—

It was clear to Lucy that Carina had broken down. She was so tense, the pages in front of her were wrinkled. Katella was only doing his job, trying to find the truth, but this was Lucy's sister. To learn about Justin's death from a cop, during an interview, at the police station. Without family to support her . . . without a lawyer.

Why didn't she have a lawyer? Andrew was an ADA at the time, their dad was still in the military, why didn't anyone protect Carina's rights?

Because innocent people never thought they needed representation. Innocent people thought the truth would set them free. And usually, it did. But legal representation wasn't just to find the truth. It was to make sure that all the rules were followed, that everyone had a fair and just system at their disposal. A lawyer wouldn't have let Carina answer questions she'd already answered. It was clear that Katella was first trying to find any inconsistencies with Carina's statement from the night before when Justin first went missing, and second trying to fluster Carina to see if guilt would prompt her to confess.

KATELLA: Can you continue?

CK: I want to go home.

KATELLA: I have just a few more questions.

CK: What?

KATELLA: What did you do after Justin went to bed?

CK: I studied. Then I fell to sleep.

KATELLA: What time did you fall asleep?

CK: I don't know.

KATELLA: Can you give me an approximate time?

CK: Around eleven. Maybe earlier. Maybe later. I
   don't remember. I had a headache and went to sit
   down on the couch and watch television until
   Nelia or Andrew came home. I fell asleep.

KATELLA: What were you watching when you fell
   asleep?

CK: Sports. Baseball highlights or something.
   There was nothing on and I hate the news. It's
   so depressing. And Patrick plays baseball in
   college, so I like to keep up with baseball. He
   might be drafted, he's that good.

KATELLA: When did you wake up?

CK: What? Um . . . when Nelia came in. She shook
   me awake. Said, "Sorry I'm so late." I sat up
   and started gathering my books. Nelia ran back

screaming. "Where's Justin? Carina, where is Justin?"

KATELLA: And then?

CK: We searched the house. Then I called 911 and Nelia called Andrew and . . . and now you tell me Justin is dead. And it's my fault. I can't believe I fell asleep. I am so sorry. God, I am so, so sorry.

Chapter Twenty-two

Max was famished and Lucy was late.

Max weighed the etiquette instilled in her by her grandmother versus her need for food. Was this an actual planned dinner? Or was it a suggestion? Was it more, "I'm eating at 8:00 P.M., join me if you can" or "We'll meet at eight to dine together?"

No matter how she sliced it, they'd planned on eating together. Damn, she was going to implode from lack of food. What was the etiquette for waiting? Twenty minutes? Thirty? She was pretty certain there was a rule about it somewhere . . . but she certainly wouldn't be calling her grandmother to ask.

Max was on the verge of summoning the waiter when Lucy walked into the dining room. The fed stopped briefly, assessed the venue and everyone in it. She scanned the room as if she had a photographic memory, pausing over every table—not looking for Max, but knowing where everyone was. Was she doing a threat assessment? She was an odd duck and Max didn't know exactly what to make of her.

Max *always* understood people. She was beginning to grow frustrated with the fact that she hadn't been able to pin Lucy Kincaid Rogan into a corner. The not knowing was going to drive her up a wall. She knew why. So much about her childhood was still a mystery to her that she sought answers where she could find them.

Lucy sat down next to Max instead of across from her where the place setting was laid out. Lucy moved it over herself. Typical law enforcement—

Max's ex-boyfriend Marco and current boyfriend Nick—was he still her boyfriend, she wondered . . . she didn't know and that saddened her—would have done the same thing.

"I'm sorry I'm late—I ended up reading the rest of Justin's file."

"And what did your brother say?"

"He'll talk to Nelia."

"Very well."

"I didn't expect you to be so reasonable about it."

"I am always reasonable."

Lucy smiled and almost laughed. When had Max given her the impression that she wasn't reasonable? Maybe almost walking out yesterday to interview Detective Katella alone . . . but that was one time.

"All I care about is the truth," Max said. "I don't much care how I get it, either, as long as I trust the information. Your brother has a long and distinguished career and I have a sense that he's extremely honest. I think he's the best person to find the answers we need." She paused, just a beat. When Lucy didn't say anything, Max added, "He holds back. During the call, I could see that he wanted to say things, but refrained. He'd be easy to beat in poker."

"And why is this bad? If people took a minute to think before speaking, most conflicts would be avoided."

"I suppose I could learn that lesson, but in my business when I make people angry, I tend to get the truth."

The waiter came over and Max ordered two appetizers and a second glass of wine. "I'm famished," she told Lucy, "but I'll share and give you time to look at the menu."

"I know what I want," Lucy said. She ordered and Max was surprised that Lucy added a glass of wine. When she said, "Any red wine is fine," Max interrupted.

"Bring her a glass of the Trefethen cab."

"Ordering for me?"

"The house wine is fine here, but trust me."

"I don't drink very much."

"All the more reason to enjoy good wine when you do."

197

Max waved off the waiter and finished her own glass of chardonnay. She generally preferred a lighter white, but they offered one of her favorite chardonnays by the glass.

"So, is everything okay with you and your brother?" Max asked.

"Yes."

Again Lucy offered nothing else. Answer the question and get out. She would be a lousy interview.

So Max got down to business. "I spoke to Andrew. My producer put in the FOIA request and Andrew will expedite it. Probably cutting a few corners, but he'll have the files ready for us tomorrow."

"You," Lucy said. "I can't—I mean, what you choose to share with me after you review the files is fine, but for now I think it would be safer for you and Andrew to go through the employee records. If we end up with a viable suspect, I don't want to jeopardize a conviction because of a warrant issue."

"What do you plan to do?"

"I'm going to talk to my sister. Carina."

"About?"

"It's personal."

The waiter came back with the two wines, and Lucy sipped the cabernet that Max had ordered. She took a second sip. "Okay, this is delicious."

Max smiled. "I know wine."

"After you and Andrew go through the files, I want to touch base with Katella—see how far he's gotten. And if you have names—we should run the names by him as well. Then I'll contact Santa Barbara and see if I can get information without making a formal request."

"Does your boss know what you're doing?"

"No," Lucy said. Again, nothing more.

"On 'vacation'?"

"I called in sick. I don't have any more vacation time—I used it all for my honeymoon."

"Where did you go?" Max asked.

"Vail, Colorado."

"I love skiing."

"No snow in October and I'm not very good on the slopes."

"So you're really a newlywed."

"I suppose we are." Lucy averted her eyes and smiled at something only she knew about. How could Max get her to open up? Even about something as little as this? Usually women loved to talk about themselves, their boyfriends or husbands. Why couldn't Lucy just bite at Max's hook?

"Your husband is very . . . intense."

Lucy laughed. It sounded genuine. Max wondered if she got Lucy drunk—or at least tipsy, since she admitted to not being much of a drinker, if she could get Lucy to talk. At this point, any information would be a win. "You had two strikes against you when we walked in. Sean isn't always so intense."

"I was doing my job."

"We're private people."

"I respect that."

"Do you?"

"I'm not going to apologize for wanting to know who I deal with." Max waited until the waiter brought out the appetizers. "Help yourself," she told Lucy.

They both dished up the small appetizer plates. Max immediately took a bite of the crab specialty, then asked, "Where did you stay in Vail?"

"Sean bought a cabin outside Vail."

"For the trip?"

"It was my wedding present, he said." Lucy smiled. It was clear to Max that she and Sean were close—not only based on seeing them together on Thursday, but how she talked about him. Yes they were married, they were newlyweds, but Max had been around enough married people to know that true love was rare.

Or maybe that was Max's own life clouding her judgment.

She said, "Private security must pay well."

"It can," Lucy said. And again, nothing more.

"How did you meet?"

"Why do I sound like I'm being interviewed?"

"I'm curious. Just in general, a curious person. I already promised your husband I wouldn't write anything about either of you without your express permission."

Lucy sipped her wine. "And you know that information is power."

"Why so evasive?"

"Just making an observation." She took another bite of the crab cakes. "You already know that two of my brothers work with Sean at RCK. Jack works out of Sacramento; Patrick and Sean opened the East Coast office a couple of years ago in Georgetown."

"But you don't still live there."

"When I graduated from the FBI Academy, I was assigned to San Antonio. Sean came with me. He can work from anywhere."

"And Patrick? He runs the office now?"

"They have a team out there now."

"So, it took more than one person to replace Sean? He must be good at what he does."

"He is."

Their dinner was served, and Max assessed Lucy as they ate. She was comfortable with not talking and she didn't ask any of her own questions.

"Is there anything you want to know about me?" Max asked.

"Is this a game of you share then expect me to share?"

"No. I'm an open book."

"That's true. It was clear after I read your book about Karen Richardson's disappearance."

"How so?"

Lucy ate for a moment and Max wondered if she was framing her response in such a way that would give Max less insight into her. Damn, Max was giving herself a headache trying to figure out this woman.

"You're very matter-of-fact," Lucy said after a moment.

"I'm a reporter."

"But you weren't then, were you? You were a college student taking leave because your best friend disappeared. You were straightforward in your writing, but you were also jaded—you have a slanted way of looking at everything."

200

"Everyone does," Max said. "If someone tells you they're not biased or unfair, they're not being completely honest with you or themselves. Everyone slants their perception based on their background, their experiences."

"In some ways. Experience is a benefit, though. I liked the book—even though the subject matter was tragic—because you had a raw honesty in how you wrote. You simply wanted answers."

"I still do."

Lucy nodded. "We're not all that different then. I just chose law enforcement."

"Why?"

"A lot of reasons."

Vague. Too vague. Lucy knew exactly why she wanted to be a cop, she just didn't want to share with Max. Max didn't like that, so she pushed. "Because of Justin's murder?"

"Partly."

That was the truth. And Lucy knew why she was a cop, she just didn't want to tell Max and she didn't want to lie, either. Interesting.

"You graduated from Georgetown."

"I did."

"I went to Columbia. Two West Coast girls moving east. How'd you like it?"

"It was . . . fine."

"You were on the swim team in college."

Lucy frowned and looked at her nearly empty plate.

"You knew I looked you up. When I found out you graduated from Georgetown, I googled your name and Georgetown. Came up with a long list of medals you won. Why does that bother you? I'd think you'd be proud of your accomplishments."

"I am," Lucy said but she wasn't looking at Max. She finished her wine. "I don't suppose you like dessert?"

This was an impossible conversation. Max was never going to learn anything about Lucy if the girl didn't talk. Even if Lucy asked questions of Max, it would give her insight. "I love dessert," Max said.

"Great. You want to know something about me? I love chocolate.

Madly in love with chocolate. Sean makes the most amazing hot choco-late. Probably why I fell in love with him. That and he always makes sure my favorite double chocolate ice cream is in the freezer."

The waiter cleared the plates and they ordered dessert and coffee.

Max was resigned to the fact that Lucy was never going to reveal anything more about herself than she wanted.

Her cell phone vibrated. She glanced at the number and frowned, sent it to voice mail.

Nick. She rubbed her eyes. She needed to figure this out, because never in her life had she been so torn about breaking up with someone.

"Is everything okay?" Lucy asked.

She probably meant was everything okay with the case, but Max decided to just spill it. If she was blunt, maybe Lucy would share something—anything. Max felt like she was going through information withdrawal.

"Boyfriend. We have a fundamental disagreement about something and I don't know that I can live with it."

"He's in New York?"

"No, northern California. He's a detective, I met him last year when I was working a cold case in my hometown. He's everything I love in a man—good-looking, smart, amazing in bed."

Lucy averted her eyes, just a bit. Was she blushing? At the mention of sex? Really, that was odd. But interesting.

"But he has an ex-wife and a son. The ex uses her son as a pawn and has Nick twisted into knots. Nick won't talk to me about it."

"He could want to spare you the details. Relationships are compli-cated."

"It's not that—trust me. He wants to keep that part of his life separate. I thought I could live with it . . . but I can't. Like you said, I'm blunt. I say what I think. I can't bite my tongue when a manipulative ex-wife uses a child to get her way. And Nick is letting her get away with it. They have joint custody and she'd been fighting in court to gain full custody so she can leave the state with her boyfriend. So far, Nick has a continuance—only because she and her boyfriend aren't married. But now apparently they're getting married. And then Nick will be screwed. And my gut is telling me this marriage is a farce—that she's doing it solely to gain full custody. And the only reason for that would be to screw Nick. I mean if she doesn't care about this guy, that means she wants to move to force Nick to leave his job and move again. She did it before—her excuse being to be closer to her family. Nick left his job and followed."

"It sounds like he shares a lot."

"No, I learned nearly everything from David, my assistant. David has a manipulative ex—this one an ex-girlfriend who's the mother of his daughter, they never married so David has even fewer rights than Nick—and he and Nick talk more about Nick's problems than me and Nick."

"That bothers you."

"Wouldn't it bother you if Sean refused to talk about something important to him? Maybe something about his personal life or his family, but he didn't want you involved at all? Told you it's an off-limits subject?"

Something flashed across Lucy's face, then it was gone. Had she and Sean had growing pains? Were they going through something now? Recently? Max's instincts hummed.

Lucy said, "We have no off-limit subjects."

Max didn't believe it. "None?" she said flatly.

"There was a time when both Sean and I would try to keep . . . secrets, for lack of a better word. I had a case last year that deeply affected me. I developed insomnia, but I kept telling Sean I was fine, that nothing was wrong, but it got to the point where I lied to him about it. Point-blank. And he knew I lied. I'm not a good liar, but I didn't want to talk about it because I didn't want to address the fundamental problem."

Max waited for Lucy to elaborate on what her fundamental problem was, but she didn't. Instead, she said, "Sean's done the same thing, ostensibly to spare me emotional pain. It took time, but we worked through all that. We couldn't possibly have gotten married if we didn't have complete trust and honesty between us. It's not who we are. But I'm certainly not one to give relationship advice. I was lucky Sean came into my life when he did. You might consider that Nick is trying to protect you or maybe doesn't share for reasons even he doesn't fully understand."

Max considered what Lucy said, not only about what Nick may or may not be thinking, but that Lucy said more about herself in that one comment than she had in the last two days Max had spent with her.

"Nick knows I'm not a woman who wants or needs to be protected— I'm a big girl, my self-confidence is stronger than most. I've asked him to tell me what's going on, and he won't. He won't even elaborate on why he won't discuss it, other than the subject is off-limits. And it's driving me crazy."

"Is it driving you crazy because you're worried about him and what he's going through, or because you can't stand being kept in the dark about anything?"

Max opened then closed her mouth. When had the conversation turned around from her digging for information to Lucy psychoanalyzing her?

"I tried a shrink for ten minutes. It didn't go over well," Max said drolly. She finished her wine. The waiter delivered their desserts and coffee.

Lucy took a bite of the chocolate concoction she ordered, the special of the day. "Oh, my God, this is amazing," Lucy said. "Take a bite."

Max did and concurred, though she wouldn't be able to eat more, it was far too rich for her taste.

Max didn't bring up Nick again and neither did Lucy. But Max couldn't stop thinking about what Lucy had said—was it simply the not knowing that drove her up a wall or how Nancy's shenanigans impacted Nick and his relationship with both his son and with Max?

She didn't know. Maybe a combination of both. Maybe she really was a selfish bitch who needed to know everything about everyone.

Or maybe she just couldn't stand the fact that Nancy was, essentially, a bully and Nick wasn't standing up for himself. He wasn't even using Max as a sounding board. If there was one thing that Max was good at it was weeding through bullshit and getting to the truth.

"Your husband is returning on Sunday?" Max said.

"Most likely."

"So you'll be leaving then?"

Lucy put her fork down and sipped her coffee. "I'm not leaving."

"Don't you have a job?"

Lucy didn't respond to the question. Instead she said, "When you get the names of the possible suspects from Andrew tomorrow, we'll talk to Katella, then to the chief in Santa Barbara and go from there."

"You're staying until we find the killer."

"Aren't you?"

"Until we find the killer or hit an impassable brick wall. My producer will throw a shit-fit if I'm not making forward progress, but I have some wiggle room." Max waited as the waiter refilled their coffees. When he left, she said, "Tell me the truth, Lucy. Are you risking your job by staying out here? You said something earlier about not having the vacation time."

"It's my job to risk. I'm okay with that."

Max believed her. Most cops Max knew were willing to risk their lives for others, they were the ones who ran toward trouble, not away from it. But they all played the game. Most wouldn't do anything to jeopardize their jobs, because they were cops not simply because they wanted to protect the public. It was a job and they had families to support. And with only a few exceptions, the agents Max had worked with in the FBI were even worse—they were bureaucrats as well as cops.

Lucy was the furthest thing from a bureaucrat.

"That said," Lucy continued, "I'm confident that the name of the killer is in those employment files. We just have to figure it out sooner rather than later. Did you find out if Peter Caldwell was buried with a stuffed toy?"

"I left John a message. He wasn't happy that I was continuing the investigation."

"He wasn't? Or his wife?"

"He wasn't happy because it upset his wife. He's going through hell and all he wants is to make everything easier for Blair. My involvement is unsettling to her, even though I assured them both that my focus was on the first three victims."

"You don't like her."

"Never did. Doesn't make her a killer."

"Andrew can get the information."

"Would he?"

"Yes," Lucy said without hesitation. "But I want him to do it right."

"I don't know what you mean by that."

"If there was no stuffed animal, that means Justin's killer didn't kill Peter Caldwell. Which means that Blair Caldwell is more than likely guilty, yet she planned this by studying the murder of my nephew. She used the pain and suffering of three other boys to inflict pain and suffering on her own child and her husband. Yet you said yourself that she has a top defense lawyer and he must think that the evidence is weak otherwise they would have pled out."

"Not all guilty people will plead. Most think they can game the system or that they're smarter than the jury."

"True, but Peter's murder was methodical. You said it had all the same elements as Justin's murder—all the same *public* elements. Though Andrew's affair was made public during the investigation, it wouldn't be something a copycat would consider part of the MO. It wasn't publicized in the Porter case, not widely. You said you believed John when he told you he wasn't having an affair."

"I did, but he could have been lying."

"Do you think he was lying? This is important, Max. You have good instincts. What do they tell you?"

Max considered everything she'd learned during her investigation into Peter Caldwell's murder. She hadn't learned much about the murder itself that wasn't already public information, but she had learned a lot about John and Blair and how the people around them perceived them.

"I don't believe he has ever been unfaithful to his wife. But there's another key point—the first three murders the husband was with his mistress during the murder and the wife was working. The Caldwells were at a party in the same neighborhood where they lived. They were seen by dozens, if not hundreds, of people. If John had disappeared long enough to have sex with someone, even if they screwed up against the wall in the bathroom, someone would have noticed he was missing. And Blair was at the same party. If John was having an affair, he would be far more discreet. And honestly, a quick fling isn't his style."

"I am positive," Lucy said, "that the affair is the primary motivation for this killer."

"You think Blair's guilty."

"I didn't say that. I haven't seen the evidence. I'm suspicious. I also want to know if John found the information about Justin's murder on his own or if Blair steered him to it."

"He told me he found it when he was doing research into like crimes. He was desperate to help the defense."

"He could have, but my guess is that Blair knew about Justin's murder, and most likely Tommy Porter as well because it's also unsolved. Porter's affair wasn't as widely reported in the press."

That was true—Max had read every press clip on the murder and the affair was only mentioned in one article, almost in passing, and in the context of the father's alibi.

"And Chris Donovan?" Max asked.

"Another similar crime, but she wouldn't have concerned herself with it because he was convicted. If she had read the trial transcripts, she would have known about the stuffed animal."

"You really do think she's guilty," Max said.

Lucy didn't comment. Max found both what she said—and what she didn't say—intriguing.

"I'll talk to Andrew," Lucy said. "If John returns your call, let me know what he says. Otherwise, we'll get the information another way. And if my suspicions are right, fair warning—I'm going to have Andrew suggest that the prosecution bring in my brother Dillon as an expert witness. Because if there is any reasonable doubt, the jury won't convict Blair Caldwell—no one wants to believe a mother can kill her son in cold blood. It's a difficult case to prosecute unless they have hard evidence."

"You're far more familiar with these cases than your brother."

"I can't testify as an expert witness—I'm a forensic *psychologist,* Dillon is a *psychiatrist*—a medical doctor—who has testified dozens of times. He has the credentials. And trust me on this, if he believes she's guilty and goes on that stand, the jury will believe she's guilty."

Max didn't doubt it for a minute. She couldn't wait to meet Dillon Kincaid in person, though he might not be as friendly as his sister.

Lucy ate almost the entire chocolate mousse before she pushed it away. "When does the trial start?"

"Week from Monday."

"Ten days. We'll have to work double-time to have answers by then. If she's guilty, we can't let her get away with it."

"We? It's not us, Lucy, it's the system—the prosecution had better have a good case."

But Max's comment fell on deaf ears, and she learned more about Lucy in that moment than she had in the last two days.

Lucy Kincaid took the world on her shoulders, as if she were solely responsible for putting every bad guy in prison. She didn't even know Blair Caldwell, she wasn't involved in the Peter Caldwell investigation, yet she wanted Blair to be punished to the fullest extent of the law. Maybe that wasn't unusual—most people wanted criminals to be caught. But this was . . . different.

We can't let her get away with it.

Interesting.

Chapter Twenty-three

Danielle bowed out of bunco with Nina, Grace, and the others. At lunch with the girls she'd made up an excuse about menopause, that her doctor had adjusted her hormones and she wasn't quite feeling herself.

She listened to the older women talk about their own menopause stories, and the younger women talk about childbirth.

It was exhausting.

But she stayed because she needed information.

For the last six weeks, ever since she'd seen Tony and Lana at the Christmas party and just *knew* what was happening, Danielle felt *off*. As if she wasn't completely in her body. As if everything was happening around her and no one actually saw her. If they did, wouldn't they see her suffering? Wouldn't they recognize that they were as much to blame for what had happened . . . what *would* happen . . . as she?

More so. She was a catalyst, nothing more.

Nina would be at bunco. Tony was staying home with Kevin.

"Having a boys' night watching some action hero movie."

That was good, right?

Just delaying the inevitable . . .

Nina didn't know the truth. Danielle almost told her about Tony and Lana, wondered if that would change anything. She was so . . . so *in love*. She was smart, why couldn't she see it?

Because she wanted it all. Career. Family. Husband. Friends. Everything.

And when she did find out, Kevin would be a pawn in the cat-and-mouse game of divorce. Because Nina and Tony were just as vindictive and angry as any other couple on earth. Friendly divorce? No such thing.

Danielle didn't trust Tony. After all, he was a cheater. A male whore. Would he bring his mistress over to the house and screw her in his wife's bed? Probably not . . . Kevin was eight.

Danielle waited until the bunco game would have started. She'd been to a half dozen over the last few years, she knew they would last until ten, sometimes longer. She drove to the Fieldstone house and parked down the block.

The Fieldstones lived in La Cresenta, in the hills above the 210 freeway. It was an older neighborhood with small, classic homes, many of which had been expanded and fixed up by the owners, increasing the value of the neighborhood. The Fieldstones were no exception. They had the money—Tony was a lawyer, Nina made in the high five figures as the senior legal secretary. They had one child.

There was one major problem with the Fieldstone house—one she hadn't encountered before, but had been thinking about a lot over the last six weeks.

The bedrooms were upstairs.

She had a couple of ideas, but neither one was ideal.

The first was the fact that Kevin spent a lot of time with his grandmother, and twice in the last six weeks had spent the night at her house. Her one-story house.

But his grandmother had two small dogs who barked whenever a fly sneezed, so that wouldn't work. And it would defeat the purpose of exposing his parents for the selfish, egotistical, undeserving, marginal humans that they were.

Danielle took a deep breath. Her head ached. She'd been drinking far too much this week, she had to stop. Relax.

But the nightmares will return . . .

She could suffer the nightmares to enact retribution. It would just be a couple of days, maybe a week. Two.

Sooner. Because Nina and Tony Fieldstone didn't want to be parents. They would leave, abandon their son.

They all did it. They all left.

The darkness deepened as she watched the house: 7:00 P.M.; 8:00 P.M.

A tap on her window made her jump.

An older man and his wife stood on the sidewalk with their leashed dog.

She turned her ignition half the way and rolled down the window. "Yes?" she said.

"Is something wrong, ma'am? Car broke down?"

"No. I was just talking on the phone. Sorry."

The man looked down at her hands. Her phone was in her purse.

"I-I had some bad news. I needed a few minutes to compose myself. I didn't meant to disturb anyone."

"You didn't, but you were here when we left for our walk nearly an hour ago. Just wanted to make sure, can't be too careful."

He stepped back from the door. Danielle didn't want to leave, but now she would have to. She couldn't afford to draw attention to herself.

She turned on the car and drove off. She glanced in the rearview mirror. The man was still watching her.

Well, shit.

She drove around for quite a while until she ended up in Burbank and saw a sign.

LAST WEEKEND FOR BLOW-OUT DEALS! LAST-YEAR MODELS CHEAP!

It was time to get a new car.

Just in case.

An hour later, Danielle drove off in a brand-new silver Nissan Ultima. Last year's model, but with only thirty-seven miles on it. She didn't care much about cars, but this was a good deal, and she'd kept her four-year-old Honda in pristine condition so got a good trade-in. She hadn't planned on getting rid of the Honda until she moved again, but it was time.

A sign.

She drove back through the Fieldstones' neighborhood, but didn't stop. She didn't know where the old folks lived, and she couldn't risk being seen again.

It was late, after ten, but Nina's SUV wasn't in the driveway. Tony always parked his sporty car in the garage, but with all their things, the two-car garage only fit one small vehicle. She couldn't tell if he was still home, but there were no other cars in the driveway or directly in front of the house. They had two babysitters, other than Kevin's grandmother—one had a small pickup truck, the other lived three blocks away and walked because she didn't have her license.

Danielle drove around the block once.

She'd been to the house several times for parties and bunco. The master bedroom had been expanded out over the garage and looked over both the front and backyard. Kevin's bedroom was in the front corner of the house. His bed was under the windows which met in the corner. Impossible to reach from ground level.

She left the neighborhood. There was only one way she could do this. She would have to go in through the front or back door. The Fieldstones had an alarm system, but they only used it when they were out of town.

As if their possessions were more important than their son.

Danielle drove home. She lived in a quaint older house in Glendale with a long narrow driveway that led to the detached garage. She didn't park in the garage—she used it for other things.

She went inside her house and poured a glass of wine, then stopped herself. She needed to be clear this week. To plan. She put the glass down but didn't pour it out. She might need just one small glass to go to sleep. To keep the nightmares at bay.

It'll take the whole bottle. You know that.

She did. But she could control herself. She had to.

She walked to the second bedroom she used as an office. It was functional, with a computer and printer and bookshelf filled with books she hadn't read.

She hadn't read a book in a long, long time.

But on the top shelf was a photo album. She took it down, sat at her desk, and opened it.

She ran her fingers over the first photo. Matthew, only hours after he'd been born. So perfect. So sweet.

Danielle couldn't do this. She flipped to the last page and pulled out the large envelope she kept there. She opened it, dumped out the contents. Keys, mostly. A few photos. Notes. Things she didn't dare leave behind, just in case.

She grabbed the key chain marked F. *Fieldstone*. It wasn't their chain—it wasn't even their key. She'd made a copy last month when Nina gave her her keys to go to the archive room to retrieve files on a case that was going to appeal.

As if subconsciously Danielle had known this was the only way.

She put everything back in the folder, including the Fieldstone security code, which she had long memorized. She'd watched Nina months ago type it in when they'd gone over to the house to prepare for a partner dinner.

Before Danielle found out the truth about Tony and Lana.

Maybe she'd always known. Maybe she had a sixth sense about cheating husbands.

You didn't know your own husband was screwing his secretary. So cliché. So disgusting.

Her hand itched to call that bastard and give him a tongue-lashing.

She put the photo album back and walked down the short hall to the kitchen. Drank half the glass of wine. Retrieved her cell phone. Dialed Richard.

He didn't answer. Was he intentionally avoiding her calls?

"Are you cheating on your wife, Richard? Does she know? Or is she as clueless as I was?"

She went off on him, going from calm to angry, long after the phone beeped to tell her the recording time was up.

She stared at the phone and almost called him back, but something tickled in the back of her mind. Something she didn't quite remember . . . but it was there.

Danielle grabbed her new car keys and went back out into the night. It was after eleven. Nina should be home by now. Danielle lived only a few minutes from La Cresenta. She turned down the Fieldstones' street and slowed when she neared their house.

Nina's SUV still wasn't there.

On a whim, because of that tickle in the back of her mind, Danielle drove to Grace's house. She lived in the Burbank Hills, in a beautiful home bought and paid for by Grace's wealthy ex-husband. Money obviously didn't buy happiness since Grace had divorced. Had he cheated on her? Probably, Grace never said. But isn't that what men did? They wanted to screw anything that moved.

At least, that's what Danielle's mom always said, and had been proven right again and again and again.

Nina's shiny Escalade was in the driveway . . . but no one else was at Grace's. Bunco would have long been over . . . and Nina was the last one here by hours?

The lights were off.

Had she been drinking? Decided not to drive?

Danielle parked on the street and closed her eyes. She was missing something. But her instincts—well-formed instincts from years of research and following cheating husbands—told her to grab her camera.

She quietly exited the car and walked up the steep slope of Grace's driveway.

She'd been to Grace's house before. Her daughter had a room upstairs, on the south; Grace's suite was on the northern ground floor. Spacious, as big as Danielle's entire house.

Why did she even work when she had made so much money on her divorce?

Danielle shook off the thought. She walked around the side of the house; there was a gate. Dammit.

She tried the latch. It wasn't locked. She quietly went down the walkway to the back of the house, then stopped.

Two sets of sliding-glass doors opened into the backyard. This was Grace's bedroom. Danielle had to tread carefully here. She walked to the far corner of the yard, on the other side of the pool, where palm trees grew up against the Verdugo Mountains. They didn't belong here; they seemed so out of place. She stood against one thick tree, aimed her camera at the bedroom, hidden by the night.

She had bought this camera years ago, but it still had some of the best features on the market. She adjusted the lens for the low-light conditions and zoomed into Grace's bedroom.

Maybe she wasn't surprised, but she involuntarily gasped.

Tony was not the only Fieldstone having an affair.

Chapter Twenty-four

Lucy dropped Max off at Andrew's office Saturday morning, then borrowed Max's rental car to drive to Carina's house. She had to pass her parents' to get there.

She slowed to a stop and sat idling across the street from the small two-story house where she'd been raised. Dillon, Jack, and Nelia had all moved out of the house before Lucy was born—Nelia married to Andrew, Jack in the army, and Dillon in college and living in the room he and their dad had built above the garage. He'd received a full scholarship to UC San Diego where he planned to study sports medicine. He'd almost finished medical school when Justin was killed. He changed his focus to psychiatry, took an extra year of school, and did his residency in a facility for the criminally insane.

Justin's murder had touched everyone in her family, not only herself and Dillon. Connor had already been a cop when Justin was killed. Patrick was in his first year of college—a full scholarship to play baseball. While he continued to play, his heart wasn't in it. He studied computer science and found he had a knack. Graduated, went to the police academy, and created what was now the modern-day cybersquad at SDPD.

Lucy couldn't remember what Carina had been studying in college when Justin was murdered. All she remembered was that she'd never gone back and instead joined the police academy. She became a cop, quickly rose in the ranks and earned her detective shield before she was thirty.

One tragedy had a profound impact on every Kincaid. It was no surprise that it affected Lucy as well.

No one was out in the yard. For years, the house bustled, people going in and out. Friends came to the Kincaids, and not just because Rosa always had enough food to feed an army. Rosa insisted. She wanted to know everyone's friends, she wanted the sound of children and laughter and fun. Lucy grew up knowing every one of Patrick's girlfriends and Carina's boyfriends; she eavesdropped on adult conversations because most everyone was an adult around her. She understood the world long before most kids her age.

And then one by one, they all moved out. Justin's death extinguished the joy for a long time, and while it gradually returned, nothing was ever the same.

How could it be?

Lucy put the car back into drive and headed for Carina's house. Lucy hadn't slept well last night. The motive of this particular killer was difficult to process. Lucy knew that she was right, and Arthur Ullman had provided another insight Lucy hadn't considered. But knowing in her heart and mind that she was right about this killer and why she was killing children did nothing to help her understand how anyone could commit such a horrific crime for the sole purpose of creating suffering among the survivors. Because it wasn't only the mothers and fathers who were shattered by the pain. It was grandparents and aunts and uncles and friends.

The killer didn't think about that. She couldn't think past her own need to inflict as much emotional pain on others as she could. Did it alleviate her own suffering? Did it give her any peace?

Lucy thought not. If murder had given her peace, she would have stopped. Instead, she continued the cycle of pain.

Lucy stopped the car in front of Carina's house. She'd bought it a few years before she met her husband, Nick. Before that, she'd lived with a boyfriend in a beachfront condo, and before that she'd lived at home. Carina had perhaps been the most affected by being raised an army brat. Lucy wasn't, she was a toddler when her family settled in San Diego. She didn't remember anything about that time in her life, only what she heard from her siblings. Part of the reason her father asked for the post in San Diego was because Nelia had married and had the first grandchild, and part of it was because Pat Kincaid had grown up in San Diego. It had always been his home base.

Carina loved having a permanent home. Her husband Nick had a career in Montana, but when they met and fell in love, he gave it up to be with Carina. Lucy's parents loved Nick like their own son. Connor and Julia had settled nearby as well.

But everyone else had left. Jack in the military, with his home base in Texas; Nelia leaving because of Justin's murder. Then Dillon moved to D.C. in part because he married Kate and in part to give Lucy a home while she was at Georgetown. She'd tried and failed to live successfully in the dorms. At the time, the trauma of her kidnapping and rape was just too much to cope with, along with having a roommate and dealing with parties and classes and gossip. If she hadn't been able to move in with Dillon and Kate, she didn't know if she'd have been able to finish school.

Then Patrick left a few years later, to work with Jack at Rogan Caruso Kincaid. First in Sacramento, then starting up the East Coast office of RCK with Sean Rogan. That's how Lucy and Sean met, and it had changed her life for the better.

Lucy hadn't realized, not until her father's heart attack when she came home and had a heart-to-heart with Carina, that Carina had been heartbroken at Patrick's move to the East Coast. She was also a little jealous of Patrick's relationship with Lucy. For their entire lives, Carina, Patrick, and Connor had been as thick as thieves, three kids born four years apart, going to school together, having friends, sticking together like glue. They'd been best friends, and then everything changed.

Lucy didn't know how much of the changes were because of her, how much because of the family, or Patrick himself. She didn't think that her relationship with Patrick should impact Carina's relationship with him, but apparently, it had, and no matter how many psych classes she took, she didn't completely understand.

Carina stepped out onto the front porch, cup of coffee in hand, and stared at Lucy sitting in the car. Busted, Lucy thought. She'd been not only thinking about the past, but working up the courage to talk to her sister.

Lucy got out of the car and walked up the short stone path. "Hi," she said.

Nick stepped out of the house behind Carina, put his hand on her shoulder. A unified front. Lucy couldn't blame him; if Sean were here, he would have done the same thing for her.

"Hi, Nick."

"You need to leave, Lucy," Nick said.

"I'd like to talk to my sister alone."

"No."

Carina turned to Nick, whispered something. He didn't look happy. But he kissed her and went back inside.

Carina came down the stairs. "Let's walk."

They walked in silence. The neighborhood was older and established. It had been an old neighborhood when the Kincaids moved in twenty-five years ago. Now it was quaint, and many of the homeowners had updated and expanded the small, post-WWII homes. American flags were displayed on more than half the homes, showing that San Diego was still a military town. Especially this neighborhood, which was so close to the naval base.

They walked in silence for a short while and then Lucy realized that Carina had steered them two blocks away, to where Dillon had once lived. His house had been destroyed by a psychopath—one who had fixated on Lucy. Dillon had nearly died because of it, and Lucy still had a hard time forgiving herself for what happened. It wasn't her fault—she almost believed that—but it haunted her because she'd lost nearly everything.

The house had been rebuilt by the new owners, and as Lucy watched a young mother came out with a jogging stroller built for two. A toddler and infant were strapped in, and the mother took off in the opposite direction, pushing the stroller as she ran while listening to music.

Life and love had replaced death and hate.

"I read the transcripts from your interview with Don Katella."

Carina didn't say anything, but continued walking past Dillon's former house. Lucy didn't comment on the direction—they were heading toward Nelia and Andrew's old house. They would pass the park where Justin's body had been found. Everything good and bad in Lucy's childhood had happened within walking distance from her home.

"I should have come to you first. Alone. I didn't fully understand, and that's on me."

Carina still didn't speak.

"I projected my own feelings and personality on you. I thought because you were a cop, you would see things the way I see them. But you were also a victim, and every survivor processes trauma differently."

"Don't try to psychoanalyze me," Carina said.

"I understand better now."

"You can't possibly understand, Lucy."

The comment burned because Lucy understood Carina—she understood everyone in her family—far better than they gave her credit for. It's why this was so hard for her, because she knew exactly what she was doing, and she knew it was going to hurt people she loved.

"I *am* sorry, Carina."

"If you were sorry, you wouldn't be doing this."

"I'm not sorry for investigating Justin's murder. I'm sorry I didn't come to you from the beginning."

Carina frowned, but didn't comment.

"I was nine when you graduated from the police academy," Lucy said. "I thought it was really cool that my big sister was going to be a police officer, just like Connor. Mom and Dad took me to your graduation. I didn't understand then why they weren't as excited as I was. Why they didn't seem happy. Now I do. They thought you'd given up something to become a cop, rather than gained something. Dad said the same thing to me the other night. That he was sad I gave up my dreams for this life.

"Dreams change. My dreams disappeared after I was raped. I didn't know if I would ever live for anything again. But I realized that even those dreams weren't real. They were what I thought I should do, what I thought I should be. I think my path was set when Justin was taken from us. From all of us." She paused. "But that doesn't mean my life is less than it could have been, or that your life was ruined because you didn't do whatever it was you thought you wanted when you were nineteen. We grow up, we change, dreams change.

"When you graduated, you put your arm around me and said something I have never forgotten. It wasn't to me, it was to Dad, who was looking both proud and sad at the same time—I know that sounds weird, but that's how I remember it. You said, 'Dad, this is what I'm meant to do. Please don't worry about me.' And Dad said, 'Cara, I will worry, and I will always love you. But I see it in your eyes. This is what you should be doing.'"

Lucy took a deep breath. "Dad has always supported us, except twice. When he disowned Jack, and when I decided to become an FBI agent."

"Dad is proud of you."

"No. He didn't come to my graduation, not because he was getting over a cold, but because he was sad for me. I saw the truth the other night. He thinks I'm torturing myself, that I do this solely because of what happened nine years ago. But this is what I'm meant to do. Maybe I didn't realize it until I was raped. What happened to me didn't turn me into a cop. It showed me who I was and who I could be. I had the best role model in you—seventeen years ago, when you became a cop, there were a fraction of the women on the force as there are now. Then you became a detective, one of the few female detectives at the time. You closed tough cases, you were strong, you were brave, and you never turned your back on those who needed your help. Never. You risked your life then, you risk your life now, because it's what you're meant to do.

"If I'd come to you first," Lucy continued, "I'm not saying I would have been able to convince you to join in this investigation. But I think I would have been better able to explain why I have to do this. Not just to solve Justin's murder. Not solely to give justice to the other families who have been torn apart. But because there is a killer out there, and she will kill again, and I cannot stand by and wait for another little boy to die."

They had reached the Justin Stanton Memorial Park. It was filled with mothers and fathers, children of all ages, because it was a cool but clear Saturday morning. A soccer game was about to begin on the field near the trees where Justin had been buried. The kids were so small—couldn't have been more than six or seven.

Lucy was going to suggest they sit on a bench, then she looked at Carina and saw the tears.

"I've never taken J. P. here," Carina said. "We go to Elm Street instead."

"You used to bring Justin and me here all the time."

"Mom made me."

"I know."

Carina turned and started walking back toward her house. Lucy took a last look at Justin's park, then caught up with her.

"Did you really read all the Katella transcripts?" Carina asked.

"Yes."

Carina rubbed her eyes. "Connor thinks you're grasping at straws. He has always believed that Justin's murder was isolated, a random act of violence."

"It's not."

"You sound so sure."

"I am."

"Why?"

"I'm not going to tell you unless you want to hear the details. You're a cop, Carina, and that's all I saw the other night. I didn't see you as an aunt, a sister, a mother. I am sorry—I never wanted anyone to be hurt because of what I'm doing. That was my own naïveté. I should have known."

They again passed Dillon's old house, and turned the corner to head back to Carina's. Carina said, "I don't know if I want the details. I'm not blind to what happened—I've read Justin's files. But tell me this, why are you working with a reporter?"

"Max found the connection between Justin's murder and at least two others. And we both know the police don't have the resources to work these cold cases."

"And your boss is letting you do this?"

Lucy hesitated. This was one of those areas she was getting nervous about, especially after the e-mail yesterday from her supervisor. "I'm doing this on my own time. When I have solid evidence—enough proof that I know it can't be ignored—I'll turn it over to the local office. It's a multijurisdictional investigation and the FBI is better equipped to handle it, but I need to have proof. And by proof, I mean the ID of the killer."

Carina stopped walking and turned to Lucy. "Do you actually think you can name the killer?"

"Yes." She didn't even hesitate. Maybe Max Revere's confidence was rubbing off on her. "I have a working profile. I know who we're looking for—at least, her general age, gender, background, and job. One of the best things about working with Max is her resources—she has a research staff that is truly amazing. They can crunch information much faster than a lone analyst at the FBI with a dozen cases on his desk. We're pooling information from the three cases we're confident are connected and one name will come to the surface."

"You said there were four cases."

"There may be four. There may be one or two cases we have yet to uncover."

Carina continued toward her house. "I reacted on emotion the other night. I didn't realize how much what happened to Justin still affected me."

"It's not just that, Carina. It's what happened to you afterward. Andrew, Nelia, and you were all suspects. Intellectually, you understand that because you would have done the exact same thing if the same crime happened today. But emotionally, you were gutted. How could anyone think that you had anything to do with Justin's murder? Even as an accident? It hurts. And that's a pain that doesn't ever really go away."

Carina stopped at her walkway. "Would you like some coffee? See J. P.?"

"Yes, but I can't right now."

She hadn't missed Nick sitting on the porch with J. P. in his lap. He was eyeing them suspiciously.

"Let me think about what you said," Carina said. "And I'm sorry about the way I reacted. You're right, I'm emotional about this. I've always had a hard time thinking like a cop when it comes to Justin."

Spontaneously, Carina hugged her. Lucy hugged her back. "I love you, Cara," Lucy said.

"I love you, too, sis. I really do." Carina smiled and wiped away tears. "Damn, I get so weepy since I've had J. P."

"Motherhood becomes you."

Lucy opened her car door and slipped inside. As she drove off, she looked in the rearview mirror. Carina and Nick were sitting together. Carina had taken J. P. from Nick and was hugging her son.

Lucy blinked back her own tears. Time to focus. She called Assistant Chief Carney with the Santa Barbara police department and knew she was about to overstep her bounds—and it could very likely cost her her job.

But if she solved Justin's murder, she could live with that.

Chapter Twenty-five

The government offices weren't empty on Saturday morning, but staff was minimal. Andrew set up his laptop in the conference room adjoining his office. He also had nine boxes stacked on the floor.

"We went completely digital ten years ago, but to save on the budget, we included only current employees. If you're right and whoever we're looking for left the office shortly after Justin was killed, then she'll be in one of these boxes. I pulled the files from the year Justin died and the following year, as you suggested." He stared at the boxes and shook his head. "Basically, those are all employees of the county of San Diego who terminated employment in those two years. It would be faster if these files were separated by department."

Max sipped her coffee. Two years ago, before she began *Maximum Exposure*, she'd been solely responsible for all her own research. Now, she did so little of it that she realized she had become lazy. The idea of spending all day sorting through spreadsheets and employee files was far from exciting. "We're two smart people, we'll figure it out," she said. "We're looking for women in which department?" She put one box in front of her.

"Lucy said anyone working in the courthouse or the district attorney's office, but I also figure the public defenders' office should be included. I know the codes, I can go through the files faster. I'll separate them and you can then look and determine if the individuals fit the profile."

"Good plan."

Andrew took the box from Max and started separating out files. He was able to sort the files based solely on the coded employee label, which saved time. They worked in silence for several minutes. Andrew was putting one in roughly every three files in front of her. She had a cheat sheet of what she was looking for: a female employee who was between the ages of twenty-five and thirty-five at the time Justin was killed. Lucy was confident she was from the East, but Arthur had suggested that it could be someone simply outside the area. Because they weren't settled on it, Max decided to leave hometown as irrelevant.

The first six files Andrew put in front of her were men, easy to put aside. The next was a woman who retired—she'd been sixty-five—out. The next a woman of thirty-three—put her in the maybe pile.

Max wanted to ask Andrew questions about Lucy, but she didn't want Andrew to know she was curious.

"I apologize for how I responded to your insistence I work with your sister-in-law," Max began, choosing her words perhaps a bit too carefully. She actually wasn't sorry for her response—it was justified, considering the circumstances—but she did wish she'd kept her cool. She'd felt blindsided.

"No apologies necessary," he said, not looking up from the files. When the first box was empty, he took the reject folders, put them back inside, and wrote on a sticky note the names and employee numbers that Max had set aside. He put it on the lid, pushed it back against the wall, and opened the second box.

"I've found her insight surprisingly helpful. My experience has been that cops don't like working with me."

Andrew glanced at her with a wry grin. "You're a reporter."

As if that explained everything.

"You say that as if I'm a used car salesman."

"I'm a lawyer, I get the same attitude."

"Yes, but you're a prosecutor. A district attorney. A lot more prestige and respect than, say, an ambulance chaser."

"Sometimes it's an uphill battle." They finished with the second box faster as they developed a rhythm, and he did the same thing as he'd done with the first, putting in the rejected files and making a note on top.

"I'll admit, I was nervous that Lucy would say no," Andrew said as he opened the third box. "Not because she doesn't want answers, but because she's finally gotten her life together. I didn't want to bring all this back on her. But the one thing I've learned about Lucy over the years is that she has a spine of steel."

"She does. She's very focused."

Finally gotten her life together. What did that mean?

"Her father had a heart attack last year—right before Christmas. The family was all here. I think that's the hardest thing for me being on the outs with the Kincaids. I had a shitty childhood. No excuses—it was what it was. My father was an alcoholic cop. A real jerk. My mom left him when I was a kid, my little brother and I bounced back and forth between them for years, until I finally said screw it, my dad didn't deserve anything from us. He died when I was in law school—broken and bitter. So when I met Nelia, I think one of the reasons I became so attached was because I fell in love with the Kincaids. Losing them on top of losing my son . . . honestly, I went through some dark times. If it wasn't for Dillon, I wouldn't be here today. He forgave me, he talked to me. He was the only one."

"We had a long conversation with Dr. Kincaid last night. They talked shrink talk—I listened."

"Dillon's a smart guy. We've been able to work together over the years, but he wouldn't even think of asking his family to forgive me. He does what he wants but I think he understood, even back then, why Nelia and I were together at all."

"Did you love her?"

"Yes, but not the right love."

"I have no idea what that means."

"It means we were friends. We ended up having sex because we were spending so much time studying together and liked each other's company. It just happened. But it wasn't a passionate love. It was comfortable. We dated because, well, we were too busy to even think about having a relationship with anyone outside of our circle of friends. So when we learned she was pregnant, we thought marriage. We liked each other, love would come. It doesn't work that way. At least, it didn't for us." He paused. "I don't know why I told you all that."

He was scared she'd spill it for the world. Sometimes she enjoyed having a conversation where people didn't think she was going to blab on the news.

"Everything we say and do in this room is off-limits, okay?"

He was obviously relieved. He stopped for a moment and looked at her. "That bothers you, doesn't it?"

Of course it did. Did people think she didn't care at all?

"I'm not a bad guy," she said. "I don't screw people for the joy of screwing them. If you lie to me, all bets are off—I really detest liars. But I work these cases because I need to solve the unsolvable. I don't know why I can't just put Karen's death behind me and lead a normal life, at least what's normal for an intelligent, independently wealthy woman. This is me, and I don't justify it to anyone."

"I respect that."

She hadn't expected a comment, or his respect, but she appreciated it.

Now how did she turn the conversation back to Lucy?

She said, "It seems that those of us who faced tragedy when we were younger turn to a version of law enforcement. I'm not a cop, but after Karen's murder I couldn't think of anything but exposing the bastard who killed her. I use the power of words. I found out I was good at it."

"I researched you after you first contacted me. You have a solid track record."

"I have a great track record." She smiled, went through the last of the files Andrew handed her. He boxed up the extras and picked up the last of the boxes. "You were already a prosecutor, but I looked into the Kincaids. Carina dropped out of college to go to the police academy, Dillon had been in medical school specializing in sports medicine, and went an extra year to change his focus to forensic psychiatry. Patrick became a cybercop. And Lucy joined the FBI."

"Lucy had other reasons for joining the FBI. She used to want to study international relations."

"Diplomacy? I can see that." What other reasons did Lucy have for joining the FBI? "Did she lose someone else to violence? After Justin?"

"You'll have to talk to her about it. But let me give you some advice: don't ask."

Now Max was even more curious. She itched to talk to Marco about Lucy—he could access her FBI records. But Sean Rogan's threat weighed heavily on her. She didn't want to blow this working relationship, and right now it *was* working.

They finished the last of the boxes and had a stack of eighteen women who had been between the ages of twenty-five and thirty-five whose last year of employment was within a year of Justin's murder.

"Eighteen is manageable," Max said.

"Hold that thought," Andrew said. He picked up his cell phone. Max hadn't heard it ring.

"Stanton. . . . Hello, Harry, thank you for returning my call on the weekend. How's Donna? . . . Great. . . . A grandson? Really? Well, congrats, Grandpa." Andrew laughed, but Max could see that this was an act for him. He might genuinely be interested in this Harry and Donna, but he was going through the motions.

Andrew continued, "I'm going to be upfront with you, Harry. I need a favor. The answer may both solve a cold case for me and help you with a pending trial. . . . Blair Caldwell. . . . Really. Well, it's a very cold case. The Justin Stanton murder. My son." Andrew pressed his fingers to his forehead, then straightened his spine as he listened. "I know you, Harry. You don't gamble at trial. But I may be able to offer you an expert witness you wouldn't be able to get otherwise. . . . Yes, I know you have your own experts. . . . I would consider this a personal favor. I only have one question. . . . All right. I understand." He paused, listening for a long minute.

"Thank you," Andrew said to Harry. "Was your victim, Peter Caldwell, buried with a stuffed animal or favorite toy?" He listened. "Interesting. . . . You have no doubts. . . . No, I wouldn't either, but the defense can work around circumstantial evidence. . . . Yes, I promised, and he's one of the best forensic psychiatrists in the country. . . . Dozens of expert testimonies, the defense won't be able to discredit him. . . . I know they're expensive, but it won't cost you a thing. He'd already agreed to do it and a nonprofit is covering his expenses. . . . I need you to keep his name under wrap for a few days, okay? . . . Dr. Dillon Kincaid. When do you have to turn it over to the defense? . . . That's fine. I'll send you Dr. Kincaid's contact information and tell him to expect your call next week. Thank you, Harry. I appreciate your help." He hung up.

Max knew what he was going to say even before he said it.

"No toy."

"Correct."

"She's guilty." Max had an odd feeling of intense rage and deep sorrow. John was going to be destroyed. She didn't want to hurt him, but she would have no choice. His wife was guilty of murder.

"Harry thinks their case is solid, but he jumped at the chance to get an expert of Dillon's caliber. Tells me they have ample circumstantial evidence but no smoking gun. Max, you can't share this information."

Again, she was angry. "I said I wouldn't. My focus is finding this killer." She rested her hand on the stack of eighteen personnel files.

"John Caldwell is a friend of yours."

"I'm not about to jeopardize the prosecution. That's not my style. And if I told John, he wouldn't be able to keep a poker face with Blair. He'd accuse her, give her a heads up, I don't know, but he wouldn't be able to sleep in the same bed as his wife. Once we find Justin's killer, all bets are off. He deserves to know—whether she's convicted or not—that his wife killed his son." She shook her head. "Why, dammit? Why would she do such a horrific thing?"

"These are the crimes I don't understand," Andrew said quietly. "It makes no sense, none. But I'll bet Lucy will have an idea."

Chapter Twenty-six

Lucy didn't say anything after Andrew shared the information about Blair Caldwell's trial. They were sitting in Andrew's office eating sandwiches that Lucy had brought in. She itched to look through the files, but didn't want to cross into that dark gray area . . . she was already on the line as it was. Andrew was typing up the information that he could legally give Max through her FOIA request. That information—which included name, date of hire and separation, previous employment, and limited personal details—would hopefully lead to answers.

Lucy hadn't been 100 percent positive that Andrew would be able to get the information from the Maricopa County DA, but Andrew had clout and respect among his peers and she'd hoped he'd be able to parlay that into valuable information.

This was valuable in more ways than one.

"Are you certain Dillon is going to be okay with this?" Andrew asked again.

"I talked to him last night. Max has a nonprofit that can pay his expenses, which won't be a conflict of interest. Expert witnesses are generally paid, and often by third parties. He's willing to testify without renumeration—he was just as angry as I was that this woman may have used Justin's murder as a blueprint for killing her own son."

"Proving it is going to be next to impossible."

"You'd be surprised, Andrew."

"Nothing surprises me anymore, Lucy."

"My guess is that she used her office computer for research because there are far stricter rules for law enforcement to obtain computers and computer records that are owned by a law office. She likely cleared her search history, and unless they were specifically looking for a connection, they wouldn't have seen it. But what most people don't know is that everything is archived somewhere. Her law firm probably automatically backs up all data at least nightly. They can't afford to lose anything in the event of a computer crash. That information includes search histories. The biggest question is whether those backups are still around after nearly a year—longer, because I suspect she's been thinking about this a long time."

"Why?" Max asked. "I don't disagree, but how can you be so certain?"

"Because she planned it. Everything she did was identical to Justin's murder, except the detail that was withheld from the public. But we'll be able to get forensics of any drugs in his system, if there were any. I suspect that Justin's killer used the same drug for Tommy Porter and Chris Donovan. It worked once, it worked twice, it worked three times—maybe more. Why change? In fact she hasn't changed anything about her MO and that troubles me more than anything."

"Why?" Andrew asked. "That's good—it makes a clearer connection for the jury."

"Because I think we're missing a victim between Tommy Porter and Chris Donovan. She may have had to improvise. She's cyclical. It also means that she's planning another murder. If we can't identify her, there will be another victim."

"She has to be older, at least in her fifties."

"Most likely she's between the ages of forty-five and fifty-five. She's determined. An eight-year-old boy might weigh sixty to eighty pounds, certainly light enough for a physically fit woman to carry. She's not going to stop until we stop her or she's dead."

Lucy's phone rang. She grabbed it, thinking it was Sean, but it was an unfamiliar number.

"Lucy Kincaid."

"Lucy, it's Don Katella."

"Hello, Don. I was going to touch base later today. Did you get the files from Andrew?" She knew he did, but they hadn't spoken since Thursday.

"Yes, and I read everything twice. I don't know that I have what you want, but I made a list of every female who was interviewed. Nothing struck me as off when I was reviewing my notes."

"I'd like to see that list. Can Ms. Revere and I come to your house this afternoon?"

"I have to run an errand for my wife, I can swing by your hotel when I'm done. Around three?"

"That would be great. If you could bring your notes as well, I might have some questions once we look through the names."

"I have everything in order. What hotel?"

"US Grant. Room Fourteen-oh-one." She gave him Max's room because of the timeline Max had on her wall—having a seasoned detective review their theories would be an added benefit.

"Snazzy place. I'll be there by three." He hung up.

"Katella?" Andrew asked.

"Yes, he didn't see anything, but he has a list of names, and that's going to help."

Andrew printed the information he'd put into the spreadsheet. It pained Lucy to watch him type so slow, but she couldn't very well offer to do it for him. "If a name pops up on Katella's list, let me know and I'll work on obtaining a warrant to use all the information in that specific personnel file."

Max grabbed the papers off the printer. "Eighteen names. Do you really think one of these women is who we're looking for?"

"Yes," Lucy said without hesitation. She looked at Andrew. "She knew you were having an affair and she stalked you and Nelia for months, if not longer. How long were you having the affair? I never asked."

"Eight months. Sheila wasn't married, we were both busy—we got together once or twice a month. It didn't even feel like that long . . . it had become routine. When Justin died, it was over."

"Did you love her?" Lucy didn't know why she asked—it wasn't her business.

He shook his head. "I liked her. A lot. Maybe I could have fallen in love, but I never planned on my marriage ending in divorce."

"I don't think love is planned. Either you do or you don't."

"Then I didn't. Because it was too easy to walk away after Justin. Maybe Justin was the only person I truly ever unconditionally loved," Andrew said quietly. "And he's gone. If you're right, Lucy, and this woman killed Justin to punish my infidelity, it worked. There hasn't been a day in the last nineteen and a half years that I haven't missed my son."

Lucy was surprised that Max was so quiet on the drive back to the hotel. No questions, no prying into her personal life, no discussion of the case. While Lucy was relieved on the one hand, she grew suspicious. One thing she'd learned quickly about Maxine Revere was that she was a sharp observer of human nature and intensely curious about every-thing. She didn't stop. She didn't slow down. She didn't let up *ever*. The dinner conversation the night before had drained Lucy, and in the back of her mind she couldn't help but think that Max wasn't going to stop prying into her life. Asking her questions didn't bother her—it was what Max might start doing without Lucy's knowledge that had her worried.

They walked through the lobby and Max made an immediate detour toward a group of chairs near the window. Lucy followed.

"You said you weren't coming down," she said to a man seated facing the lobby.

"I was done," he said and stood. "The drive wasn't bad, and I can be of more use to you here than in Santa Barbara."

"David, this is Agent Lucy Kincaid. Lucy, David Kane, my right hand."

Lucy took his hand. He was neither short or tall—just topped six feet—but with the posture of a soldier and the eyes of a cop. He had a scar down half of his right cheek and close-cropped hair. He looked like half the mercenaries her brother Jack worked with.

"Pleasure, Agent Kincaid."

"Lucy."

He nodded. "David."

"We're meeting with the lead detective from the Stanton murder," Max said, "I'll get you a room, then we'll head up to my suite."

"Ben got me a room."

"I might have something else for you to do."

"Today?"

"We'll talk about it. Let's debrief before the detective arrives."

Lucy wondered if Max was planning on going behind her back again. The reporter had been quiet ever since Lucy got back from talking to Carina. She hardly said more than two sentences in Andrew's office while they ate lunch. Something was up and Lucy didn't know what it was.

That made her very nervous.

Lucy got off on the floor before Max. "I'm going to call Sean, then I'll be up."

"You don't mind if I fill David in on the plan?"

"Go ahead."

Lucy let herself into her room and called Sean. He answered almost immediately.

"I miss you," he said.

"It's only been two days."

"Feels like two weeks."

"I talked to Carina this morning. It went well."

"I'm still mad about Thursday night."

"I had a long conversation with Dillon. I understand so much better now."

"Because you look at everyone's point of view. That still doesn't excuse the way your family treated you."

"I forgive them."

"You're a better person than me."

Sean was protective of her, and she loved him for it, but she didn't want this situation to permanently damage his relationship with half her family. Especially since he was so close to Patrick and Jack.

"Sean, I'm okay." She'd been hurt, especially the conversation with her father, but she *would* be okay.

"This is me, Luce," Sean said quietly. "How is the investigation going? Is Revere minding her manners?"

Lucy almost laughed. "We had a nice dinner last night. She was fishing for information—out of curiosity. She doesn't like that she hasn't figured me out."

"Let's keep it that way."

"We have a list of suspects. A few stand out to me. Detective Katella is coming over with his notes and then . . . I'm hoping one of the names matches." She wasn't hoping. She was almost 100 percent sure that one of the names would match. "I talked to the assistant chief in Santa Barbara—he wants to help, but he also wants a formal FBI request."

"There are a half dozen people you can have request the information."

"I'm not going to risk anyone else."

"Risk?"

"Reprimand. Suspension. I know the career risk, I'm willing to take it."

"Lucy—"

"Please, Sean." He had to understand her predicament.

"Okay. I'll drop it, for now."

"I might have a back door to get the information. If I have a name or two, the assistant chief may give me a yay or nay, and at this point, that's all I need to push forward. I can turn everything over to the local FBI office with an actual suspect, and they can get the information through the proper channels."

"That sounds like a good plan."

"It was Max's."

"You told her about your leave? Or, rather, lack of time?"

"Not in so many words, but the woman is astute."

"She raises the hackles on the back of my neck, Lucy."

"On this, I trust her."

Lucy deliberately changed the subject.

"How was the RCK meeting?"

"It's not over."

"I thought JT locked you all up until the meeting was over."

"Patrick and I led a mutiny at two. That's two in the *morning*. We bought a twelve-hour reprieve. Today should go faster. We still have a few security issues to work through, and then replacing Jayne."

Jayne had been the computer guru and primary researcher for RCK until she'd leaked information. Though she hadn't been malicious in her actions, it had created a huge problem for the group. She'd been with them for ten years and knew a lot about the organization and the people. There had even been talk about letting her stay in a different capacity, but no one was comfortable with her in the office. JT had found her a job as the IT manager for a software company. Perhaps she didn't deserve the recommendation, but Lucy understood how the situation had spiraled out of control. Jayne hadn't intended for anyone to get hurt, she didn't even know that the information she shared would put Sean and his brothers in danger—and Lucy.

"She's going to be hard to replace," Lucy concurred.

"I have someone in mind, but you'll be upset."

"Why?"

"Because I want to take him from the FBI."

She knew immediately who he was referring to. "Zach."

"He's perfect. Smart, young, loyal, and I've already run a deep background on him."

"Honestly, Sean, I wouldn't be upset except that I would miss him. He *is* good. And I don't want any more changes in my squad. But it's his decision. Maybe he doesn't want to leave."

"He has no family in Texas. His parents are semiretired in Florida. His sister is in college in Oregon. He's in San Antonio because that's where the FBI assigned him when he graduated. He's squeaky clean and has a genius level IQ. The problem is that JT has an agreement with Rick Stockton that he won't poach anyone from the FBI. He's only allowed to bring in agents who have retired, or who seek out a position on their own—like when Mitch Bianchi came over from Sac FBI a few years ago. He wanted to leave, JT and Rick hashed out the details, and it worked out. But we can't go to Zach and offer him a position."

"You're going to do it anyway, aren't you."

"I have to be sneaky about it. I probably shouldn't have even mentioned it to you."

"I won't say anything.

"Hold on."

Lucy glanced at her watch. Nearly three—she needed to meet Katella. She didn't want him talking to Max alone. She was still a little worried about what the reporter had planned because she was far too quiet.

"Luce?"

"I'm here."

"I need to go. I'll call you when we're done tonight or if it takes longer than I think, I'll call in the morning and let you know when I'll be in San Diego."

"I don't know that I'm going to leave tomorrow."

Sean didn't say anything. He knew as well as she did that her new boss wasn't going to be pleased with her.

"I can always use your brains."

"You have them. Be careful. I love you."

"Love you, too."

She hung up. Sean hadn't said it, but she could sense his reservations. He didn't like her new boss either, but he also knew how much she loved her job.

You'll find a way to make it work. You have to.

"What's going on?" David asked Max after they entered her suite.

Max shot him a narrow-eyed glance. "I'm in the middle of an investigation."

"You're quiet."

"You can tell after five minutes?"

"I can see you thinking."

"Psychic, too."

"What job do you have for me? You seemed unhappy that I came down today. Should I head back up to Santa Barbara?"

"No, I was going to get you a plane ticket direct to Scottsdale."

"What do you want me to do?"

"Blair killed her son."

"You're certain?"

"We know Justin's killer is not Peter's killer. And Lucy—she has a profile on Blair, though she didn't share."

"Profile? You didn't tell me she was a profiler."

"She's not, at least not officially. She started talking about Blair, but then clammed up, as if I was going to broadcast every word."

"Don't hold that against her."

"I'm not."

David arched his eyebrow. He was actually *smiling* at her frustration. She ignored his unspoken commentary and said, "I'm going to take the trial. Ace will be angry with me, but that's hardly news."

"You need me to lay the ground work."

"Ben will send someone later in the week. The trial starts a week from Monday. I need you to do what you do best."

"Making sure no one takes a shot at you?"

"Hardly." Where had that come from? "Talk to the cops. They know me, I ran the circuit when I got there last week. I want insight. Personal stories. You know what I need."

"I'm not the best person."

"Cops like you."

"They don't dislike me. Big difference."

"You can fly out on Monday. Take tomorrow off."

David grunted. "What would I do?"

"Relax."

David smiled. "I relax about as well as you do."

Max turned on the Keurig in the kitchenette and waited for the water to heat.

"You okay?" David asked.

"About what?"

"You're off today."

Was she? Maybe. She wanted Blair to be innocent. Not because she liked the woman, but because of John.

"How can a woman kill her child?" Max stared at the counter. "Blair has money. They're comfortable. She didn't even *snap*. At least how I think of someone snapping. She planned it all—researched the murders of other children, planned when and where and how, then executed it. Then, when it was all done, she went back to a fucking *party* and put on a happy face so no one knew any different. No one knew she'd killed a child. Her *son*. Went back for another martini and made small talk then came home and pretended she was stunned to find Peter missing. Why, David? How could she do that? And keep up the farce?"

David didn't say anything. What could anyone say? How could anyone make sense of this crime? Max couldn't even make sense of the profile Lucy Kincaid had created on the woman who killed Justin and two other little boys. But at least there was a *reason*. The woman was crazy—maybe not legally, but certainly she was twisted—but she at least had a reason for killing. Some perverse sense of punishment for the men who cheated on their wives . . . cheated on their families. While Max didn't understand it, at least the bitch had a *reason*.

Blair had no reason. She killed her son and pretended she didn't. She pretended she was a victim as much as Peter and John. She was cold. Calculating. She expected to get away with it, to be found not guilty, to continue to live her life of privilege married to a man she had emotionally gutted. And there was nothing that Max wanted more than to watch the justice system destroy her with the rope she handed them. Blair Caldwell would not get away with murder. If the justice system didn't take care of it, Max would destroy her life, piece by piece.

Max prepared coffee black for David, then put another pod in for herself.

"I take it things are working out with Agent Kincaid," David said.

"I made lemonade," Max said.

"You copied me into your memo to Ben. I know about the meeting with the shrinks last night."

"She's smart. She doesn't act like a rookie."

"So what's her story? I was surprised you didn't give Ben something more about her. She seems . . . interesting."

"To say the least." Max took her coffee and added cream and sweetener, then sat on one of the stools. "The woman shares nothing about herself. She'll talk about the case until the cows come home, but the only personal thing I could get out of her is that she loves chocolate."

"I'm sure you observed more."

"No. That's it—she's closed off. Like a veil is hanging around her. I can put some things together, like she was more upset about her failed meeting with her family than she wanted me to know. She and her husband have what seems like a too-perfect relationship that makes me want to gag—it's straight out of a fairy tale. Except then she shares one little tidbit about how they don't keep secrets. I pushed—I had to—and she was deliberate in how she answered. She doesn't drink too much alcohol, she loves coffee almost as much as I do, and she seems to know me better than I know her."

"I can see why that would bother you."

"I just want to know what makes her tick. She's said a few things that stuck with me—particularly related to the case. Like, when we were talking about Blair possibly being guilty, she said *we won't let her get away with it.* Maybe it was the way she said it—the intensity. I don't know exactly what, but she's like me in some ways—a dog with a bone, as you once said—and in other ways she is my polar opposite. I pushed Andrew this morning—we had a good conversation while sorting through files— and he wouldn't tell me squat. He let slip that it wasn't Justin's murder that pushed Lucy into the FBI. So what was it? He told me he wouldn't tell me and not to ask about it."

"Is it relevant to this case?"

"No, but—"

"Then leave it alone. Some things are better left buried."

David might be right, and there was nothing about Lucy's past that impacted this particular investigation. Well, Max didn't know that, did she? She didn't know anything *about* Lucy's past.

"I think you're ticked off because her husband pushed your buttons, made you promise something you didn't want to promise."

"You mean I can't say word one about either of them."

David was right. That had rubbed her the wrong way.

There was a knock at the door, and David answered. Lucy walked in. "Don Katella's not here?"

Max shook her head. "Coffee?"

"Yes, thank you."

Max made the coffee, then said, "I should have just ordered up a pot from room service."

Lucy sat across from David. He said, "Max said your brother was in the army."

"Yes, my oldest brother, Jack."

"Where?"

"I was practically a baby when he enlisted—I know he went to boot camp at Fort Bragg, then did a tour in Central America. Became Delta a couple years later."

"I was army. Rangers."

Lucy smiled. "I thought so. There's something familiar about you."

"We haven't met."

"No, but there's a familiarity in those who served, especially career. My brother-in-law Duke was in the army for three years, he doesn't have the same edge that Jack does."

"But they both work for RCK."

Lucy glanced at Max. Max ignored the question in her eyes—was David actually getting more information out of Lucy than she could?

"Yes."

"Max has their press kit. Made me read it."

Lucy laughed. "RCK does a lot more than hostage rescue and personal security."

"But that's what they're known for."

"True, it's how they started the business. They employ many former servicemen and women. The transition years, especially if you were deployed overseas, are difficult. Being able to use those skills can help bridge the gap between service and civilian life. Some can never fully leave."

"It's a way of life."

"But you left."

"I hadn't planned to, but it was the right time."

There was another knock on the door and Max inwardly groaned. David was expertly working Lucy, and she wanted more . . . but she didn't dare interject because Lucy was sharp enough to figure it out. Max didn't even think that David was knowingly pumping Lucy for information about herself and her family.

Max let Katella in. "We're glad you could make it," she said. "We have some names and want to compare them to your list."

"I'll do whatever I can to help," he said, but it was clear to Max that he was skeptical.

"Coffee?"

"Thank you."

Why hadn't she ordered room service? She made Katella a cup with the Keurig and David introduced himself.

Katella seemed impressed with her wall of information. "This is extensive."

"Nothing we didn't tell you on Thursday, but I like the visual," Max said.

"You said four victims, but you crossed off this last victim."

"Not the same killer," Max said. "We now have two different cases, and Caldwell is already on trial. I don't want to focus on her right now"—she handed Katella the mug—"we have a lead on Justin Stanton's killer."

"Possibly," Lucy qualified. "Max used the Freedom of Information Act to obtain information about certain county employees, and Andrew expedited the request—he pulled the information himself. But we wanted to make sure that if there were any legal issues, we had the paperwork as backup. We have all the information that we're legally able to obtain on eighteen employees. Women, between the ages of twenty-five and thirty-five at the time of Justin's murder, who left employment within a year of his death."

Katella handed Lucy a two-page list of handwritten names. "These are all the women who were interviewed—their personal information, such as their address at the time of their interview is in the files. I didn't think to copy it."

"We'll double-check the addresses if we have a common name. How do you verify identity when you interview someone?"

"Driver's license, though if we're canvassing we wouldn't ask for ID. We make note of the house we approached."

Max hadn't thought to ask that question, but it made sense. Double-checking the information they obtained from Andrew with the information Katella gleaned at the time of the murder.

Lucy read the names and immediately said, "Danielle Sharpe."

"How did you see that so quickly?" Max ran a finger down the print out that Andrew had given her.

"I had a few names in my head based on the information on the spreadsheet." Lucy asked Katella, "What do you remember about her?"

Katella seemed to be surprised that they'd narrowed the suspect pool down so quickly. And to be honest, Max was surprised herself. It was never this easy.

Easy? Was this really easy? Or did you just have someone who knew exactly what to look for?

"Um—" Katella seemed flustered. He opened the box he'd brought and dug through loosely organized notepads, most of which had sticky notes with names written on the tabs. "I marked each of those interviews. Let me find it . . ."

It took him a minute, but he located the notebook. "Here—I didn't interview her myself. Oh, yeah. First responders interviewed her that morning. She was a neighbor who helped in the search. Remember, we didn't find Justin's body until late the next day. For a time we thought he might have left the house on his own and got lost."

"We?" Lucy asked.

"I didn't—kids his age don't usually wander out of the house in the middle of the night, and I wasn't called until the body was found. However, because he had his blanket some people thought maybe he got it in his head to camp or something. His mother told us he loved camping and was planning for a sleepaway camp with his best friend."

Max looked at Lucy and saw pain. Bittersweet memories? Was she the best friend?

"Sharpe handed out flyers to all the neighbors."

"You said she was a neighbor, but was she interviewed at Andrew's house?"

"Correct."

"Did she give her address?"

"No. We were in a different mode then—search."

"And you never interviewed her again."

"Yes, I did. I had her number, called her on the phone and asked follow-up questions. She didn't have anything that helped. Here." He handed Lucy his notepad.

While Lucy scanned the interview shorthand, Max looked at the line item that Andrew had prepared. Danielle Sharpe, age thirty-one, had left employment at the end of the year—six months after Justin's murder. She was a legal secretary, but it didn't indicate if she worked for Andrew or another prosecutor.

"How do the legal secretaries get assigned?" Max asked.

Lucy looked at her in confusion. "I have no idea."

"Depends," Katella said. "Andrew would know best. I know he has his own dedicated legal secretary, and a few of the other senior attorneys do as well, but it's more a pool system. They get assigned based on workload and experience."

"Andrew was a new ADA, so he would have been part of that process. He could have crossed paths with her. Max, there was no line item about marital status."

"It wasn't in the employee records, though there was emergency contact information."

"We need that, but I want to pick Andrew's brain. Give me two more legal secretaries on the list, I don't care who, and I'm going to run all three by Andrew."

"I don't understand," Katella said. "Why not just ask him?"

"Because if I'm right, this woman killed his son, and Andrew isn't going to be thinking like a prosecutor—he's going to be thinking like a grieving father."

"There's one more name in Katella's notes," Max said. "This woman—Jan DuBois. Why didn't you home in on her?"

"She doesn't live in the neighborhood."

"Does that have to be a factor?"

"Her previous employment was as dispatcher in the sheriff's department of San Diego County. I'm confident that whoever killed Justin came from out of state. Danielle fits that."

Max was skeptical. She believed in instincts—depended on them—but she was also methodical in her approach.

"But," Lucy continued, "I'll include her in my questioning to Andrew. Good?"

"Yes."

There were no other common names to both lists. Max pulled one other legal secretary who had left employment one year almost to the day of Justin's murder and Lucy called Andrew and put him on speaker.

"Andrew, I'm here with Max, her assistant David Kane, and Detective Katella."

"Don, how've you been?"

"Can't complain."

"Thank you for your help."

"Andrew," Lucy said, "I have three names I want to run by you."

"You think one of them killed Justin."

"Not necessarily. I don't want you to overthink it, okay? Just tell me if you know them, what you remember about them, first recollection."

"Who?"

"Jan DuBois."

"Jan? Don't tell me—"

"Don't read into this, Andrew. Just spill it."

"I've known Jan for years. She's been married to Bill DuBois since before I met her. He's now the assistant sheriff. She was a legal secretary for several years after she had two girls, thirteen months apart, then when they started school she went to law school. She's in private practice now. The girls—jeez, I haven't seen them in ages. They're probably in college. They were a few years younger than Justin, if I recall. I see Bill and Jan at least once a year."

"Katella interviewed her about whether she knew of your relationship with Sheila and about your marriage."

"He interviewed a lot of people on staff." There was a tone of bitterness in his voice.

"Buddy," Katella said, "I was doing my job."

"I know, Don. Sorry. It was a miserable year."

"Christina Hernandez."

"I don't remember her."

"She was the legal secretary to the DA, left employment in June the year after Justin's murder."

"I don't remember, seriously. I vaguely remember the DA's legal secretary, but I didn't interact with her much. Hold on." Max heard him rummaging through files.

Lucy said, "Don't give me anything I shouldn't have."

Max was going to tear her hair out if they had to walk the straight and narrow. *This* was the reason she didn't like working with cops.

"You could leave the room," Max said.

Lucy gave her such a look that Max almost did a double take.

"Just an idea," Max mumbled.

Andrew said over the phone, "I can tell you that she doesn't fit your profile, does that help?"

"Yes, just keep her information handy. Last name. Danielle Sharpe."

Silence.

"You don't know her, either?" Max said. Damn, and she thought it had been a good lead. Didn't mean she was innocent, but she would be harder to investigate if they had to go back to square one.

Andrew said, "I remember Danielle."

"It was nearly twenty years ago," Lucy said. "That's a really good memory."

Lucy sounded almost like she was interrogating Andrew. It was subtle, but Max didn't miss the tone.

"She almost screwed up one of my biggest cases in my early career. Not something I would forget."

"Explain."

"It was more my fault for trusting her with something so crucial, but she'd done outstanding work for one of my colleagues, and I was still new—I'd only been in the DA's office for two years at that point, still making a name for myself."

"What specifically did she do?"

"I had her researching cases to back up a fraud case I was prosecuting. She screwed up every citation. *Every single one.* I called her on the carpet for it—she blamed the computer program she was using, that it had shifted columns so everything was one off. Still, the DA pulled the case from me and gave it to one of my rivals."

"Did you believe her?"

"Why shouldn't I have? Mistakes happen—I was furious at the time."

"When was this?"

Andrew took a long pause. "I got the case at the beginning of the year. It would have been around April. Before Justin. Are you saying she killed my son because I got her in trouble?"

"No," Lucy said. "I'm not saying anything."

"Then why all these questions?"

"Do you know if she was married?"

"I didn't know anything personal about her. I never worked with her again. I considered her incompetent, but ultimately, it was my responsibility to double-check her research."

"Thank you. I'll let you go and—"

"Stop. Don't you dare hang up, Lucy! Is this the woman who killed my son? Why? Dammit, Lucy, you owe me that!"

Lucy bristled, and Max said in a calm, controlled voice, "Andrew, I'm sure you don't mean that."

He swore in the background. Something crashed to the ground.

"Listen to me," Lucy said. "*Back off.* I know exactly what you're thinking."

"You don't."

"Yes, I do. I didn't want to tip you off because you would go off half-cocked and try to find her. Confront her. She killed your son and everything you felt then, you're feeling now. I will find her, Andrew, and if she is guilty, *I will prove it.* I promise you, Andrew. I'm not letting this go."

"Okay. Okay." He took a deep breath. "I'm sorry—I'm just—you're right. I haven't felt myself since Max called and told me she was looking at Justin's murder. I have a question, though."

"Of course."

"Are you saying Don interviewed her? Is that why her name came up?"

"Yes."

"Why?"

Katella spoke up. "She was at your house the morning after Justin disappeared. There were dozens of people there—she said she was a neighbor, but I don't have her address in the files."

"A neighbor. I didn't know. I never saw her there."

"You weren't home that morning. According to my notes, you were out looking for Justin with one of the first responding officers, then insisted that he take you to the station so you could run all sex offenders. Then I believe you went to your office to find out who might have been released recently that you put away. All the things I would have done—and did do—after he turned up dead."

"Those days are a blur. All I really remember was when Nell called me and said Justin was gone. I remember bits and pieces . . . but the pain is always here. Always."

"Andrew," Lucy said, "you know me. You know I'll never back down. I will find Danielle Sharpe, and if she killed Justin, she will be punished to the fullest extent of the law."

"I think it's time you bring this to the police," Andrew said.

Max leaned forward. She wasn't giving this up, not yet. She was close, and as soon as the police got involved, she'd be shut out.

"We don't have enough," Lucy said before Max could comment. She shot Max a look and shook her head. What did she think Max was going to say or do?

"What do you mean? We have a suspect! She matches all of your criteria."

"Andrew, we have no idea what her background is, where she's from, if she's married or was married or lost a child. We don't know where she is or what she's doing. We have no physical evidence to tie her to the murders. *None.* We turn this over to the police—even here in San Diego where you have clout—they will be stymied because they don't have the resources to pursue this out of the area. They'll pass it along to whichever jurisdiction she lives in now, and they'll talk to her—and that will get us nowhere. She's never been interviewed as a suspect to our knowledge, and I don't want to spook her—not until we have something solid. This is a multijurisdictional case, and as soon as I have *anything* tangible, I'll give everything to the FBI. You know they'll be able to expedite this—I'll call in every favor to make it happen. We don't have it, not now. But we will."

"You believe that."

"Yes," Lucy said without hesitation.

"Let me know what I can do. Anything."

"Right now, go home. Do something to take your mind off this."

"That won't happen, but I have a charity event I'm supposed to go to tonight. That'll distract me for a bit."

"I'll call you later."

Lucy hung up. "David, would you be able to contact the assistant sheriff in Santa Barbara? I talked to him this morning. I don't want to put in a formal request, but he seemed to be open to answering yes or no questions if we have a name."

"You want me to ask if he interviewed Danielle Sharpe."

"Yes."

"Tommy's uncle has been helping—he's a cop."

"Can he talk to the parents about her? I would like to talk to them myself if possible."

"I'll feel him out, see what he thinks, but I suspect they want him to mediate."

"That'll work for now, but later, they may need to come forward, go on record about this woman."

"Understood," David said. He stepped out of the main room and onto the balcony to make the calls.

"She didn't give me the vibe," Katella said. "I don't even really remember her."

"That's exactly what she wants and expects." She snapped her fingers. "I can't believe I didn't think of this." She got back on the phone. "Andrew, do you have employee photos? Would those be covered under the FOIA Max filed?" She listened, then said, "Send it to both me and Max. Thanks."

She hung up. Max was watching her closely. Lucy was certainly in her element, but there was something more—a maturity she hadn't really noticed before. The focus? Yes. The borderline obsession? Yes. But she'd smoothly taken over the investigation. Had it just happened or had it been happening all along?

What surprised Max more than anything was that she didn't care as much as she thought she would. Yes, she wanted to write about these cold cases. Yes, she wanted to give justice to these innocent victims and their families. In the past, she would have fought tooth and nail against bringing in any law enforcement agency until she had practically solved their case and turned it over with a pretty monogrammed Maxine Revere bow. She would have fought and won—she knew how the game was played, she knew how to manipulate the system, and she firmly believed—because it had been proven to her over and over again that when the police got a cold case, nothing would happen, even if she gave them some juicy facts.

Maybe it was Lucy herself. Max had the distinct impression—based on little things here and there—that Lucy was putting her career on the chopping block by working with Max. Not specifically because she was here with Max, but because she was pursuing an investigation without sanction from her office, way out of her jurisdiction. The more Max learned about the rookie, the more she realized she didn't know—and damnit, she wanted to know everything. Lucy Kincaid was one of the most mysterious and interesting people Max had met in a long, long time.

She had to convince Lucy to let her interview her for *Maximum Exposure*. She had to find a way. Max would work through the FBI's media office, and she usually got what she wanted.

"I can find Danielle Sharpe," Max said.

"How?" Lucy asked.

"The power of the media."

Lucy frowned. "You can't expose her, not yet."

"No, I should say, the power of my research staff. They're the best, and I don't say that lightly. Give me a couple hours."

"Okay, thank you. I need to call Dillon."

"Why?" Why was Max even worried about it? Dillon Kincaid was not only helping, he was going to testify for the prosecution against Blair Caldwell. He was on their side.

"Andrew didn't know she was at the house after Justin was kidnapped. But Nelia would. She might not remember, but Dillon needs to talk to her. What if Danielle Sharpe kept in contact with her? What if she has another connection to my sister? There's *something* that set her off, something that made her target Justin. Without more, there's no way the FBI or any other agency is going to touch this."

"Okay, you're right," Max said, relieved. Lucy *did* understand, and they were on the same page.

"I should go," Katella said. "I still need to do those errands for my wife, though this conversation has been far more interesting." He picked up his box of files. "If you need anything else, call me."

Lucy walked him to the door, said something Max couldn't hear, then let him out.

"Can I use this office to call Dillon?" Lucy asked Max, gesturing to the small den off the living room.

"Of course," Max said. She waited until Lucy closed the door, then she called Ben.

"Hello, darling," Max said.

"You want something."

"I always want something, it's why you love me."

"It's six thirty on Saturday night."

"The news never sleeps. I need to find a person, and it needs to be hush-hush."

"Research staff is off. It can wait until Monday."

"No, it can't."

"What did you do before you had a staff?"

"I didn't have to commit any time to filming a show, writing three articles a week for a Web page, or covering trials. I took one case at a time and hired people to get me information I needed when I needed it. I could always go back to my old life."

"You'd hate it."

"I'd love it, and you damn well know it."

Ben sighed. "What."

"I'm sending you the photograph, name, and basic statistics of a person of interest, we'll call her. I need to know where she lived prior to Justin Stanton's murder and where she is now."

"You don't ask—you have a suspect?"

His tone changed midsentence.

"You did it, didn't you?" Ben continued, excited.

"Not alone."

"And the fed is letting you run with this?"

"She's not *letting* me do anything. We need more information. You can't air a word of this—we don't want to spook her. But I'll give you one more thing—I'll cover the Blair Caldwell trial."

"What? Really? That's terrific!"

"You're going to have to tell Ace, I'm not going to get in another shouting match with him."

"I can handle Ace, but why the change?"

"She's guilty. I know it. Kincaid got her brother to agree to be an expert witness, the DA is considering it, and we may even be able to help."

"Can you solve Justin Stanton's murder before the trial starts?"

"If we can find this person, yeah. I think so." So she was stretching a bit. But Ben needed to be fully committed and see the potential of the show. The trial, with bonus content of Max being involved in solving a similar cold case and through that proving that Blair Caldwell is a cold-blooded killer. Max didn't have to explain the potential—he usually saw it before her.

"I want Lucy Kincaid on tape."

"So do I." She glanced at the closed door. "That might be trickier."

"I've been exceptionally discreet, but I'm learning more about her."

Max felt uncomfortable. She wanted the information, but she had promised Lucy and Sean that she wouldn't dig around.

No, you promised them you wouldn't quote them or mention them without express permission. You never promised you wouldn't dig around.

"She has a thick sealed FBI file."

"Before or after she graduated?"

"Both, seems to go back to when she was eighteen."

"And?"

"I don't have it—I'm not going to touch it with a ten-foot pole. My contact at the FBI office gave me a heads-up about it, as a way of steering me away from pursuing it. Seems people asking about the file are reprimanded or reassigned. It's—extremely odd."

It most certainly was. It was a situation Max would pursue in a heartbeat. Instead, she said, "Drop it."

"I never in a million years thought you'd say that."

"I want to tread carefully."

"I'm sending you a report I dug up on a California crime blog. I don't know how much of it is accurate, but the guy who writes it seems to be in the know."

"What's it about?"

"Last Christmas, Kincaid was held hostage by a gunman at the hospital morgue and apparently saved the lives of the other hostages, then helped catch a mercy killer. The crime blog pulled from articles and an interview with an unnamed source, but according to him, no one figured it out until Kincaid came along and put disparate information together. And then I was talking to a friend of mine in Texas—"

"Texas? I thought you hated the South."

"I didn't go down to visit him, good God, I used the phone. He was privy to the details of Operation Heatwave, which was a multiagency sting in the greater San Antonio area. Took down wanted felons, bail jumpers, et cetera. Kincaid was part of it—not only part of it, but word is she went undercover to rescue a group of orphaned boys who were being used by the cartels as mules. He wasn't positive about the details— he thinks they might have been foster kids, because shortly after Heatwave was over, details came out about a corrupt social worker and he suspects there was a connection. But without making inquiries, we won't know the truth. But I did find out one fact."

"Tell me," Max said, watching the door closely. The last thing she wanted was Lucy walking into the room while she was talking about it.

"She solved the murder of Harper Worthington."

"The husband of that corrupt congresswoman? Who was caught taking bribes but then was killed or something?" Max hated politics, and she hadn't followed the case considering it was Texas.

"She was murdered by the cartels she was laundering money for."

"I hate politics."

"Which is why you don't remember the case. But it was huge. And your pal Kincaid was in the middle of it."

"As a rookie."

"Apparently."

The door opened and Max said, "I have to go, can you get that information on Sharpe? I sent you everything I have."

"I'll call in Debbie."

"Is she the one who likes baseball?"

"That's Trinity. Debbie is the best fact-checker we have and adopts every stray animal on the planet."

"I owe her."

"Buy her a year supply of dog and cat food and I think she'd be happy." Ben hung up.

"All good?" Max asked Lucy.

"Dillon is calling Nelia." Lucy was distracted. She glanced out the window to where David was still on his phone.

"That doesn't really answer my question," Max said. "You look troubled."

"Let's say we get everything we want—proof that Danielle Sharpe was in each city at the time of the murders. That she worked with one of the parents. That she lost her son. Even if we can prove that her husband was having an affair, none of that proves that she's the killer. We have no physical evidence. We don't have probable cause for a search warrant. We have some circumstantial evidence that doesn't really mean anything, except to us. She gets a good lawyer, we don't even get to talk to her."

"Then we'll talk to her before she even knows she's a suspect."

"I can't. I'm a federal agent, if I go and talk to her I'm going to be tipping my hand. And if I lie about who I am, then anything I learn can be thrown out."

"I can talk to her. I'm a reporter. Believe me, I'm used to pulling information out of people who don't want to talk."

"Maybe," Lucy said, but she didn't seem happy about it.

"This is my job, and I usually don't work with a cop for this exact reason—you can't do what I can do."

David walked back inside. "In a word, yes. Danielle Sharpe was interviewed by Santa Barbara PD. She worked for the same law firm as Doug Porter, joined six months after she left San Diego. She was interviewed not because she was a suspect, but because she was Porter's personal legal secretary and was required to turn over certain documents and calendars. She's also the one who told the police about the affair—though she didn't call it that. She said he was out with a client and gave the name and location. According to Porter's brother-in-law—the cop I've been talking to—Porter was surprised she knew the information, but she said she thought Porter was working off-book for a client, against the policy of the law office. She claimed she didn't know he was cheating on his wife."

"She knew because she stalked him," Max said, glancing at Lucy for confirmation.

Lucy nodded. "That's exactly right."

"Why didn't he know?" Max asked. "Porter admitted he didn't know she had the information."

"Because his son was dead," David said. "He wasn't thinking about anything else but his son and his family."

"David's right," Lucy said. "Unless the police had a reason to draw his attention to his assistant, he wouldn't have thought about it. David, I really would like to talk to Chris Donovan's mother."

"I haven't attempted to contact her," David said.

"My staff did," Max said, "and she blew us off. But I have her contact information."

"She knows this woman, I'm positive."

"Danielle worked with the fathers."

"Chris's father worked in computers. His mother is an attorney, right? Private practice?"

Max confirmed. "She and her partner worked in tax law."

"Partner?" Lucy asked.

"Yes," Max flipped through her binder of background information. "Sandra Gillogley."

"We talk to her, then. Are they still partners?"

"Yes."

"There's loyalty there, especially since they have a small office. Okay,

I think the primary goal is to confirm that Danielle Sharpe worked there when Chris Donovan was murdered, then ask about the circumstances of employment."

"As if we're looking to hire her?" Max asked.

"Yes."

"I'll do it," David said.

"Why you?" Max countered.

"Because you're too damn nosy and you'll make a lawyer nervous," David said. "I know exactly what information you need."

"It's Saturday," Max said. "She's not going to be in the office. What's your excuse calling her at home?"

"I don't need one. We have her cell phone number. It's what we pay that research staff of yours for."

David sat down at the desk, wrote some notes, and dialed. He put his finger to his lips, then put his phone on speaker.

"Hello."

"Sandra Gillogley, please."

"This is Sandra. Who's this?"

"David Kane, assistant to Mr. Revere at Sterling Revere Hopewell in Menlo Park."

Max was impressed. David had used her family's law firm.

"What can I do for you, Mr. Kane?"

"I'm calling regarding a résumé that has come across my desk. I'm fact-checking details."

"Go ahead."

"Did Ms. Danielle Sharpe work for your firm from 2011 through 2013?"

"Yes, she did. July of '11 through December of '13."

"Under her duties she listed legal secretary responsibilities as well as light office work, preparation of filings, and the like."

"Correct."

"What was the workload of your office? Light, moderate, heavy?"

"Light, though during tax season extremely heavy."

"Was Ms. Sharpe capable if handling the variety of workloads?"

"Mostly."

"Can you elaborate?"

"She did her job well, she was meticulous—absolutely essential when working in tax law—but during crunch time, she became testy. We're a small office and even my partner and I are irritable in April."

"She indicated that she left to pursue another opportunity, but it's unclear if it was voluntary or if she was asked to leave."

"I would say it was mutual."

"Can you elaborate?"

"Danielle was a good employee, and more competent and mature than most legal secretaries we've had over the years. But my partner went through a traumatic event early in 2013, and I felt Danielle was far too interested in her personal life. At first, she was very kind, even commiserated with my partner. But it turned a bit . . . well, let's just say, too interested."

"That's a little vague. Would you say she was personally involved in your partner's life? Perhaps to the point of being uncomfortable."

Silence. Had David tipped his hand?

"That's a pointed question."

"I apologize—while Sterling is a civil law firm, I originally came from criminal law and tend to look at situations from that viewpoint."

"I can say this. My partner lost her son in early 2013. Apparently, so did Danielle, years before. I suspect that Cindy's loss triggered some deep emotions in Danielle and she felt the need to overshare details with Cindy, which caused my partner distress. I suggested that Danielle find someone else to talk to about it—it was clear to me she was deeply pained—and Danielle did not take my suggestion in the way I intended. We decided that it would be best if she leave. I assured her I would give her outstanding recommendations—because she did a good job for us—and I have been called twice for a reference, which I happily gave. In fact, two years ago one of my law school classmates hired Danielle into his law firm and thanked me for the referral."

"What is his name?"

Again, silence. "If she didn't list it on her resumé, perhaps they left on less than stellar terms."

"It's even more important that I speak with him."

"Don't hire her. If anyone lied on a resumé, they'd go into the trash bin. If there's nothing else?"

"No, ma'am. Thank you for your time."

David hung up.

"Sorry," he said.

"Sorry?" Lucy said. "That was perfect. Any more and she would have become suspicious. But I need that name. Two years—she's still there, I'm certain of it."

"How do you find out?"

Max already was on it. She googled Sandra Gillogley. "She graduated in 1989 from Whittier Law School." She typed in another search bar. "They average about seven hundred students in enrollment, full- and part-time."

"I don't suppose the Web site had a way to sort by graduates within two years of her," Lucy said.

"No, but if he's a member of the bar, my staff can track him down. Or, at least, a list of potentials."

"She's in California," Lucy said. "Most likely she's going to stick with what she's familiar in, and working for fifteen years in the law in California between Andrew, Doug Porter, and Donovan means she's not going to venture too far."

"You'd be surprised how small the number could be," Max said. "But it's still going to take time." She sent a message to Ben, then immediately shut down her e-mail so she didn't have to read a rant. He wouldn't be happy.

"We have exactly what we need." Lucy walked over to Max's timeline and wrote details about Danielle Sharpe's employment. Max fought the urge to object—she never let anyone else write on her timeline. "I'll bet Andrew can talk to human resources and find out if there were any inquires into Sharpe's employment." She made notes on a small pad. "Sandra said she suggested that Danielle talk to someone, probably a psychologist. That would set Danielle off. To her, there's nothing wrong with her. It's everyone else who has a problem. But I also suspect that deep down she has a fear that someone will be able to see through her, see what she's done." She continued writing.

Max hadn't made the connection, but as soon as Lucy said it, it was obvious.

"Why hasn't anyone seen through her?" Max wondered out loud.

"Because she has no friends. No one who can get close. That two-lawyer office was as close to friends as she had, but Sandra didn't sound like the type of person would would get chummy with her support staff. And Danielle would have put up walls to ensure there was no personal connection. She has no close friends, everyone is superficial. If she stayed in any one place for a long time, people would notice, but they might not think much of it. Most people aren't that observant."

"Yet Katella said she was at the Stanton house helping with the search."

"A criminal often goes back to the scene of their crime."

"Why?"

"Different reasons. For arsonists it's usually sexual, or a way to see their handiwork in full glory. For killers it's more complicated. Either to absorb the pain of others, or to gloat, or to make sure no one suspects them. For Danielle? A combination of regret and gloating. She needed validation. She wanted Andrew's affair to be revealed, she wanted him to suffer, and she wanted—needed—to see that."

"But Andrew didn't see her at the house."

"That he remembers. She was there, at least once, and saw Nelia turn Andrew away. It validated her. Finally, the woman has some sense, sees the truth, too bad it took the death of her only son to notice her husband is a cheating asshole."

Lucy stopped suddenly and looked from Max to David. "I-I didn't mean that literally. I'm just thinking like the killer."

"Why didn't you go into BSU?" Max asked spontaneously. Lucy seemed surprised by the question. "I mean, you sound like Arthur Ullman, just more . . . intense. You understand these people."

"It's a gift and a curse," Lucy said and averted her eyes.

"Still, it seems you would be a natural for that unit."

"I'm starving," David said.

Max wanted to throttle him. She was getting Lucy to open up—finally. It wouldn't have taken much more prodding. She sensed Lucy was weakening, maybe because she was so emotionally involved with this case. There was something about her that drew Max in . . . and she would find the answers she was looking for.

"Let's go downstairs. Lucy?" David asked her.

"Give me a minute, I want to take a few more notes." She glanced at her phone. "And Dillon's calling me."

"We'll meet you down there," Max said. She grabbed her purse and walked out with David. "Why?" she demanded as soon as they closed the door.

"You were about to overstep, and I didn't want you damaging your relationship with that girl."

"I was not overstepping. It was a natural question to the situation. You heard her—she's not like most feds we know."

"Sometimes for the most observant person on the planet, you're obtuse."

"Insults. Really." She pressed the elevator button. "Don't interfere with this. I want to know everything about Lucy Kincaid."

"Then step back and watch, don't question. I guarantee you, Max, that if you give her room to work, you'll see her shine—and figure out why she's so damn good at her job."

Chapter Twenty-seven

Lucy watched Max and David leave, then answered Dillon's call. "That was fast."

"I have Nelia on the line with me," Dillon said.

Lucy's heart pounded. "Nelia?"

"Hello, Lucy," Nelia said.

"Hi." Lucy sat down heavily at the desk. Dillon wouldn't blindside her like this, would he?

"Dillon explained to me what you're doing, and I wanted to talk to you about it."

"I—" What did she say? That she wasn't going to stop? That no matter what Nelia said, Lucy wasn't turning back? Why would Dillon do this to her? Her stomach twisted in knots.

"I remember Danielle Sharpe. Dillon told me you suspect her in Justin's murder."

"Yes," Lucy said quietly. "You actually remember her? How?"

"How is Andrew?"

Non sequitur, but Lucy took the moment to regroup. "He's the same. At least how I've always remembered him."

"I mean, how is he now that he's looking into Justin's murder?"

"Resolved is the best word."

"That's Andrew. He always controlled his emotions better than me."

Lucy didn't think that was true—she remembered Nelia as being cool and aloof most of her life.

"Justin's murder hurt Andrew as much as me. Only, he dealt with his pain and I didn't. I need to explain something, Lucy, I've apologized to you and Carina for the way I treated you both after . . . after Justin's murder. But I've never discussed it with anyone. When I say that Andrew controlled his emotions I meant it—I didn't. My emotions controlled me. I didn't show it, but I lived inside my broken soul. That's how I felt when Justin died—broken. A million pieces that I couldn't put back together, so I pulled them all together, one big bag of messy pieces, and carried them around hoping they'd find someway to heal. They did, but not in the right way. It took me years—honestly, until Tom came into my life—before I stopped waking up every morning with my first thought being about Justin. Not the good parts, but losing him. It took a long time before I learned to manage my grief."

"No one blames you for anything, Nelia."

"I just wanted you to understand. Mom and Dad still see me as broken."

Lucy could relate to that.

"Dillon told me what happened the other night," Nelia said. "I'm so sorry. They reacted that way because they thought I would be hurt. I'm calling them tonight. They had no right to treat you so poorly. Just like I had no right to ignore you for all those years. I meant what I said in my letter before you got married. I admire you, and what you've done with your life to seek answers for victims . . . I couldn't do that. And I realized when Andrew called you, and not me, that he thought I was still too fragile to handle any news related to Justin. But I can. It's been nineteen and a half years. I will always miss him."

"Me, too," Lucy said and blinked back tears.

"You know most everything about what happened then. About Andrew and me, how I got pregnant in law school, how I knew about his affairs. Sheila wasn't the first. What you don't know—what no one knows—is how it was just as much my fault. Andrew tried to make it work, but all I saw was my own failures. That I was pregnant and so was my mother. That I *had* to get married. I was in a daze, I think, because I knew Andrew and I didn't love each other, but he tried—he tried harder than I did. Andrew put me through law school. Andrew hated corporate law, but he worked there to make the money to put me through law school because I'd lost my scholarship when I left to have Justin. Mom watched him so I could go to school, then she watched him so I could work. I thought that's what would fulfill me, but slowly I realized that all I really cared about was my son.

"Andrew and I talked about separating. But in the end, he didn't want to divorce because his parents had a bitter divorce, and I didn't want to divorce because I thought it would prove that I was a failure. And we had one thing in common. We loved Justin so much. We thought that love would be enough. We never fought. Never argued. Andrew bent over backwards to help around the house, and I knew part of it was because of his guilt for sleeping around. I didn't care. What does that say about me?"

"It doesn't say anything, Nelia," Lucy said. "Except you need to forgive yourself."

"Dillon told me Justin's killer targeted him because of Andrew's affair. And I knew about it."

"Do you blame Andrew?"

"Of course not. I never did, because I knew where he was and I still choose to work that night. I could have stayed home. I could have worked from home. I should have."

"Nelia, what have we talked about?" Dillon interjected.

"I know. I'm doing better." She took a deep breath.

Lucy said, "Nelia, are you really okay with this? With me investigating Justin's murder?"

"It's not going to bring him back, it's not going to take away the pain, but I can handle the truth. Would you do it even if I didn't want you to?"

"Yes."

"Good."

Lucy didn't know what to make of that, but she said, "Danielle Sharpe."

"It's odd that I remember her, because I don't remember a lot about those weeks—months—after Justin died. I remember Danielle not because she was at the house, as Dillon told me she was. I honestly don't remember anyone at the house, though I knew Mom was there, Carina, Andrew . . . but I remember her because of the funeral."

"She was at Justin's funeral?"

"She came to me in the bathroom and I might have recognized her. I didn't make the connection then and I couldn't swear to it now. Same old condolences that everyone else gave me, except . . . she said she'd lost her son. He'd been eight years old, only a year older than Justin, and when she looked at me I knew she felt the same pain I felt. I don't know why that made me feel better—it didn't last, but in that moment I realized that there were other people with the same pain I had. She gave me a note with her name and number and said I could call her anytime."

"Did you?"

"No. Remember, I was broken. I forgot all about the conversation. I went to see a psychiatrist but that didn't last. I didn't want to go. I think I wanted the pain because grief is feeling something, and without it, I would have nothing.

"Then," Nelia continued, "a year or so later—I can't swear to the time, I was already in Idaho living in my shell—Mom sent me a package. She was always doing that—cookies, jams she recently canned—"

"She still does," Lucy said. "I get something almost every month."

"I do, too." Lucy could hear the smile in Nelia's voice, and somehow, that made the conversation a little bit better, a little bit easier. "In the package was a letter from Danielle. She wrote that she'd raised money from the neighborhood and donated it to the parks district to rename the park where Justin died. The Justin Stanton Memorial Park. She said she debated asking my permission, but in the end didn't want to hurt me so did it on her own, but wanted me to know. I've never gone back—I visit Justin's grave once a year, but I haven't been to the park. I can't."

"I went yesterday," Lucy said.

"Is it nice?" Nelia whispered.

"It's clean, larger, safe. They play soccer there."

"Good." Nelia's voice cracked and Lucy found her own eyes moist. "Did she kill him, Lucy? Did she really kill him?"

"Yes."

"Why?"

How much should Lucy tell her?

"I can take it," Nelia said. "Tom's here with me. I'm not broken, not like before."

She still hesitated. How much to say? How to say it?

"It's okay, Lucy," Dillon said.

She sighed. Having Dillon validate her theory helped, but it was still dark and twisted. "There's a lot we don't know about Danielle Sharpe," Lucy began, "but I believe she lost her son. I suspect something happened to him when he was young—either an accidental death or murder, and that's when she found out about her husband's infidelity. Maybe her husband was supposed to be watching him, or maybe her motives go back even further, to her own childhood. I'm sure there's more about her past that we need to know. But it's clear her husband was with his mistress when their son died and she blames him. She's completely blocked out her own grief to the point that she doesn't feel emotions like you and I do." Lucy knew she processed emotions differently than other people. Maxine Revere had been looking at her in that odd, inquisitive way when Lucy talked about motive . . . and it bothered Lucy that she'd revealed so much about herself. But she couldn't dwell on it now, and had to trust that Max would honor her privacy.

"She moved," Lucy said, "we're still working on finding out where she's from. She moved to San Diego and possibly shut out her past life. Worked, did what was expected of her, kept a distance from people. She was friendly but quiet and aloof. Something triggered her—she may have figured out Andrew was having an affair."

"Andrew was discreet, out of respect for me."

That was interesting—Donovan hadn't been discreet, but he also hadn't worked with Danielle Sharpe. "We believe she stalked Andrew for some time. It could be she stalked several men who fit her profile—men who had a son and a working wife—and when she confirmed Andrew was having an affair, it caused her to relive her own pain discovering her husband had an affair."

"Why kill Justin? I don't understand."

Lucy did. She understood this woman—at least how Danielle Sharpe thought. Normal people didn't understand these disorders. Normal people didn't feel like they were sharing their skin with psychopaths.

Dillon spoke up, "To you and I and Lucy, it makes no sense. But to Danielle Sharpe, it does. She couldn't stop what happened to her son—and she couldn't do anything to her husband, at least back then. I suspect she may have gone after him at some point, however. There could be a restraining order against her, or maybe she really did kill him—though killing her husband does nothing to make him suffer. I think that's how she's thinking—she wants to make these men suffer. And the best way to do that was to take from him the one thing they love the most—their child."

"Does Andrew know this?" Nelia's voice cracked. She was crying.

"Yes," Lucy said.

"Dear God, he must be in so much pain right now."

"He's strong. He's a good man, Nelia, faults and all."

"I know he is. I'd like to call him."

"I think he'd like that, too."

"You're going to find her, right?"

"Yes. Do you still have that letter?"

"No, I threw it away long ago."

"That's okay."

"It was postmarked Tallahassee, Florida."

"Are you certain? You remember that after all these years?"

"I'm certain. It stuck out to me."

"That helps. Thank you, Nelia."

"Lucy, I'm not good with people anymore. Honestly, I never was a people person. But I'd like to see you sometime. Without the family, without pressure. If you're up near me, please let me know, okay?"

"I'd like that, Nelia. Thank you. Good-bye, Dillon."

She hung up and immediately called Max.

"Max, I have something that takes priority for your research staff." It irked Lucy that she could do this herself if she could access her FBI account—but she didn't want to cross that line, not yet. Not until she had to.

Max didn't say anything for a moment.

"Are you there?" Lucy asked.

"I'm here. What is it?"

"Danielle Sharpe in Tallahassee, Florida. I think that's where she's from, that's where her son died."

"You're a psychic, aren't you?"

"My sister Nelia got a letter from Danielle a year after Justin's murder—which was *after* she left San Diego. It was postmarked Tallahassee. Danielle is the one who paid for Justin's memorial at the park. Not Andrew like I had assumed. She killed Justin, stayed for a few months, then went back to visit her son's grave or her ex-husband. Maybe there was another reason, but my educated guess is that Tallahassee is her home base. It's where she goes after she kills. Sharpe may be her maiden name, I don't know, but if she was married there should be a record of that."

"I'll do what I can. Are you joining us for dinner? We haven't ordered."

Lucy wasn't that hungry, but she hadn't eaten much today. She should eat.

"I'll join you—sorry, I'm distracted. Dillon had Nelia on the phone as well."

"And Nelia is . . . good?"

"She gave me her blessing."

"And yet everyone thought she was going to fall apart at the mention of an investigation."

Lucy wasn't certain she appreciated Max's tone, but she didn't comment. "I'll be down in five minutes. Thank you." She hung up.

She got up from the desk and looked at the timeline again. She wrote at the beginning under Victim 0: *Tallahassee, Florida.*

She was about to walk away when she saw something on the desk. A note, in Max's bold handwriting.

What makes Lucy Kincaid tick?

That was it. Nothing more, as if she were doodling.

Lucy was furious. How dare she . . . hadn't anything that Lucy or Sean said sunk in? Lucy thought Sean had made it perfectly clear that they would tolerate no prying into their personal lives. None.

Lucy didn't want her past dragged through the media. What happened when she was kidnapped. That she'd been raped repeatedly. That her rapes had been aired over the Internet. That she'd killed her rapist while he was unarmed. In cold blood. Because if she didn't, he would still be out there. Maybe in prison, but he would be walking the earth and he didn't deserve it. He would have killed her if her brothers hadn't found her. . . .

She took a deep breath. Yes, she was angry, but she didn't see Max doing anything about it, even if she knew the truth. Which she'd never get—not the whole truth, at any rate. It was Max's nature to seek answers. And Lucy had deliberately avoided conversations about herself and her past. No wonder Max was curious—Lucy would be if the roles were reversed.

What *did* make her tick? Her past as a victim? Her need to stop people from hurting each other? Her ability to get into the heads of psychopaths?

She may never know. Maybe a combination of the above. All she knew was that she couldn't see herself doing anything but what she did. She'd long ago given up hope of being normal, but that was okay. Sean had taught her she had value outside of what she did. That she could love and be loved like everyone else.

She walked out of Max's suite and while in the elevator sent Sean a text message: *I love you.*

It made her feel good, to let him know she loved him just because.

But what made her feel even better was when Sean responded immediately: *What's not to love?* and a wink emoji.

He knew how to make her smile.

Chapter Twenty-eight

It was late, so late Saturday that it was probably already Sunday morning, but Danielle didn't care what time it was, she had proof. The final piece of evidence she needed.

She poured the rest of the red wine into her water glass and sipped. She had the photos now, boy, did she have the photos. Tony Fieldstone *and* Nina Fieldstone.

Sex was obviously more important to both of them than their own son.

It was only a matter of time before they abandoned him to screw around with their respective lovers.

Danielle Sharpe had never been so angry as she was right now. She almost confronted Nina this morning when she ran into her at the gym.

Yes, it was on purpose. She had to look at her, see her, talk to her.

Find out what her plans were.

Find out what day her life would end as she knew it.

It was only a matter of days.

It might be only a matter of hours. . . .

Chapter Twenty-nine

Lucy didn't go to church as often as she used to, but being back in San Diego where she grew up, she felt a need to reconnect with a part of her life that had always been clear. Even through tragedy—Justin's murder, then when she was raped at the age of eighteen—she'd found a peace within the walls of God's house. It wasn't something Sean shared with her, and that was okay—her prayerful life was as private as she wanted to keep her personal life.

She went to the earliest Mass, knowing that her mom always went to a later Mass. She didn't want to see her family. Not yet. She wasn't certain Nelia would be able to change their minds about what Lucy was doing, but that the one person she thought would hate her for her actions actually thanked her meant more to her than anything else. She and Nelia would never be close—but for the first time Lucy felt a true connection to her oldest sister.

She sat in the last pew and left as soon as the priest gave the final blessing. She'd seen several people she recognized from her parents' circles—it was hard to walk into a church you attended most of your life and not recognize people. The last thing she wanted was small talk. As soon as she turned her phone back on, she had a text message from Max.

My staff came through. Come upstairs ASAP.

Lucy called Max as she drove back to the hotel. "I got your message."

"Sleeping in?"

270

"I was at church."

Max didn't speak. Odd, Max had a comment about everything. Lucy almost laughed that she'd stumped her.

"Okay. Well, I have news. Danielle Sharpe—and you were right, Sharpe is her maiden name—was married to Richard Collins. They had a son, Matthew Collins, a year after their marriage. When he was eight, he disappeared from his bedroom—while his father was with his mistress, Danielle at work, and a babysitter watching him. Both parents were interviewed extensively but ultimately cleared by police. At least according to the press reports. A week later Matthew's remains were found in an open field—police arrested a known sex offender, who ultimately pled guilty in exchange for a reduced sentence."

Lucy felt ill and angry. "How reduced?"

"Twenty-five to life."

"It's a special circumstances homicide—you said sex offender— why would they do that? He could have been eligible for the death penalty."

"I don't have the case files, all I have are press reports. His name was Paul Borell and he died in federal prison. You could probably get the details faster than I can. Danielle filed for divorce shortly after Matthew's funeral. Uncontested."

"Do you have the autopsy report?" Lucy asked.

"No, everything I learned about Matthew's disappearance and murder was in a couple of articles and two newscasts my staff dug up from the era—not easy, by the way, because it was a small affiliate outside of major media markets."

"Your staff is obviously good."

"They are the best," Max concurred. "I learned that Danielle worked for the city attorney in Tallahassee."

"And she was working late at night?"

"She was a legal secretary for the city attorney but going to law school part-time at night. She had classes that night, they got out at nine thirty. She went to the library to study until it closed at midnight, then she went home and found her son was missing."

"I assume the police verified her alibi."

"We can assume, but in my line of work, I never make an assumption like that. Still, they arrested Borell and he pled."

"And the father?"

"A businessman. Some sort of high-end insurance broker."

"Was Matthew's body found close to the house?"

"About five miles."

"Why did it take them a week to find the body?"

"I don't know, the press reports were vague on the details, likely because there was a sexual component to the crime. My guess is that maybe Borell kept the boy prisoner for a while. Again, it's a guess, and not something I'm going to run with until I get it confirmed."

"I'll see if I can track down the autopsy report," Lucy said.

"Is it important?"

"I don't know, maybe." Yes, but Lucy didn't say it. It was important because she needed to know everything Danielle Sharpe knew about her son's murder. To lose a child to violence was awful, but what had turned her into a killer? "Did you learn anything about Danielle's family? Her parents?"

"That's been more difficult. During the investigation, her mother was quoted in one of the papers—Natalie Hoover of Orlando. Big city, common name, we haven't found her yet. And that was nearly twenty-five years ago. She could have died, been remarried—"

"I get it. It might not be important. What about her ex-husband?"

"More there—Richard Collins moved to Denver a year after the divorce was finalized. Remarried, though I don't know when. He and his wife bought a house fifteen years ago in a Denver suburb. Property records have them still owning it."

Lucy's gut twisted. "Kids?" Danielle would certainly go after Richard Collins's kids.

"His new wife has two kids from her first marriage, both now adults."

"We need to talk to him. You have his contact information?"

"Yes, but this is the one time I'm going to suggest that you're better suited to make this contact. He has no reason to talk to a reporter, and you have the authority to compel him to talk."

"I have no authority."

"All you have to say is you're an FBI agent investigating a crime."

Max was right—it wasn't an outright lie, but it was deceptive. Still, this was the closest they'd gotten to Danielle Sharpe.

The woman who killed Justin.

"Let me think about how to approach him. We may want to see how it goes, work together to get the information we need. I'll be back at the hotel in ten minutes."

Max didn't like eating in her room, but the suite at the US Grant was spacious, and there was a separate dining area, so she didn't feel like she was eating in bed. She had room service bring up a nice buffet of food and extra coffee. It was ready before Lucy returned.

David walked in in his typical pressed polo shirt and slacks. He took one look at the food and said, "Are you having a party?"

"We have work to do. Any word from Ben about Danielle Sharpe's current location or employer?"

"I'm supposed to tell you that they worked all night to track down the information about Richard Collins and his son and you can go to hell."

"And?"

"They're working on it."

She knew she was asking a lot of her staff, but she constantly rewarded them.

"Ben wants to know when you're going to let him hire you an assistant."

"You're my assistant."

"You know what I mean."

She did. She had gone through a half-dozen assistants during the first two years she'd been with NET. Then she found one she liked, but Riley left after six weeks. Max had been trying to entice her back—Riley had so much potential. But she'd also nearly been killed during one of Max's investigations. Max had gone to visit her in Boston and while Riley spoke to her—a first since she left—she said that investigative reporting wasn't her "thing." Whatever that meant. Even though Max insisted that danger was rare, Riley didn't budge.

"I'll think about it," Max said.

"Office staff. Not field staff."

"I said I'll think about it."

She was getting testy, and she knew both David and Ben were frustrated that she refused to bring on anyone else. But what happened with Riley had affected her. Max was willing to risk her own life—and even David, because he was trained for it—but she'd unwittingly risked Riley's life. It didn't matter that Riley had gone off on her own, she'd done it because she thought that's what Max would have wanted. Having that kind of influence over a young, impressionable reporter made Max nervous.

Lucy was more than ten minutes, but Max didn't say anything. She looked like she'd had about as little sleep as Max, but without Max's skill of hiding her fatigue with makeup.

"I ordered up extra coffee," Max said.

"I need it." Lucy walked over to the small buffet and seemed surprised. "Coffee and breakfast."

"Hope you didn't eat yet."

"No, thank you for thinking of it."

Lucy poured coffee and dished up a small plate of food. She looked preoccupied.

"Bad news?" Max asked.

"Excuse me?"

"You're a million miles away."

"Thinking."

"About?"

Lucy sipped her coffee and sat down at the conference table. "Whether Richard Collins has any loyalties to his wife. Whether he's still in contact with her, and whether he'll call her as soon as I hang up."

Max had to admit, she hadn't thought of that. But she wasn't a cop—she was all about information.

"Would that be a problem?"

"Yes. We have no probable cause to detain Danielle Sharpe. If he alerts her, she could disappear."

"Not easy to do. She hasn't changed her name—she may not be able to up and disappear."

"We don't know that she hasn't changed her name, but I agree, it's likely she's still using the name because of her work history. Still, just because she worked for three people who all lost a son while she was there is still circumstantial. A good lawyer would stonewall a police investigation, and Sharpe has gotten away with murder for twenty years. She has an exit plan. I want to take the direct approach, and honestly over the phone isn't going to work."

"You want to hop a plane to Denver?"

"Yes. I know it's asking a lot, but in my experience, face-to-face is the only way we're going to get answers. I spoke to Sean, and he says he could fly us, but it would take him a few hours to get down here, and I had a feeling he was still working."

"Don't worry about the plane, I'll get us there." She looked at David and he picked up the phone. "Did you think I wouldn't like the idea?" Max poured fresh coffee. "I much prefer face-to-face interviews. It's easier to know if someone is lying."

Lucy smiled. "We agree."

"But we're not going unless I can confirm he's there—David is working on it now."

Lucy excused herself—ostensibly to call her husband—and Max waited until David was off the phone. "I have a local PI checking out the Collinses' residence, he'll get back to us within an hour. In the meantime, I have reservations on a twelve thirty flight, which only gives us two hours to get to the airport. Puts you in Denver just before four local time. I also got you a driver."

"I don't need a driver."

"You need someone who knows the area and is used to driving in snow."

"Good point. I'll pack an overnight bag just in case, but I expect to be back here tonight."

"It's snowing. Or were you not listening to me?"

"I still want to come back tonight."

He sighed. "I have you booked on the last flight out, but don't blame me if you get stuck at the airport all night."

———

By the time Lucy and Max arrived in Denver, it was no longer snowing, but the roads were slow going. Getting from the airport to Richard Collins's house in the suburbs took well over an hour. Max talked to Ben, the research staff, David—he'd landed in Phoenix before Max and Lucy arrived in Denver—and proofread the article she'd written on the plane. Not about this case—she always had an article up on Monday mornings about something of interest to NET viewers. The articles were available through the wire and often got picked up by newspapers, but NET subscribers received them in their e-mail the night before public release.

Max hadn't thought there'd be so much interest in crime issues on the Internet—while she was tech-savvy, she didn't track consumer data like Ben did. He'd had a vision, and it had more than been fulfilled. While Max enjoyed most of what she did for the network, she had grown frustrated that she couldn't always work the cases she wanted, she didn't have the time to spend on the ground like she used to, and while her name and face weren't a household name, she had enough recognition that going undercover like she'd done before the television show was now impossible.

Give and take, she realized. Through NET's Internet and television platforms, she'd been able to give a larger voice to crime victims than in the books and articles she used to write exclusively. That meant something.

While Max worked in the car, Lucy was silent and stared out the window. She'd been quiet all morning, and on the plane appeared to be sleeping—perhaps to avoid conversation? Lost in thought? Max didn't know. But something seemed to be going on with her partner.

Max almost snorted at the thought. Partner? With a *federal agent*? She had worked with law enforcement in the past, but it was a grind. She'd expected the same with Lucy Kincaid—yet this was different. Maybe because Lucy was working off the clock. Maybe because Lucy had a personal stake in the outcome. Or maybe because Max liked her.

More likely, you're just curious.

Max got a lot done in the car, and by the time the driver pulled up to the Collinses' residence, she felt like she'd accomplished more than her fair share for the week.

The Collinses' well-maintained house matched all the other suburban houses in the neighborhood. It had been built fifteen years ago, and according to the property records Max's staff had pulled, Richard Collins and his second wife, Patricia, had purchased it new. Not Max's idea of home, but then again, she hadn't had much of a *home* growing up—at least not until her mother dumped her on her grandparents.

The Collinses' side of the street backed up to the mountainside, the one thing that distinguished it from the other streets.

"You ready?" Max asked Lucy.

"Of course."

"You've been quiet."

"Thinking."

Lucy hadn't dressed like a cop. She wore jeans with knee-high boots and a twin-set sweater. Max noticed she carried her gun—she'd checked it on the plane, which caused them some delay, but Lucy was a federal agent and everything went smoothly. Yet the gun was in her purse, not holstered, so Collins wouldn't immediately think *cop.* Max hardly thought they'd need a gun, and when she commented on it, Lucy had ignored her.

Chalk it up to another curiosity about Agent Kincaid.

Neither Max nor Lucy had more than a light jacket—they'd left San Diego when it was eighty degrees. Max didn't care—she preferred the cold—but Lucy was shivering.

"Didn't expect snow when you flew to San Diego," Max joked.

"I don't particularly like the humidity in Texas, but I love the heat."

Max knocked on the door. A moment later an older woman answered. She was trim, fifty, with blond hair expertly dyed by a talented stylist. "May I help you?"

"Patricia Collins?"

"Yes?" She wasn't suspicious. She looked like every other middle-class empty nester that Max could picture.

"I'm Maxine Revere. I'm an investigative reporter from New York and I'd like to speak to your husband, Richard."

She stared at Max as if it took her a minute to process what she'd said. "A reporter? About what?"

Richard stepped into the doorway. He'd heard Max, and he had a frown on his face. "What's this about?" he said, perhaps more harshly than he intended. His hand was on his wife's back and he put his other hand on the door, as if he would slam it on them without hesitation.

"About your son, Matthew."

"I don't speak to the press about my son. No one has even asked about him in years. Why?"

He was curious, as well as suspicious.

"I investigate cold cases. I've been working a case in San Diego that is similar in many ways to your son's disappearance and murder. That's why I brought Lucy Kincaid with me—she's the aunt of one of the victims and she's been helping me with my research and investigation."

Max was prepared to argue her case. Richard was skeptical, and he couldn't mask the pain in his eyes.

"A pervert killed my son. I don't want to talk about it."

Lucy said, "Mr. Collins, I know talking about your son is difficult. And we don't have to talk about him if you don't want to."

Max almost blew her top. Of course they needed to talk about Matthew Collins—what was Lucy saying?

Lucy continued. "But it's very important that we talk to you about your ex-wife, and in doing so, we'll need to discuss your son's murder. If you would give us just ten minutes of your time, you will help us find and stop a killer."

"Are you saying that Paul Borell didn't kill my son?"

"No, I'm not. All the evidence, including his plea agreement, confirms that he is guilty."

Patricia said, "It's cold outside, Richard, let them come in."

He didn't want to, but he listened to his wife. "Ten minutes," he said. "No more."

Max and Lucy stepped in and he closed the door behind them. Pictures framed the entry—mostly of two people Max presumed were Patricia's daughters. Photos of them as children and one of them in her wedding gown with the second as the maid-of-honor. They looked to both be in their midtwenties.

There was one photo of Matthew. It was a picture of him and his father, when he was about six. They were smiling and each holding up a fish. Max noticed that Lucy looked at it for a long minute, then turned away.

Patricia led them to the living room. It was the type of room reserved for formal guests. The couches barely looked used, though the style was more than a decade old. Through the open archway Max would see the family room—more cluttered, with comfortable furniture and many more photos.

"Coffee? Water?" Patricia offered.

"No," Richard said. "Ten minutes—I'm not entertaining them."

"I do appreciate your time, Mr. Collins, so I'll get to the point," Max said. "I became interested in the Justin Stanton murder in San Diego when my staff uncovered two other similar cases. Justin was murdered nearly twenty years ago, when he was seven years old. He was taken from his bedroom while his parents were out, drugged, suffocated, and buried in a shallow grave a short distance from his house. He was found within twenty-four hours, but there was little to no evidence, and while the police looked at the parents and family members, no one fit.

"As my staff and I investigated, we realized there were several unusual similarities. But there's one key fact that connects with your son's death: in each of these cases, the fathers of the boys were having an affair."

Max let that information sink in. Richard immediately understood what she was saying.

"It's not the same," he said, his voice scratchy with emotion.

"Justin's father is the district attorney of San Diego, so we had assistance in putting together information that wasn't available to the general public. And because these murders were all five or more years apart and in different California jurisdictions, the police didn't make the connection."

"How did you?" Patricia asked. Her hands were entwined with her husband's, but she was far more in control. "Poor Matthew was killed in Florida."

"Because Lucy's brother is a forensic psychiatrist and was able to help us form a profile of sorts. When we had that, we went back to Stanton and he went through employee records looking for a woman who left employment shortly after Justin's murder. We followed up with the other two connected cases. One woman worked with either the mother or father of each dead boy."

"Then why aren't the police here?"

"Because," Lucy said, "we have no hard evidence. But we think you can help—you know this woman."

"We? Are you a cop?"

Lucy showed her badge. "FBI. But I'm not here officially—I'm here because I'm Justin's aunt."

"I don't understand," Richard said. "What does this have to do with Matthew's death?"

Patricia bristled. "You can't think that Richard has anything to do with any of this."

"Of course not," Lucy said. "Have you been in contact with your ex-wife, Danielle Sharpe, at any time after you left Florida?"

Both Patricia and Richard stared at Lucy.

"Danielle?" Richard said.

Lucy said, "We have a theory, but no proof. We know that you were with your mistress the night Matthew was killed—"

Patricia jumped up. "I can't believe you would do this to my husband! Hasn't he suffered enough? First his son is molested and murdered, then his ex-wife makes his life a living hell, and now this? You have to bring it up again?"

"It's okay," Richard said, taking his wife's hand.

"It's not okay!"

"A living hell?" Max said, needing to take the emotion out of the room. "How so?"

"No, I'm not doing this again. Don't, Richard."

Richard stood up and said to Max and Lucy, "Can you excuse us for a minute?"

Max didn't want to let them out of the room—there was something here, she could feel it buzzing around the room. But Lucy spoke before Max could stop them. "Take all the time you need," she said.

They walked out.

"What are you doing?" Max said. "Did you hear them? Bet you a million bucks that Danielle has been tormenting him for years. 'Living hell.' And now they're going to clam up and sanitize whatever they tell us. Maybe call a lawyer. Maybe he's calling the police right now to have us removed."

"You have a vivid imagination," Lucy said.

"We were so close!" She cleared her throat to lower her voice. "You should never have let them walk out."

"We are close, Max, and I'm definitely not taking your bet. He's heard from his ex recently."

"How do you know that?"

"His face when I mentioned her name. I don't think he told his wife, but Danielle has reached out to him."

"I don't understand what you're saying. They're not—screwing around or something?"

"No. I think Patricia was right—Danielle tried to make Richard suffer. But Richard remarried, moved, was able to get on with his life. Danielle couldn't. But there's more here than hatred of her ex-husband. She blames herself as much—or more—than her ex."

"How do you get that?"

"It's everything, Max—it's not just the husbands who are cheaters. The wives were all working. In a traditional household, the father works and the mother stays home with the kids."

Max almost laughed. "It's the twenty-first century—certainly not the status quo now." And she couldn't imagine not working. But something on Lucy's face had her asking, "If you had kids, would you quit your job and raise them?"

"I can't answer that question," Lucy said.

"What I'm saying is, in this day and age there are many two-income households. It's common. Sometimes because both parents want to work, and sometimes because both parents have to work. Either way, even twenty years ago no one batted an eye when a mother went back to work after having a kid."

"It's not about the mother working, it's about the mother not being home when her son was in danger. It's a primal instinct to protect our young. We talk anecdotally about mother bears and their cubs, but it's based on observable truths. Danielle certainly blames Richard because he was with another woman when Matthew was killed. But she blames herself even more. There is an intense self-loathing, which she has projected onto other families."

Max glanced up and saw Richard in the entry of the living room. Lucy had to have seen him when they were talking. Why had she continued? Did she want Richard to hear?

Patricia wasn't there. "I need to talk to you without Patricia," Richard said. His eyes were moist. "You think Danielle killed someone. A child."

"Yes," Lucy said. "Do you think she's capable?"

"I don't know." He sat back down heavily on the couch. "What do you want to know?"

Max had a million questions, but she glanced at Lucy. Lucy was running this show. Maybe she had from the minute she stepped into the lounge at the US Grant on Thursday afternoon. Max's control was only an illusion that Lucy wanted her to keep until they broke the case open.

"Let's start at the beginning," Lucy said. "You were young when you married."

He nodded. "We were both in college. I was a senior, she was a freshman. Love at first sight, I suppose."

This was no happy reminiscing.

"We married because Danielle got pregnant. I loved her, and the baby. I wanted to do the right thing. We were happy, I thought. But Danielle was always clingy. Needy, I guess. I chalked it up to her being young and insecure about our marriage, but I tried. And Matthew, we loved him. After he was born, it was good, really good. I'd already graduated. She took a year off, then finished school. Juggled Matthew and classes. I was working for a major insurance company, nine-to-five mostly, but I was promoted when Matthew was five and started traveling. I told Danielle she didn't need to work if she didn't want to—I was making more money, and she really hated her job. She said she wanted to go to law school, and I supported that. She was working and going to school and I was traveling and she was always suspicious. Several times she'd show up at my hotel room. Said she wanted to surprise me, and the first time I was thrilled—it was fun and exciting. But then . . . it turned weird."

"How so?"

"She would show up at work in the middle of the day. She would call at odd times. If I didn't answer right away, she'd leave a long message. If I called her back she would accuse me of avoiding her. I wasn't, but then I began to. It was awkward. She showed up at a company dinner with one of our biggest clients and made a scene. It was after that I suggested we separate . . . and she almost had a breakdown. I found out then that her mother had been married twice—and each time her father or step-father had an affair and left her mom for another woman. Her mom and I never got along—the woman was bitter and manipulative and what is it called? Passive-aggressive? Say things to Danielle like, 'Oh, I love your haircut, it covers your big forehead,' or 'That dress is amazing, it hides your fat ass beautifully.' I'm sure growing up like that had to wear her down, and she was always self-critical and critical of me. But she begged me to forgive her, and we had Matthew—I loved that kid so much."

"And yet you still had an affair."

"I'm not proud of it. It just happened . . . and I didn't know how to get out of it."

"It wasn't with Patricia."

"God, no. Someone I worked with. She was married as well, neither of us were happy, it started innocuously . . . and then well, you can guess."

"What happened the night Matthew was kidnapped?"

"I had a dinner meeting. Marlena and I stayed after for drinks. Her husband was out of town—he was a pilot and he took extra legs because their marriage was so bad. She knew he was having an affair, too, and I think she wanted to stick it to him by screwing me in their bed. I planned on being home by ten—we had a high school girl who babysat, and I knew Danielle had a late class and then would study until the library closed. But I fell asleep. Woke up when Danielle called at twelve thirty and said Matthew wasn't in his bed. I—I lied to her at first, but when the police came everything came out, because I didn't know what happened to my son and I wanted the police to find him."

"We have the basics from the investigation," Lucy said, "but no details."

"He was found five days later in an open field, under a pile of construction garbage. But . . . the police said after the autopsy that he'd been only been dead for twenty-four hours. They arrested Paul Borell. Found Matthew's clothes. His blanket . . . his favorite stuffed animal . . . in Borell's basement. And blood. My little boy . . . he was hurt, then Borell killed him."

"How did he die?" Lucy asked, her voice so soft Max almost couldn't hear her.

"He was strangled."

"And he was sexually assaulted."

Richard's voice cracked. "Y-yes."

"Patricia said that Danielle made your life a living hell. How?"

"She blamed me. I blamed myself. I should have been home."

"But she knew you were working late legitimately."

"Yes. But I was supposed to be home by ten. And I wasn't, and my son was kidnapped."

"What about the babysitter?"

"She fell asleep on the couch. She was sixteen—she didn't hear or see anything. Poor girl fell apart, too. Danielle was so cruel to her, and she got into drugs and drinking. I don't know what happened—they moved away a year later."

"And you?"

"I had to move. Danielle would show up at my house, she'd come to the office, she left awful messages on my door, on my phone. The police arrested her once when she attacked me, but I dropped the charges. I mean—I hated myself. So a year later, I moved here. I met Patricia at a grief support group through a community church. Her husband had died—he was young, it was a tragic highway accident—and it took a while, but I finally forgave myself."

"Have you seen or heard from Danielle since you left Tallahassee?" Lucy asked.

"I haven't seen her, but she calls me every once in a while. The first time—I talked about it in grief counseling, so Patricia knows about it.

She was worried about me so I never told her that Danielle has called me many times over the years."

"Define many?" Max said.

"At first she would call me on the anniversary of Matthew's murder and yell at me, blame me. I took the calls because I wanted to be punished. But then it stopped. Years pass and I don't hear from her, then she'll call every day for a couple weeks. The first time she called after Patricia and I married, she was in the room and made me promise never to answer the phone again if it was Danielle."

"But you did."

"I had to—I mean, she was Matthew's mother. She was grieving. And I suspected she called me after she was drinking or something, because she didn't sound right. And it would stop. And then I'd almost forget, but it would start up again."

"When was the last time you talked to her?"

"Wednesday."

"Last week Wednesday?" Max asked. "What did she say?"

"That she hates me. That she wishes I'd died instead of Matthew. She always asks me if I'm cheating on my wife." He sighed. "She left messages on my phone the next couple of days. I still have them."

"I need to hear them," Lucy said.

Richard looked pained, and he was confused. "I don't understand. What's going on? Is Danielle in trouble?"

Max had thought it was perfectly clear. Was Richard being deliberately obtuse? Or was he in denial?

"You ex-wife has killed at least three young boys," Max said.

Lucy tensed. "We suspect," Lucy clarified.

"You suspect, I know," Max said. Before Lucy could backtrack into cop speak, Max said, "We have evidence that your wife worked with the parents of three specific victims at the time the boys were killed. Within a year, she moved to another town, in another job, found another adulterer, and stalked the family until she found the opportunity to kidnap their child in the middle of the night, drug and suffocate him, and bury him in a park with his favorite stuffed animal."

Tears rolled down Richard's face.

"Excuse me for being blunt, but if we're right she's going to do it again." Max wasn't sorry. She needed information and Richard was playing the woe-is-me card and stonewalling them.

Lucy looked at Max with a flash of anger Max hadn't seen in the cop before. Then Lucy turned to Richard. "Danielle blames you for Matthew's death, but she hates herself more. She's stuck in this violent cycle, and she will continue until we stop her. You can help. Do you know where she is?"

He shook his head. "I really don't. The phone she calls me on is blocked."

"That's okay. If you have a record of the calls, I can get a warrant for your phone records."

"I'll give them to you. If you're right—if Danielle—I don't believe it, but . . . I thought if anything she would come after me. Or maybe she was suicidal. The first time she called, she was so hysterical I really thought she was going to kill herself. I talked to her because I didn't want her to die, I wanted her to get help. I thought I calmed her down. She didn't call for a long time after."

"We need a warrant to build a case against her, but you can certainly help expedite it," Lucy said. "Do you have those voice mails?"

He pulled his phone from his pocket.

"May I record them as they play?"

He nodded.

Lucy took out her own phone and pressed a record button, then Richard played his messages.

"I miss Matthew," a faint female voice whispered. "I miss him so much."

Then nothing, but the call wasn't terminated. Thirty seconds later it beeped and the message was over.

"That's it?" Max said.

Richard shook his head and pressed the next saved message.

"I hate you!" The voice sounded completely different than the pained voice before it. It disconnected immediately.

"How long between calls?" Lucy asked. "What day?"

"On Thursday. Two minutes, according to my phone."

Lucy frowned. "Next, please."

"There was a series of six calls that night where she didn't leave a message—hung up before voice mail."

Lucy nodded. "Same day as those two?"

"Yes. And then this on Friday night, late." He looked at the phone. "Two A.M. Saturday morning. I was asleep, I turn my phone off at night."

"Play it."

He hesitated, then pressed Play.

The recording started in the middle of a sentence, as if Danielle had been talking as soon as she hit Send.

"—fucking bitch. Liar! Just like her husband. Just like you. I loved you, and you fucked around. How many, Richard? How many were there before *Marlena*. How many? How many times have you cheated on Patricia? Or maybe she's cheating on *you*. Ha! Serves you right. Why even have children? Why can't people just do what they promised? They'll suffer, I hope they suffer as much as you, I hope they—" *Beep.* The voice mail ended.

"Every day?" Lucy said.

He nodded. "And last night—again, late, my phone says the first three calls came in at two oh-two, two oh-five, and two thirteen. But there's nothing there. You can hear her moving around or moving things around, but she doesn't say anything. Until the call at two thirty-five."

He pressed Play. The first five seconds were silence. Then: "While you were with your whore, a pervert walked into Matthew's bedroom and carried him off to do awful, awful things to him. He suffered, Richard. He was so hurt. Broken . . . no child should suffer like that. They don't deserve him. They don't care. They're never home. I hate you. I hate you!" The harsh sound of breaking glass, then the call was cut off.

"Is that the last one?" Lucy asked.

"Yes."

"She's going to call again tonight. You're going to need to answer it."

"I—I can't. You don't understand."

"I'm going to call the local FBI office and have them here. I want

287

them to see if they can trace the call. She may not stay on the phone long enough, but they might be able to get the area she's calling from. Even a general region will help us."

"She sounded drunk," Max said.

"Possibly. It's the weekend, she doesn't have to keep herself together on the weekends," Lucy said. "Richard, listen to me. This is important. Do you remember the months and years she called you in the past."

"I do," Patricia said as she walked in.

Richard jumped up and went to his wife. "Honey—"

"Richard, you tried to protect me, but I know you've talked to her. I didn't want to say anything, but I could tell by how depressed you got." Patricia turned to Lucy and handed her a piece of paper. "I was really scared for a while that Danielle was going to try and hurt Richard. Physically hurt him. The first time was twenty years ago."

"Are you sure?" Lucy asked.

"June—so nineteen and a half years I guess. I know because my husband died June fifteenth and our anniversary had been June twenty-ninth, so it's always been a really hard month for me. I hadn't been to the grief group in a while, and I went then and Richard talked about the calls. He was shaken."

Lucy stared at the paper, then handed it to Max.

The pattern was clear. Every four to five years, Danielle called her husband for a week to ten days in a row, then stopped. Three of the four time periods matched perfectly with the three murders they were certain Danielle had committed.

And now she was calling again.

"What does this mean?" Patricia asked.

"It means that Danielle has found another cheating spouse and is making plans to kill his son," Max said.

"Why would she do this? Why would she kill an innocent child?" Richard said. He sank down onto the couch.

Lucy said, "She saw how much you suffered after Matthew's death; she wants others to suffer the same way. She blames you, but she mostly blames herself because she wasn't there, either."

"Dear Lord, how are you going to find her?" Richard asked.

"With your help. Please."

"Anything. Anything you need."

Lucy asked Max to wait with the driver while she went into the local FBI headquarters. Max didn't want to—in fact, she was more than a little angry to be kept out of it—but Lucy persuaded her that it would be easier for everyone if she didn't have to explain why she had a reporter interviewing a potential witness.

This was the point of no return, Lucy realized. She presented the information to the local office and the request to work with Richard Collins to obtain his phone records and trace any calls coming from a blocked number for the next week. Lucy didn't have to work hard to get them to cooperate—she simply dropped some names. Then she called the San Diego FBI office and spoke to the SSA, Ken Swan, who she'd worked with in the past. It took her a while to get through to him—he wasn't on call—but when she did, he listened with minimal questions until the end.

"How certain are you that this woman is going to kill in the immediate future?"

"I'm positive."

"When are you going to be back in San Diego?"

"Late tonight."

"Let's meet tomorrow morning, you can give us everything you have. You've been busy on your vacation."

Lucy had led him to believe that she was on vacation visiting her family when this all came up. She didn't want to lie any more than she had to. "I took time off specifically to work with this reporter—she did most of the background work."

"You forget, Agent Kincaid, I've worked with you before. I'll call the Denver office and we'll coordinate. See you tomorrow."

An hour later, Lucy was back in the car with Max. The reporter glared at her. "You damn well better give me something if you're going to bench me."

"I checked our flight—it's delayed ninety minutes."

"You know what I mean."

Lucy did. "I'm sorry, but I had to tread carefully in there. Dot my i's, cross my t's. I'm not leaving you out of the loop—I didn't tell them anything you don't already know."

The driver started for the airport. Max was still irritated. "I'm used to getting the shaft from cops."

"I'm sorry you think that's what I did."

Max was silent, perhaps thinking the cold shoulder would affect Lucy, but it didn't. The peace was . . . refreshing. And gave Lucy time to think and process everything she learned.

After twenty minutes, Lucy said, "You wanted to know what made me tick."

Lucy didn't know what she expected of Max—maybe to justify the notes she'd taken and left on her desk? Apologize? But she did neither. All she said was, "Yes, I do."

"You want the truth, Max. I understand that drive. I really do. I'm always seeking the truth—but more than that, I'm looking for answers. I'm driven by a much darker force than *truth*. I need justice. I need to know that killers will be caught, that they will be punished. That they'll be in prison or in a grave."

"That doesn't tell me why."

"But it is the truth. Is the *why* of the truth more important than the truth itself?"

"It's part of the whole."

"Perhaps."

She didn't expand. She could tell that Max wanted to know more—it would bug her because she couldn't put Lucy in a predefined box.

Max didn't need to know. She wanted to, but she didn't need to, and Lucy wasn't going to become one of Max's projects.

Lucy said, "What is more important to you—that Karen's killer is brought to justice, or that you find out why he killed her in the first place?"

Max opened her mouth, then closed it. Lucy didn't smile, though she wanted to because she realized something about Max that Max thought she hid from everyone.

She cared more about justice than she did about exposing the truth.

"I want him in prison," Max said.

"So justice."

"But in putting him in prison, I'll find out why."

"You know why. I read your book, Dr. Ullman had a profile of the killer—that he was a sexual sadist. She'd been heavily drugged—that according to the toxicology report on the blood found at the scene. He had her somewhere for up to thirty-six hours before he killed her. Do you have to know why he held her in captivity? Why he drugged her? Why he most likely raped her repeatedly? Is that important? Because I can tell you right now, there are millions of sick people just like him, whether they kill or not. People are tools to them. Is he any different than a pervert who has sex with children? Like Paul Borell, who raped and murdered Matthew Collins? We can put a label on it—sexual deviancy, pedophiles, sadists, psychopaths—but it all comes down to one lone truth: that their needs, however sick and twisted they are, are supreme. That no one has the right to deny them their satisfaction.

"Danielle Sharpe has a dark need to make other people suffer because she suffered. She has separated herself from the act of murder. I guarantee you that the man who killed Karen has done the same thing. Karen's death served the larger purpose, he can move on. He doesn't care about the pain he caused because he doesn't feel pain. Danielle doesn't *want* to feel pain, but it's all she *can* feel. She believes that if she gives the pain to others—her ex-husband, other broken families—that it'll somehow make her feel better. For a while, it works. But the pain returns and she has to make people suffer again. And we—you and I—are going to stop her."

Chapter Thirty

Max never had trouble falling asleep at night, but no matter what time she woke up, even if it was three in the morning, she couldn't go back to sleep. She'd stopped trying to force herself, which usually resulted in a headache and daylong irritability.

Monday morning she slid out of bed just after four in the morning. Three hours of sleep. She was going to need extra makeup to hide the dark circles.

There was one benefit to waking early, and that was no one was trying to reach her. She made a cup of coffee and filled up the Jacuzzi bathtub. She turned on the jets and relaxed in the hot water. The tension left over from yesterday disappeared. One of her ex-boyfriends had suggested she work out in the morning when she couldn't sleep, but nothing was better than a hot bath, morning or night, to clear her mind.

Thirty minutes later, she took a shower, washed her hair, and then spent a good hour getting ready for the day. She could get ready faster, but why rush? Lucy wasn't meeting her until ten. By seven she was ready and decided to go downstairs for breakfast instead of calling room service.

She'd just ordered and was enjoying orange juice and coffee while reading a book—one that she'd started on the plane ride to Scottsdale a week ago, but hadn't picked up since—when her cell phone vibrated. *So the day begins,* she thought as she closed the book. She assumed it was Ben, but it wasn't.

"Nick," she said when she answered.

"You're still alive," he said.

"I'm sure you would have heard it on the news if I wasn't."

"I left a couple of messages."

He sounded an odd cross between upset and irritated.

"Busy case." Her food arrived and she wished she could eat without the stress of this conversation.

Since when did talking to Nick become stressful? You always looked forward to his calls.

"When will you be done?"

"I'm going to cover the Caldwell trial in Arizona. It starts next week."

"And then?"

"And then . . . I don't know."

"I'd like to see you. Even if you just fly in for a day . . . I miss you, Max."

He sounded sincere. He was sincere, at that moment. Max knew they had a certain chemistry that worked.

"I miss you, that's why I keep myself so busy."

He laughed. "You wouldn't know how to relax, sweetheart. Tell me you'll be here for the weekend after the trial and I'll take it off. Switch shifts with someone if I have to. You and me. I think we need a little time alone."

"I agree." And she did . . . on the one hand. When she and Nick were alone and didn't talk about his life, everything was good.

But if she was going to be part of his life, she had to be part of *all* his life.

Lucy's comments about Nick's motivation for keeping her out of his personal life came back.

"Nick, I want to see you. Spend time with you. Talk. Really talk."

He didn't say anything.

"Do you have the idea that you're somehow sheltering me or protecting me by keeping me out of the loop about your custody battle?"

"I told you, Max, I'm not talking about Nancy with you."

"I know. And you know I don't like these off-limits subjects. I'm a big girl, and I've been making great strides to keep my opinions to myself."

"You don't need to speak to make your opinions known."

"I care about you, Nick. You need to be able to talk to me about anything. God knows I don't hold back when something is bothering me."

"Max, I know what you'll say. You'll tell me Nancy is manipulating me, using Logan as a pawn, and I know it. I know it, dammit! But I will do anything to be in my son's life. Any damn thing. And if we talk about it, the conversation will just frustrate both of us. We don't have much one-on-one time, so why do you insist that when we do it's filled with conflict and arguments? Why can't you just let it go?"

Why? Good question. Max was only beginning to understand why, and it went right to the heart of what she really wanted in a relationship. Trust. Respect. Honesty. How could there be any of those things when Nick shut her out of what troubled him the most?

"I don't know, Nick."

"Can we talk about it when you visit? I don't want to fight with you over the phone. It's much more fun when we fight and make up."

And he nailed it. The crux of her problem with all her relationships. Nick was one of the longer-term relationships she'd had, other than Marco. And Marco fit the same pattern. Fight, make up, live in different states, so dealing with the day-to-day relationship commitment had never been a thing for her.

Before Nick, she didn't care to be intimately involved in the personal lives of any of her lovers. But she recognized that if she was going to have anything permanent—if she wanted anything more than casual, long-distance affairs—she needed to be a real part of another person's life. The good and the bad.

"Max," Nick said quietly, "I promise. We'll talk."

She didn't know if he meant it. Really meant it.

"I'll call you when the trial's over."

"Call me before then—I miss our late-night conversations."

Why? She wanted to ask. The conversations were superficial, sexy, fun . . . but nothing substantive.

Max wanted substantive. She wanted what Sean and Lucy Rogan had.

"Okay," she heard herself saying. "I gotta go." She hung up because she was feeling too melancholy and off her game. She needed to get it together before the meeting at SDPD later this morning.

She put her pleasure book aside and pulled out her notes on Danielle Sharpe while eating her cold omelet. Ten minutes later, all thoughts of Nick were pushed aside.

But not forgotten.

Lucy spoke to her boss, SSA Rachel Vaughn, at 7:00 A.M. Monday morning—9:00 A.M. San Antonio time.

She'd been dreading this call, and she knew that it would be worse when she returned and Rachel found out she was working on an investigation. But she didn't want to share that information now.

"I have a family issue in San Diego," she said. "I won't be back for another day or two."

"Does that mean you were lying to me on Thursday when you said you were sick?"

Lucy rubbed her stomach. She hadn't eaten breakfast yet, but she felt nauseous. "I know I don't have any vacation time."

"You left two active cases that the squad has to now scramble to catch up."

"I left detailed notes—"

"That's irrelevant, Agent Kincaid. We are understaffed and overworked, and while I have sympathy for family issues, I don't have sympathy for my staff lying to me. You need to decide whether you really want to be a federal agent."

"Yes, ma'am."

"Since you are not actually ill or caring for an ill child or spouse, I can't allow you to use sick time."

Lucy didn't comment. Though technically sick time was only for illness, the squad had used it for what one of Lucy's colleagues called "mental health" days. Since it was rare to use two weeks' sick leave—which didn't accrue year to year like vacation time—their former boss let them use sick time whenever they wanted.

"I'm new, and I understand that you and my predecessor were

friends." The way she said *friends* made Lucy angry—she implied far more in the tone. "You have become used to a certain level of autonomy and, if I may be blunt, freedom that I'm certain SSA Casilla would never have allowed. That ends now. When you return from resolving whatever *family issues* you have, we'll have a discussion as to what exactly is expected of you should you want to continue working as a federal agent. Do you understand?"

"Yes, ma'am."

"Good. I am writing this incident up for your file. It'll be up to ASAC Durant as to whether you'll be formally reprimanded, but I will be recommending such. Good-bye."

She hung up. Lucy stared at the phone with a mixture of anger and frustration and guilt. Her boss was right. Lucy had operated fairly autonomously, even before Noah Armstrong took over when Juan went on paternity leave. She'd overstepped, she'd been put on administrative leave, she'd put herself in the crosshairs of a violent drug cartel that, risked the lives of everyone she worked with.

But the crux of the problem was that she didn't regret the decisions she made. Every tough choice she'd made ultimately saved lives. She'd resolved herself to live with the consequences of her actions, but that meant that she may not have a long career in the FBI.

What else could she have done? Justin was her nephew. Andrew was still family. Three other little boys deserved justice. And she knew, in her gut, that they didn't have enough information to turn over to the police.

Until now.

Lucy and Max had stayed up half the night putting together all the evidence—all of which was circumstantial. But it was certainly compelling. And Lucy knew, as soon as she was confronted with the evidence, that Danielle would incriminate herself. All it took was the right questions, the right focus, and Danielle's guilt would make her break.

Dillon needed to come to California and break her. There was no one better than him, and he was a civilian consultant for the FBI. He had the certifications and credentials necessary. He'd already agreed to go to Arizona and assess Blair Caldwell—she might not agree, but that was fine—Dillon didn't need to have her agreement. He could give the prosecution more information into the mind of the killer, and testify as to the type of person who could commit this crime. He couldn't flat-out say that Blair was guilty—without a psychological evaluation that he administered it would be problematic—but Lucy was pretty certain that there *was* a psych eval done at some point. That would help Dillon with his assessment.

Her phone rang. Caller ID informed her it was Carina.

Lucy took a deep breath and answered.

"Hello."

"It's Carina. Connor and I are in the lobby. Can we come up?"

Lucy wanted to say no. She was nervous about her presentation this morning, she didn't want anyone else in her head. Nothing they could say would deter her from this path, but at the same time, this was family. She'd hoped that after her conversation with Carina on Saturday, her sister understood why she was pursuing this.

"I don't have a lot of time," Lucy said.

"I know, my chief called me this morning."

Dammit. Lucy knew that might be a possibility because Carina was well respected on the police force. She'd only hoped that Andrew had convinced the chief to keep everything under wraps until they officially took over the case, or it was officially an FBI case.

"Lucy, Connor and I want to be there. We want to help. Can we just come up and explain?"

"All right." Lucy gave Carina her room number and hung up. She sent Max a text message and said she'd meet her in the lobby at ten. Their meeting at SDPD was at eleven. Andrew was also talking to the special agent in charge of the local FBI office, after Lucy's conversation with SSA Ken Swan yesterday. Lucy suspected her boss, SSA Vaughn, would hear about this before the day was out, but there was nothing else she could do.

A murderer would be in prison and that was the most important thing.

Lucy answered the door as soon as Carina knocked. She was dressed for work—slacks, a button-down shirt, and a blazer. Connor was right behind her in jeans and a leather jacket.

"I'm meeting Max downstairs in twenty minutes," Lucy said.

"Nelia called me last night," Carina began. "She told me about your conversation with her. She also talked to Dad."

"I didn't ask her to do that."

"Connor and Julia were over for dinner when she called, and we all had a long talk. I don't think Nelia and I have talked in years . . . not like that. Nothing more than superficial conversation. While I was thinking of her when you announced you were investigating Justin's murder, I was thinking more about myself. What I went through, that the police suspected me, that I looked into Justin's murder as soon as I became a cop and there was nothing—no evidence, no suspects, nothing. I assumed that if I couldn't find anything and I was there at the time that you certainly wouldn't be able to find anything, but that all this shit would be dredged up again and I would be . . . I don't know. I really don't know what I was thinking, but I was being selfish."

"I understand." In part. Maybe she wouldn't completely understand why her family had been set against her on this, but she didn't hold it against any of them, especially Carina.

"We're also concerned about the reporter," Connor said. "Reporters are not our friends."

"Max is . . . different."

Connor snorted and Carina shot him a look.

Lucy said, "Max is going to write about Justin's murder when we catch Danielle Sharpe and she's been arrested for her crimes."

"And what about you?"

"What about me?"

"Is she going to write about you?"

"No."

"You trust her that much? That she won't dig up your past?"

Why did everything come back to her past? Was she supposed to hide and cower for fear that someone would find out that she'd been kidnapped and brutally raped? That she'd nearly died? That her injuries were so severe that she lost her uterus and could never have her own children? The truth was out there, if someone knew where to look and were really, really good at it. Max could find it if she wanted to. It would take her time, but she could figure it out.

Through clenched teeth, Lucy said, "Not everything is about me."

"That's not what we meant—" Carina began.

Lucy cut her off, forced herself to relax. "Whether she finds out the truth about what happened isn't what's important. She won't write about it."

"How can you be so damn sure?"

"Because Sean had her promise not to write about him or me without our permission."

"And she'll stick to it?" Connor shook his head. "A verbal agreement means nothing, especially to someone like her. I looked her up, she's a bitch. What people have said about her—sure, she's solved some cold cases and she doesn't back down. But she's all about ratings. What's going to help her show. And if she thinks you will help her show, she'll exploit you. We both know you've been involved in some situations that really wouldn't be so great to be public. And I'm not talking about what happened when you were eighteen."

"She's not all about the ratings. Yes, she is focused on her show and what she can use for it, but she made me a promise, and I believe she will live up to it. But truthfully, even if she did find out everything there is to know about me, should I let that stop me from bringing Danielle Sharpe to justice?"

"There are other ways."

"We would have nothing if Max hadn't found the connection between Justin and two other boys. We would have nothing if Max hadn't come in and asked the hard questions. She wouldn't have a case without my help—she would have theories, but no one here was going to help her because Justin's murder was essentially off-limits for fear of upsetting the Kincaids."

"That includes you, Lucy," Carina said softly.

"And Andrew asked me for my opinion. Max has a keen eye, and she has included me from the beginning. We're presenting our evidence with Andrew's blessing, with Nelia's blessing, and the help of Detective

Katella. Dillon is going to be on speakerphone because he helped with the profile. A representative from the FBI is going to be there. But this wouldn't have happened if Max and I didn't work together." She looked from her sister to her brother. "You called not ten minutes ago and said you wanted to help. Now you're challenging me? I don't have time for this or time to doubt myself."

"We're not—" Carina began.

"You are. You're testing my resolve or, hell, I don't know! But I'm not going to back down."

"I want to be there," Carina said.

"I don't know," Lucy said. "I'd like you to be, but I don't know that I can trust you."

The sorrow that crossed Carina's face was real. "Lucy, you're a great cop. I really believe you found Justin's killer. I want to listen to the evidence. I want to help stop her. It'll give me closure, too. I need it—but if you really don't want me there, fine. I'll stand down."

What could she say? No? Could she even keep Carina out of the room considering that she was an SDPD detective on good terms with her chief?

Sometimes, she still felt like a little girl. Her brothers and sisters were so much older than she was. Even Patrick, the next youngest, was nearly eleven years older than her. Was that what Thursday night was about? Lucy didn't back down when her family ganged up on her, but would they ever see her as someone other than the lost girl she'd been after she'd been raped? Someone other than the little kid who tagged along with her older siblings?

She'd thought after last year, when she mitigated the hostage crisis at the hospital, that they finally saw her as a grown woman, a cop who knew what to do and when to do it.

"I'm not going to ban you," Lucy said. "If you want to be there, I want you there. But if you undermine me, I will ask you to leave."

Carina clearly wasn't expecting that answer—whether that she wanted her there or that she would really ask her to leave. Lucy couldn't have someone second-guessing her when she was already nervous about everything that they'd done. Not that she'd done anything wrong, but her job was on the line and she wasn't going to allow her family to turn a difficult situation into an impossible situation.

"Thank you," Carina said.

"Are you joining us?" Lucy asked Connor. She had never been as close to Connor as Patrick. Maybe because fifteen years separating them was too much, she didn't know. And then after Patrick's coma, Connor had distanced himself even further. It wasn't his fault—he had watched Patrick nearly die when they went to rescue Lucy and walked into a trap. Lucy sensed that he was conflicted about a lot of things, and it was just better if she steered clear. Yet, there were many things she loved about him, including his loyalty to his family.

"No," Connor said. "I shouldn't have been involved in any way—this wasn't my decision to make."

"You're family."

"I was being overprotective of Carina, but in doing so, I hurt you. And I'm sorry."

"Apology unnecessary but accepted."

"It's hard to see you all grown up. You aren't the little girl who followed Patrick and me everywhere. You left for the East Coast practically a child and came back a woman, and it's been . . . difficult, I suppose, to see you so focused and mature. And you're close to Jack when no one else is. No one quite knows what he does or even if it's legal."

Lucy was surprised to hear that from Connor, but he was right about one thing—when her father disowned Jack, it had taken Jack years to start building a relationship with his family again. Lucy wasn't part of that—and she and Jack had bonded. Over tragedy and adversity, but he was a rock. Her rock.

Connor continued. "If you trust this reporter, I'll accept your judgment. And it's clear you found something solid, otherwise the chief would never meet with you."

"It is solid. Danielle will break as soon as she's questioned—I'm ninety percent certain. So is Dillon. We'll get her. We just have to find her, and we have enough information to turn over that the police should be able to locate her. We suspect she's in California."

Connor said, "Can Carina go with you? I drove her over here."

"Sure."

Carina was relieved, and they all walked down to the lobby together. Max was waiting—talking on her phone—and raised her eyebrows when Lucy approached.

"I'll call you when I have something solid," she said into the phone, then ended the call. "Isn't this a pleasant surprise," she said drolly.

"Carina is going to join us for the meeting with Chief Causey," Lucy said.

Max didn't say anything.

Lucy gave Connor a hug. "Thank you for understanding," she said.

"If you need me, for anything"—he gave Max a sidelong look full of suspicion—"call me. Anytime."

"I will."

Connor left and Max said, "Ready?"

"Yes."

Max turned and strode out of the lobby. Her rental car had already been brought around to the front. It was all Lucy could do to keep up with her long stride.

"Carina wants to be involved," Lucy said quietly. "She wants to help."

"I hope you're right."

"I am."

Max slid into the driver's seat. It didn't take long to arrive at SDPD headquarters, but Max was silent the entire drive. So she was irritated. Lucy didn't regret bringing Carina along. Knowing the truth would only help her sister—and the rest of her family.

As soon as they arrived, Carina spotted her longtime partner and excused herself.

"I'm not going to apologize," Lucy said to Max as they waited for their escort to the chief's office.

"For what?"

"You're mad that I brought Carina."

"Not mad. Mildly irritated. She could have been helping from the beginning, but I'm not upset that she's here. Truthfully, the more law enforcement on board, the better chance we have of building the case and for the DA or AUSA to get a conviction. I may not be a cop or a lawyer, but I've followed enough trials and investigations to know that with something like this, more cooks makes for a better meal."

Lucy wasn't sure she'd have used that analogy, but she understood what Max meant.

"Then why the silent treatment?"

"Truthfully? I had an argument with my boyfriend this morning. He's in northern California and wants me to come up for a few days after I'm done with Blair Caldwell's trial."

"And? What's the argument?"

"I took what you said to heart—that he might have this twisted thought that he's protecting me or that he doesn't want the negativity in our relationship or some such nonsense. So I told him as much. And he finally told me why he won't share." She glanced around, then lowered her voice. "He said he knows what I will say, that I will tell him he's being manipulated by his ex-wife. But ultimately, he'll do anything to keep joint custody of his son, and it would only frustrate both of us if we discuss it."

"Is he right?"

"Partly. He is being manipulated, but it's more than that. It's like extortion. Nancy has something that Nick desperately wants—time with his son—and he's willing to do anything for it. He's going by the rules—the legal process, the court system—and she then changes the rules midgame. It's wholly unfair, and Nick is being hung by his balls because he won't call her bluff."

"He doesn't want to risk his son."

"I get that. I don't want him to risk his relationship. He says we'll talk, but it's more of the same. It's tearing Nick apart and I can't watch, especially when he won't let me be involved."

In a mere whisper, Max said, "And maybe I just don't love him enough to ignore all this."

Lucy felt for Max—it was clear she had feelings for Nick, but it was also clear that she was losing respect for him. "Sometimes, when I have a difficult decision, I consider each possible choice I could make and run through the outcomes—not what will happen, but how I will feel about each outcome. How would you feel if you ended the relationship?"

"I've thought about it a lot, especially since September. I would miss our conversations, I would miss the sex even though we don't see each other all that often. Definitely miss the sex. But I don't think I would be torn apart by ending the relationship. And I don't think Nick would be, either."

"I'm sorry."

A uniformed officer came out to escort Lucy and Max to a large conference room. Lucy was surprised that they had such a large group of people. Andrew, Carina, Don Katella, two uniformed officers, and three detectives—or so she thought—that she didn't recognize. The chief then walked in with FBI SSA Ken Swan. Lucy had met him a year ago when she was visiting her dad in the hospital over Christmas and became embroiled in a hostage situation.

"Agent Swan," Lucy said.

"Agent Kincaid. Good to see you again. Do you have a minute?"

Lucy almost panicked, suspecting that this was going to be bad news considering her conversation with her boss an hour ago. "Of course."

She stepped out of the room with Swan.

"Just wanted you to know that I got word from Denver—Sharpe made contact with her ex last night, and as you suggested, he spoke to her. When you're right, you're right—the woman is certifiable."

"Were you able to trace it?"

"It lasted less than two minutes. Collins tried to extend the conversation, but no dice. We know what region, however—it came from Southern California. The techs narrowed it to Los Angeles, Orange County, or San Bernardino."

"That's more than we had before."

"You need to hear it. She called just after midnight Denver time."

"We have to present—"

"Two minutes." He pulled out his phone and earbuds and handed it to Lucy. She put the earbuds in and Swan pressed Play.

Lucy closed her eyes.

"Hello," Richard Collins said. Lucy could hear the strain in his voice.

Danielle didn't say anything for several seconds.

"Who is this?" Richard said.

"Me," Danielle said.

"It's after midnight. You can't keep calling me so late. I have to work."

"Matthew would have been thirty on Friday."

"I never forget his birthday, Danielle."

"We didn't deserve to have him."

"That's not true. We loved him."

"No, we didn't. If we loved him, we would have been there that night."

"You don't believe that. Listen, I have an idea. Let's meet in Tallahassee on Friday, okay? Have lunch? Talk about this—talk about Matthew. You have to find a way to put this behind you."

"Behind me? He was murdered, Richard! Because I wasn't there to protect him. Because you were fucking another woman! He's dead and it's all our fault!"

That was new, Lucy realized. On the previous conversations, she hadn't said anything about her blame. She was either escalating or something had happened with the family she was stalking.

"It's not your fault or my fault. It was Paul Borell and he's in hell."

"I'm in hell! And I wish you were there with me!"

She disconnected the call. She said to Ken, "Can you send that to Dr. Dillon Kincaid? He's going to be on the conference call, but I want him to listen to it first."

"E-mail?"

She gave him Dillon's contact information.

"She has a victim," Lucy said. "She has a plan—we have to find her fast."

"Denver is working on the tech, but I don't think they're going to get any closer."

"We have a room full of smart people, we'll figure it out before the morning is over," Lucy said.

"How long can you stay here? I can clear it with your SSA— Richardson already gave me the approval."

She needed to be honest with Ken from the beginning. "I took time off to be here, but I didn't tell my boss why."

"And he would have a problem with it?"

"She might. She's new to the office. We've been in a bit of flux this year—my SSA left on paternity leave, we had a temporary guy, and now the original SSA is retiring early. I don't want to make waves."

"I can smooth over anything, but if you don't want me to call, I won't. Still, I can't guarantee that your name isn't going to come up. If we arrest this person and there's a trial, you'll have testimony, briefing the AUSA, any number of things."

She hadn't even thought that far ahead.

"Did you lie to her about what you were doing?" Ken asked.

"No, not really. I said family issues. I don't lie well, so I thought being vague would be best."

"I'll talk to Richardson, see what she thinks we should do. I'd like you to be part of this—you earned it."

"I just want this woman stopped."

"You and me both."

Lucy let Max present their findings—how she became interested in the cold cases, what she put together and when, and then the timeline. Lucy presented the profile of Danielle Sharpe—a woman so destroyed by grief and anguish that she had a need to spread the suffering to others. She had turned her actions into punishment of sorts—not only for herself, but for anyone who mirrored her own failed life.

They were in the middle of questions when Ken Swan excused himself from the room.

Something was definitely up—he had his phone to his ear before the door closed.

Chief Causey said, "Ken, Andrew, and I already hashed out jurisdictional details—the FBI is taking lead, our office is providing whatever support they need. Andrew has a conflict of interest, and it would be far better for the federal government to prosecute—especially since we're dealing with a minimum of three jurisdictions and potentially more. But, Ms. Revere, I have a question for you. Do you think in any way that my squad was incompetent or made critical mistakes after Justin Stanton was killed?"

"No, sir," Max said. "I've reviewed all of Detective Katella's reports and he investigated Justin's murder not only to the full extent of the abilities of his team, but went above and beyond. There were simply too many variables they couldn't have known at the time. It was random on the one hand and highly personal on the other."

Interesting way to analyze the case, but Lucy concurred with Max.

Ken came back into the room. "We may have a break. When we got Sharpe's name yesterday, we ran her. Clean record, no criminal record. We ran all DMVs in California—got a hit. She has a driver's license renewed in Sacramento, and owns a black Honda Accord registered to the same address. I have agents already en route to her house."

"Good work, Ken, and everyone." Causey asked Katella if he would work with a detective to bring them up to speed, and then dispersed the team. "Ken, do you need my office?"

"No, sir, I'm going to head back to headquarters. Kincaid, can you join me?"

Lucy glanced at Max, then Carina. She had a few things to do first. "Yeah, give me a minute."

"I'll meet you out front in five minutes." He walked away, again on the phone.

"Give me a minute with Carina, okay?" Lucy asked Max.

"Take all the time you want." Lucy watched as Max pulled Andrew away from the group and out of the room. Lucy couldn't worry about either of them. She went over to her sister who looked frozen. There was no other word. She hadn't spoken the entire meeting, hadn't asked a question, just watched and listened.

"Are you okay?" Lucy asked.

She nodded. "You and Max built the case. It's solid. I didn't think it could be done . . . I'm floored."

"Fresh eyes," Lucy said. She sat down. "Carina, you can't go back. You weren't a cop then, you did everything you could. Don Katella did everything he could, believe me. At the time, there was no way of knowing that Danielle Sharpe had killed Justin. No evidence, no witnesses, no connection to Andrew or Nelia—except a tenuous connection at the district attorney's office. She fixated on the family but except for one incident at work, she never did anything to tip her hand."

"Incident?"

"Andrew can explain. Then she left months later and waited years before she killed again."

"You did an amazing job, Lucy, really. And I guess you get along with that reporter."

"She's very smart. She thinks like a cop, but doesn't have to follow the rules." Lucy realized that she didn't always follow the rules, either. Maybe she was a little jealous of Max's freedom. Except that while Max could expose a killer, only Lucy and other law enforcement agents could bring a killer to justice.

"I don't know if Mom and Dad are going to be satisfied," Lucy said, almost surprising herself.

"I'll talk to them. Nelia did, but they worry."

About Nelia and Carina, Lucy thought. Did they worry as much about her? After what her father said, she realized she had a different place in the family than she'd thought. There were some things that couldn't be forgotten, some things that—maybe—would never be forgiven. Lucy had made peace with what happened on her high school graduation. It had taken her years, but she was stronger now. Maybe her father was right and it changed her in a fundamental way. But she couldn't go back. She couldn't undo the past. She was who she was because of how she was raised—if she hadn't been raised as she was, would she have been able to overcome her attack?

"I'll come by before I leave San Diego," Lucy said.

"When are you going back to work?"

"After we find Danielle Sharpe."

Max was waiting for Lucy when she walked away from Carina. "I'm not cutting you out," Lucy said. "But this is now an official FBI investigation. And I promise, they're not going to drop it."

"Oh, I know that. And I have what I need from Chief Causey and from Andrew."

"What?"

"Promises of quotes and interviews. An exclusive. And I talked to your brother earlier."

"Which one?"

"Dillon. The one who doesn't want to strangle me."

"You haven't met them all," Lucy said, trying to lighten the conversation.

"I've done enough research to know I don't want to be on the bad side of *any* Kincaid—or Rogan, for that matter."

"You're not. Without you, we'd never have identified Danielle Sharpe and we'd never have known what really happened to Justin."

"We still don't. We have theories, but you need to stop her. I have complete faith in you, Lucy. And I don't say that to a lot of people."

"I appreciate it. I'll let you know what's happening."

"Thanks. And if my staff or I learn anything new, I'll shoot it to you." Lucy extended her hand. "Thanks for everything."

Max tilted her head. "I'm sure I'll see you tonight or tomorrow."

"It might be a zoo, especially if we arrest her."

"Before you leave, I'd like to take you—and your husband if he's back—out to dinner."

Lucy smiled. "I'd like that."

Lucy left the police station and walked outside. A brief horn alerted her to Ken's location parked in a red zone. She slid into the passenger seat.

"Where are you staying? Your parents'?"

"The US Grant."

"Wow. They must pay you better in San Antonio."

"Why?"

"You need to pack a bag, just in case." He pulled rapidly from the curb and immediately into traffic. "I always have an overnight in the trunk—been stuck too many times in the boondocks."

"In case of what?"

"We have three departments working double time on this right now. Sacramento already reported back that Sharpe no longer lives in the house up there—the landlord said she moved out more than two years ago. They're getting her rental agreement and interviewing the neighbors and talking to her former employer, but it's not going to get us anywhere. So I followed up with the lawyer in L.A.—Gillogley? Donovan's partner, the tax lawyer. She'll talk to us, but only with a warrant. Gave us a bone—said the lawyer is in Los Angeles. My boss is working with the AUSA, we should have it in an hour or two."

"Andrew can expedite it."

"Yeah, but we have to keep him out of it from here on out."

"Then why am I involved?"

"You're not the kid's mother. You were related to him, but it's a degrees of separation thing." He glanced at her. "Do you want out?"

"No."

"Good. So we're heading to L.A. If we hit the road now I'm hoping to miss most traffic, though it'll still be a mess once we reach Orange County."

"Backtrack—why can't the L.A. office interview Gillogley and her lawyer friend?"

"First, it's going to take time—I'll take bets on whether we get the warrant before or after we hit the L.A. County line. We're going to talk to Gillogley about whom she referred Sharpe to—the lawyer who called to thank her, according to your reporter friend. L.A. can handle it, but we'd have to get them up to speed, and then we have the not-so-sensitive information about this chick. That she may be stalking another family. It could take a day to put together a team from L.A.—why take the time? By the way, based on the timeline that referral call was only a short time after Sharpe left Sacramento."

"She's built another nest," Lucy muttered.

"Nest. Sure, I guess. Whatever it is, it's likely she's still there. She stays two to five years in each place. I got another agent building on the reporter's timeline with addresses, employment records, filling in the blanks. By the time we get to L.A. we'll have a broad warrant. Talk to Chris Donovan's mother, the lawyer, and follow up with what we learn. Boots to the ground and all that. Sacramento may have been a dead end—but if her MO holds, she'll be entrenched somewhere else. That's what you said, right?"

"Yes."

Lucy left Ken in the car and ran up to her room. She packed a bag, sent Sean a text message, and was back in the car in less than ten minutes. Sean responded.

I'll see you when you get back, Princess. I'll make sure Maxine doesn't get out of line.

She rolled her eyes and almost laughed.

"All good?" Ken said.

"Good."

"Want to take that bet?"

"About the warrant? It's what, two hours to L.A.?"

He laughed. "If you want."

"We'll have it before."

"Or you buy dinner."

"Fair enough."

Chapter Thirty-one

Max arrived back at the hotel and admitted to herself that she felt a little lost. She'd turned everything over to the police and now she had nothing to do except wait.

She took her laptop to the hotel bar and ordered soup, salad, and a glass of wine while she started her article on the case. She believed the FBI when they said they'd give her the exclusive, but sometimes even when they had the best of intentions, they let information slip. She wanted to be ready to run with the article as soon as they arrested Danielle Sharpe, and she could fill in the details—hopefully with solid quotes—on the fly.

Her phone rang, it was John. Why was he calling her? He had made it clear he wanted her to no longer pursue the case he'd put in her lap. He'd avoided her calls all weekend. And now, here he was.

She almost ignored his call. But she couldn't do that—she owed him something, didn't she? Except she couldn't give him what he wanted—peace of mind.

"Hello," she answered.

"Hi, Max, it's John."

"How are you doing?"

"I haven't been able to sleep. I promised Blair I wouldn't contact you, but I need to know—have you found anything?"

"I tried calling you this weekend. I had questions, but you didn't answer."

"Blair had been with me. She's so stressed—the trial starts in a week. I didn't want her to know we were talking, further upset her."

"We're not doing anything wrong," she snapped. "I'm trying to get answers."

"For me. And I appreciate it."

"No, for Justin Stanton and the other victims."

"And? Do you have answers?"

"Yes, John." She paused, considered what she should say and how to say it. Tact wasn't her strong suit. "I don't know if they're the answers you want."

"Anything will help—I'm at my wit's end."

"Why? Honestly, John, why? Blair's attorney is competent and he thinks the prosecution isn't going to be able to make the case. Me? I'll give it fifty-fifty. Circumstantial cases are hard to prove, but not impossible."

"But I have to know who killed my son. We've been over this, Max—I have to know. I can't sleep. I can barely eat. The last nine months have been hell. Peter is dead. My son—" His voice cracked. "I don't expect you to understand."

"I understand grief, John."

"Then tell me what's happening."

"I solved Justin Stanton's murder, John."

"Oh, my God—Max, that's great. Who?"

"I can't tell you yet. I promised the police I wouldn't talk about the case until they give me the okay to release the information."

"This is me, Maxine! What am I going to do with the information?"

"I don't know—"

"This person killed my son!"

"No, John, the person who killed Justin Stanton and the other boys didn't kill Peter. It's not the same person."

"Of course it is."

"It's not. I can prove it to you, but not until I get the okay. You're going to have to trust me on that."

"I don't. I don't trust you! It *has* to be the same person!"

He was losing it. "John," she said in a calm, quiet voice. "I don't have the answers you want, but I'm still looking. You need to go into this trial with your eyes open."

"They are. Max, I'm dying here. I don't know how to keep it together. I need to help my wife."

John was clinging to these cold cases because he wanted proof that his wife wasn't a killer. But deep down, he had doubts.

"I have to go," he said and hung up.

She put her phone down and asked the waiter to bring her a martini.

When he returned with her drink, she thanked him and saw a familiar face in the doorway.

Sean Rogan.

He walked over to her and sat down. "Hello, Max."

"Lucy isn't here."

"I just talked to her. She said the meeting today went well and she's on her way to interview the suspect."

"Did you just fly in?"

"Came right from the airport."

"Have you eaten?"

"I could use food."

Max signaled for the waiter and he took Sean's order. At least the PI ordered a beer so Max wasn't drinking alone. Not that she cared.

"Did Lucy fill you in?"

Sean nodded. "We talked last night, after you two put together the presentation. She asked me to cut you some slack, that you had developed a symbiotic relationship."

"I suppose we did. But I don't care if you cut me any slack, Sean. I'm not fragile."

He smiled. "No, you're certainly not."

They didn't talk anymore about the case, and Max was relieved. Sean asked about some of her other cases, and admitted he'd read a couple of her books while he was in Sacramento. He particularly liked her last book, which she'd written about a nursing home director who had killed several patients.

"Why that one?" she asked, curious.

"First, the subject matter. You made me laugh with some of the antics of Lois Kershaw and her band of octogenarian sleuths."

Max smiled. "Lois is a hoot. I visited her a couple of weeks ago after she had surgery. You'd think she was getting younger."

"And the way you stood up to the local police. I have a healthy respect for law enforcement and some deep distrust. You seemed to balance that well."

"It's like the nursery rhyme."

"What is?"

"When the police are good, they are very, very good; when they are bad, they are horrid."

Sean laughed. "I like that."

Max considered pumping Sean for more information about his wife, but realized he'd recognize any ploy she came up with. Instead, she sipped her drink.

"What is it you want to ask?" Sean said.

"Everything, but I won't. And—I'm not digging around. I did, before your threats, and I'm curious about a lot of things, but I can let it go."

"You can? That doesn't seem to be in your personality."

"I have a lot of respect for your wife, and I don't say that about a lot of people. On the one hand, I am curious. I'm curious how Lucy became involved as a consultant for two major cases in New York before she was ever an FBI agent. I'm curious about why you were expelled from Stanford. I'm intrigued by the cases the staff dug up that Lucy worked last year in San Antonio."

As she spoke, Sean didn't move. He didn't change much of anything, except he was watching her closely. Trying to assess her angle? Her game plan?

"Yes, I want to know what makes Lucy tick, but I realized it's just because I hate not knowing *anything*. I like facts and proof and truth. But I'm really okay not knowing. Maybe for the first time in my life."

"Why?" he asked sharply.

"Because whatever brought Lucy here, to this point in her life, isn't an unsolved mystery. It's not a cold case. Justice doesn't need to be served, because it already has been. So it's really only me, Maxine Revere, being curious just because I want to know."

Sean didn't say anything, and Max ordered another round of drinks. She wasn't positive he believed her, but she didn't care. *She* believed herself. That she wanted to know didn't mean she had to know, and for the first time she was really okay with that.

When the drinks came, Max took a long sip, then ate one of the three olives. "You read my books, you know about my mother."

"You don't hold back."

"Rarely. I don't like secrets and hidden agendas and people I don't understand. I never understood my mother—why she moved all the time, why we never had a home, why she even had me in the first place. I created all these fantasies in my head about her being a spy, a fugitive, in witness protection—I had an active imagination. And then I find out she has a huge trust fund and lived on the money my great-grandparents had worked so hard for. The Sterlings came from nothing and made something wonderful. I didn't know any of it until I was nearly ten and my mom left me with my grandparents and never came back. And my mother? She did nothing for it except to be born. Because I believed so many lies growing up, I'm skeptical of everything now."

"Did you ever look for her?"

"On and off. She used to send me birthday cards—I was born December thirty-first. She said my birthday would always be a party. But I don't even know if that's my real birthday, I don't have a real birth certificate. My grandparents had one filed with the courts—I mean, I exist—but even they don't know where I was born or what day. They didn't know about me until my mom left me with them."

"So you solve cold cases because your life is one big cold case."

"Pretty much." She ate a french fry. "I know you and Lucy want to stay off the grid, as much as you can, and I will continue to respect that wish. Like I said, I have a lot of admiration for your wife, and I don't want to blow her trust."

Sean drained his beer. "You want to know why I was expelled from Stanford?"

She raised an eyebrow. "Of course I do. I said I wouldn't dig around, not that I didn't want to know." She smiled, and was relieved when Sean smiled back.

"I learned that one of my professors was a pedophile. I hacked into a cybercrime symposium on campus and exposed not only the professor, but the flaws in the new FBI cybercrime software."

She didn't doubt Sean had done exactly that. She was about to comment when her phone vibrated.

"It's my producer."

"You want me to leave?" he asked, though he made no move to get up.

She shook her head. "Ben, I hope you have something good."

"Depends how you define good. I found another victim."

She sighed. It wouldn't end, would it?

"Where?"

"San Jose, California. A seven-year-old boy went missing from his bedroom eleven years ago. He was found in a shallow grave but several weeks later, and his body was not in good shape. They determined he died of a drug overdose, not suffocation, but he was wrapped in his own blanket with a stuffed animal. Father was having an affair. But it didn't originally pop up on our radar because there was one other distinct difference."

When Ben didn't immediately tell her, she said, "You're killing me, Ben."

"There was a second victim. The babysitter was shot to death. The police went with the theory that a sexual predator broke in, killed the babysitter and grabbed the kid. When they found his body, they determined there was no sexual assault but attributed it to the fact that the sexual predator had accidentally overdosed him."

"Was there any forensic evidence?"

"No. The police rounded up all the sexual predators in the neighborhood, but couldn't get anyone to confess and with no physical evidence they couldn't make a case."

"The babysitter caught her in the act—wow. Okay, I'm going to pass that information on to Agent Kincaid."

"The San Jose Police Department has ballistics—according to Nick, they ran them through the federal database and didn't get a hit, but tell your agent that if they find the gun, they can match. I just forwarded you everything we have."

"Nick? You called Nick?"

"Yeah, is that a problem? If I had to get information in Florida, I would have called Marco."

"Don't do that again."

"You're breaking up with him, aren't you?"

"None of your business."

"Everything about you is my business, Maxine."

She hung up without comment and checked her e-mail. As Ben said, he'd sent her the file—she forwarded it to Lucy, then sent her a text message.

> Found the missing victim—Jonah Oliver. Eleven years ago. His babysitter
> was shot and killed. There are some differences in the MO, but nothing
> substantial. San Jose police have ballistics, should be in the FBI database.
> Be careful, you now know she has a gun.

"Another victim?" Sean said.

"Yes. I sent everything to your wife."

"Does it bother you not to be in the middle of things?"

"Who says I'm not?" She smiled and turned her laptop toward him. "I have my work done, just need to layer in the details."

Sean's face darkened. Before he could threaten her again—which she wouldn't appreciate—she said, "I'm not mentioning Lucy. Your brother-in-law—Dr. Kincaid—has already agreed to give me something good, and I'm going with that. I stick by my promises."

Sean relaxed and smiled. The smile didn't quite reach his eyes, but he was softening toward her . . . as much as anyone as curious and suspicious as he was could soften.

"I guess we have time while we wait—another drink?"

"Absolutely."

She wasn't holding out hope that she'd get more information out of Sean Rogan than she had out of Lucy, but it would be fun trying to figure him out.

He was just as interesting as his wife.

Maybe even more so.

Chapter Thirty-two

"I'm never going to complain about traffic in San Antonio again."

Ken glanced at Lucy. "You were raised in San Diego, right? We have awful traffic."

"You have to admit, San Diego isn't as bad as *this*."

They were driving slow—at two in the afternoon—on I-5 through downtown L.A. Ken made Lucy nervous with the way he juggled two phones while he navigated traffic, but she didn't say anything. She had to admit, she was a nervous driver. She had been in a car accident when she was five, and another just two years ago when she had taken a witness into protective custody. The person who wanted her dead ran them off the road. The only time she wasn't nervous was when Sean was driving—not because Sean was unusually safe, but because he generally distracted her with conversation and jokes.

"There's this great burger place in Burbank, which is probably where we're going to stay tonight. My office reserved two rooms at a Residence Inn, just in case. I don't mind driving back late, but I think we'll need a day or two of interviews."

"Burger place—I can afford a better meal than fast food," Lucy said. She'd lost the bet—the warrant hadn't come through yet, and they were already ten miles over the L.A. border.

"Sure, but they have the *best* burgers I've ever had. I just have to remember the name. Anyway, hold on."

He picked up his phone. "Wham-bam! Got the warrant."

"Call Gillogley," Lucy said. "We can then hit the law office first."

"You don't want to talk to Donovan?"

"I do, but the last call Danielle made to her ex-husband has been bothering me. I'd like to locate Danielle Sharpe immediately—interviewing Cindy Donovan will help for the prosecution, but it's not going to get us closer to finding Danielle."

He handed her his phone. "Her number's there, you can forward her the warrant."

Lucy called Sandra Gillogley. "Ms. Gillogley, my name is Lucy Kincaid, with the FBI. You spoke to my associate earlier—SSA Kenneth Swan."

"Yes. Are you here?"

"On our way in traffic. The warrant just came through. I'm hoping I can forward you the digital copy and we can expedite getting the name of the lawyer you referred Danielle Sharpe to. It's imperative we find her soon."

"Why?"

Lucy glanced at Ken.

He said, "I didn't give her details. Go ahead."

"She's wanted for questioning in three homicides."

"Danielle?"

It didn't sound like she believed it.

"I can't give you more details, but we are following up on evidence uncovered in a recent investigation. Will you give us the information or are we going to have to see you in person?"

Lucy didn't usually get testy with people, but she didn't like people who stonewalled just for the sake of maintaining a level of power over others.

"Send it to me, I'll call you back after I read it."

Lucy hung up. "What a piece of work," she mumbled and forwarded Gillogley the warrant.

"She's just doing her job."

"No, she's being deliberate. I know people like her—they need to always have the upper hand. She doesn't need a damn warrant to give us the name of a friend she referred an employee to. She just wants to feel important and intellectually superior to others."

"Never stop profiling people, do you?"

320

"I'm not a profiler," Lucy said.

Her phone rang. It was Max.

"Hi, Max," Lucy answered.

"You sound irritated."

"Lawyers."

Max laughed. "Well, at least you didn't say *reporters* in that tone. I just e-mailed you information about a similar case in San Jose that fits the timeline. Boy, kidnapped from his bedroom, wrapped in a blanket with his stuffed animal. Father having an affair, mother working late—she was a nurse and worked twenty-four-hour shifts—but there are two key discrepancies. First, the babysitter was shot and killed. Second, the autopsy specified drug overdose—same narcotic found in the other victims."

"We can possibly exhume the body, though proving suffocation might be difficult. Inconclusive at best."

"The body wasn't found for three weeks. Buried in a wooded area behind the house, three miles away."

"I take it the boy liked the woods?"

"I have no confirmation on that—something to talk to the parents about. But I think you're missing the key point."

"What?"

"She shot and killed the babysitter."

"We don't know that it was Danielle."

"You said there would be another victim between Tommy Porter and Chris Donovan—this could be the one. And get this—my staff, as fabulous as they are and as careful as Danielle Sharp is—learned that she worked for a start-up company in the Silicon Valley, as the assistant to one of the lawyers. Jonah's father was that lawyer. Read what I sent, if you disagree, be prepared to have a damn good reason."

Max hung up. And she thought Lucy was testy?

Maybe she was. "Max's staff may have found another victim," Lucy said. She didn't have time to bring up the e-mail because Gillogley called back on Ken's phone.

Ken answered. "This is Kenneth Swan. You're on speaker with me and my partner, Agent Kincaid."

"My friend is Archie Frank, a partner with Duncan, Fieldstone, Frank and Devereaux. I do a lot of audit work with him. I gave him a list of three legal secretaries who had tax backgrounds, which is what he was looking for, and we ran into each other at a holiday function a year ago. He told me he'd hired Danielle and she was just what his office needed—meticulous, focused on the fine details. That's all we discussed related to Danielle."

"When did he hire Danielle?" Lucy asked.

"I didn't ask; he didn't say."

Lucy really didn't like this woman. She was more specific. "When did you refer Danielle to Mr. Frank?"

"I don't recall. I would say it was two years ago, before April but after New Year's. I don't keep records of every call or referral."

Ken said, "What's the address?"

"Their offices are on North Brand, in Glendale."

Ken suddenly swerved over three lanes and exited the freeway, making Lucy dizzy.

"Agents?"

"Here," Ken said. "I almost missed the Glendale exit."

I'm sure there would have been another, she thought. Lucy couldn't wait to get out of the car.

"Exact address?" Ken asked.

Gillogley read it off; Lucy wrote it down but suspected Ken had memorized it.

"Should I expect you today?" the lawyer asked.

"We'll call you back and let you know. Is this your cell phone?"

"Yes."

"Keep it with you." Ken hung up. "That should give her something to stew over."

Other than his driving, Lucy liked Ken. He was chatty, but didn't expect her to talk or share. He was easygoing, but could play hardball. He was smart, but also fun.

Why couldn't she have a boss like Ken?

You could, if you wanted to move back to San Diego.

She couldn't. Even before this week, she didn't want to, and now she knew it would add more stress and conflict in her life. She and Carina might be able to get along, but Sean would be much happier working with Patrick in D.C. or Jack in Sacramento. Lucy had seriously been thinking of requesting a position in the D.C. or Virginia office. She had one more year to get through here, but after working with Dillon again on this case, she realized how much she missed him and Kate.

But she loved San Antonio, and the only reason she'd been thinking of leaving was because of the conflict with her new boss. She didn't want to run away because a situation became too difficult. She ran into trouble and danger head-on, why couldn't she manage her professional life in the same way?

Ken was back on the phone. "Hey, I need the second warrant—the one to get Danielle Sharpe's employment records, personnel file, address, whole nine yards. Where is it?" He listened a minute. "You have ten minutes, we know where she works. If she's there, we're arresting her—if she's not, we need all her data and it's a fucking law office. They're not going to give us shit without a warrant."

He hung up. "I explained exactly what I needed, and they put it all in one warrant—Archie Frank will laugh us out the front door."

"You read it?" *While driving?*

"I read fast. I can just tell at the beginning that they were being too general, thinking I could use this with anyone other than Gillogley, but I know lawyers, and if this guy has a stick up his ass, he'll bark just because he can. Text Richardson all the vitals—name, address, yada yada."

Lucy typed on his phone, happy to do it so Ken didn't take his eyes off the road.

"So you think your reporter buddy was right about this other victim? What's-his-name?"

"Jonah. I haven't read her evidence yet. But she wouldn't have sent it if she wasn't certain. The babysitter was shot and killed, she wanted me to be careful because that changes Danielle's MO. She's willing to kill whoever tries to stop her from taking the kid."

"Do we need backup?"

"The chance that she has a gun with her at her place of employment is slim—we need to be cautious. I don't want us to tip our hand. We ask to see her, we don't tell anyone why, and we arrest her immediately."

"Works for me. The L.A. office has been alerted."

"If she's not at the office, we call in backup for her house."

"Why wouldn't she be? It's Monday afternoon."

"You heard her on the phone—she's cracking. I suspect this is part of the cycle—her ex-husband said her calls were emotional, ranging from calm reminiscing to verbal attacks. In fact, we should get Glendale PD to take her into custody while we find out who she's targeting. The more information we have when we interrogate her, the better."

"Fine by me. This is your show, Kincaid."

"It's really not."

"Hey, you're the one who ID'd Danielle. We're lucky Revere didn't swoop in for an interview with the killer before we had a chance to nab her."

"That's not her style."

"I haven't had many—okay, I haven't had *any* good experiences with a reporter, and I've been in the FBI for . . . thirteen? Fourteen? Wow, *fifteen* years this June. Damn. I'm going to be forty in July."

Lucy had never had a case partner who chatted or jumped around the conversation as much as Ken, but it was informative to know that he'd been in the FBI since he was twenty-five. Most agents these days started the FBI as a second career and were already over thirty when they entered Quantico, including half her graduating class. Many came from the military.

"This is it," Ken said as he pulled in front of a high-rise in downtown Glendale, a city northeast of Los Angeles. He popped an official duty placard in the dashboard so he could park in the loading zone. "My favorite part of the job," he said with a wink.

Lucy almost laughed.

They got out and went into the building. "Eighteenth floor," Ken said to the guard and flashed his badge, "and don't alert the tenants." He showed the guard a photo of Danielle Sharpe. "If this woman attempts to leave the building, please detain her and call me." He dropped his card on the desk.

Ken didn't wait for an argument, he simply passed the desk and hit the elevator button. "Sometimes," he said when they stepped into the elevator, "they want to argue with you or flex some muscle, pretend they're real cops or some such nonsense. Some of them are cool beans, some have been on the job, I can usually tell by looking. That skinny kid was a rent-a-cop."

Lucy ignored most of Ken's commentary, mentally preparing herself for the interview with Danielle Sharpe. How to approach the woman, how to get her to confess. It went back to the eyes—Danielle couldn't face her victims. She couldn't watch as she killed the children because she had to distance herself—and that was going to be Lucy's in. Photos of the crime scenes, photos of the autopsies.

Lucy's stomach twisted in knots. She would have to look at them, too. She would have to steel herself against the pain and rage she would feel looking at the young lives cut short. At looking at Justin in death.

They exited the elevator into a small lobby. Double glass doors led to the pricey law offices. Two receptionists had large desks in front of a stunning view of Los Angeles to the south. Stunning, Lucy supposed, because she expected to see a layer of smog, but today was crystal clear blue.

They walked in through the doors and approached the first receptionist, who was clearly surprised at the visitors. "You need to check in with the guard downstairs," she said formally.

Ken flashed his badge, then showed the warrant which was on his phone. "Danielle Sharpe's office—don't call her, just lead us to her desk."

"Ms. Sharpe isn't in today."

"Who's her direct supervisor?"

"Uh, Nina. Nina Fieldstone is the office manager—she supervises all paralegals and legal secretaries."

"Contact her and Archie Frank."

"Mr. Frank?"

"Just do it."

The receptionist immediately got on the phone. "Nina, there are two FBI agents here asking to see Danielle. They'd like to speak with you and Mr. Frank." She didn't say anything for a long minute. "Yes, ma'am."

She hung up and said, "Nina will find Mr. Frank and she asked me to bring you to a conference room."

"Actually, we'll check out Danielle Sharpe's desk first. It's covered under the warrant."

"I can't allow that," the receptionist said. "We have privileged information—"

"Don't care, it's covered."

"Mr. Frank will want to read the warrant."

The stately young receptionist was nervous, but Lucy had to admire the way she stood up for her employer and protocols.

"Sharpe's desk," Ken said. "Now."

The receptionist got back on the phone. It took longer to reach Nina this time, and when she did, she said, "They want to go to Danielle's desk. They have a warrant."

She hung up and less than fifteen seconds later, a tall, burly man with a shocking head of white hair reminiscent of Albert Einstein came through an almost hidden set of doors on the far side of the lobby. Immediately behind him was a willowy brunette in impossibly tall spike heels.

"I'm Archie Frank," he said in a deep voice.

Ken and Lucy showed their ID, the warrant, and explained that they needed to speak with Danielle Sharpe.

"I'm Nina Fieldstone, Danielle's supervisor. What's this about?"

Ken was about to speak, but Lucy was painfully aware of the two receptionists listening to the entire conversation. "Is there someplace we can go in private?" Lucy said.

Frank turned and walked back through the doors. They followed. The first door on the left was a small conference room with the same stunning view. "I don't appreciate the FBI coming in unannounced and terrorizing my staff."

"An overstatement," Ken said. "Danielle Sharpe is wanted for questioning in a homicide investigation."

"Murder?" Nina said. "*Danielle?*"

Frank shot her a look that said to shut up, and he said, "Warrant."

Ken handed him his phone. "We drove up from San Diego, I didn't have time to print it."

Frank scrolled through. "This is vague."

"Not for me."

"Where is Ms. Sharpe?" Lucy asked.

Nina looked at Frank, he nodded, and she said, "She called in sick this morning."

"Is that common?"

"No—she had a doctor's appointment last week, she has been under the weather—so I'm not surprised she took a sick day."

Was Danielle suspicious? Did her ex-husband say or do anything on the phone call that may have tipped her off? Lucy would have to listen to it again. Something wasn't right.

"We need her address immediately," Lucy said, "and we have some questions for you both."

"I barely know Ms. Sharpe," Frank said.

"Sandra Gillogley gave her a recommendation two years ago and you hired her."

"Sandra is a longtime friend and colleague. She's given many recommendations. Ms. Sharpe worked for her for a couple of years and did a good job, we needed someone with her experience."

"And that's it?"

He paused for a few seconds, then said, "Nina, I'm going to ask Trevor Banks to be our legal representative for this investigation." He then said to Ken and Lucy, "Mr. Banks is one of our senior associates, he came from the Los Angeles City Attorney's office and has extensive experience with criminal law and warrants. He'll be your contact between this law firm and the FBI for the duration of the investigation into Danielle Sharpe. If you'll excuse me."

He walked out. Lucy wanted to say no, she *didn't* excuse him, because he was a pompous jerk. But Ken let him go. He turned to Nina.

"I-I'm just stunned," Nina said.

"Are you friendly with Danielle?" Lucy asked.

"Yes, we go out after work occasionally."

"Did you speak to her this morning when she called in?"

"Briefly, she called on my cell phone, told me she was sick. She sounded sick, I told her to take the day off and if she needed another day to just let me know. She's put in a lot of extra hours since the New Year for an important client."

"When was the last time you saw her?" Lucy asked.

"Friday. Here at the office—she looked tired. She was supposed to come to Grace's house—she's another legal secretary—for a game of bunco. We have a group that plays once a month. But she said she hadn't slept well, and felt under the weather."

"So you would say that you and Danielle are close?" Lucy didn't buy it. Danielle wouldn't be close to anyone.

"I'm probably closer to her than anyone else here. Danielle is quiet, keeps to herself."

"But *are* you close? Like girlfriend, tell-each-other-secrets close?"

"No, not like that."

"Did you know that her only son was murdered by a sexual predator twenty-three years ago?"

Nina's eyes widened. "No. All she ever said was that she was divorced."

The door opened and a young, attractive male in a suit walked in. "Trevor Banks." He handed his card to both Ken and Lucy.

"Kincaid," Ken said, "go with Ms. Fieldstone and get Sharpe's home address and phone number. Banks, take me to Danielle's desk."

"Mrs. Fieldstone can't be alone with one of your agents. Which is more important to you?"

"Both," Ken said. "A child's life is in immediate danger and I'm not going to play one-upmanship with a bunch of lawyers."

"Agent Swan, there's no need for—"

"No bullshit, or I'll arrest you for obstruction."

"You hardly have a case—"

Lucy said, "If we don't find Danielle Sharpe quickly, the son of one of your employees will be killed. We have evidence that she's a serial killer, and every second you delay is a second closer to another murder."

Nina sucked in her breath.

"I don't think theatrics are necessary," Banks said, though he looked both shaken and suspicious. "Nina, get Agent Kincaid what she needs. Agent Swan, with me."

Wasn't that what Ken just asked for? Banks turned it around as if the order came from him. Ken winked at Lucy as he and Banks walked out.

"Were you lying?" Nina asked as she led Lucy down a long hall and through a series of turns.

"No."

"Dear Lord, I have a son."

"Where is he?"

She looked at her watch. "My mother-in-law is picking him up from school. She watches him until I get off work. I need to call her."

"Call her, and then get me the file."

She shook her head. "She doesn't have a cell phone. She walks to pick him up at school. She'll be home a few minutes after three."

That was still nearly twenty minutes away.

Nina's office was private and spacious. She opened a file cabinet, pulled out a slender folder and handed it to Lucy.

Lucy immediately opened it. A photo of Danielle—much more current than her driver's license. Lucy took a picture of it and sent it to the team that Ken and Chief Causey had assembled this morning.

She flipped through. Hiring dates, reviews, previous employer, address. "Address in Glendale—is this far?"

"I haven't been over there, but it's just south of the Galleria."

Lucy had no idea where that was, but Nina made it sound like it was close.

She sent Ken a text message with the information.

Lucy asked Nina if she could have a copy of the file. Nina took the documents and left the room.

Lucy looked around. Nina didn't have the view of the L.A. skyline, but of the freeway below and hills beyond that. Her desk was immaculate, with a pen and pencil set, her name plate, and a grouping of pictures. Lucy noted one of Nina with a man she presumed was her husband and a cute boy of about six. They were at Disneyland and Minnie Mouse and

Mickey Mouse had joined the family for a photo op. A school picture of the boy, this maybe a year more recent. His two front teeth were missing and one had just started to grow in. A wedding photo of a much younger Nina and her husband.

Nina came back and handed Lucy the copy. "I had to get Banks to approve this, but it's okay—it's covered under the warrant."

Lucy could have told her that, but instead focused on the photos. "Your family?"

"Yes. My husband—he's a partner here. And our son, Kevin. He'll be nine next month. The time sure goes . . . did you really mean that a child is in danger?"

"Yes." Lucy looked at her phone. Ken said he had sent over two agents with Glendale PD to Danielle's residence and to let him know when she was done.

Lucy wasn't done. Banks wasn't here, and Nina was thinking about something . . . Lucy had to get it out of her.

"How many employees with your law firm? It's public information, please don't make me do the research."

"Um—well, with the partners, junior partners, associates, support staff . . . between sixty-five and seventy employees. I could get you exact numbers if you need them, but I'd need to run a report."

"The warrant didn't specify employee information," Lucy said, "but Danielle targets a specific type of family. The family has one child, a boy, under the age of ten, and both parents work. Who else—other than your family—fits that profile?" She didn't want to mention the adultery—that would raise the woman's hackles and she might not talk.

"Oh, God—Kevin." She pulled her cell phone out and dialed. "Mom? Mom—it's Nina. Do you have Kevin? . . . I know, you always pick him up on time, I just . . . okay. Okay, I'm sorry, I was just thinking about him . . . yeah, I won't be late, I know Monday is your bingo night. . . . Thanks, Mom." She hung up and let out a deep breath. "Kevin's safe. He and my mother-in-law just walked in the house. They're making oatmeal raisin cookies."

She was nervous. Why?

"What other families?"

"I have to think . . ." She sat down heavily at her desk. Lucy sat across from her.

"Carly has a boy. I don't remember how old he is, maybe four now. She started working here after he was born."

Lucy took a note. "Carly what?"

"Um, Carly Milligan. She works part-time, her husband is a surgeon. And then . . . no, they have a girl. Bruce Zarian has a boy. He's one of the junior partners. Really nice guy. Melinda Cage—she's an associate, she has a son. Well, she has two sons. The oldest is a teenager. I think she's going through a divorce, I can find out—"

"Look at the employee list if that helps. One child, a boy, under ten and over five. Married." She paused. "And in each case, the father had been having an affair."

Nina's face paled. "Wh-what? Sh-she kills husbands?"

"No. She kills their son."

"Oh, God. Oh, God. This can't be happening."

It clicked. "Is your husband having an affair?"

"I-I don't know. I don't know. But . . . I am. I have to go to my son."

"I will have an agent pick him up at your mother's house and bring him here. Okay?"

"Okay. Okay. I have to talk to my husband. I can't believe—"

"Hold on one second, okay?"

Lucy called Ken on the phone. "Ken, I need someone to pick up the Fieldstone boy at his grandmother's house. He may be Danielle's next target."

"I'll call you right back. Send me the address."

"Plainclothes, discreet. If she's stalking him, we don't want her to become suspicious."

"Roger that."

Lucy got the address from Nina, sent it to Ken. "You and your husband are not in trouble here, but I need you to be completely honest in all your answers."

"Always. Are you getting my son?"

"Yes, and my partner will get the names so you can give your mother-in-law the information."

"Can I call Tony?"

"Yes."

She made a brief call.

"I'm sorry about this," Lucy said after she hung up, "but all the secrets need to come out."

"Tony knows. I've been having an affair with Grace for three years, since her divorce. It's . . . comfortable. Tony and I are happy, we make it work. We're talking about having another baby. I love him."

"And if he's having an affair?"

"I-I'll deal with it. I still love him. I can't very well say he can't screw around if I'm doing it."

But Lucy could tell she was hurt. Either because he hadn't told her or because she really was a hypocrite, Lucy couldn't be certain.

"From what we know, Danielle targets families where the husband is the adulterer. There are four known victims over twenty years."

"Twenty *years*?"

"I can't go into details, but we're confident we have the right person." Lucy looked at her phone. "Can you call your mother-in-law and tell her to expect two FBI agents within twenty minutes, a man and woman. They'll be dressed casually and show their photo identification and badges. If Danielle is stalking your son—and she has stalked the other victims—we don't want to tip her off. If anyone calls or asks your mother about Kevin leaving early, she needs to tell them that friends picked him up because his mother had to work late."

"What? Why?"

"We don't want Danielle knowing that we've identified her. She's on edge, she may snap and do something unpredictable. The agents will bring Kevin here."

"But you're going to find her, right?"

The door opened and Tony Fieldstone walked in. Lucy recognized him from his photos. He was several years older than Nina, in good shape, and dressed impeccably.

"What's going on with Kevin?"

He looked at Lucy, then said to his wife, "Nina, you can't talk to the

FBI without Trevor here. Archie told me they have a warrant, but that doesn't mean—"

"It's Kevin."

He blinked. "What?"

"Danielle's wanted for murder. And Agent Kincaid thinks that she's planning to hurt Kevin."

"*Danielle?*" He shook his head.

"Sir, we've sent two agents to pick up your son at your mother's house, and it's imperative that we find Danielle Sharpe as soon as possible. I need to be blunt. She targets families who have one child and—"

Nina said, "Tony, are you and Lana sleeping together?"

The look on Tony's face said it all. He couldn't even respond to the blunt question.

"I thought so," Nina said. "I just—why didn't you tell me?"

"Not here, Nina! Not now—"

"It's as much my fault as yours," Nina said, her voice cracking. "She kills children of couples who are unfaithful. Four boys already, and Agent Kincaid thinks that she's been stalking *us*. But my affair with Grace has been going on longer—I never thought—God, I never thought—"

Lucy said, "This is *not* your fault, Nina." Her voice was sharper than she intended. "Neither of you are to blame. I can tell you more later, after we find her, but casting blame isn't going to help."

Tony went to his wife and hugged her tightly. "Are you certain?" he asked over the head of his wife.

"Yes."

Ken came into the office, Trevor Banks on his heels. "Kincaid, a minute."

Banks wasn't happy. "Nina, have you been talking? I told you."

Ken shut the door on Banks and said quietly, "She's not there."

"She bolted? Who tipped her off?"

"Address is a mail drop. We need another warrant to get her mail and records to see if there's a physical address associated with it, but that's going to take time."

"Both Fieldstones are having affairs—but it seems they know, or sort of knew. We have to find her house."

"Ask them."

Lucy and Ken walked back into Nina's office. Lucy asked, "Have you ever been to Danielle Sharpe's house?"

They all shook their heads.

Nina said, "I can call her. She'll recognize my number—she always picks up."

"No," Banks said at the same time as Lucy said, "Good."

Lucy stared at the lawyer. "This woman may not seem like a threat, but she has the capacity for violence. She has killed four young boys and a babysitter. That we *know* about. Don't ask me for proof, don't ask me for evidence, that's not your call. The AUSA issued a search warrant for her desk, her house, her car. We have an arrest warrant. We are going to find her, and the more you delay and play around with legal bullshit, the greater chance she'll disappear. If Mrs. Fieldstone is willing to help us, then dammit, let her!"

Lucy stunned herself. She didn't know what came over her, but she couldn't backtrack now. She turned to Nina because Banks didn't say a word, and said, "We need to trace the call—"

Ken snapped his fingers. "Cell phone! We didn't have her phone number until now, we can trace it without a call. Brilliant. Call, but I'll also get the local office on it. One way or the other, we'll get her."

He left the office.

Lucy said to Nina, "Call her and ask how she is, and if she can at all come in to take care of something, or if you can bring work to her. Is there anything that only she can do?"

"Noooo," Nina said. "What if I tell her I want to bring her chicken soup?"

"She put a false address on her employment records, she's not going to let you visit her." Lucy didn't even think she was at home, but Lucy wanted her address because there was going to be evidence there that would help convict her. Lucy wanted to get it before she had a chance to destroy anything.

House.

"Hold on one second," Lucy said and followed Ken out the door.

She found him around the corner on his phone. He put the person on hold. "Have something?"

"Electricity. Water. She has to have them in her name. Can we get those records?"

"Absolutely. I'll get the L.A. office working on it."

Lucy went back into Nina's office. "Okay. Call her, ask her to come in. Is there something only she would know where it is? Or did she work on something that you can plausibly say got deleted? Misfiled? A client that only wants to work with her? It has to be believable, or she'll catch on."

"She's been preoccupied," Nina said. "I had to call her on Thursday, after her doctor's appointment, because she hadn't filed a document properly."

"Use it. But don't push too hard. I don't want her to get suspicious."

Nina paused a minute, then dialed the number.

She listened. "Voice mail," she said.

"Just ask her to call you back," Lucy said.

Nina nodded. "Hi, Danielle, it's Nina. Can you give me a call when you get this message? I have a question about the Carroll file, and I can't find the docs on your desk. It's important—thanks." She hung up. "Okay?"

"Perfect," Lucy said.

Ken walked back in and said, "Kevin Fieldstone is here. He's in Mr. Fieldstone's office."

"Can I—?" She looked at Lucy.

"Yes, but I need to talk to him."

"Why?"

"Danielle stalked her other victims. He may have seen her."

She could see Tony Fieldstone wanted to argue, but he simply put his arm around his wife's shoulders and led the way to his office.

Ken whispered to Lucy, "I'm going to follow up on the address. We may need to bolt quickly."

"I want to get the Fieldstones into protective custody," she said. "As soon as Danielle figures out we're onto her, she may change her MO or disappear."

"I'll work on getting a detail to sit on them at their house." Ken walked off and Nina and Tony led Lucy to Fieldstone's office.

Lucy asked Banks to stand aside and not interject. "I don't want to scare Kevin," she said quietly, "and too many grown-ups getting angry will do that."

She also said that for Nina and Tony's benefit—they meant well, but they were an intimidating couple, especially together.

"Hi, Mom! Hi, Dad! I brought you Grandma's cookies."

He had a Tupperware in his hands.

"Great, they're my favorite," Nina said and took the box.

"Did you know that two FBI agents were picking me up? Grandma said you did, but it was so totally cool. They have guns and everything. They have a cool radio in their car, but their car isn't like a police car. It's all stealthy."

"Yes, we asked them to bring you here."

"Why? Is something wrong, Mom?" He looked more curious than worried.

"No," Nina said. "Not with us, but this FBI agent would like to talk to you. She came all the way from San Diego."

"Really? Why?"

Kevin was a cute kid. He was small for an eight-year-old, fidgety, with huge blue eyes and a mop of dark blond hair.

Lucy sat in the chair next to Kevin. "It's good to meet you, Kevin," she said. "You can call me Lucy, and you can ask me anything. I think that's only fair because I'm going to ask you questions."

"Do you have a gun?"

"Yes. I have two."

"Really? Like a backup gun?"

"Exactly like that."

"So it's not just in the movies."

"No. The movies don't always get things right, but that one is true for some of us. My turn?"

He nodded.

"Do you know a woman named Danielle Sharpe—Ms. Sharpe—who works with your mom and dad?"

"Yeah, sort of."

"What does that mean?"

He shrugged. "Sometimes I come to the office here, like when we have a minimum day or Christmas break and my grandma has things to do like buying me Christmas presents so I can't stay with her. It's fun. So I know people here."

"When was the last time you saw Ms. Sharpe?"

"Today after school."

Nina sucked in her breath and Kevin frowned.

"You have a good memory," Lucy said. "Where were you when you saw her?"

"Grandma picks me up at school every day and we walk to her house. Unless it's cold, then she brings the car because Grandma doesn't like it too cold."

"And Ms. Sharpe was standing outside your school?"

"No, she was in her new car."

"New car?"

"Yeah, she used to have a black Honda now she has a brand-new silver car. Like Uncle Eric's."

Lucy glanced at his parents. Tony said, "My brother has a Nissan Altima."

Lucy made a note, and asked Kevin, "Do you see her at your school often?"

"A few times. I just thought she has a kid or something. Ashley's dad is a lawyer, too."

"That's the daughter of one of the senior associates," Tony said. "She's a couple years older."

"Sixth grade," Kevin said. "I'm in third grade."

"So a few times—is that a few times lately? Since the school year started?"

He squinted. "Well, maybe since break. I don't think I saw her before Christmas. But, you know, I might not have noticed. I saw her the first day we got back—I remember only because my grandma was a couple minutes late. The dogs got out because the gardener left the gate open. Grandma called the school and my teacher waited with me. I didn't really think about it, just thought she looked familiar, but then the next week I saw her again sitting in the car and remembered she was a friend of my mom's and worked here."

"Why didn't you tell me?" Nina asked. "Ms. Sharpe doesn't have a child."

Kevin shrugged, but looked a little uncertain. "I didn't think to?"

"You're not in trouble, Kevin," Lucy said. "I promise."

"Did she do something wrong?"

Now he was getting worried, but she didn't want to lie to him, either. Kids picked up on lies sometimes faster than adults. "Well, a long time ago Ms. Sharpe had a little boy who died. We're just a bit concerned because she misses him so much we think she might want to find herself another little boy."

"Like me?"

He was quick. She didn't want to scare him. "Yes. But she isn't thinking straight, and I don't want you to get hurt. So it's really important that you stick with your mom and dad for a while, stick to them like glue, until we find her and make sure she isn't going to hurt anyone."

"So I don't have to go to school tomorrow?"

"We'll see."

"Because I'm a straight-A student. I don't have to go and I'll still have A's because school is really easy."

Lucy almost laughed. The comment reminded her of something Sean might have said when he was a precocious eight-year-old.

"You should probably also know that I saw Ms. Sharpe at Grandma's."

"Talking to Grandma?" Tony asked.

"No, just out front. She was in her car, talking on her cell phone. The old car, last week. Before she got the new car."

"Any other time?"

"Nope, that's all the times I've seen her. Well, except here at Mom and Dad's office."

"That's good, Kevin, thank you," Lucy said. "I'm going to talk to your mom and dad for a minute alone, okay? The agents who picked you up will sit with you for a while."

She stepped out of Tony's office. When she was alone with the two of them, she said, "When you're ready to leave, two agents will take you to your house and keep an eye on the place tonight. Tomorrow, if you can't stay home for the day, I'd like Kevin to stay here in the building with you. It's easy to secure, and we can post agents in the lobby. You might want to cancel Danielle's access into the building."

"I'll talk to Archie, we'll take care of it," Tony said. He was holding Nina's hand. Lucy didn't know how they could do it—hold it together when they'd violated each other's trust. Except . . . had they? She didn't understand open relationships and how they worked. She couldn't do it.

But they loved Kevin. It was clear by their fear and worry for him, and their unity in front of him. Just like Andrew and Nelia. Their marriage wasn't perfect, but they had a shared love for the child they'd created.

Ken came running down the hall. "We know where she lives. Units are on their way, let's go."

Chapter Thirty-three

Danielle let herself into the Fieldstones' empty house. The alarm beeped repeatedly. She walked over to the panel and typed in the code Nina Fieldstone had used months ago.

The beeping stopped and the light turned green.

She had done a little research on alarms because she didn't know if they had motion detectors or door alarms or what, but she figured out how to set the house for exterior doors only. She did, so when they came home they wouldn't think anything was out of the ordinary. The same code turned on and off the alarm, whatever alarm was set.

She stood in the entry and stared at the wedding portrait that took up one wall. They looked so happy, but they weren't happy. They were miserable human beings, they cheated on each other, they put their own selfish needs above their only child. The one thing they should care for. The one being they should love above all others.

But they loved themselves first and foremost.

Like Richard.

Like herself.

It was over. It was truly over.

No!

She walked slowly through the house. Since the last time she'd been here, they'd moved the furniture around a bit. Added the third-grade portrait of Kevin to a wall of photos that framed the staircase.

Soon, all they would have of Kevin were the photos. Then they would be very, very sorry.

340

But she didn't have time. She'd seen those people walk up to Kevin's grandmother's house and take him away. They were cops. They may not look like cops—no uniform, no cop car—but Danielle had been around enough cops when they were looking for Matthew that she had a sense of how they walked, how they moved, always looking around but not really seeming to. And why would Kevin go off with anyone? Friends? Maybe. Maybe, but she didn't think so.

Danielle went upstairs to Kevin's room. It took her a long minute before she could actually walk in.

Such a little boy. He liked football, it seemed. A poster of a quarterback in a black uniform—who were they?—hung above his bed. She stepped closer. Carr, Raiders. She didn't know anything about football.

It looked like Kevin had every *Goosebumps* book ever written—they took up two long shelves in his bookshelf. A hodgepodge of other books filled the remaining space, plus a football signed in Sharpie, but Danielle couldn't read the signature.

He had a computer in his room . . . what parent let a child have a computer in their room? There were predators out there, predators like that evil man who stole Matthew and hurt him.

Remembering the pain when the police told her what had happened . . . Danielle had to sit down. She sat on Kevin's bed and took a deep breath. And then another. She picked up an old, ratty, stuffed Pooh Bear. The bear had seen better days, but it was obviously well loved.

Danielle held it close and, hands shaking, pulled her cell phone from her pocket.

Richard answered on the second ring. Her instincts buzzed. He rarely answered the phone when she called, as if, even though her number was blocked, he knew it was her.

"Hello, Richard."

"Danielle."

He sounded different.

"You betrayed me again, didn't you?"

"What? What do you mean? Honey—"

"Don't call me that!"

341

Her head pounded and she squeezed her eyes shut. Something was wrong, and she knew her husband—*ex-husband*—was part of it.

"Danielle, you sound agitated. Tell me what I can do to help you. I'll do anything. Matthew was my son, too. I loved him."

"You'd do anything? Really? Anything?"

"Yes, Danielle. Name it. We can talk, we can see a counselor, we can visit his grave—whatever you need."

"Go kill yourself."

She ended the call. That's when she saw that she had a missed call and voice mail.

She listened to it.

Nina.

Something was very, very wrong.

Danielle turned off her phone, but what if someone could trace it? She'd read in an article that law enforcement could trace phones even if the phone was off.

She went back downstairs and filled a pot with water. She immersed her phone and hoped that killed it completely.

She had one more job to do. One more . . . and then maybe, just maybe, she could rest in peace.

She was so, so tired.

She brought the pot back upstairs and put it on the top shelf of the linen closet, then sat back on Kevin's bed and took the gun out of her purse.

Surprisingly, her hands were steady.

Because she was doing the right thing.

Chapter Thirty-four

Danielle lived in a small two-bedroom post-WWII house in Glendale only blocks from the mail drop. Two Glendale PD squad cars, a locksmith, and two teams of FBI agents were already there when Ken and Lucy arrived. One of the FBI agents, who identified himself as SSA Tim Nelson, said, "We didn't attempt contact, as you asked, but we haven't seen any movement in the house, and a neighbor informed us that Ms. Sharpe left the house shortly before noon today and she hasn't returned. She's driving a silver Nissan Altima with new dealer plates."

"Thanks, Tim," Ken said. "Do you have an extra vest for Kincaid here? She's from out of the area and doesn't have her gear."

Tim nodded and motioned for Lucy to come to his trunk. "It might be too big."

"Thanks," Lucy said and put the vest over her T-shirt and left her blazer in his trunk. FBI was printed on the back and front in large yellow letters. She adjusted it. Big, but not cumbersome.

Ken, Lucy, and Tim approached the front door. Tim had Glendale PD covering the back. Ken knocked on the door. "Danielle Sharpe, this is the FBI. We have a search warrant for these premises. We're coming in."

He waited to make sure she really wasn't home, then Tim had the locksmith crack open the lock. They entered the premises, guns drawn, and did a complete search of the house.

"Clear," they called out one by one.

They met back in the living room. "I'll clear the garage," Tim said and left Ken and Lucy to begin the search.

They both pulled on gloves and Lucy found the light switch.

The house was sparsely furnished. There were no pictures on the walls, nothing personal. A television was in the corner, a couch, and a coffee table. The far wall had a faint stain on it. Lucy approached, at first thinking it might be blood, but when she got closer she realized that it was a wine stain. On the floor was a broken wine stem.

"She threw a full wineglass at the wall." Lucy touched the carpet. "It's dry."

Ken was in the kitchen. "She drinks a lot of wine—the recycling bin has twelve, no thirteen, empty bottles."

"She may not have emptied it recently." But it also could be part of her process, building herself up to take another human life. Yet Lucy didn't see how she could be intoxicated and still be sharp enough to commit these murders without leaving any evidence.

"Refrigerator is almost empty—a couple of take-out boxes," Ken said. "Cabinets—looks like my first apartment. Minimal dishes, glasses—just enough to get by."

Lucy opened the first door—it was a den. Danielle spent far more time in here—there were books and photo albums and the distinct smell of sour grapes. The desk was a mess. Two wineglasses with residue were positioned on the bookshelf.

Lucy went through the papers on the desk. A photo album had been destroyed—pictures cut out and shredded. Lucy put a couple of the photos back together—they were of Danielle and her ex-husband. The photos of Matthew were still intact, yet if one of his parents was in the photo, they had been cut out.

Both Richard and Danielle.

What did that mean? Was she suicidal? Had she already killed herself? Something had tipped her off—she wasn't sick, she wasn't home, she hadn't returned Nina Fieldstone's call, and she likely had a gun.

Lucy's phone rang and she jumped.

"Hello?" she answered.

"This is Richard Collins.

"Mr. Collins. Do you have information?"

"Danielle just called me. It wasn't a long call, and she sounded . . . strained."

"What did she say? Did you record it?"

"Yes, the FBI recorded it. She asked me if I had betrayed her again. Then she told me to kill myself. What's going on?"

"Has she ever told you to kill yourself?"

"No, I mean, she told me repeatedly that I should have been the one to die, but not like this."

"We're looking for her. Stay put, Richard, okay? Stay in your house with your wife. The FBI will stick with you for tonight, just in case." Lucy didn't see why Danielle would go after Richard now, after twenty-three years, but something had tipped her off. Then she realized.

"Richard," she asked, "when we talked yesterday you said she left voice mails, but you only talked to her once."

"Yes, so?"

"What about the other times she called? Five years ago? Before then?"

"I don't know what you mean."

"Did you talk to her every time she called, or not?"

He paused. "No, I usually only answered the phone once or twice. Then I started sending all blocked calls to voice mail. It got to be . . . stressful for me."

"Thanks. If she calls again, let me know immediately. I'll get the tape from the Denver office." Lucy wanted to listen to her voice.

Ken said, "I have it—they sent it to me."

He played the recording. It was short—not even a minute long.

"Betrayed me again," Ken mumbled. "What does that mean? They're not married, they haven't been."

"She knows he's talked to us."

"How?"

"Because he's been answering all her calls. That's something he hasn't done in the past. She's not an idiot, it's a change, and any change of behavior she's going to pick up on. I think she realized it last night when she talked to him, which is why she left this morning. And last night she sounded intoxicated, she may have needed time to sober up and plan. She's not irrational—not in the way we might think. She had a plan, but now she changed it. Just like she had a plan for Jonah Oliver, but had to change it when his babysitter confronted her."

But what exactly was she going to do?

Lucy looked around the room. She noticed there were seven photo albums on the top shelf of the bookshelf that all matched the one that was torn apart on her desk. She took them down. Inside all the pictures of Richard had been cut out, but Matthew's pictures—and Danielle's pictures—were intact. "She might have kept a diary, kept something that can help us find her."

"I'll take the desk."

Tim Nelson turned in to the doorway. "You gotta see what's in the garage."

Lucy and Ken followed him out the back door. An officer guarded the door, and another was standing by the side door into the small, detached garage. The lone window had been blacked out.

The garage was set up as a war room—one wall were photos of Kevin Fieldstone and his parents. Kevin with his grandmother after school. Kevin going into his house. Kevin playing on the playground at school.

Pictures of the Fieldstone house. Of Nina at work. Of Tony at a party. Of another woman, older, blond, pretty. Of Tony and the woman in bed.

Of Nina and a woman in bed.

Hundreds of photos, all printed at home on photo paper. A computer stood in the corner of a workplace. A color printer next to it.

Lucy turned and couldn't stop herself from gasping.

The other wall had photos of Danielle's previous victims and their families. A stalker's paradise. Photos of people having sex, but it was clear they were taken either through a Web camera or a zoom lens. Lucy grew increasingly uncomfortable, and then she recognized a much younger Andrew. Andrew with Nelia. Andrew with Justin. Andrew naked in bed with another woman.

Lucy couldn't process any more when her gaze rested on a photo of her and Justin nearly twenty years ago. Playing at the park where Justin had been buried.

She heard Tim and Ken talking, but didn't hear any words.

She remembered that day vividly. She didn't realize how vividly until now—it had been the last time she'd seen Justin alive. The day he died.

Lucy sat in the sand and pushed the grains back and forth with her shovel. She didn't feel good, her stomach hurt and her head hurt and she just wanted to go home.

Justin plopped down next to her. "Wanna play tag?"

"No."

"Climb trees?"

"No."

"Ask Santa for Christmas presents?"

She looked up at him and wrinkled her nose. "It's June, months before Christmas."

"I'm gonna ask Santa for a Nintendo. Or a Game Boy. I don't know which one's better. But if I got a Nintendo we could play together."

"You should ask Patrick. He plays video games all the time. He knows about those things. He's really smart."

"Uncle Patrick said he'd help coach my baseball team. Isn't that great? He said he'd come to at least one practice a week and help with batting. He had a three-sixty batting average last year. Daddy said he'll probably get a major league contract when he graduates if he keeps it up. Wouldn't that be cool? If he plays for the Padres? And we can get free season tickets? They do that, right? Give the players free tickets for their family?"

"I'd think they would," Lucy said. *She sighed.*

"Hey, are you okay, LuLu?"

"I feel sick. But don't tell my mom, because she'll tell your mom and you'll have to go home."

"Grandma calls my mom nervous Nellie." Justin giggled. *"Nellie, because her name is Nelia."*

"I think it's an expression," Lucy said. *"I've heard it before."*

"I think it's funny."

"Can you do me a favor?"

"Sure."

"I really want to go home, but I don't want my mom to know I don't feel

good because then she won't let me go swimming tomorrow. I don't want to be stuck inside all day. But if you tell her you're hungry or something, she'll take us home."

"You look green."

"Do not."

On the way home from the park, Lucy threw up in the bushes and started crying, and when they got home her mom took her temperature and it was 102. When Nelia called to say she was going to be late, Lucy's mom mentioned in passing that Lucy was sick and in bed. Nelia asked Carina to pick up Justin and watch him.

And that was the last time Lucy had seen her nephew—her best friend—alive.

"Lucy, you okay?"

Ken was right behind her.

"Do you see something important?"

Lucy cleared her throat and squeezed her eyes shut. "I—dammit."

She stepped out of the garage. She had to, her emotions were so overwhelming she almost didn't know how to process them. It was dark; at some point the sun had set and only a faint blue was evident in the west.

She sat down on the ground and put her head between her legs. She didn't even know how she felt. Rage? She had it. Sorrow? Yes, in spades. And helpless. Absolutely helpless, and she didn't know why.

She felt seven again.

She didn't know how long she sat there, but Ken came for her. "We can't get into her computer. Nelson is calling in the cybersquad. There may be something that tells us where she went."

"Did you find a gun?"

"No."

"She's going after the Fieldstones."

"I just got off the phone with the two agents sitting on them. They took them home—they have an alarm system. All's clear. They're sitting out front keeping an eye on the place."

"She has a plan. Something tipped her off—her ex-husband talking to her, seeing the agents pick up Kevin this morning. She's circling around. You saw her den, and this . . . this obsession. How long until we get into her computer?"

"Hour, maybe two. I don't have an estimated time when the ERT unit will be here."

"I'd like to call an expert."

"Your husband."

"He's worked with the FBI before, and we have a warrant to get into her computer."

"He's in San Diego, right?"

"He can do it remotely—I'm almost positive."

"Call him."

Lucy had Sean on speaker. He walked her through which cable to use to connect her phone to Danielle's computer so he could hack into the hard drive. In less than five minutes, he'd opened her computer up to the FBI.

"That's pretty damn amazing," Ken said to Sean.

"Thank you," Sean said. "What are you looking for specifically?"

"Any clue as to where she is now," Ken said.

"Search histories? Purchases?"

"We have the airports alerted, but it would help if we knew if she bought a ticket. Does she have a cloud account and if so when was the last time she uploaded anything?"

"Not bad, Swan," Sean said.

As they watched, the computer screen flipped through a bunch of programs and suddenly photos scrolled across the page. Lucy saw one of the two agents with Kevin.

"Stop, Sean."

Ken said, "Well, shit, she was outside the grandmother's house."

"She saw the agents. They may have been discreet, but she knew."

"Good news, bad news," Sean said. "I can tell you that her phone is not operational—it's set to sync with her cloud account every hour, and the last time it pinged was at four."

"She called her husband at about four forty," Lucy said.

"That's an hour after these photos were taken. She called her husband? Okay, hold on a sec."

The screen shifted and Sean was working within the operating system. A minute later a map popped up. "She made the call to her husband within a thousand feet of this point."

"You didn't hack—" Ken began.

"No, because she syncs her entire phone to her cloud account, which is cloned on her hard drive. All the data gets copied over. You just have to know where to look, then convert the code."

"I didn't know that."

"It's why I get paid the big bucks," Sean said.

Lucy zoomed in on the map. "Ken, that's the Fieldstones' neighborhood, and their house is in the middle of that circle. We have to get over there, she's watching them."

"Thanks, Rogan, appreciate the help," Ken said. "You can write this all up for my report, right?"

"I know what you need. Lucy? You can disconnect your phone—I removed all security protocols on Sharpe's computer so that your people can dig deeper."

Lucy picked up her phone and took Sean off speaker. "I have to go."

"Be careful. I love you."

"I love you, too."

Max was duly impressed with Sean Rogan. They'd been sitting in the lounge for the last four hours alternatively working on their respective laptops and talking. She hadn't been able to get him to say much about Lucy personally, though he shared a few stories. Didn't give Max much insight into what exactly made these two people tick, but she enjoyed them. Sean didn't repeat the warning he issued on Thursday, which Max respected. He didn't treat her like an idiot.

When he hung up with Lucy, she said, "You're really good."

"I know."

She laughed. She appreciated well-placed confidence. "Do you work often with the FBI? Private consultant?"

"When they need me."

"How close are they?"

"Close."

"You're worried about Lucy. She seems to be a woman who can take care of herself."

"I am, and she is." Sean stared at her, as if trying to read her intentions. "Lucy trusts you. Why, I have no idea, but she does."

That only partly surprised Max. She'd thought she and Lucy had developed a good working relationship, but from the beginning she recognized that trust wasn't something that either of these people gave freely.

Sean continued, "Danielle Sharpe is most likely in the Fieldstones' house."

Max almost jumped out of her seat. "What? Lucy said that?"

"I did. Lucy knows—I didn't have to tell her. It's obvious, and Lucy fears Sharpe is going to up her game and take out the whole family. She's been working up to it."

"Why isn't Lucy in the BSU? Arthur—my friend Dr. Arthur Ullman who is retired from the BSU—said they take only the best and brightest with that certain extra that makes them good profilers. And you can't tell me that Lucy doesn't have that extra. She has it in spades."

Sean didn't say anything for a minute. He was looking at something on his phone, but Max couldn't see what it was. Or was he thinking about what to tell her and how to say it?

He said, "There's only so much darkness a person can take before it consumes them." He looked up from his phone and his dark, vibrant blue eyes spoke volumes. Max had never believed in true love and soulmates and all that romantic bullshit. Until now.

There was nothing Sean Rogan wouldn't do for his wife. And it was clear the feeling was mutual.

He turned his phone to Max and she read the text message from Lucy.

The agents aren't responding and we can't reach the Fieldstones. Ken and I are on our way with L.A. FBI. We don't know yet if we're dealing with a hostage situation or something far worse. I'm going in to talk her down. I will be okay, but . . . well, I love you.

"I'm going to L.A.," Sean said. "If you can be ready to leave in five minutes, you can join me."

Chapter Thirty-five

The two agents watching the Fieldstones' weren't in their vehicle. "Dammit, I told them to check on the family—how'd they get ambushed? Why didn't they call for backup?"

"We don't know what happened." But Lucy knew time was not on their side. Last contact with the agents was ten minutes ago. She'd told Ken they needed to check on the family immediately; he'd acted based on her advice. Because he trusted her.

Now two agents were in danger. Or already dead.

Tim Nelson was calling in FBI SWAT. Their ETA was a minimum twenty minutes. Lucy didn't know if the family had twenty minutes. She didn't know if they were already dead.

"I have to go in," Lucy said.

"Fuck no," Ken said. "I'm not putting another FBI agent in the line of fire."

"She's going to kill them. She knows she's not getting out of this and she has nothing to lose. She's been spiraling down for twenty-three years, Ken—she's been careful, methodical, but one thing changed: her ex-husband started talking to her. She sensed there was something wrong, and even if he didn't say something specifically to set her off, she unconsciously knows that something is different. And this family is different. The mother was having an affair. It's a deviation. Kevin cannot die. I can't let him die."

"You're not going in there and risking your life."

Lucy pulled out the photo of her and Justin playing at the park the afternoon before Danielle killed her nephew. "This is my card inside. She will know who I am—I can talk her down. Make sure the agents are alive. If anyone needs medical help, I will try to get them out. Ken, we can't sit here and wait for a tactical team! There are three and potentially five hostages inside. Dead? Alive? Danielle Sharpe has drugs, a gun, and nothing to lose."

Tim Nelson came over to them. "Glendale PD is working with us until the sheriff's deputies arrive. They've blocked off the street both sides, and are notifying the neighbors to stay indoors. SWAT is nineteen minutes out—I had them on call, so they were ready to roll."

"Nineteen minutes is too long—I'm a hostage negotiator," Lucy said. "I'm a rookie, I'm not supposed to negotiate without a senior negotiator, but I don't think we should quibble about the damn bureaucracy when everyone in that house will be dead in nineteen minutes if we don't do something now."

"Agent Kincaid, I don't think you can make that call," Nelson said. "Going in blind, without intelligence, is going to put another life in danger."

"A word," Ken said to Nelson and pulled him aside.

Lucy knew she was right—Danielle had changed her MO. She went into the house because she knew law enforcement had tracked her down. The calls to her husband coupled with the agents taking Kevin from his grandmother's house gave it away. So she went to her Plan B—Danielle already knew about the alarm, knew how to bypass it. Nina Fieldstone probably didn't realize that Danielle might have the alarm code. Danielle was inside the house when she called her husband the last time.

Did you betray me again?

Only this time, it was a different betrayal. Instead of another woman, it was talking to the police.

Ken and Nelson came back. "One condition," Nelson said. "You get her on the phone. I'm not sending you anywhere near that house if I don't know that the hostages are alive."

Lucy nodded. How could she get Danielle to pick up?

She dialed the Fieldstones' house phone. It went to voice mail after six rings. She tried Nina's cell phone; it went direct to voice mail.

"Bullhorn?" she asked Nelson.

He retrieved one from his trunk. Lucy took a deep breath and spoke into the bullhorn.

"Danielle, my name is Lucy Kincaid. You know me. Justin called me Lulu. No one else has ever called me Lulu. Pick up the phone. I need to talk to you. You owe it to me to pick up the phone."

She nodded to Ken, who called the house phone again. It rang four times. Lucy thought she was too late, that they were already dead.

On the fifth ring Danielle answered.

"Are you lying to me?"

The phone was on speaker, and Lucy motioned for everyone to quiet down.

"No, Danielle. I found the picture of me and Justin playing in the park. I was playing in the sand and didn't feel well. I didn't remember until today that Justin called me Lulu. I blocked it out because I miss him so much."

"I need more than a photo. How do I know it's really you and you're not just lying to me like everyone else?"

Lucy considered what she wanted. What would she know that the average person wouldn't know?

"You know it's really me, Danielle. I was born two weeks before my nephew. Nelia was twenty-two when she had Justin, she got pregnant in college—just like you. She married Justin's father—just like you married Matthew's father. And Andrew had an affair just like Richard had an affair. I don't know how to prove to you I am who I am."

"Justin broke his arm. Which arm did he break and how?"

Bile rose in Lucy's throat. Justin broke his arm nearly a year before he was killed. She was there, at the park, and she'd told him not to climb so high. Coming down he'd slipped and fell more than twenty feet. It was a clean break, healed quickly, but he had a cast for several weeks.

"His left arm. He fell out of a tree." She closed her eyes. She wouldn't have remembered if she and Max hadn't gone back to the park last week. "He was buried next to that tree."

"It is you."

"Yes. I'm now an FBI agent and I really need to talk to you. Please,

Danielle, let the family go and I'll come in and we'll talk. As long as you need to talk, I'll listen." She didn't want to listen to the woman—she didn't want to hear her justify why she killed Justin and all the other boys. She didn't want to hear her justify why the Fieldstones needed to die.

"No."

"They're not going to let me come in unless you let the family leave. Can they leave, Danielle? Is anyone hurt?"

"You can have the two FBI agents. They're in the garage. But Tony and Nina are going to suffer for what they have done to their family."

"Wait—Danielle, we need to talk."

"Fine, come here and talk, but they're still going to die. You know they have to. You of all people know that they need to be punished!"

Lucy? *Of all people?* That made no sense. Was Danielle thinking of someone else when she thought of Lucy? Or was she truly having a psychotic break?

"We're going to come in and retrieve the FBI agents," Lucy said, "then I'm going to come inside."

"No guns."

"I'll leave my weapon out here. Is Kevin okay?"

"He's sleeping. He's so peaceful. So perfect."

Sleeping? No, it wasn't even seven. Had she already drugged him?

Nelson was already in the process of retrieving the two agents from the garage. Lucy prayed this wasn't a trap, but a minute later, they all came out. The agents had been duct-taped together. Danielle couldn't have overpowered them—she must have used Kevin's safety as a threat and forced Tony Fieldstone to do it.

A parent will do anything to protect their child.

And when they can't protect them? Like Danielle? Is this what happened? A twisted vengeance to punish everyone else because she couldn't punish the man who killed her son?

"I'm going in," Lucy said. She handed her gun to Ken.

He looked worried. "This is suicide."

"No, she said Kevin is sleeping. She drugged him, I'm certain of it. She's waiting either for him to die, or for herself to build the courage to suffocate him. Get an ambulance here, tell them which drugs she's used in the past, we need an antidote and paramedic—a doctor if they can get out here. I can't let him die, and you can't either. You know it."

She prayed Kevin wasn't already dead.

"Wire," Ken said. Another agent who worked with Nelson handed Ken a communications piece. "Pull up your shirt.

Lucy did, burying any embarrassment she had over the request. Ken taped on the thin wire, then handed her the mic. "I'll let you attach this to your bra. It's very sensitive, but small, she shouldn't be able to see it. It's wireless with a range of five hundred feet, so as long as you're in the house, we should be able to hear everything."

Lucy attached it and pulled down her shirt. Ken handed her a small earpiece. "You need to be able to hear us. Take your hair down, she won't be able to see it."

Lucy did what Ken said, and started up the front walk of the Fieldstone house.

"Can you hear me?" Lucy said quietly.

"Loud and clear. Don't get killed, Kincaid."

She didn't plan on dying today.

Nina Fieldstone opened the door. She had a bruise on her face and dried blood on her mouth, but she was alive.

Nina closed the door as soon as Lucy walked in and locked it. Her hands were shaking and her eyes were wide and wild.

Lucy looked around. She didn't see anyone else. "Go," she told Nina. "Get out."

"She'll kill Tony. She told me to come down here and let you in but she'll kill Tony."

"She's upstairs?"

"Kevin's room. She was here all along!"

"Nina!" a female shouted from upstairs. "I'm counting."

"Please," Nina whispered, tears in her eyes. "I don't know what to do—Kevin won't wake up. I-I—"

"Follow my lead," Lucy said.

Lucy told Nina to stay behind her. Lucy went upstairs. One door was closed. She pointed and Nina nodded.

Lucy knocked once on the door then slowly opened it.

The first person she saw was Tony Fieldstone. His entire body sagged in the desk chair in the corner of the room, wrists and ankles duct-taped. His head was bleeding from the scalp—likely pistol-whipped. Conscious, but clearly injured. His mouth had been duct-taped as well.

Lucy stepped over the threshold. Danielle sat on Kevin's bed. She had a gun in hand; her hands were steady as she pointed the gun at Lucy.

Kevin lay under his blankets, but Lucy could see his face. He wasn't sleeping; he was unconscious. If she used the same drugs as before, they could kill him, depending on the dosage.

But the good news was that Danielle was looking at his face. She was more than a little conflicted about killing him, and Lucy had to capitalize on that doubt.

"Let Kevin go," Lucy said. "Let Nina carry him out."

"No," Danielle said. "We just need to wait a few more minutes. Then they'll finally understand how selfish they are." Danielle looked at Lucy for several seconds. "It really is you. You grew up very pretty."

"I understand why you're doing this, Danielle, and I'm here to tell you that you have no idea of the repercussions of your actions. I understand that Tony and Nina have failed as parents in your eyes. They betrayed their marriage vows. They put their needs and their careers before their son. Selfish, right?"

"You do understand." She seemed surprised.

"You are so narrow in your focus that you have no idea the pain you cause to innocent people. To people like me."

"You had parents who respected each other, who loved you. Your mother not only took care of you, but Justin, too, because your sister was too busy to be bothered with a child."

Lucy had to let that pass, because if she defended Nelia or Nina or any other parent, Danielle would get angry and Lucy wouldn't be able to gain her trust.

"You killed Justin to punish Andrew and Nelia. But you punished me, too. And my mother and father. And my other brothers and sister.

And all the kids in my school who had to face the dark truth that one of their classmates and friends was dead. That one of their friends—the happy, joyful, smart Justin Stanton—had been murdered."

"This isn't about that," Danielle said, but she averted her eyes, just for a moment.

"Look at me!" Lucy ordered.

Danielle straightened and scowled, but she looked at Lucy.

"I speak four languages fluently, and several others I can pass with. I wanted to be a linguist, or go into diplomacy. I was a championship swimmer—I won dozens of blue ribbons and swam for my college team. I thought I could put Justin's murder behind me, but I couldn't. I became an FBI agent. You did that, Danielle. You made me an FBI agent."

It was clear Danielle hadn't expected this conversation, nor had she seen the impact of her actions on anyone but the immediate family.

"My life changed the minute you killed my best friend. My mother—Justin's grandma—cried every day for a year. She aged. My sister Nelia didn't speak to me until last year—not once—because in the back of her mind, I was partly to blame for Justin's death. Why? Because I got sick that day and my mom couldn't keep Justin. When Carina fell asleep on the couch the night you climbed in through Justin's bedroom window, it was because she was up late studying. She was in college, on a full scholarship, and she had to maintain good grades to keep that scholarship. That's why she fell asleep after eleven at night. That's why she didn't hear you take her nephew out the window.

"My brother Patrick was a major league baseball prospect. Instead of pursuing a baseball career—something he had dreamed about ever since he could throw a ball—he joined the police academy and became a detective. My brother Dillon was in medical school and stayed longer in order to become a psychiatrist—a forensic psychiatrist—because he had a deep need to understand why people kill children. All this, because of *you*."

As Lucy spoke, she was inching closer to Danielle. Danielle still had the gun. The gun was still pointed at Lucy, but Lucy had to take the risk. She might anger Danielle so much that she just pressed the trigger to make Lucy shut up, but Lucy had to push because this was the only way she could save Kevin's life.

"Your selfish, immature, criminal acts touched all of us. I was seven and a half years old and I faced murder for the first time. Justin was closer to me than my own brothers and sisters. You took him away from his parents—and they suffered, so I'm sure you're very proud of yourself—but you took him away from *me*. And *I* suffered. Your actions have far more consequences than your small, petty, selfish mind can process."

"You do not know me! You have no idea what I have suffered!" Now Danielle was shaking. But she wasn't looking at Kevin or Nina or Tony. She was looking only at Lucy. As if seeing her for the first time. Or maybe seeing herself.

"I have made my career out of studying sexual predators like Paul Borell who raped and murdered your son. I put men like Borell in prison—and in the grave if they fight back. I know your pain. I have felt it. You want other mothers to feel the pain that you feel. You could have stopped it. You could have gotten help, you could have forgiven your ex-husband, you could have done anything else but kill. Yet you choose to kill.

"What do you think Matthew would think of you now? He would have been thirty last week."

"How—"

Danielle's voice cracked. Lucy took one more step toward her.

"Do you think he would be proud of his mother? The woman who loved him? Or do you think he would be horrified that you killed four little boys in his name?"

"I—"

The gun dipped and Lucy pounced.

She leapt forward and grabbed Danielle's gun hand, tightening her grip on Danielle's wrist so hard she heard a bone crack. The gun fell from her hand as Danielle screamed in rage. She tried to hit Lucy with her free hand, but Lucy had adrendaline on her side. And her own inner rage fueling her. She pulled Danielle forward, keeping her off balance, and pushed her to the ground. She kicked the gun away with her left foot, then put her right knee firmly on Danielle's back.

"Backup! Now!" she shouted. "And medics, stat!"

Danielle fought and cried underneath Lucy. Lucy didn't dare take a hand off the thrashing woman to retrieve the cuffs out of her back pocket.

It didn't take more than thirty seconds before Ken Swan and Tim Nelson came into the room. Lucy held Danielle down while Swan cuffed her. Nelson went over to Kevin and felt his pulse. "I feel a very faint pulse. I need medics up here!"

Two other agents came in.

Nina was sobbing and trying to reach her son. "Get them out!" Nelson ordered.

"I need to be with my baby! Kevin!"

"Get them out!" Nelson repeated.

Lucy searched Danielle. She found two syringes, one full and one empty. As soon as the medics came in, she handled them the vials. "She drugged the boy, you may need to confirm with what, but in the past she used a narcotic, likely chloral hydrate. We need to get him on a respirator stat."

The paramedic said, "I have a doctor online. We need room in here."

Ken wrestled a struggling Danielle Sharpe down the stairs. Nina and Tony were holding each other on the couch of their living room, two agents and a medic with them.

"This is your fault, Nina! You don't deserve to have a son, you don't deserve to have anyone!"

Ken pushed Danielle through the door. Lucy was behind them.

She'd found Justin's killer.

She stopped walking and sat on the lawn, her back against the lone tree. She couldn't take another step for fear of collapsing. She just needed a minute. She ripped off the mic and took the receiver out of her ear. She didn't want to talk to anyone, didn't want to listen to the chatter. She wanted—needed—silence.

You found Justin's killer.

It wasn't peace she felt.

She felt satisfaction that she had stopped a killer and saved Kevin's life. Relief that Justin's murder had finally been solved. And, yes, deep down, a modicum of peace.

But mostly, she felt a deep, numbing sadness.

She didn't know how long she sat there, but she was grateful everyone let her be. Everything she said to Danielle was the truth, but it wasn't something that she consciously thought about all the time. When she did remember Justin and her childhood, it was always bittersweet. Bringing it all up, talking about it, reminded Lucy of everything she'd lost because one person made one bad decision that spiraled into many bad choices. Evil choices.

But not everyone who loses someone can kill. Danielle had it in her all along, it just took the right trigger and she snapped.

Ken Swan came over to her and cleared his throat. "Danielle is on her way to jail. Kevin is stable and on his way to the hospital. Tony Fieldstone has a concussion and is in a separate ambulance. Nina is with her son. We'll need to debrief them—I'll give them a little time, but we should do it tonight. Are you up for it?"

"Yeah, I am. Just a couple more minutes?"

"Take all the time you need. You did good, Lucy. Really good. I, um, I didn't know all that about your family."

"It's the truth. The butterfly effect, I suppose. One act of violence changes everthing."

Ken spoke into his mic. "Let him through." To Lucy he said, "Thirty minutes, then I should be wrapped up here and we'll go to the hospital."

"Thanks."

She put her head on her knees and closed her eyes. She didn't know how long she sat until she heard a familiar voice.

"Lucy."

She looked up and blinked back tears she hadn't realized had been falling. She smiled. "Sean."

He sat down next to her and wrapped his arms around her. "Swan told me the basics. And the boy is okay."

She nodded and put her head on his shoulder. "I'm so glad you're here."

She closed her eyes and let the peace finally seep in.

Chapter Thirty-six

BLAIR CALDWELL'S TRIAL

Blair Caldwell's trial started promptly at nine Monday morning. Max recorded a segment before the trial began, including a montage of photos and stories about Peter Caldwell. She ended with a hook: "Did Blair Caldwell kill her son? District Attorney Harrison Trotter believes so. In a statement to the press this morning, Trotter said, 'I'm confident we'll prove beyond a shadow of a doubt that Blair Caldwell planned and executed this horrific crime.'"

During each break in the trial, Max posted on her NET blog a summary of testimony—the judge hadn't ordered a media blackout, which Max would have fought—then she recorded a one-minute video segment. She was working with a lone cameraman who also handled all the other technical details.

The first day of trial went pretty much as Max expected. Opening statements, then a methodical outline of the events from the moment the 911 call came in. They listened to the recording, the responding officer took the stand, the officer who had found the body, the coroner. The coroner spoke about how Peter died and the lead detective spoke to how they determined Peter was taken from his room. The final step was a timeline of Blair's whereabouts the night of the murder. It took more than an hour—with all of Charles North's objections—but ultimately, it would be up to the defense to find someone who saw Blair Caldwell in the twenty-two-minute window where no one was on record as having seen her.

While the twenty-two minutes didn't point to Blair's guilt, it was enough to establish that she had the time to kill—if she had everything planned out ahead of time. The prosecution had to set the stage for premeditated murder.

Max had just wrapped up her live evening segment outside the courthouse—always a good background—and sent her cameraman off to pack up the tech. She was famished and planned to eat a hearty dinner and get some sleep. It had been a long two weeks. She missed New York and her apartment. Though the Biltmore was one of the nicest resorts to stay in, she was more than ready to go home.

"Ms. Revere," a voice said.

She turned and recognized Dillon Kincaid, Lucy's brother. She'd seen him in the courtroom earlier, but when she tried to introduce herself, he'd disappeared.

"Dr. Kincaid. Good to finally meet you in person." She shook his hand.

"Dillon, please."

"Call me Max."

"Do you have some time? Can I take you to dinner?"

She was surprised at the offer. "I'm famished, but I should be taking you to dinner."

"Your foundation paid for my expenses, I can return the favor."

She laughed. "Not my foundation—I funded it, but I don't run it. One of those conflict-of-interest things lawyers don't like when the foundation pays for experts or private forensic reports."

"Still. One of the detectives told me about a wonderful Mexican food restaurant he swears by—says it's the best in Phoenix."

The restaurant was two blocks from the courthouse so they walked. Conversation was light—how pleasant the weather was in Arizona considering it was thirty degrees on the East Coast; what they both missed about the West Coast considering they'd both grown up in California. By the time they were seated and had ordered—Max joining Dillon for a margarita, though she rarely drank anything other than wine—Max asked, "What did you think of the first day?"

"Honestly? Boring. But I understand why they had to go through the case step-by-step."

"I found a few nuggets."

"I saw. I signed up for your blog alerts."

"I hope the DA knows what he's doing. If he can prove everything he said during the opening statement I think they'll get the conviction, but it's still a difficult conviction. Andrew says this guy—Harry Trotter— is good, but they all tend to support each other, and Trotter did share information with Andrew that was private."

"The stuffed animal."

"My gut told me Blair was guilty, but I've been known to make snap judgments about people. Because of John, I was willing to consider her innocence—in fact, look at Peter as another victim of Sharpe's. But no toy in the grave sealed it."

"It's not going to be enough to convict her."

"No, but it's enough to convince John." She munched on the delicious tortilla chips. She rarely went out for Mexican food—there weren't many good Mexican restaurants in her neighborhood in New York. If she could find a place like this, she would change her habits.

"I'm concerned about him."

Max hadn't spoken to John since she returned to Arizona. She called him when she came back, the night before *Crime Watch* aired, to give him the heads-up that she solved Justin Stanton's murder, but he said he didn't want to talk to her unless she could clear Blair's name. It hurt—it was as if she was the bad guy here, when all she did was find the truth.

"I didn't talk to him about your nephew's case."

"But you wrote about it, and aired a segment on your crime show. You revealed key information that would tell John that Danielle Sharpe didn't kill his son."

She wasn't certain John had seen it. She'd sent him an e-mail about the show with a link to the archived segment, but she didn't know if he had watched it.

"Danielle didn't kill Peter."

"We know that, but John was positive his wife was innocent."

"I don't think so." She sipped her margarita. Tangy. She still preferred wine—or a really good martini—but an occasional change was nice.

"Why?"

"John was desperate when he called me. He found the cold cases—but I think that Blair planted the idea in his head. That there were other cases like Peter's. Lucy thinks she used her work computers, which would have stronger protections against police search and seizure. Still erase the history, though nothing is truly gone forever. Blair never expected John to follow up on the cases or to call me. She wanted him to believe in her innocence so that he would stand by her through the investigation and trial. Not only do I think she didn't expect him to call me, she never expected me to take the case. Or solve the crime." She ate more chips. The salsa was amazing. She needed the recipe. Would they share?

"If he watched your report, or read the article—which seemed to be picked up by every major newspaper for the weekend—he's going to know that the details of his son's murder don't match the details of the other murders."

"I tried to call him and give him a heads-up, but he didn't want to talk to me."

"How well do you know him?"

"I knew him well, but until two weeks ago I hadn't seen him in nearly ten years."

"I couldn't read him in court today. He kept a poker face."

"Yet he sat behind her for the entire trial."

"I'm afraid he might do something he can't come back from."

Max wasn't sure what Dillon meant by that. "Like?"

"I mean," Dillon clarified, "his wife is still living in his house, but he must have doubts at this point. You made it quite clear that the only detail held back by police was that Danielle Sharpe's victims were buried with a stuffed animal. And we know that Peter was not."

"John is a smart guy, but we all have blind spots, don't we?"

"I don't want him to enact his own justice."

Usually Max was faster, but it took her several seconds to realize what Dillon was actually saying.

"Kill her?" She shook her head. Could he? *Would* he?

"Grief, betrayal, rage—it makes good people do bad things."

"You can't possibly be comparing John with Danielle Sharpe. She had problems long before she killed those boys."

"True. Her problems went back to her youth, and no one saw them. She hid her natural tendencies extremely well. Yet, everything that happened combined to create the perfect storm for her to snap."

"I still don't think that John would kill Blair." She paused. "He might confront her."

"And what would she do?"

"Deny. She will never admit that she killed Peter. Even if she is convicted, she'll tell everyone she was innocent, railroaded, maybe take a cheap shot at me. File for an appeal until her money runs out."

Dillon smiled. "I think you're right."

"I may not have your advanced training, but I know people."

"I'll admit, I was skeptical when Lucy first called me about your theory. Not that you didn't have something backing it up, but what your real motives were."

"I'm a reporter. I report."

"No, you're not."

"Excuse me?" Max didn't know whether she should be insulted or not.

"I hardly think the word *reporter* does you justice. I've had run-ins with reporters in the past when I've consulted on criminal cases, and my impression has never been positive."

"I gather you don't have a problem with the way I reported on Justin's murder."

"No. I may have done things a little differently, but I truly appreciate how you wrote about my family. I was worried it could have been . . . more sensational."

"You should have read my archive."

"I have. And sometimes you're more sensational than others."

"Then I probably didn't like who I was writing about," she said, irritated.

"I'm sorry I offended you."

She was bothered, and she tried to shake it off. Dillon was being open and honest, she respected that. It's just that this was the same old, same old. She was tired of her motives always being questioned. Tired of people doubting her, criticizing her for things she didn't even do—but what they perceived of her doing.

The food came and she ordered a second margarita. Dillon was still on his first. When the waiter left, she said, "I should be used to it by now. Sometimes it bothers me more."

"I told Lucy a long time ago that there were very few people like us—her and me—who can separate ourselves from horrific crimes and get inside the mind of the criminal. It's both a blessing and a curse. We have both had to face others looking at us with skepticism, suspicion, worry, fear. Lucy says it's not normal, but I tell her what *is* normal? So I do apologize for offending you, but not for protecting my sister or my family."

"Lucy asked me not to quote her or write about her, and I didn't, except the brief paragraph that she gave me permission to use. She got no credit for what she did on this case. If it weren't for her—and you—Danielle Sharpe would still be out there. Another little boy would have died."

"Lucy didn't want credit."

"I figured that out really early in our relationship. I appreciate that you gave me some good insight and quotes. I still would like to have you on the show for an interview, and though I don't like being hamstrung by off-limit topics, I would be willing to give you a little leeway there. Out of respect for your sister."

"I'll think about it, but I'm not one for the spotlight."

"You'd be a good interview."

"How about this—after this trial, I'll give you an interview. We can talk about both Blair Caldwell and Danielle Sharpe—provided we leave Lucy out of it."

"Thank you."

They ate in silence for a few minutes. Then Max asked, "I sensed that Lucy might have some problems when she went back to work. She didn't say specifically, but . . ." She let the sentence drop, looking at Dillon.

"She has a new boss. They've haven't found their rhythm yet."

Max raised an eyebrow. "That sounds like an understatement."

"Lucy is a private person."

Max laughed. "That's definitely an understatement."

"Last week, she asked me what makes her tick. From our conversation, I sensed that the question came from you."

Why did Lucy ask her brother? Max thought she was being evasive because she didn't want to discuss her past. Did she not really understand her most fundamental drive?

"I'm exceptionally curious. I told Lucy I wouldn't dig any more than I already did before I met her. I learned a few things only because I'd already set my research staff on it, but I didn't push. Her husband made it perfectly clear he would have my head."

"Sean is protective."

"Is that what you call it?" Max shook her head. "It doesn't matter—I'm not going to push. Yes, I'm still curious. But only because I admire Lucy. Several reasons, but a few stick out. First, she's just as sharp as you are—no offense."

"I concur."

"Yet, when she spoke to Richard Sharpe, she gave you complete credit for the profile. She came up with several points during that conversation that we hadn't even discussed, yet she drew on her experience and knowledge to reach conclusions that I don't know that I would have made—and I'm fairly intelligent."

Dillon smiled. "You certainly are."

"On the one hand, she thinks like a cop. She has that edge. I've been around enough law enforcement to know. Yet, there's something else. I can't put my finger on it, and that's why I asked her what makes her tick." Max paused. "And you're not going to tell me."

"You already know the answers, you just don't want to ask the questions, and I respect that."

No more. He essentially dropped the subject. Did Max know? Maybe. She had some theories about Lucy, but she wouldn't voice them. Because she did respect the rookie fed, and she hoped if their paths crossed again, she would have an ally.

"About John Caldwell."

Dillon didn't say anything else.

"You want me to talk to him."

"Let's just say I watched him closely and I'm concerned."

Max had watched him as well, but she didn't see anything but a rigid supporter of his wife.

"I'll see what I can learn."

Chapter Thirty-seven

Max didn't have an opportunity to talk to John before the trial started Tuesday morning. She was riveted, however, by Dillon Kincaid's testimony. While Monday had been an exercise in boredom, today was the reverse. She watched the jury as well—they, too, listened closely.

After the prosecutors established Dillon's credentials, they asked him a series of questions related to the psychology of the killer. Since they'd already established the crime scene, the method, and the window of time that Blair Caldwell could have killed her son—which matched with the window the coroner also established—they focused on the mind-set of the killer.

"Considering your experience, do you have a profile of Peter Caldwell's killer?"

"Yes, I do."

"I submit exhibit Thirty-four B, Your Honor," the prosecution said.

"With no objections, Dr. Kincaid's profile will be included in the record."

"Will you please summarize your findings?"

"The key fact that stood out to me is that Peter was not sexually assaulted in any way. This stands out because overwhelmingly, close to ninety percent of homicide victims under the age of fourteen are sexually assaulted or killed in a failed sexual attack. Right there that tells me that this crime was not sexually motivated. Another key fact is that over ninety percent of homicide victims under the age of fourteen are killed by someone they know—a friend of the family or a relative.

"There is one primary fact related to Peter's death that tells me his killer is female. Peter was drugged with a benzodiazepine that, in the dose he was given, would have made him lethargic to the point of unconsciousness. Poison or drugs are a female weapon—when used as a murder weapon, virtually all these killers are women."

"Dr. Kincaid," the DA said, "have you reviewed the psychiatric evaluation of Mrs. Caldwell?"

"I have. As well as the recordings of her interviews with police."

"Objection," the defense said. "The psychiatric evaluation of Mrs. Caldwell did not indicate that she was capable of murder."

The judge said, "Counselor, you may use your cross-examination to discuss the report already submitted into evidence. Overruled."

"Dr. Kincaid, what was your conclusion based on your readings and viewings?"

"The original psychiatric evaluation was conducted several weeks after the murder and in my opinion should have less weight placed on it than the interviews conducted by first the police and then by the detective at the station, shortly after Peter's death. The reason is that time slants bias. Meaning, a person's recollection of events differ and they have a different emotional response over time. However, several things stood out during the initial interview. May I use the projector?"

The prosecution inserted a disk into the DVD player after submitting it officially into evidence. Evidently, Dillon had already spliced the recording to highlight the points he wanted to make.

"I'm going to show you three segments that tell me that Blair Caldwell lied to police."

"Objection," the defense said. "Dr. Kincaid is a psychiatrist, not a psychic."

Laughter in the courtroom, but Max noted that only one of the jurors cracked a smile.

"Overruled," the judge said.

"Go on, Dr. Kincaid," the DA said.

Dillon played a short segment on the projector. In it, Blair was sitting in the interview room in Scottsdale with two detectives, one female and one male. She also had her lawyer with her.

The detectives asked Blair about the night her son was killed and specifically who she spoke to at specific times. Blair was clearly annoyed by the questions and almost flip in her responses.

Dr. Kincaid didn't make a comment, but started a second segment. The detectives asked Blair about the home security system and whether they habitually had it on when someone was home. Again, her responses were filled with annoyance, as if the police were idiots to even be asking the questions. Yet, she answered them.

"Objection," the defense said after the second brief clip. "Relevance. The transcript of Mrs. Caldwell's interviews with police have already been entered into the record."

The prosecutor said, "Your Honor, the point we're trying to make will be clear momentarily."

"Make sure it is," the judge said. "Objection overruled. Dr. Kincaid, please get to your point.

"Yes, your Honor. One more clip." He nodded to the prosecutor who began the tape again.

The last clip was the most damning.

On it, Blair was poised and almost regal. She was also belligerent with law enforcement and clearly looked down at them in how she spoke.

"Mrs. Caldwell, there's a block of time you cannot account for. You can see why we're suspicious. Tell us where you were and we're done."

"I cannot believe you've had me here for over an hour because you couldn't find anyone who saw me for a few minutes at a party."

Her attorney said, "Mrs. Caldwell has answered all your questions to the best of her ability. If you're not going to charge her, you need to let her go."

"We have a witness who says she saw you on the porch of the clubhouse at twelve thirty-five the night of the party. The witness said she told you that your husband had been looking for you and you said you were getting fresh air. Yet a group of businessmen were smoking cigars on the porch from approximately twelve ten until twelve thirty and none of them saw you."

"I know who you're talking about. Misty Vale. I was getting fresh air, and it wasn't at twelve thirty-five—it was earlier. The businessmen weren't on the porch, they were off to the side, on the patio."

"Yes, they were, up until twelve ten when they moved to the porch."

"And that's when I spoke to Misty. I don't keep a schedule of every person I speak to for two minutes at a function like this."

"We were able to verify the witness's timeline based on other witness statements that put her in the ladies' lounge prior to twelve thirty-five."

"We're going to quibble over a few minutes? This is ridiculous!"

Blair was getting agitated on the recording, but she was also growing agitated in the defendant's chair. It was clear that she felt she was being ridiculed or attacked.

"Charles," Blair said on the disk, "I want to leave. Now."

"Detective," the attorney said, "do you have any physical evidence tying my client to her son's murder?"

"We're still in the middle of our investigation."

"Then we will be leaving until such time as you have any evidence—because it sounds to me like you're fishing."

"You're free to leave, but be available for more questions, Mrs. Caldwell."

She rolled her eyes. "Really. *More* asinine questions."

The lawyer put his hand on Blair's arm. "Blair, we should go."

The detectives rose, gathered their files, and stepped out.

The recording continued to play.

"Where's John?" Blair asked.

"He's in the waiting room."

"Why aren't they asking him these questions? Why me?"

"They did interview him."

"This is the most—"

John entered the room. He looked a mess—there was no better description. His clothing was rumpled, his shirt stained—perhaps coffee—and he had dark circles under his eyes as if he hadn't slept in a week. "The detectives said you can go. Blair—"

In less than a blink of an eye, Blair started crying. She threw her arms around John and sobbed. "Oh, God, John, it was awful! Why are they doing this to me? Why aren't they looking for the real killer? Why ask me all these awful questions?"

John patted her on the back. "It's okay, Blair. It'll be okay. I'll take you home."

The clip ended.

Max stared at John. The shock on his face was clear—seeing Blair in action with the detectives and then with him.

Max already suspected what Blair's defense would be—she was an attorney, she was used to rigid questions—but it was also clear that she was manipulating her husband.

At least to Max it was clear. Was it clear to the jury?

Dillon said, "What you witnessed here is classic sociopathic and narcissistic behavior. First, the indignation of being detained and questioned—she's above it. Everyone else's recollections are wrong, not hers, and if she's wrong it's because they're nitpicking her. Second, the complete reversal of emotions when her husband walks into the room. Her body language and tone immediately changed."

"What could be her motive for killing her son?" the DA asked.

"I can't speak to motive without personally evaluating Mrs. Caldwell—"

"Objection," the defense said. "Mrs. Caldwell is innocent until proven guilty."

"Sustained. Jury will disregard. Please rephrase the question or move along."

The DA said, "Dr. Kincaid, considering that Peter Caldwell was not sexually assaulted, what motive could there be for his death?"

Dillon paused long enough that the judge asked him if he understood the question.

"Yes, Your Honor, I understand. The answer is both simple and complex. What we need to remember is more what *didn't* happen. He wasn't sexually assaulted. It wasn't a crime of anger—such as an abused child who is beaten to death, or someone in a violent rage. He wasn't brutalized in any way. It wasn't spontaneous. In fact, his murder was almost serene. He was drugged to the point of losing consciousness. He was suffocated and didn't struggle, telling us that he never regained consciousness.

Whoever killed him didn't want him to suffer, but also clearly didn't want him to live. Why? I can only speculate."

"Yet you're an expert witness," the DA said. "You can speculate."

"Based on the original psych evaluation of Mrs. Caldwell and her interviews with police, not once did she ask any specific questions about her son's murder. She showed no emotional connection to her son. In her outburst to her husband, she specifically said, 'Why are they doing this to me? Why ask me all these awful questions?' While on the one hand it's absolutely normal for a parent to be frustrated with law enforcement for not being out looking for their child's killer, not once did she ask the police why they weren't doing more to find the *real* killer, as she said to her husband. She reserved those statements *solely* for her husband.

"Narcissists want to be the focus of everyone in their lives. They need the attention. Peter Caldwell was, by all accounts, a loved and exceptional child. He was a good student. He and his father shared a love of baseball. His father doted on him. Took him on field trips. Volunteered in the school. Spent time with him. One thing stood out in the original psych evaluation. When Dr. Opner asked about time spent with her son, Mrs. Caldwell responded . . ." Dillon looked down at his notes. "This is on page seventeen of the evaluation, Your Honor. 'We do everything with Peter. Our lives revolve around him. In fact, John brought him on our anniversary vacation to Cabo last year.' She said *John brought*. Not *they brought*. I suspect this was a sore point with her, and one of the triggers in her plan to remove her son from the family unit."

"Objection."

"Sustained. The jury will disregard the last sentence and it will be stricken from the record."

"Dr. Kincaid, do you think that Blair Caldwell was jealous of the attention her husband gave to her son?"

"Yes, I do."

"Is this common in other cases you've consulted where a parent killed a child?"

"Objection!"

The DA said, "Your Honor, I'm simply asking Dr. Kincaid based on his extensive experience and already stipulated credentials to offer an expert opinion as to cases similar to this."

"The question itself prejudices the jury."

The judge said, "Jurors, the question presented to Dr. Kincaid reflects a generic observation regarding all suspects and victims within Dr. Kincaid's scope of knowledge, not specifically the defendant. Proceed."

"Dr. Kincaid?" the DA prompted.

"There is not one answer to that question," Dillon said. "I would focus specifically on premeditated homicides. There are surprisingly few. Most parental-involved deaths involve neglect or gross abuse, and most of those involve very young children who are more fragile. In the cases where an older child—over the age of six—is killed, if the parent is not addicted to alcohol or drugs, which impairs their judgment or creates a violent home, or where there is no history of abuse, there are sometimes cases that are technically child abuse called Munchausen syndrome by proxy, where a parent or caregiver fabricates or creates symptoms in a child. In eighty-five percent of the cases, the mother is responsible for causing the illness, usually through poison."

"Peter Caldwell didn't die of a medical condition."

"No, and Munchausen syndrome by proxy is a mental illness that is extremely rare. I don't believe this is specifically what we're dealing with here—I bring it up because of the reason behind the illness. It is solely for attention. Where some people will fabricate stories about grand adventures or accomplishments to the point that they will create false narratives that they believe—pathological liars—someone who suffers from Munchausen will create false illnesses in those in their care in order to gain attention. However, in this case Peter was extremely healthy. I've reviewed his medical records and he was rarely sick, statistically less than most children of his socioeconomic position. Yet I think the underlying cause—the need for attention—is the primary reason for his death. Secondarily, there is the complete disassociation of Mrs. Caldwell from her son."

"What do you mean by disassociation?"

"In all of her interviews and in the psych eval, not once did Mrs.

Caldwell express any emotions related to questioning about Peter and his death. She did not once refer to Peter as *our son* or *my son*. She never asked police during the three interviews she had before her arrest what happened to Peter. She never asked about the autopsy or what the police were doing in their investigation—the only person she appears to have shown any emotion toward was her husband. And even then, as the clip showed, she didn't mention Peter by name or even by association as their son. The subject of the sentence was 'they' meaning the police."

"No further questions, the state reserves the right to redirect."

The judge allowed the defense to cross-examine.

"Dr. Kincaid, psychology is not a real science, is it?"

"It's sometimes called a soft science, but it's based on research and observation, like all sciences."

"But human beings are complex. They don't all react to the same situations in the same way."

"Correct."

"So Mrs. Caldwell's seemingly cold or haughty interview with the police could be a defense mechanism because she felt attacked."

"I do not think so."

"But that's just your opinion."

"Correct, my opinion based on years of experience."

"You showed eleven minutes of interviews out of more than three hours."

"I viewed all recorded interviews and read every transcript."

"So we're relying on what is essentially your nonscientific opinion."

"Objection," the DA said. "Dr. Kincaid's credentials have already been stipulated by the defense. I can read them for the record."

"Withdrawn," the defense said. "Dr. Kincaid, the original psych evaluation indicated that there were no clear signs that Blair Caldwell was capable of killing her son."

"Let me read the conclusion." Dillon flipped a few pages. "According to Dr. Opner, 'After spending two hours with Mrs. Caldwell, I've determined that there are no clear signs as to her guilt or innocence. This observation is due in large part to the fact that four weeks has passed since Peter Caldwell's murder and the stages of grief manifest in different ways. At this point, I would say that Mrs. Caldwell is in the denial stage. She is cool, refined, polite, but not willing or able to discuss her son's murder.'"

The defense counsel said, "Because she was grieving."

"She could have been. I wasn't there during the evaluation."

"No further questions."

"Redirect?" the prosecutor said. He stood. "Dr. Kincaid, based on the evidence, would you concur with the lead detective who testified yesterday that Peter Caldwell's murder was premeditated?"

"Yes."

"Why do you believe it was premeditated?"

"For all the reasons Detective Jackson said, and one more: whoever killed Peter had to grind and dissolve the Valium that was used to incapacitate him. Based on the coroner's report, the drugs were originally in pill form. They had to be crushed, dissolved in water, then administered to Peter. Nothing was found in the house with any residue. That means the killer brought the drug into the house already prepared to be used."

"Would that mean that Mrs. Caldwell is not guilty? After all, she didn't even have a prescription for Valium."

That was good, Max thought—already working to destroy one of the key defense arguments.

"It doesn't go to her guilt or innocence," Dillon said. "It's a fact. It means that every step of this murder was planned including preparing the drugs, how long it would take to get to the Caldwell house, take Peter to the sand pit, bury him, then disappear. It was planned carefully, down to the minute. The amount of drugs in his system was excessive. They would take approximately ten to fifteen minutes to affect an adult, shorter for a child. The drugs were administered in sweetened water. That still wouldn't have masked the bitter taste, and suggests that the killer was someone Peter trusted. The babysitter testified that she heard Peter cough and use the bathroom. When she went to check on him, he was back in bed. I would postulate that he was already drugged at that time, and the killer was hiding in the adjoining bathroom. Such a theory fits the timeline established by the police and the medical examiner." Dillon sipped water that was at the podium.

"So my question has been from the beginning, who has a motive? Who would go to such lengths to kill Peter Caldwell? Someone who simply didn't want Peter to exist. The crime had no passion, no anger or rage or hesitation. It was cold, methodical, and carried out to the letter—as it was planned."

Max couldn't find John during the break. Her cameraman was following her because she had a scheduled two-minute clip to air live.

She was worried about John—his expression during Dillon Kincaid's testimony had changed from stoic to disbelieving to pain-filled. She didn't want him to do anything stupid. She wasn't as worried about him killing Blair as she was about him hurting himself. Maybe that's what Dillon had meant last night. She sent David a brief text message that she needed his help to track down John.

The docket after the lunch break was for a computer expert. Max knew the only reason to bring in a computer expert was to confirm what had originally been Lucy Kincaid's theory that Blair Caldwell knew the details of Justin Stanton's murder and copied them—all except for the stuffed animal because that wasn't in the public reports.

"Max, we need to do this now. Ben is yelling at me."

"Fine," she said and looked around. She pointed to a corner of the second floor. "That should be sufficient."

Once lighting and sound were established, and her cameraman set up the live feed with NET, Max began.

"We're in the middle of the second day of the trial of Blair Caldwell, the corporate attorney accused of murdering her eight-year-old son last April. This morning's testimony focused on Dr. Dillon Kincaid, a renowned criminal psychiatrist who was called by the prosecution as an expert witness. In the two hours, nine minutes of testimony, Dr. Kincaid provided the court with . . ."

She went through the key points of his testimony in a clear, concise and unemotional way—reporting the facts as he represented them without his extensive details. She had two minutes, not the two hours that Dillon Kincaid was ultimately on the stand.

Max wrapped up with: "Dr. Kincaid ended with a possible motive: whoever killed Peter Caldwell simply wanted Peter to no longer exist." She paused for effect, then said, "For more about the trial, visit the NET Web site at the address on your screen and click on 'Maxine Revere' for all my articles, commentary, and nightly in-depth report about the day's events. This is Maxine Revere for NET."

She waited a moment until her cameraman told her she was off-air, then she continued her hunt for John.

Dillon was at the bottom of the courthouse stairs talking to the district attorney, Harrison Trotter. Max said, "Dillon, I can't find John."

Trotter said, "He was the first person out of court after the judge."

"I'm worried," Max said. "I watched him during your testimony and I saw the change in him."

"I'm the last person he'll want to see," Dillon said.

"You can explain this to him."

"He's not going to be receptive. I gave him the most devastating news in his life—that the woman he loved and trusted killed his son. You need to find him."

"He's not happy with me, either."

"But he knows and trusts you, Max. Why do you think he contacted you in the first place? Because he believed you would learn the truth. And you did. It just wasn't the truth he wanted. Remember what you said last night—that deep down he suspected she was guilty. He *wanted* to be wrong, he convinced himself his doubts weren't valid, but now he knows. We didn't prove it, but we created the plausibility in court." Dillon glanced at the DA. "I'm prepared to return to the stand to confirm what your computer expert learned."

The DA was clearly uncomfortable with Max standing there. "Be in the courtroom after lunch. Excuse me." He walked away.

"Find him," Dillon said.

Max stepped outside. It was overcast and looked like it would be raining—and decidedly colder than even yesterday.

David called her. "I found him. Parking garage, second floor."

"Is he okay?"

"He's just sitting in his car. I'll keep an eye on him until you get here."

It had started raining. She pulled her umbrella from her purse as the rain pounded. One minute, completely dry. The next minute, torrential downpour. Fortunately, she had on boots because she'd checked the weather report that morning. She walked half a block to the pedestrian entrance of the parking garage.

John drove a white Volvo. Practical, just like John. Max collapsed her umbrella and took the stairs to the second floor. She looked up and down each row. She found the Volvo at the row closest to the courthouse entrance. Of course there would have been an entrance leading directly to the courthouse—if she'd know that, she wouldn't have even had to venture out into the rain.

David was standing next to the courthouse. He looked at her oddly as she approached. "I didn't expect you to come from the street," he said.

They both looked at John sitting behind the wheel. "I'll take care of him."

"I'm not leaving."

"David—"

"Look, Max, I was in the courtroom. I saw his face. He owns two guns. I'm not leaving you with a grieving man who may or may not plan to kill himself—or plan to kill his bitch of a wife. Or his friend, the messenger with bad news. This is what you pay me for. Deal with it."

She looked at him and smiled. "Thank you."

He seemed surprised that she had acquiesced so easily. She left David by the courthouse doors and walked over to John's Volvo. She opened the passenger door and sat in the leather seat, then closed the door behind her.

John barely glanced at her.

"I've been avoiding your calls because I knew. After I read that article on Saturday, I knew."

He put his head on the steering wheel and cried. Max had never heard such a gut-wrenching sound come from a man, as if his pain and grief had found a voice. Max rarely cried, but she felt tears roll down her face.

She didn't tell John everything was going to be okay. She put her hand on his back and sat there. She would stay with him as long as it took, because he shouldn't be alone.

Chapter Thirty-eight

After three days of trial and a day and a half of jury deliberations, the jury returned a guilty verdict Friday after lunch.

John Caldwell was not in the courtroom. He didn't return Tuesday afternoon, or any day since. He checked into a hotel room and hadn't returned home.

Max met with him each night because she was worried about him—and what he might do. But after the guilty verdict came down, he said he would be okay.

"It's over," he said.

"I can stay for the weekend. We can talk. Or just—do nothing."

He actually gave her a small smile. He hadn't slept, he'd barely eaten except when Max pushed food on him, and his hair looked gray. Did people really get stress gray?

"I will be okay, Max. My sister is coming tomorrow. She's going to help me pack up the house and get it on the market. I can't live there anymore."

"How about dinner tonight?"

He shook his head. "I can't—I need to make plans. I'm going to move. Not just out of the house, but out of Scottsdale. A friend of mine has been trying to get me to work for them. Their headquarters are in Seattle. I need a change. A real change."

"Well, if you want to talk, or have dinner, or breakfast, call me. I'm leaving in the morning."

John walked her to the door. "Did you know? From the beginning, did you know that Blair was guilty?"

What could she say? "Suspecting is different than knowing. I was suspicious, but I wanted her to be innocent."

"Why?"

"Because I knew it would break your heart, and I didn't want you hurt like this."

"Nothing could hurt me more than losing Peter. Even knowing that Blair killed him—killed him for no reason I can understand other than a deep selfishness that I ignored for years—doesn't hurt as much as the fact that he's gone."

"Nothing good can come from this, and I won't even tell you that there is a silver lining. *But,* if you hadn't called me, four other boys wouldn't have seen justice. Another little boy would have died. This trial ended with two killers in prison. It won't give you peace, but it might give you some satisfaction."

"However much it hurts, it's better to know the truth. I'll never understand why. *Why.* Your friend, Dr. Kincaid, came by last night. I think he wanted to give me answers, but there are no answers."

She hadn't known that Dillon went to see John, but that was so like him. She had grown to like and respect the man over the last two weeks. He showed a deep compassion but tempered it with logic and reason. He didn't raise his voice. Nothing seemed to fluster him. He'd agreed to come to New York for an interview in two weeks, and she would be filming her next *Maximum Exposure* show about Danielle Sharpe and Blair Caldwell—mothers who kill. That was Ben's tag. Max planned to take the show far deeper than a simple tagline could suggest. Dillon's involvement would help tremendously. She also had agreements with Blair's attorney (to talk generally, not specifically about her case because he planned to appeal—though she didn't mention that to John), DA Harrison Trotter, Stanton, Detective Katella, and Danielle's ex-husband. There were others she might be able to nab as well.

Except the one she really wanted. Lucy Kincaid. Max was going to have to be satisfied with her brother.

"The truth is an answer," she said.

"It's not enough, but it has to be."

She gave John a hug good-bye, and went down to the parking garage to get her rental car. She considered staying the weekend to pamper herself at the Biltmore resort. But she'd already been gone for over two weeks, and it was time to go home.

She had wanted to stay—not only for John, but because Nick was expecting her this weekend. Why had she told him that she would visit when the trial was over? She didn't want to see him. She knew their relationship was over. It was over the minute he told her he would never discuss his ex-wife and custody arrangement with her. It wasn't that she had to know, it was that his problems with Nancy were integral to his life, and she realized that she wanted to share all or nothing with the man she loved.

And she couldn't love anyone who closed half his life to her. Arguably, the most important half of his life, his child.

She was sad on the one hand because with Nick she saw something that could have been. There was something about him—and who she was when she was with Nick—that made her want to make it work. But at the same time, a weight lifted. She hadn't realized the emotional stress she'd put on herself trying to justify Nick's silence about Nancy. She'd made excuses to herself and for him, and she refused to do it anymore. She valued honesty—she couldn't settle for less in her own relationships.

Maybe part of it was because of Lucy and Sean. She'd not only observed them, but listened to Lucy when she spoke of her husband. Their relationship was built on trust and honesty. No secrets. Maybe that was a near impossible goal, but it was still a goal. And one that Max was willing to pursue.

Because for the first time in her life, Max was thinking about the future. Before, her relationships had always been superficial. Passionate and intelligent relationships with men who could stand up to her, men who weren't intimidated by her independence or confidence. But they were still superficial because to Max, the job always came first. To Max, her job was her vocation and there was no room for anything else.

Nick taught her one thing: that she wanted more. That while she wouldn't give up her career, she definitely had room for another person.

Someone who was more than an occasional lover. And Lucy taught her that Max didn't have to settle for a relationship that was one-sided or based solely in sexual gratification. Max would rather be alone for the rest of her life than love a man who didn't trust her with both the good and the bad in his life.

The freedom in that revelation gave Max a rare peace that she hadn't expected.

She left her rental with the valet at the Biltmore, then walked through the lobby and out the back doors to her expansive suite. She was surprised when she found David sitting in her living room reading the book she had only half finished.

"Don't tell me how it ends, I'll read it on the plane tomorrow," she said, kicking off her heels and sitting across from him. "I thought you left this afternoon."

"I changed it to tomorrow. We'll head back together." He put the book down. "I thought you were seeing Nick this weekend."

"I'd planned on it, but . . ." David and Nick were friends, which made this harder than she thought. "I'm done."

"It's not as simple as that."

"It is. But I'm okay. You can take the weekend, visit Emma, do whatever you need to do. I don't need a babysitter."

"What changed?"

"Nothing. I thought I could tolerate being shut out of his life, and I can't. I guess . . . I have too much respect for myself. It got to the point where I cared too much. And I was giving up too much just to spend time with him."

"Nick cares. This is a hard time for him."

"I know. But I'm supposed to let him shut me out on this? What else? Let's say Nick and I stick it out. I have to shut my ears and close my eyes every time Nancy is mentioned? Every time she interferes with his life? Would I even be allowed to have a relationship with Logan? I don't want to live like that. It's not like he's my employee."

She didn't realize what she'd said until she'd said it.

"Is that what I am, Max? An employee?"

Last September, David had hurt her so deeply, but she hadn't realized it still bothered her. Bothered her? She was still hurt.

"You were my friend, David," she said. "And I thought—I don't know. That we were family, in a way. But you made it clear I'm not. And I get it—Brittney gave you an ultimatum. She didn't want me anywhere around Emma. You couldn't risk losing your daughter to that vindictive bitch. I understand, David—and I tried to keep it all in perspective. You work for me. I'm not part of your life. I don't have a right to expect to be part of your family dinners or spend time with you and Emma outside of our job. We're not lovers, we're not in that kind of relationship, and now our friendship is . . . I don't know."

"I am really sorry I hurt you, Max," David said. "I didn't realize when I shut you out of Emma's birthday dinner that you took it personally. I had to make that promise to Brittney, that you wouldn't be there, that you wouldn't be in Emma's life. I have no rights with Emma. None except what Brittney gives me."

"I'm okay."

"Yet you're dumping Nick."

"Because I'm not going to be cut out. Not in something so important to Nick."

David nodded. "Okay."

"Dinner?"

"Sure." He got up. "Max, I'm sorry about the situation with Emma. But we are friends, we will always be friends. I knew something was wrong, you talked to me different, but I didn't make the connection. Forgive me."

"All is forgiven," she said. And she meant it. Another weight lifted off her heart. "I mean it. I'm going to call Nick, tell him I'm not coming tomorrow. Meet you in the restaurant? An hour?"

"See you there."

Max's cell phone rang Friday night after she returned from dinner. It had been really good to connect with David again.

"Max Revere," she answered.

"Hi, it's Lucy Kincaid."

Max sat down at her desk and smiled. "I'm glad you called."

"It was a zoo in Glendale after we arrested Danielle Sharpe, and then you left the next morning. I felt bad I didn't get a chance to say good-bye."

Max didn't tell Lucy that she'd negotiated a copy of the transcript from Lucy's hostage negotiation with Danielle. She wasn't going to use it—she'd promised Andrew she wouldn't—but it gave her a new insight into how she investigated cold cases.

And great insight into Lucy Kincaid. There was more to her story, Max was certain, but for the first time she was okay with letting it go.

"Sean and I had breakfast before I left, while you were debriefing and doing all the boring paperwork."

Lucy laughed. "Definitely not the fun part of my job."

"What now?"

"Back to work—well, I'm not on call, so I have a couple days. Dillon's here—he flew in this afternoon after the verdict and is going to stay for the weekend."

"Tell him I said thank you. Again. He sealed the conviction."

"He said it was three things—his testimony, the computer expert who confirmed that Blair Caldwell had read articles about Justin's murder on her work computer, and the fact that her husband didn't return to court after Dillon's testimony. The jury noticed."

"John knew from the beginning, but he was in denial. He wanted me to prove that she didn't do it, to give him peace."

"I figured that. Have you spoken to him?"

"This afternoon. He's picking up the pieces. His sister is coming to town, they'll sell the house, he's been offered a job in the Pacific Northwest. He isn't going to just get over his son's murder."

"No, he won't. He doesn't want to hear that it'll get easier, but there will be a time when he'll wake up and his first thought won't be Peter. It'll take time. Years, perhaps. The sorrow will always be there. But he'll learn to find joy in his life. There will be balance, and that's really all any of us can hope for."

"Is everything okay with you? Your work?"

Yes, she was prying. But she was curious, and a bit concerned. Lucy was instrumental in solving her nephew's murder and preventing the death of another young boy; she didn't deserve to be raked over the coals by a boss who didn't know what she'd accomplished.

"I'm fine."

Talk about a vague answer! But Max didn't press.

"I wanted to ask you something," Lucy continued.

"As you told me, I'm an open book."

"Sean is a private investigator and rather exemplary at his job. You told him about how your mother disappeared. You have a lot of information on your Web site as well."

"I've never kept it a secret. I recognize that one of the reasons I've chosen this job—to solve crimes for other people—is because I can't solve the mysteries in my own life. I've never lied to myself about it."

"Sean has a lead. But we didn't want to send you the information he uncovered without asking if you really want it."

Max's heart skipped a beat. "A lead? What kind of lead?"

"You told Sean your mother never wrote to you after your sixteenth birthday, and shortly after that she stopped withdrawing money from her trust account. She was legally declared dead seven years and three months after your sixteenth birthday—seven years after the last withdrawal she made from her trust—so Sean dug around and found out where she was living after April first."

"She withdrew the money in Florida, but I lived with her for ten years. She would withdraw the money then immediately leave. Why, I don't know. I thought at the time so that my grandparents couldn't track her. But I've wondered if she was running from someone else. Or just running from herself."

"She bought a car in Florida the day she withdrew the money. She bought it under a false identity. The car was found abandoned in Virginia two weeks later."

Max's stomach twisted in knots. She had looked into her mother's disappearance, but she'd never truly devoted a lot of time or energy. Maybe part of her didn't want to know the truth. Could that be? Could it be that Max herself didn't want answers to the one question that had driven her for so long?

"Max?"

"I'm here."

"Sean didn't get this information strictly legally. I know what you're thinking."

"You don't."

Lucy laughed, though there was no humor. "Max, do you really think you intentionally thwarted yourself?"

Maybe Lucy Kincaid really could read minds. "Yes."

"Maybe you could have found it. Maybe not. This was sixteen years ago. And Sean is—well, let's just say *he* would say he's the best in the business."

"It sounds like he is."

"Do you want the information he found?"

Did she? Did she want to know the truth about her mother? Why she left her when she was ten, why she never returned, never called, and sent her a birthday card every year until she disappeared off the face of the earth?

Would the answers give her closure? A sense of peace? *Justice?*

Except . . . if she was murdered, that meant there was a killer out there. And even after sixteen years, that killer needed to be found. And prosecuted. Justice had to be served. Because no matter how selfish and irresponsible Martha Revere was, she didn't deserve death.

"Yes, Lucy. I'd like the information. And thank you. Thank you both."